WOLVES EAT DOGS

Pasha Ivanov, one of Russia's richest oligarchs, is lying dead on the pavement outside his luxury high-rise apartment in Moscow. His death, it seems, is a straightforward case of suicide. Senior Investigator Arkady Renko, however, has never been one to take evidence at face value and there's something puzzling him that he simply refuses to ignore: a mountain of salt found in Ivanov's wardrobe . . .

Renko's investigations take him to the notorious exclusion zone, the area around Chernobyl deserted and forgotten for almost two decades. "The Zone" is a place of mystery, danger – and sometimes – unimaginable beauty. When the body of Lev Timofeyev, Pasha Ivanov's former research partner, is discovered in a contaminated cemetery, it is only the beginning of Renko's journey into this labyrinthine netherworld of crime – and an investigation that is about to uncover some of the nation's most closely guarded secrets.

WOLVES EAT DOGS

Martin Cruz Smith

WINDSOR
PARAGON

First published 2004
by
Simon & Schuster
This Large Print edition published 2005
by
BBC Audiobooks Ltd by arrangement with
Macmillan

ISBN 1 4056 1128 6 (Windsor Hardcover)
ISBN 1 4056 2115 X (Paragon Softcover)

British Library Cataloguing in Publication Data available

Printed and bound in Great Britain by
Antony Rowe Ltd., Chippenham, Wiltshire

For Em

1

Moscow swam in color. Hazy floodlights of Red Square mixed with the neon of casinos in Revolution Square. Light wormed its way from the underground mall in the Manezh. Spotlights crowned new towers of glass and polished stone, each tower capped by a spire. Gilded domes still floated around the Garden Ring, but all night earthmovers tore at the old city and dug widening pools of light to raise a modern, vertical Moscow more like Houston or Dubai. It was a Moscow that Pasha Ivanov had helped to create, a shifting landscape of tectonic plates and lava flows and fatal missteps.

Senior Investigator Arkady Renko leaned out a window the better to see Ivanov on the pavement ten floors below. Ivanov was dead but not particularly bloody, arms and legs at odd angles. Two black Mercedeses were at the curb, Ivanov's car and an SUV for his bodyguards. It sometimes seemed to Arkady that every successful businessman and Mafia hood in Moscow had been issued two Nazi-black Mercedeses.

Ivanov had arrived at 9:28 p.m., gone directly up to the safest apartment in Moscow and at 9:48 p.m. plunged to the sidewalk. Arkady had measured Ivanov's distance from the building. Homicides generally hit close, having expended their energy in trying not to fall. Suicides were single-minded and landed farther out. Ivanov had almost reached the street.

Behind Arkady, Prosecutor Zurin had brought drinks from the wet bar to a NoviRus senior vice president named Timofeyev and a young blonde in the living room. Zurin was as fussy as a maître d'; he had survived six Kremlin regimes by recognizing his best customers and smoothing out their problems. Timofeyev had the shakes and the girl was drunk. Arkady thought the gathering was a little like a party where the host had suddenly and inexplicably dived through the window. After the shock the guests carried on.

The odd man out was Bobby Hoffman, Ivanov's American assistant. Although he was worth millions of dollars, his loafers were split, his fingers were smudged with ink and his suede jacket was worn to a shine. Arkady wondered how much more time Hoffman had at NoviRus. An assistant to a dead man? That didn't sound promising.

Hoffman joined Arkady at the window. "Why are there plastic bags around Pasha's hands?"

"I was looking for signs of resistance, maybe cuts on the fingers."

"Resistance? Like a fight?"

Prosecutor Zurin rocked forward on the sofa. "There is no investigation. We do not investigate suicides. There are no signs of violence in the apartment. Ivanov came up alone. He left alone. That, my friends, is a suicide in spades."

The girl lifted a dazed expression. Arkady had learned from the file he had on Pasha Ivanov that Rina Shevchenko was his personal interior designer, a twenty-year-old in a red leather pantsuit and high-heeled boots.

Timofeyev was known as a robust sportsman, but he could have been his father, he had shrunk so much within his suit. "Suicides are a personal tragedy. It's enough to suffer the death of a friend. Colonel Ozhogin — the head of NoviRus Security — is already flying back." He added to Arkady, "Ozhogin wants nothing done until he arrives."

Arkady said, "We don't leave a body on the sidewalk like a rug, even for the colonel."

"Pay no attention to Investigator Renko," Zurin said. "He's the office fanatic. He's like a narcotics dog; he sniffs every bag."

There won't be much left to sniff here, Arkady thought. Just out of curiosity, he wondered if he could protect the bloody prints on the windowsill.

Timofeyev pressed a handkerchief against his nose. Arkady saw spots of red.

"Nosebleed?" asked Zurin.

"Summer cold," said Timofeyev.

Opposite Ivanov's apartment was a dark office building. A man walked out of the lobby, waved to Arkady and gave a thumbs-down.

"One of your men?" Hoffman asked.

"A detective, in case someone over there was working late and might have witnessed something."

"But you're not investigating."

"I do whatever the prosecutor says."

"So you think it was suicide."

"We prefer suicides. Suicides don't demand work or drive up the crime rate." It also occurred to Arkady that suicides didn't expose the incompetence of investigators and militia who were better at sorting out dead drunks from the living than solving murders committed with any amount of forethought.

Zurin said, “You will excuse Renko, he thinks all of Moscow is a crime scene. The problem is that the press will sensationalize the death of someone as eminent as Pasha Ivanov.”

In which case, better the suicide of an unbalanced financier than assassination, Arkady thought. Timofeyev might lament the suicide of his friend, but a murder investigation could place the entire NoviRus company under a cloud, especially from the perspective of foreign partners and investors who already felt that doing business in Russia was a dip in murky water. Since Zurin had ordered Arkady’s financial investigation of Ivanov, this U-turn had to be executed with dispatch. So, not a maître d’, Arkady thought, but more a skillful sailor who knew when to tack.

“Who had access to this apartment?” Arkady asked.

“Pasha was the only one allowed on this level. The security was the best in the world,” Zurin said.

“Best in the world,” Timofeyev agreed.

Zurin said, “The entire building is covered by surveillance cameras, inside and out, with monitors that are watched not only at the reception desk here but, as a safeguard, also by technicians at the headquarters of

NoviRus Security. The other apartments have keys. Ivanov had a keypad with a code known only to him. He also had a lock-out button by the elevator, to keep out the world when he was in. He had all the security a man could wish for."

Arkady had been in the lobby and seen the monitors tucked into a round rose-wood desk. Each small screen was split in four. The receptionist also had a white phone with two outside lines and a red phone with a line direct to NoviRus.

"The building staff doesn't have Ivanov's code?" Arkady asked.

"No. Only the central office at NoviRus."

"Who had access to the code there?"

"No one. It was sealed, until tonight."

According to the prosecutor, Ivanov had ordered that no one enter the apartment but him — not staff, not a housecleaner, not a plumber. Anyone who tried would appear on monitors and on tape, and the staff had seen nothing. Ivanov did his own cleaning. Gave the elevator man the trash, laundry, dry cleaning, lists for food or whatever, which would be waiting in the lobby when Ivanov returned. Zurin made it sound like many talents.

"Eccentric," Arkady said.

"He could afford to be eccentric.

Churchill wandered around his castle naked."

"Pasha wasn't crazy," Rina said.

"What was he?" Arkady rephrased the question. "How would you describe him?"

"He had lost weight. He said he had an infection. Maybe he had a bad reaction to medication."

Timofeyev said, "I wish Ozhogin were here."

Arkady had seen a glossy magazine cover with a confident Lev Timofeyev sailing a yacht in the Black Sea, carving through the waves. Where was *that* Timofeyev? Arkady wondered.

An ambulance rolled discreetly to the curb. The detective crossed the street with a camera and shot flash pictures of Ivanov being rolled into the body bag and of the stain on the pavement. Something had been concealed under Ivanov's body. From Arkady's distance it looked like a drinking glass. The detective took a picture of that, too.

Hoffman watched Arkady as much as the scene below.

"Is it true, you treat Moscow like a crime scene?"

"Force of habit."

The living room would have been a

forensic technician's dream: white leather sofa and chairs, limestone floor and linen walls, glass ashtray and coffee table, all excellent backgrounds for hair, lipstick, fingerprints, the scuff marks of life. It would have been easy to dust and search before Zurin genially invited in a crowd and tainted the goods. Because with a jumper, there were two questions: was he alone, and was he pushed?

Timofeyev said to no one in particular, "Pasha and I go far back. We studied and did research together at the institute when the country suffered its economic collapse. Imagine, the greatest physics laboratory in Moscow, and we worked without pay. The director, Academician Gerasimov, turned off the heat in the buildings to save money, and of course, it was winter and the pipes froze. We had a thousand liters of radioactive water to discharge, so we sent it into the river in the center of the city." He drained his glass. "The director was a brilliant man, but you would sometimes find him inside a bottle. On those occasions he relied on Pasha and me. Anyway, we dumped radioactive water in the middle of Moscow, and no one knew."

Arkady was taken aback. He certainly hadn't known.

Rina took Timofeyev's glass to the bar, where she paused by a gallery of photographs in which Pasha Ivanov was not dead. Ivanov was not a handsome individual, but a big man full of grand gestures. In different pictures he rappelled off cliffs, trekked the Urals, kayaked through white water. He embraced Yeltsin and Clinton and the senior Bush. He beamed at Putin, who, as usual, seemed to suck on a sour tooth. He cradled a miniature dachshund like a baby. Ivanov partied with opera tenors and rock stars, and even when he bowed to the Orthodox patriarch, a brash confidence shone through. Other New Russians fell by the wayside: shot, bankrupted or exiled by the state. Pasha not only flourished, he was known as a public-spirited man, and when construction funds for the Church of the Redeemer ran low, Ivanov provided the gold foil for the dome. When Arkady first opened a file on Ivanov, he was told that if Ivanov was charged with breaking the law, he could call the senate on his mobile phone and have the law rewritten. Trying to indict Ivanov was like trying to hold on to a snake that kept shedding skin after skin and grew legs in the meantime. In other words, Pasha Ivanov was both a man of his time and a stage in evolution.

Arkady noticed a barely perceptible glitter on the windowsill, scattered grains of crystals so familiar he could not resist pressing his forefinger to pick them up and taste them. Salt.

"I'm going to look around," he said.

"But you're not investigating," Hoffman said.

"Absolutely not."

"A word alone," Zurin said. He led Arkady into the hall. "Renko, we had an investigation into Ivanov and NoviRus, but a case against a suicide doesn't smell good in anybody's nostrils."

"You initiated the investigation."

"And I'm ending it. The last thing I want is for people to get the idea that we hounded Pasha Ivanov to death, and still went after him even when he was in the grave. It makes us look vindictive, like fanatics, which we aren't." The prosecutor searched Arkady's eyes. "When you've had your little look around here, go to your office and collect all the Ivanov and NoviRus files and leave them by my office. Do it tonight. And stop using the phrase 'New Russian' when you refer to crime. We're all New Russians, aren't we?"

"I'm trying."

Ivanov's apartment took up the entire

tenth floor. There weren't many rooms, but they were spacious and commanded a wraparound view of the city that gave the illusion of walking on air. Arkady began at a bedroom upholstered in linen wall panels, laid with a Persian rug. The photographs here were more personal: Ivanov skiing with Rina, sailing with Rina, in scuba-diving gear with Rina. She had huge eyes and a Slavic shelf of cheekbones. In each picture a breeze lifted her golden hair; she was the kind who could summon a breeze. Considering their difference in ages, for Ivanov their relationship must have been a bit like making a mistress of a leggy girl, a Lolita. That was who she reminded Arkady of — Lolita was a Russian creation, after all! There was a nearly paternal humor in Pasha's expression and a candy-sweet flavor to Rina's smile.

A rosy nude, a Modigliani, hung on the wall. On the night table were an ashtray of Lalique glass and a Hermès alarm clock; in the drawer was a 9mm pistol, a Viking with a fat clip of seventeen rounds, but not a whiff of ever having been fired. An attaché case on the bed held a single Bally shoe sack and a mobile-phone charger cord. On the bookshelf was a decorator's selection of worn leather-bound collections of Pushkin,

Rilke and Chekhov, and a box that held a trio of Patek, Cartier and Rolex watches and gently agitated them to keep them running, a definite necessity for the dead. The only off note was dirty laundry piled in a corner.

He moved into a bathroom with a limestone floor, gold-plated fixtures on a step-in spa, heated bars for robes large enough for polar bears and the convenience of a toilet phone. A shaving mirror magnified the lines of Arkady's face. A medicine cabinet held — besides the usual toiletries — bottles of Viagra, sleeping pills, Prozac. Arkady noted a Dr. Novotny's name on each prescription. He didn't see any antibiotics for infection.

The kitchen looked both new and forgotten, with gleaming steel appliances, enameled pots without a single smudge and burners with not one spot of crusted sauce. A silvery rack held dusty, expensive wines, no doubt selected by an expert. Yet the dishwasher was stacked with unwashed dishes, just as the bed had been loosely made and the bathroom towels hung awry, the signs of a man caring for himself. A restaurant-size refrigerator was a cold vault, empty except for bottles of mineral water, odds and ends of cheese, crackers and half a loaf of sliced bread. Vodka sat in the freezer. Pasha was a busy man, off to business dinners every day. He was, until recently, a famously sociable man, not a wealthy recluse with long hair and fingernails. He would have wanted to show his friends a shining up-to-date kitchen and offer them a decent Bordeaux or a chilled shot of vodka. Yet he hadn't shown anyone anything, not for months. In the dining room Arkady laid his cheek on the rosewood table and looked down its length. Dusty, but not a scratch.

At the twist of a rheostat, the next room turned into a home theater with a flat screen a good two meters wide, speakers in matte black and eight swivel chairs in red velvet with individual gooseneck lamps. All New Russians had home theaters, as if they were auteurs on the side. Arkady flipped through a video library ranging from Eisenstein to Jackie Chan. There was no tape in the tape player, and nothing in the mini-fridge but splits of Moët.

An exercise room had floor-to-ceiling windows, a padded floor, free weights and an exercise machine that looked like a catapult. A television hung over a stationary bike.

The prize was Ivanov's apartment office,

a futuristic cockpit of glass and stainless steel. Everything was close at hand, a monitor and printer on the desk, and a computer stack with a CD tray open beneath, next to an empty wastebasket. On a table lay copies of *The Wall Street Journal* and *The Financial Times*, folded as neatly as pressed sheets. CNN was on the monitor screen, market quotes streaming under a man who muttered half a world away. Arkady suspected the subdued sound was the sign of a lonely man, the need for another voice in the apartment, even while he banned his lover and nearest associates. It also struck Arkady that this was the closest anyone in the prosecutor's office had ever come to penetrating NoviRus. It was a shame that the man to do so was him. Arkady's life had come to this: his highest skill lay in ferreting out which man had bludgeoned another. The subtleties of corporate theft were new to him, and he stood in front of the screen like an ape encountering fire. Virtually within reach might be the answers he had been searching for: the names of silent partners in the ministries who promoted and protected Ivanov and their account numbers in offshore banks. He wouldn't find car trunks stuffed with dollar bills. It didn't work that way anymore. There was no paper. Money flew through the air and was gone.

Victor, the detective from the street, finally made it up. He was a sleep-deprived man in a sweater that reeked of cigarettes. He held up a sandwich bag containing a saltshaker. "This was on the pavement under Ivanov. Maybe it was there already. Why would anyone jump out a window with a saltshaker?"

Bobby Hoffman squeezed by Victor. "Renko, the best hackers in the world are Russian. I've encrypted and programmed Pasha's hard drive to self-destruct at the first sign of a breach. In other words, don't touch a fucking thing."

"You were Pasha's computer wizard as well as a business adviser?" Arkady said.

"I did what Pasha asked."

Arkady tapped the CD tray. It slid open, revealing a silvery disk. Hoffman tapped the tray and it slid shut.

He said, "I should also tell you that the computer and any disks are NoviRus property. You are a millimeter from trespassing. You ought to know the laws here."

"Mr. Hoffman, don't tell me about Russian law. You were a thief in New York, and you're a thief here."

"No, I'm a consultant. I'm the guy who

told Pasha not to worry about you. You have an advanced degree in business?"

"No."

"Law?"

"No."

"Accounting?"

"No."

"Then lots of luck. The Americans came after me with a staff of eager-beaver lawyers right out of Harvard. I can see Pasha had a lot to be afraid of." This was more the hostile attitude that Arkady had expected, but Hoffman ran out of steam. "Why don't you think it's suicide? What's wrong?"

"I didn't say that anything was."

"Something bothers you."

Arkady considered. "Recently your friend wasn't the Pasha Ivanov of old, was he?"

"That could have been depression."

"He moved twice in the last three months. Depressed people don't have the energy to move; they sit still." Depression happened to be a subject that Arkady knew something about. "It sounds like fear to me."

"Fear of what?"

"You were close to him, you'd know better than I. Does anything here seem out of place?"

"I wouldn't know. Pasha wouldn't let us in here. Rina and I haven't been inside this apartment for a month. If you were investigating, what would you be looking for?"

"I have no idea."

Victor felt at the sleeve of Hoffman's jacket. "Nice suede. Must have cost a fortune."

"It was Pasha's. I admired it once when he was wearing it, and he forced it on me. It wasn't as if he didn't have plenty more, but he was generous."

"How many more jackets?" Arkady asked.

"Twenty, at least."

"And suits and shoes and tennis whites?"

"Of course."

"I saw clothes in the corner of the bedroom. I didn't see a closet."

"I'll show you," Rina said. How long she had been standing behind Victor, Arkady didn't know. "I designed this apartment, you know."

"It's a very nice apartment," Arkady said.

Rina studied him for signs of condescension, before she turned and, unsteadily, hand against the wall, led the way to Ivanov's bedroom. Arkady saw nothing different until Rina pushed a wall panel that clicked and swung open to a walk-in closet bathed in lights. Suits hung on the left, pants and jackets on the right, some new and still in store bags with elaborate Italian names. Ties hung on a brass carousel. Built-in bureaus held shirts, underclothes and racks for shoes. The clothes ranged from plush cashmere to casual linen, and everything in the closet was immaculate, except a tall dressing mirror that was cracked but intact, and a bed of sparkling crystals that covered the floor.

Prosecutor Zurin arrived. "What is it now?"

Arkady licked a finger to pick up a grain and put it to his tongue. "Salt. Table salt." At least fifty kilos' worth of salt had been poured on the floor. The bed was softly rounded, dimpled with two faint impressions.

"A sign of derangement," Zurin announced. "There's no sane explanation for this. It's the work of a man in suicidal despair. Anything else, Renko?"

"There was salt on the windowsill."

"More salt? Poor man. God knows what was going through his mind."

"What do you think?" Hoffman asked Arkady.

"Suicide," Timofeyev said from the hall, his voice muffled by his handkerchief.

Victor spoke up. "As long as Ivanov is

dead. My mother put all her money in one of his funds. He promised a hundred percent profit in a hundred days. She lost everything, and he was voted New Russian of the Year. If he was here now and alive, I would strangle him with his own steaming guts."

That would settle the issue, Arkady thought.

By the time Arkady had delivered a hand truck of NoviRus files to the prosecutor's office and driven home, it was two in the morning.

His apartment was not a glass tower shimmering on the skyline but a pile of rocks off the Garden Ring. Various Soviet architects seemed to have worked with blinders on to design a building with flying buttresses, Roman columns and Moorish windows. Sections of the facade had fallen off, and parts had been colonized by grasses and saplings sowed by the wind, but inside, the apartments offered high ceilings and casement windows. Arkady's view was not of sleek Mercedeses gliding by but of a backyard row of metal garages, each secured by a padlock covered by the cutoff bottom of a plastic soda bottle.

No matter the hour, Mr. and Mrs.

Rajapakse, his neighbors from across the hall, came over with biscuits, hard-boiled eggs and tea. They were university professors from Sri Lanka, a small, dark pair with delicate manners.

"It is no bother," Rajapakse said. "You are our best friend in Moscow. You know what Gandhi said when he was asked about Western civilization? He said he thought it would be a good idea. You are the one civilized Russian we know. Because we know you do not take care of yourself, we must do it for you."

Mrs. Rajapakse wore a sari. She flew around the apartment like a butterfly to catch a fly and put it out the window.

"She harms nothing," her husband said. "The violence here in Moscow is very bad. She worries about you all the time. She is like a little mother to you."

After Arkady chased them home, he had half a glass of vodka and toasted. To a New Russian.

He was trying.

2

Evgeny Lysenko, nickname Zhenya, age eleven, looked like an old man waiting at a bus stop. He was in the thick plaid jacket and matching cap that he'd been wearing when he was brought by militia to the children's shelter the winter before. The sleeves were shrinking, but whenever the boy went on an outing with Arkady, he wore the same outfit and carried the same chess set and book of fairy tales that had been left with him. If Zhenya didn't get out every other week, he would run away. How he had become Arkady's obligation was a mystery. To begin with, Arkady had accompanied a well-intentioned friend, a television journalist, a nice woman looking for a child to mother and save. When Arkady arrived at the shelter for the next outing, his mobile phone rang. It was the journalist calling to say she was sorry, but she wasn't coming; one afternoon with Zhenya was enough for her. By then Zhenya was almost at the car, and Arkady's choice was to either leap behind the wheel and drive away, or take the boy himself.

Anyway, here was Zhenya once again, dressed for winter on a warm spring day, clutching his fairy tales, while Olga Andreevna, the head of the shelter, fussed over him. "Cheer Zhenya up," she told Arkady. "It's Sunday. All the other children have one kind of visitor or another. Zhenya should have something. Tell him some jokes. Be a jolly soul. Make him laugh."

"I'll try to think of some jokes."

"Go to a movie, maybe kick a ball back and forth. The boy needs to get out more, to socialize. We offer psychiatric evaluation, proper diet, music classes, a regular school nearby. Most children thrive. Zhenya is not thriving."

The shelter appeared to be a healthful setting, a two-story structure painted like a child's drawing with birds, butterflies, rainbow and sun, and a real vegetable garden bordered by marigolds. The shelter was a model, an oasis in a city where thousands of children went without homes and worked pushing outdoor market carts or worse. Arkady saw a circle of girls in a playground serving tea to their dolls. They seemed happy.

Zhenya climbed into the car, put on his seat belt and held his book and chess set tight. He stared straight ahead like a soldier.

"So, what will you do, then?" Olga Andreevna asked Arkady.

"Well, we're such jolly souls, we're capable of anything."

"Does he talk to you?"

"He reads his book."

"But does he talk to you?"

"No."

"Then how do you two communicate?"

"To be honest, I don't know."

Arkady had a Zhiguli 9, a goat of a car, not prepossessing but built for Russian roads. They drove along the river wall, past fishermen casting for urban aquatic life. Considering the black cloud of truck exhaust and the sluggish green of the Moscow River, for optimism fishermen were hard to beat. A BMW shot by, followed by a security team in an SUV. In fact, the city was safer than it had been in years, and chase cars were largely for form, like the retinue of a lord. The most ferocious businessmen had killed one another off, and a truce between the Mafias seemed to be holding. Of course, a wise man took out all forms of insurance. Restaurants, for example, had both private security guards and a representative of the local Mafia at the front door. Moscow had reached an equilibrium, which made Ivanov's suicide all the harder to understand.

Meanwhile, Zhenya read aloud his favorite fairy tale, about a girl abandoned by her father and sent by her stepmother into the deep woods to be killed and eaten by a witch, Baba Yaga.

" 'Baba Yaga had a long blue nose and steel teeth, and she lived in a hut that stood on chicken legs. The hut could walk through the woods and sit wherever Baba Yaga ordered. Around the hut was a fence festooned with skulls. Most victims died just at the sight of Baba Yaga. The strongest men, the wealthiest lords, it didn't matter. She boiled the meat off their bones and when she had eaten every last bite she added their skulls to her hideous fence. A few prisoners lived long enough to try to escape, but Baba Yaga flew after them on a magic mortar and pestle.' " However, page by page, through kindness and courage, the girl did escape and made her way back to her father, who sent away the evil stepmother. When Zhenya was done reading he gave Arkady a quick glance and settled back in his seat, a ritual completed.

At Sparrow Hill, Arkady swung the car in sight of Moscow University, one of Stalin's skyscrapers, built by convict labor in such a fever for higher learning and at such wholesale cost of life that bodies were said to have been left entombed. That was a fairy tale he could keep to himself, Arkady thought.

"Did you have some fun this week?" Arkady asked.

Zhenya said nothing. Nevertheless, Arkady tried a smile. After all, many children from the shelter had suffered negligence and abuse. They couldn't be expected to be rays of sunshine. Some children were adopted out of the shelter. Zhenya, with his sharp nose and vow of silence, wasn't a likely candidate.

Arkady himself would have been harder to please, he thought, if he'd had a higher opinion of himself as a child. As he remembered, he had been an unlovable stick, devoid of social skills and isolated by the aura of fear around his father, an army officer who was perfectly willing to humiliate adults, let alone a boy. When Arkady came home to their apartment, he would know whether the general was in just by the stillness in the air. The very foyer seemed to hold its breath. So Arkady had little personal experience to draw on. His father had never taken him for outings. Sometimes Sergeant Belov, his father's aide, would go with Arkady to the park. Winters were the best, when the sergeant, tramping and puffing like a horse, pulled Arkady on a sled through the snow. Otherwise, Arkady walked with his mother, and she tended to walk ahead, a slim woman with a dark braid of hair, lost in her own world.

Zhenya always insisted on going to Gorky Park. As soon as they'd bought tickets and entered the grounds, Arkady got out of the way while Zhenya made a slow perambulation of the plaza fountain to scan the crowd. Fluffs of poplar seed floated on the water and collected around the stalls. Crows patrolled in search of sandwich crusts. Gorky Park was officially a park of culture, with an emphasis on outdoor performances of classical music and promenades among the trees. Over time, the bandshell had been claimed by rock bands and the promenades covered by amusement rides. As ever, Zhenya returned from the fountain dejected.

"Let's go shoot something," Arkady said. That generally cheered boys up.

Five rubles bought five shots with an air rifle at a row of Coke cans. Arkady remembered when the targets had been American bombers dangling on strings, something worth blazing away at. From there they went into a fun house, where they followed a dark walkway between weary moans and swaying bats. Next came a real space shuttle that had truly orbited the earth and was tricked out with chairs that lurched from side to side to simulate a bumpy descent.

Arkady asked, "What do you think, Captain? Should we return to earth?"

Zhenya got out of his chair and marched off without a glance.

It was a little like accompanying a sleep-walker. Arkady was along but invisible, and Zhenya moved as if on a track. They stopped, as they had on every other trip, to watch bungee jumping. The jumpers were teenagers, taking turns soaring off the platform, flapping, screaming with fear, only to be snapped back the moment before they hit the ground. The girls were dramatic, the way their hair rippled on the way down and snapped as the plunge was arrested. Arkady couldn't help but think of Ivanov and the difference between the fun of near death and the real thing, the profound difference between giggling as you bounced to your feet, and staying embedded in the pavement. For his part, Zhenya didn't appear to care whether the jumpers died or survived. He always stood in the same spot and glanced cagily around. Then he took off for the roller coaster.

He took the same rides in the same order: a roller coaster, a giant swing and a ride in a pontoon boat around a little man-made lake. He and Arkady sat back and pedaled, the same as every time, while white swans and black swans cruised by in turn. Although it was Sunday, the park maintained an uncrowded lassitude. Rollerbladers slid by with long, easy strides. The Beatles drifted from loudspeakers: "Yesterday." Zhenya looked hot in his cap and jacket, but Arkady knew better than to suggest the boy remove them.

The sight of silver birches by the water made Arkady ask, "Have you ever been here in the winter?"

Zhenya might as well have been deaf.

"Do you ice-skate?" Arkady asked.

Zhenya looked straight ahead.

"Ice skating here in the wintertime is beautiful," Arkady said. "Maybe we should do that."

Zhenya didn't blink.

Arkady said, "I'm sorry that I'm not better at this. I was never good at jokes. I just can't remember them. In Soviet times, when things were hopeless, we had great jokes."

Since the children's shelter fed Zhenya good nutritious food, Arkady plied him with candy bars and soda. They ate at an outdoor table while playing chess with pieces that were worn from use, on a board that had been taped together more than once. Zhenya didn't speak even to say "Mate!" He simply knocked over Arkady's king at the appropriate time and set the pieces up again.

"Have you ever tried football?" Arkady asked. "Stamp collecting? Do you have a butterfly net?"

Zhenya concentrated on the board. The head of the shelter had told Arkady how Zhenya did solitary chess problems every night until lights-out.

Arkady said, "You may wonder how it is that a senior investigator like myself is free on such a glorious day. The reason is that the prosecutor, my chief, feels that I need reassignment. It's plain that I need reassignment, because I don't know a suicide when I see one. An investigator who doesn't know a suicide when he sees one is a man who needs to be reassigned."

Arkady's move, the retreat of a knight to a useless position on the side of the board, made Zhenya look up, as if to detect a trap. Not to worry, Arkady thought.

"Are you familiar with the name Pavel Ilyich Ivanov?" Arkady asked. "No? How about Pasha Ivanov? That's a more interesting name. Pavel is old-fashioned, stiff. Pasha is Eastern, Oriental, with a turban and a sword. Much better than Pavel."

Zhenya stood to see the board from another angle. Arkady would have surrendered, but he knew how Zhenya relished a thoroughly crushing victory.

Arkady said, "It's curious how, if you study anyone long enough, if you devote enough effort to understanding him, he can become part of your life. Not a friend but a kind of acquaintance. To put it another way, a shadow has to become close, right? I thought I was beginning to understand Pasha, and then I found salt." Arkady looked for a reaction, in vain. "And well you should be surprised. There was a lot of salt in the apartment. That's not a crime, although it might be a sign. Some people say that's what you'd expect from a man about to take his life, a closet full of salt. They could be right. Or not. We don't investigate suicides, but how do you know it's a suicide unless you investigate? That is the question."

Zhenya scooped up the knight, revealing a pin on Arkady's bishop. Arkady moved his king. At once, the bishop disappeared into Zhenya's grasp, and Arkady advanced another sacrificial lamb.

"But the prosecutor doesn't want complications, especially from a difficult investigator, a holdover from the Soviet era, a man on the skids. Some men march confidently from one historical era to the next; others skid. I've been told to enjoy a rest while matters are sorted out, and that is why I can spend the day with you." Zhenya pushed a juggernaut of a rook the length of the board, tipped over Arkady's king and swept all of the pieces into the box. He hadn't heard a word.

The last regular event was a ride on the Ferris wheel, which kept turning as Arkady and Zhenya handed over their tickets, scrambled into an open-air gondola and latched themselves in. A complete revolution of the fifty-meter wheel took five minutes. As the gondola rose, it afforded a view first of the amusement park, then of geese lifting from the lake and Rollerbladers gliding on the trails and, finally, at its apogee, through a floating scrim of poplar fluff, a panorama of gray daytime Moscow, flashes of gold from church to church and the distant groans of traffic and construction. All the way, Zhenya stretched his neck to look in one direction and then the other, as if he could encompass the city's entire population.

Arkady had tried to find Zhenya's father, even though the boy refused to supply the first name or help a sketch artist from the militia. Nevertheless, Arkady had gone through Moscow residence, birth and draft records in search of Lysenkos. In case the father was alcoholic, Arkady asked at drying-out tanks. Since Zhenya played so well, Arkady visited chess clubs. And, because Zhenya was so shy of authority, Arkady went through arrest records. Six possibles turned up, but they all proved to be serving long terms in seminaries, Chechnya or prison.

When Zhenya and Arkady were at the very top of the wheel, it stopped. The attendant on the ground gave a thin shout and waved. Nothing to worry about. Zhenya was happy with more time to scan the city, while Arkady contemplated the virtues of early retirement: the chance to learn new languages, new dances, travel to exotic places. His stock with the prosecutor was definitely falling. Once you'd been to the top of the Ferris wheel of life, so to speak, anything else was lower. So here he was, literally suspended. Poplar fluff sailed by like the scum of a river.

The wheel started to turn again, and Arkady smiled, to prove his attention hadn't wandered. "Any luck? You know, in Iceland there's a kind of imp, a sprite that's just a head on a foot. It's a playful imp, very mischievous, likes to hide things like your keys and socks, and you can only see it from the corner of your eye. If you look straight at it, it disappears. Maybe that's the best way to see some people."

Zhenya acknowledged not a word, which was a statement in itself, that Arkady was merely transportation, a means to an end. When the gondola reached the ground, the boy stepped out, ready to return to the shelter, and Arkady let him march ahead.

The trick, Arkady thought, was not to expect more. Obviously Zhenya had come to the park with his father, and by this point, Arkady knew exactly how they had spent the day. A child's logic was that if his father had come here before, he would come again, and he might even be magically evoked through a re-creation of that day. Zhenya was a grim little soldier defending a last outpost of memory, and any word he passed with Arkady would mute and dim his father that much more. A smile would be as bad as traffic with the enemy.

On the way out of the park, Arkady's mobile phone rang. It was Prosecutor Zurin.

"Renko, what did you tell Hoffman last night?"

"About what?"

"You know what. Where are you?"

"The Park of Culture and Rest. I'm resting." Arkady watched Zhenya steal the opportunity to take another turn of the fountain.

"Relaxing?"

"I'd like to think so."

"Because you were so wound up last night, so full of . . . speculation, weren't you? Hoffman wants to see you."

"Why?"

"You said something to him last night. Something out of my earshot, because nothing I heard from you made any sense at all. I have never seen a clearer case of suicide."

"Then you have officially determined that Ivanov killed himself."

"Why not?"

Arkady didn't answer directly. "If you're satisfied, then I don't see what there is for me to do."

"Don't be coy, Renko. You're the one

who opened this can of worms. You'll be the one who shuts it. Hoffman wants you to clean up the loose ends. I don't see why he doesn't just go home."

"As I remember, he's a fugitive from America."

"Well, as a courtesy to him, and just to settle things, he wants a few more questions answered. Ivanov was Jewish, wasn't he? I mean his mother was."

"So?"

"I'm just saying, he and Hoffman were a pair."

Arkady waited for more, but Zurin seemed to think he had made his point. "I take my orders from you, Prosecutor Zurin. What are your orders?" Arkady wanted this to be clear.

"What time is it?"

"It's four in the afternoon."

"First get Hoffman out of the apartment. Then get to work tomorrow morning."

"Why not tonight?"

"In the morning."

"If I get Hoffman out of the apartment, how will I get back in?"

"The elevator operator knows the code now. He's old guard. Trustworthy."

"And just what do you expect me to do?"

"Whatever Hoffman asks. Just get this

matter settled. Not complicated, not drawn out, but settled."

"Does that mean over or resolved?"

"You know very well what I mean."

"I don't know, I'm fairly involved here." Zhenya was just finishing his circuit of the fountain.

"Get over there now."

"I'll need a detective. I should have a pair, but I'll settle for Victor Fedorov."

"Why him? He hates businessmen."

"Perhaps he'll be harder to buy."

"Just go."

"Do I get my files back?"

"No."

Zurin hung up. The prosecutor might have shown a little more edge than usual, but, everything considered, the conversation had been as pleasant as Arkady could have wished.

Bobby Hoffman let Arkady and Victor into the Ivanov apartment, moved to the sofa and dropped into the deep impression already there. Despite air-conditioning, the room had the funk of an all-night vigil. Hoffman's hair was matted, his eyes a blur, and tear tracks ran into the reddish bristle on his jowls. His clothes looked twisted around him, although the jacket given to him by Pasha was folded on the coffee table beside a snifter and two empty bottles of brandy. He said, "I don't have the code to the keypad, so I stayed."

"Why?" Arkady asked.

"Just to get things straight."

"Straighten us out, please."

Hoffman tilted his head and smiled. "Renko, as far as your investigation goes, I want you to know that you wouldn't have touched Pasha or me in a thousand years. The American Securities and Exchange Commission never hung anything on me."

"You fled the country."

"You know what I always tell complainers? 'Read the fine print, asshole!' "

"The fine print is the important print?"

"That's why it's fine."

"As in 'You can be the wealthiest man in the world and live in a palace with a beautiful woman, but one day you will fall out a tenth-floor window'?" Arkady said. "As fine as that?"

"Yeah." The air went out of Hoffman, and it occurred to Arkady that for all the American's bravado, without the protection of Pasha Ivanov, Bobby Hoffman was a mollusk without its shell, a tender American morsel on the Russian ocean floor.

"Why don't you just leave Moscow?"

Arkady asked Hoffman. "Take a million dollars from the company and go. Set up in Cyprus or Monaco."

"That's what Timofeyev suggested, except his number was ten million."

"That's a lot."

"Look, the bank accounts Pasha and I opened offshore add up to about a hundred million. Not all our money, of course, but *that's* a lot."

A hundred million? Arkady tried to add the zeroes. "I stand corrected."

Victor took a chair and set down his briefcase. He gave the apartment the cold glance of a Bolshevik in the Winter Palace. From his briefcase he fished a personal ashtray fashioned from an empty soda can, although his sweater had holes that suggested he put out his cigarettes another way. He also had put, in a light-fingered way, drinking glasses from the evening before in plastic bags labeled "Zurin," "Timofeyev" and "Rina Shevchenko," just in case.

Hoffman contemplated the empty bottles. "Staying here is like watching a movie, running every possible scenario. Pasha jumping out the window, being dragged and thrown out, over and over. Renko, you're the expert: was Pasha killed?"

"I have no idea."

"Thanks a lot, that's helpful. Last night you sounded like you had suspicions."

"I thought the scene deserved more investigation."

"Because as soon as you started to poke around, you found a closet full of fucking salt. What is that about?"

"I was hoping you could tell me. You never noticed that with Ivanov before, a fixation on salt?"

"No. All I know is, everything wasn't as simple as the prosecutor and Timofeyev said. You were right about Pasha changing. He locked us out of here. He'd wear clothes once and throw them away. It wasn't like giving the jacket to me. He threw out the clothes in garbage bags. Driving around, suddenly he'd change his route, like he was on the run."

"Like you," Victor said.

"Only he didn't run far," Arkady said. "He stayed in Moscow."

Hoffman said, "How could he go? Pasha always said, 'Business is personal. You show fear and you're dead.' Anyway, you wanted more time to investigate. Okay, I bought you some."

"How did you do that?"

"Call me Bobby."

"How did you do that, Bobby?"

"NoviRus has foreign partners. I told Timofeyev that unless you were on the case, I'd tell them that the cause of Pasha's death wasn't totally resolved. Foreign partners are nervous about Russian violence. I always tell them it's exaggerated."

"Of course."

"Nothing can stop a major project — the Last Judgment wouldn't stop an oil deal — but I can stall for a day or two until the company gets a clean bill of health."

"The detective and I will be the doctors who decide this billion-dollar state of health? I'm flattered."

"I'd start you off with a bonus of a thousand dollars."

"No, thanks."

"You don't like money? What are you, communists?" Hoffman's smile stalled halfway between insult and ingratiation.

"The problem is that I don't believe you. Americans won't take the word of either a criminal like you or an investigator like me. NoviRus has its own security force, including former detectives. Have them investigate. They're already paid."

"Paid to protect the company," Hoffman said. "Yesterday that meant protecting Pasha, today it's protecting Timofeyev. Anyway, Colonel Ozhogin is in charge, and he hates me."

"If Ozhogin dislikes you, then I advise you to get on the next plane. I'm sure Russian violence is exaggerated, but it serves no one's purpose for you to be in Moscow." Ozhogin's displeasure was a cue for any man to travel to foreign climes, Arkady thought.

"After you ask some questions. You hounded Pasha and me for months. Now you can hound someone else."

"It's not that simple, as you say."

"A few fucking questions is all I'm asking for."

Arkady gave way to Victor, who opened a ledger from his briefcase and said, "May I call you Bobby?" He rolled the name like hard candy. "Bobby, there would be more than one or two questions. We'd have to talk to everyone who saw Pasha Ivanov last night, his driver and bodyguards, the building staff. Also, we'd have to review the security tapes."

"Ozhogin won't like that."

Arkady shrugged. "If Ivanov didn't commit suicide, there was a breach in security."

Victor said, "To do a complete job, we should also talk to his friends."

"They weren't here."

"They knew Ivanov. His friends and the women he was involved with, like the one who was here last night."

"Rina is a great kid. Very artistic."

Victor gave Arkady a meaningful glance. The detective had once invented a theory called Fuck the Widow, for determining a probable killer on the basis of who lined up first to console a grieving spouse. "Also, enemies."

"Everyone has enemies. George Washington had enemies."

"Not as many as Pasha," said Arkady. "There were earlier attempts on Pasha's life. We'd have to check who was involved and where they are. It's not just a matter of one more day and a few more questions."

Victor dropped a butt in the soda can. "What the investigator wants to know is, if we make progress, are you going to run and leave us with our pants down and the moon out?"

"If so, the detective recommends you begin running now," Arkady said. "Before we start."

Bobby hung on to the sofa. "I'm staying right here."

"If we do start, this is a possible crime scene, and the very first thing is to get you out of here."

"We have to talk," Victor told Arkady.

The two men retreated to the white

runway of the hall. Victor lit a cigarette and sucked on it like oxygen. "I'm dying. I have heart problems, lung problems, liver problems. The trouble is, I'm dying too slowly. Once my pension meant something. Now I have to work until they push me into the grave. I ran the other day. I thought I heard church bells. It was my chest. They're raising the price of vodka and tobacco. I don't bother eating anymore. Fifteen brands of Italian pasta, but who can afford it? So do I really want to spend my final days playing bodyguard to a dog turd like Bobby Hoffman? Because that's all he wants us for, bodyguards. And he'll disappear, he'll disappear as soon as he shakes more money out of Timofeyev. He'll run when we need him most."

"He could have run already."

"He's just driving up the price."

"You said there are good prints on the glasses. Maybe there are some more."

"Arkady, these people are different. It's every man for himself. Ivanov is dead? Good riddance."

"So you don't think it was suicide?" Arkady asked.

"Who knows? Who cares? Russians used to kill for women or power, real reasons. Now they kill for money."

"The ruble wasn't really money," Arkady said.

"But we're leaving, right?"

Bobby Hoffman sank into the sofa as they returned. He could read the verdict in their eyes. Arkady had intended to deliver the bad news and keep going, but he slowed as bands of sunlight vibrated the length of the room. A person could argue whether a white decor was timid or bold, Arkady thought, but there was no denying that Rina had done a professional job. The entire room glowed, and the chrome of the wet bar cast a shimmering reflection over the photographs of Pasha Ivanov and his constellation of famous and powerful friends. Ivanov's world was so far away from the average Russian's that the pictures could have been taken by a telescope pointed to the stars. This was the closest Arkady had gotten to NoviRus. He was, for the moment, inside the enemy camp.

When Arkady got to the sofa, Hoffman wrapped his pudgy hands around Arkady's. "Okay, I took a disk with confidential data from Pasha's computer: shell companies, bribes, payoffs, bank accounts. It was going to be my insurance, but I'm spending it on you. I agreed to give it back when you're done. That's the deal I made with Ozhogin and Zurin, the disk for a few days of your help. Don't ask me where it is, it's safe. So you were right, I'm a venal slob. Big news. Know why I'm doing this? I couldn't go back to my place. I didn't have the strength, and I couldn't sleep, either, so I just sat here. In the middle of the night, I heard this rubbing. I thought it was mice and got a flashlight and walked around the apartment. No mice. But I still heard them. Finally I went down to the lobby to ask the receptionist. He wasn't at his desk, though. He was outside with the doorman, on their hands and knees with brushes and bleach, scrubbing blood off the sidewalk. They did it, there's not a spot left. That's what I'd been hearing from ten stories up, the scrubbing. I know it's impossible, but that's what I heard. And I thought to myself, Renko: there's a son of a bitch who'd hear the scrubbing. That's who I want."

3

In the black-and-white videotape, the two Mercedeses rolled up to the street security camera, and bodyguards — large men further inflated by the armored vests they wore under their suits — deployed from the chase car to the building canopy. Only then did the lead car's driver trot around to open the curbside door.

A digital clock rolled in a corner of the tape. 2128. 2129. 2130. Finally Pasha Ivanov unfolded from the rear seat. He looked more disheveled than the dynamic Ivanov of the apartment photo gallery. Arkady had questioned the driver, who had told him that Ivanov hadn't said a word all the way from the office to the apartment, not even on a mobile phone.

Something amused Ivanov. Two dachshunds strained on their leashes to sniff his attaché case. Although the tape was silent, Arkady read Ivanov's lips: *Puppies?* he asked the owner. When the dogs had passed, Ivanov clutched the attaché to his chest and went into the building. Arkady switched to the lobby tape.

The marble lobby was so brightly lit that everyone wore halos. The doorman and receptionist wore jackets with braid over not too obvious holsters. Once the doorman activated the call button with a key, he stayed at Ivanov's side while Ivanov used a handkerchief, and when the elevator doors opened, Arkady went to the elevator tape. He had already interviewed the operator, a former Kremlin guard, white-haired but hard as a sandbag.

Arkady asked whether he and Ivanov had talked. The operator said, "I trained on the Kremlin staircase. Big men don't make small talk."

On the tape, Ivanov punched a code into the keypad and, as the doors opened, turned to the elevator camera. The camera's fishbowl lens made his face disproportionately huge, eyes drowning in shadow above the handkerchief he held against his nose. Maybe he had Timofeyev's summer cold. Ivanov finally moved through the open doors, and Arkady was reminded of an actor rushing to the stage, now hesitating, now rushing again. The time on the tape was 2133.

Arkady switched tapes, back to the street camera, and forwarded to 2147. The pavement was clear, the two cars were still at the curb, the lights of traffic filtering by. At 2148 a blur from above slapped the pavement. The doors of the chase car flew open, and the guards poured out to form a defensive circle on the pavement around what could have been a heap of rags with legs. One man raced into the building, another knelt to feel Ivanov's neck, while the driver of the sedan ran around it to open a rear door. The man taking Ivanov's pulse, or lack of it, shook his head while the doorman moved into view, arms wide in disbelief. That was it, the Pasha Ivanov movie, a story with a beginning and an end but no middle.

Arkady rewound and watched frame by frame.

Ivanov's upper body dropped from the top of the screen, shoulder hitched to take the brunt of the fall.

His head folded from the force of the impact even as his legs entered the frame.

Upper and lower body collapsed into a ring of dust that exploded from the pavement.

Pasha Ivanov settled as the doors of the chase car swung open and, in slow motion, the guards swam around his body.

Arkady watched to see whether any of the security team, while they were in the car and before Ivanov came out of the sky, glanced up; then he watched for anything like the saltshaker dropping with Ivanov or shaken loose by the force of the fall. Nothing. And then he watched to see whether any of the guards picked up anything afterward. No one did. They stood on the pavement, as useful as potted plants.

The doorman on duty kept looking up. He said, "I was in Special Forces, so I've seen parachutes that didn't deploy and bodies you scraped off the ground, but someone coming out of the sky here? And Ivanov, of all people. A good guy, I have to say, a generous guy. But what if he'd hit the doorman, did he think about that? Now a pigeon goes overhead and I duck."

"Your name?" Arkady asked.

"Kuznetsov, Grisha." Grisha still had the army stamp on him. Wary around officers.

"You were on duty two days ago?"

"The day shift. I wasn't here at night, when it happened, so I don't know what I can tell you."

"Just walk me around, if you would."

"Around what?"

"The building, front to back."

"For a suicide? Why?"

"Details."

"Details," Grisha muttered as the traffic went by. He shrugged. "Okay."

The building was short-staffed on weekends, Grisha said, only him, the receptionist and the passenger elevator man. Weekdays, there were two other men for repairs, working the service door and service elevator, picking up trash. Housecleaners on weekdays, too, if residents requested. Ivanov didn't. Everyone had been vetted, of course. Security cameras covered the street, lobby, passenger elevator and service alley. At the back of the lobby Grisha tapped in a code on a keypad by a door with a sign that said STAFF ONLY. The door eased open, and Grisha led Arkady into an area that consisted of a changing room with lockers, sink, microwave; toilet; mechanical room with furnace and hot-water heater; repair shop where two older men Grisha identified as Fart A and Fart B were intently threading a pipe; residents' storage area for rugs, skis and such, ending in a truck bay. Every door had a keypad and a different code.

Grisha said, "You ought to go to NoviRus Security. Like an underground bunker. They've got everything there:

building layout, codes, the works."

"Good idea." NoviRus Security was the last place Arkady wanted to be. "Can you open the bay?"

Light poured in as the gate rolled up, and Arkady found himself facing a service alley wide enough to accommodate a moving van. Dumpsters stood along the brick wall that was the back of shorter, older buildings facing the next street over. There were, however, security cameras aimed at the alley from the bay where Arkady and Grisha stood, and from the new buildings on either side. There was also a green-and-black motorcycle standing under a No Parking sign.

Something about the way the doorman screwed up his face made Arkady ask, "Yours?"

"Parking around here is a bitch. Sometimes I can find a place and sometimes I can't, but the Farts won't let me use the bay. Excuse me." As they walked to the bike, Arkady noticed a cardboard sign taped to the saddle: DON'T TOUCH THIS BIKE. I AM WATCHING YOU. Grisha borrowed a pen from Arkady and underlined "watching." "That's better."

"Quite a machine."

"A Kawasaki. I used to ride a Uralmoto,"

Grisha said, to let Arkady know how far he had come up in the world.

Arkady noticed a pedestrian door next to the bay. Each entry had a separate keypad. "Do people park here?"

"No, the Farts are all over them, too."

"Saturday, when the mechanics weren't on duty?"

"When we're short-staffed? Well, we can't leave our post every time a car stops in the alley. We give them ten minutes, and then we chase them out."

"Did that happen this Saturday?"

"When Ivanov jumped? I'm not on at night."

"I understand, but during your shift, did you or the receptionist notice anything unusual in the alley?"

Grisha took a while to think. "No. Besides, the back is locked tight on Saturdays. You'd need a bomb to get in."

"Or a code."

"You'd still be seen by the camera. We'd notice."

"I'm sure. You were in front?"

"At the canopy, yes."

"People were going in and out?"

"Residents and guests."

"Anyone carrying salt?"

"How much salt?"

"Bags and bags of salt."

"No."

"Ivanov wasn't bringing home salt day after day? No salt leaking from his briefcase?"

"No."

"I have salt on the brain, don't I?"

"Yeah." Said slowly.

"I should do something about that."

The Arbat was a promenade of outdoor musicians, sketch artists and souvenir stalls that sold strands of amber, nesting dolls of peasant women, retro posters of Stalin. Dr. Novotny's office was above a cybercafe. She told Arkady that she was about to retire on the money she would make selling to developers who planned to put in a Greek restaurant. Arkady liked the office as it was, a drowsy room with overstuffed chairs and Kandinsky prints, bright splashes of color that could have been windmills, bluebirds, cows. Novotny was a brisk seventy, her face a mask of lines around bright dark eyes.

"I first saw Pasha Ivanov a little more than a year ago, the first week in May. He seemed typical of our new entrepreneurs. Aggressive, intelligent, adaptable; the last sort to seek psychotherapy. They are happy to send in their wives or mistresses; it's popular for the women, like feng shui, but the men rarely come in themselves. In fact, he missed his last four sessions, although he insisted on paying for them."

"Why did he choose you?"

"Because I'm good."

"Oh." Arkady liked a woman who came straight to the point.

"Ivanov said he had trouble sleeping, which is always the way they start. They say they want a pill to help them sleep, but what they want me to prescribe is a mood elevator, which I am willing to do only as part of a broader therapy. We met once a week. He was entertaining, highly articulate, possessed of enormous self-confidence. At the same time, he was very secretive in certain areas, his business dealings for one, and, unfortunately, whatever was the cause of his . . ."

"Depression or fear?" Arkady asked.

"Both, if you need to put it that way. He was depressed, and he was afraid."

"Did he mention enemies?"

"Not by name. He said that ghosts were after him." Novotny opened a box of cigars, took one, peeled off the cellophane and slipped the cigar band over her finger. "I'm not saying that he believed in ghosts."

"Aren't you?"

"No. What I'm saying is that he had a past. A man like him gets to where he is by doing many remarkable things, some of which he might later regret."

Arkady described the scene at Ivanov's apartment. The doctor said that the broken mirror certainly could have been an expression of self-loathing, and jumping from a window was a man's way out. "However, the two most usual motives of suicide for men are financial and emotional, often evidenced as atrophied libido. Ivanov had wealth and a healthy sexual relationship with his friend Rina."

"He used Viagra."

"Rina is much younger."

"And his physical health?"

"For a man his age, good."

"He didn't mention an infection or a cold?"

"No."

"Did the subject of salt ever come up?"

"No."

"The floor of his closet was covered with salt."

"That *is* interesting."

"But you say he recently missed some sessions."

"A month's worth, and sporadically before then."

"Did he mention any attempts on his life?"

Novotny turned the cigar band around her finger. "Not in so many words. He said he had to stay a step ahead."

"A step ahead of ghosts, or someone real?"

"Ghosts can be very real. In Ivanov's case, however, I think he was pursued by both ghosts and someone real."

"Do you think he was suicidal?"

"Yes. At the same time, he was a survivor."

"Do you think, considering everything, he killed himself?"

"He could have. Did he? You're the investigator." Her face shifted into a sympathetic frown. "I'm sorry, I wish I could help you more. Would you like a cigar? It's Cuban."

"No, thank you. Do you smoke?"

"When I was a girl, all the modern, interesting women smoked cigars. You'd look good with a cigar. One more thing, Investigator. I got the impression that there was a cyclical nature to Ivanov's bouts of depression. Always in the spring, always early in May. In fact, right after May Day. But I must confess, May Day always deeply depressed me, too."

It wasn't easy to find an unfashionable restaurant among the Irish pubs and sushi bars in the center of Moscow, but Victor succeeded. He and Arkady had macaroni and grease served at a stand-up cafeteria around the corner from the militia headquarters on Petrovka. Arkady was happy with black tea and sugar, but Victor had a daily requirement of carbohydrates that was satisfied best by beer. From his briefcase Victor took morgue photos of Ivanov, frontal, dorsal and head shot, and spread them between the plates. One side of Ivanov's face was white, the other side black.

Victor said, "Dr. Toptunova said she didn't autopsy suicides. I asked her, 'What about your curiosity, your professional pride? What about poisons or psychotropic drugs?' She said they'd have to do biopsies, tests, waste the precious resources of the state. We agreed on fifty dollars. I figure Hoffman is good for that."

"Toptunova is a butcher." Arkady really didn't want to look at the pictures.

"You don't find Louis Pasteur doing autopsies for the militia. Thank God she operates on the dead. Anyway, she says Ivanov broke his neck. Fuck your mother, I could have told them that. And if it hadn't been his neck, it would have been his skull. Drugwise, he was clean, although she thought he had ulcers from the condition of his stomach. There was one odd thing. In his stomach? Bread and salt."

"Salt?"

"A lot of salt and just enough bread to get it down."

"She didn't mention anything about his complexion?"

"What was to mention? It was mainly one big bruise. I questioned the doorman and lobby receptionist again. They have the same story: no problems, no breach. Then some guy with dachshunds tried to pick me up. I showed him my ID to shake him up, you know, and he says, 'Oh, are they having another security check?' Saturday the building staff shut down the elevator and went to every apartment to check who was in. The guy was still upset. His dachshunds couldn't wait and had a little accident."

"Which means there was a breach. When did they do this check?"

Victor consulted his notebook. "Eleven-ten in the morning at his place. He's on the ninth floor, and I think they worked their way down."

"Good work." Arkady couldn't imagine who would want to pick up Victor, but applause was indicated.

"A different subject." Victor laid down a picture of two buckets and mops. "These I found in the lobby of the building across from Ivanov's. Abandoned, but the name of the cleaning service was on them, and I found who left them. Vietnamese. They didn't see Ivanov dive; they ran when they saw militia cars, because they're illegals."

Menial tasks that Russians wouldn't do, Vietnamese would. They came as "guest workers" and went into hiding when their visas expired. Their wardrobe was the clothes on their back, their accommodations a workers' hostel, their family connection the money they sent home once a month. Arkady could understand laborers who slipped into the golden tent of America, but to sneak into the mouse-eaten sack that was Russia, that was desperate.

"There's more." Victor picked macaroni off his chest. The detective had changed his gray sweater for one of caterpillar orange. He licked his fingers clean, gathered the photos and replaced them with a file that said in red: NOT TO BE REMOVED FROM THIS OFFICE.

"Dossiers on the four attempts on Ivanov's life. This is rich. First attempt was a doorway shooting here in Moscow by a disgruntled investor, a schoolteacher whose savings were wiped out. The poor bastard misses six times. Tries to shoot himself in the head and misses again. Makhmud Nasir. Got four years — not bad. Here's his address, back in town. Maybe he's got glasses now.

"Second attempt is hearsay, but everyone swears it's true. Ivanov rigged an auction for some ships in Archangel, got them for nothing and also bent some local noses out of shape. A competitor sends a contract killer, who blows up Ivanov's car. Ivanov is impressed, finds the killer and pays him double to murder the man who sent him, and shortly after, supposedly, a guy falls in the water in Archangel and doesn't come up for air.

"Third: Ivanov took the train to Leningrad. Why the train, don't ask. On the way, you know how it is, someone pumps sleeping gas into the compartment to rob the passengers, usually the tourists. Ivanov is a light sleeper. He wakes, sees this guy coming in and shoots him. Everyone said it was an overreaction until they found a razor and a picture of Ivanov in the dead man's coat. He also had some worthless Ivanov stock.

"Fourth, and this is the best: Ivanov is in the South of France with friends. They're all zipping back and forth on Jet Skis, the way rich people carry on. Hoffman gets on

Ivanov's Jet Ski, and it sinks. It flips upside down, and guess what's stuck to the bottom, a little limpet of plastique ready to explode. The French police had to clear the harbor. See, that's what gives Russian tourists a bad name."

"Who were Ivanov's friends?" Arkady asked.

"Leonid Maximov and Nikolai Kuzmitch, his very best friends. And one of them probably tried to kill him."

"Was there an investigation?"

"Are you joking? You know our chances of even saying hello to any of these gentlemen? Anyway, that was three years ago, and nothing has happened since."

"Fingerprints?"

"Worst for last. We got prints off all the drinking glasses. Just Ivanov's, Timofeyev's, Zurin's and the girl's."

"What about Pasha's mobile phone? He always had a mobile phone."

"We're not positive."

"Find the mobile phone. Ivanov's driver said he had one."

"While you're doing what?"

"Colonel Ozhogin has arrived."

"*The* Colonel Ozhogin?"

"That's right."

Victor saw things in a different light. "I'll

look for the mobile phone."

"The head of NoviRus Security wants to consult."

"He wants to consult your balls on a toothpick. If Ivanov was pushed, how does that make the head of security look? Did you ever see Ozhogin wrestle? I saw him in an all-republic tournament — he broke his opponent's arm. You could hear it snap across the hall. You know, even if we did find a mobile phone, Ozhogin would take it away. He answers to Timofeyev now. The king is dead, long live the king." Victor lit a cigarette as a digestif. "The thing about capitalism, it seems to me, is, a business partner has the perfect combination of motive and opportunity for murder. Oh hey, I got something for you." Victor came up with a plastic phone card.

"What's this for? A free call?" Arkady knew that Victor had strange ways of sharing a bill.

"No. Well, I don't know, but what it's great for . . ." Victor jimmied the card between two fingers. "Locks. Not dead bolts, but you'd be amazed. I got one, and I got one for you, too. Put it in your wallet."

"Almost like money."

Two young men settled at the next table with bowls of ravioli. They wore the jackets and stringy ties of office workers. They also had the shaved skulls and scabby knuckles of skinheads, which meant they might be office drudges during the day, but at night they led an intoxicating life of violence patterned on Nazi storm troopers and British hooligans.

One gave Arkady a glare and said, "What are you looking at? What are you, a pervert?"

Victor brightened. "Hit him, Arkady. Go ahead, hit the punk, I'll back you up."

"No, thanks," Arkady said.

"A little fisticuffs, a little dustup," Victor said. "Go on, you can't let him talk like that. We're a block from headquarters, you'll let the whole side down."

"If he doesn't, he's a queer," the skinhead said.

"If you won't, I will." Victor started to rise.

Arkady pulled him back by his sleeve. "Let it go."

"You've gone soft, Arkady, you've changed."

"I hope so."

Ozhogin's office was minimalist: a glass desk, steel chairs, gray tones. A full-size model of a samurai in black lacquered armor, mask and horns stood in a corner. The colonel himself, although he was packaged in a tailored shirt and silk tie, still had the heavy shoulders and small waist of a wrestler. After having Arkady sit, Ozhogin let the tension percolate.

Colonel Ozhogin actually had two pedigrees. First, he was a wrestler from Georgia, and at wrapping opponents into knots Georgians were the best. Second, he had been KGB. The KGB may have suffered a shake-up and a title change, but its agents had prospered, moving like crows to new trees. After all, when the call went out for men with language skills and sophistication, who better to step forward?

The colonel slid a form and clipboard across the desk.

"What's this?" Arkady asked.

"Take a look."

The form was a NoviRus employment application, with spaces for name, age, sex, marriage status, address, military service, education, advanced degrees. Applying for: banking, investment fund, brokerage, gas, oil, media, marine, forest resources, minerals, security, translation and interpreting. The group was especially interested in applicants fluent in English, MS Office, Excel; familiar with Reuters, Bloomberg, RTS; IT literate;

with advanced degrees in sciences, accounting, interpreting/translation, law or combat skills; under thirty-five a plus. Arkady had to admit, he wouldn't have hired himself. He pushed the form back. "No, thanks."

"You don't want to fill it out? That's disappointing."

"Why?"

"Because there are two possible reasons for you being here. A good reason would be that you've finally decided to join the private sector. A bad reason would be that you won't leave Pasha Ivanov's death alone. Why are you trying to turn a suicide into a homicide?"

"I'm not. Prosecutor Zurin asked me to look into this for Hoffman, the American."

"Who got the idea from you that there was something to find." Ozhogin paused, obviously working up to a delicate subject. "How do you think it makes NoviRus Security look if people get the idea we can't protect the head of our own company?"

"If he took his own life, you can hardly be blamed."

"Unless there are questions."

"I would like to talk to Timofeyev."

"That's out of the question."

Besides an open laptop, the sole item on

the desk was a metal disk levitating over another disk in a box. Magnets. The floating disk trembled with every forceful word.

Arkady began, "Zurin —"

"Prosecutor Zurin? Do you know how all this began, what your investigation of NoviRus was all about? It was a shakedown. Zurin just wanted to be enough of a nuisance to be paid off, and not even in money. He wanted to get on the board of directors. And I'm sure he'll be an excellent director. But it was extortion, and you were part of it. What would people think of the honest Investigator Renko if they heard how you had helped your chief? What would happen to your precious reputation then?"

"I didn't know I had one."

"Of a sort. You should fill out the application. Do you know that over fifty thousand KGB and militia officers have joined private security firms? Who's left in the militia? The dregs. I had your friend Victor researched. It's in his file that on one stakeout he was so drunk, he went to sleep and pissed in his pants. Maybe you'll end up like that."

Arkady glanced out the window. They were on the fifteenth floor of the NoviRus building, with a view of office towers under construction; the skyline of the future.

"Look behind you," Ozhogin said. Arkady turned to take in the samurai armor and helmet with mask and horns. "What does that look like to you?"

"A giant beetle?"

"A samurai warrior. When Japan was opened up by the West, and the samurai were disbanded, they didn't disappear. They went into business. Not all; some became poets, some became drunks, but the smart ones knew enough to change with the times." Ozhogin came around the desk and perched on its corner. For all his grooming, the colonel imparted the sense that he could still wring a bone or two. "Renko, did you happen to see *The Washington Post* this morning?"

"Not this morning, no. Missed it."

"There was a considerable obituary for Pasha Ivanov. The *Post* called Pasha a 'linchpin figure' in Russian business. Have you considered the effect a rumor of homicide would have? It would not only harm NoviRus, it would damage every Russian company and bank that has struggled to escape Moscow's reputation for violence. Considering the consequences, I think a person should be careful about even whispering 'homicide.' Especially when there isn't the slightest evidence that there was one. Unless you have some evidence you'd like to share with me?"

"No."

"I didn't think so. And as for your financial investigation of NoviRus, didn't the fact that Zurin chose you as investigator suggest to you that he wasn't serious?"

"It crossed my mind."

"It's laughable. A pair of worn-out criminal detectives against an army of financial wizards."

"It doesn't sound fair."

"Now that Pasha is dead, it's time to let go. Call it a draw if you want. Pasha Ivanov came to a sorry end. Why? I don't know. It's a great loss. However, he never asked for any increase in security. I interviewed the building staff. There was no breach." Ozhogin leaned closer, a hammer taking aim on a nail, Arkady thought. "If there was no breach in security, then there's nothing to investigate. Is that clear enough for you?"

"There was salt —"

"I heard about the salt. What sort of attack is that? The salt is an indication of a mental breakdown, pure and simple."

"Unless there was a breach."

"I just told you there wasn't."

"That's what investigations are for."

"Are you saying there was a breach?"

"It's possible. Ivanov died under strange circumstances."

Ozhogin edged closer. "Are you suggesting that NoviRus Security was, to any degree, responsible for Ivanov's death?"

Arkady picked his words carefully. "Building security wasn't all that sophisticated. No card swipes or voice or palm ID, just codes, nothing like the security at the offices here. And a skeleton crew on weekends."

"Because Ivanov moved into an apartment meant for his friend Rina. She designed it. He didn't want any changes. Nevertheless, we staffed the building with our men, put in unobtrusive keypads, fed the surveillance cameras to our own monitors here at NoviRus Security and, any hour he was home, parked a security team in front. There was nothing more we could do. Besides, Pasha never mentioned a threat."

"That's what we'll investigate."

Ozhogin brought his brows together, perplexed. He had pushed his opponent's head through the wrestling mat, but the match went on. "You're stopping now."

"It's up to Hoffman to call it off."

"He'll do what you say. Tell him that you're satisfied."

"There's something missing."
"What?"
"I don't know."
"You don't know, you don't know." Ozhogin reached out and tapped the disk so it fluttered in the air. "Who's the boy?"
"What boy?"
"You took a boy to the park."
"You're watching me."
Ozhogin seemed saddened by such naïveté in a Russian. He said, "Pack it in, Renko. Tell your fat American friend that Pasha Ivanov committed suicide. Then why don't you come back and fill out the form?"

Arkady found Rina curled up in a bathrobe in Ivanov's screening room, a vodka bottle hanging from one hand and a cigarette from the other. Her hair was wet and clung to her head, making her appear even more childlike than usual. On the screen Pasha rose in the elevator, floor by floor, briefcase clasped to his chest, handkerchief to his face. He seemed exhausted, as if he had climbed a hundred stories. When the doors parted, he looked back at the camera. The system had a zoom capacity. Rina froze and magnified Pasha's face so that it filled the screen, his hair lank, his cheeks almost powdery white, his black eyes sending their obscure message.

"That was for me. That was his good-bye." Rina shot Arkady a glance. "You don't believe me. You think it's romantic bullshit."

"At least half of what I believe is romantic bullshit, so I'm not one to criticize. Anything else?"

"He was sick. I don't know with what. He wouldn't see a doctor." Rina put down her cigarette and pulled the robe tight. "The elevator operator let me in. Your detective was going out as I came in, looking pleased with himself."

"A gruesome image."

"I heard Bobby hired you."

"He offered to. I didn't know the market price for an investigator."

"You're no Pasha. *He* would have known."

"I tried to reach Timofeyev. He's not available. I suppose he's picking up the reins of the company, taking charge."

"He's no Pasha, either. You know, business in Russia is very social. Pasha made his biggest deals in clubs and bars. He had the perfect personality for that. People liked to be around him. He was fun and generous. Timofeyev is a lump. I miss Pasha."

Arkady took the seat beside her and relieved her of the vodka. "You designed this apartment for him?"

"I designed it for both of us, but all of a sudden, Pasha said I shouldn't stay."

"You never moved in?"

"Lately Pasha wouldn't even let me in the door. At first I thought there was another woman. But he didn't want anyone here. Not Bobby, no one." Rina wiped her eyes. "He became paranoid. I'm sorry I'm so stupid."

"Not a bit."

The robe fell open again, and she pushed herself back in. "I like you, Investigator. You don't look. You have manners."

Arkady had manners, but he was also aware of how loosely tied the robe was.

"Did you know of any recent business setback? Anything financial that could have been on his mind?"

"Pasha was always making deals. And he didn't mind losing money now and then. He said it was the price of education."

"Anything else medical? Depression?"

"We didn't have sex for the last month, if that counts. I don't know why. He just stopped." She stubbed out one cigarette and started another off Arkady's. "You're probably wondering how a nobody like me and someone as rich and famous as Pasha could meet. How would you guess?"

"You're an interior designer. I suppose you designed something for him besides this apartment."

"Don't be silly. I was a prostitute. Design student and prostitute, a person of many talents. I was in the bar at the Savoy Hotel. It's a fancy place, and you have to fit in, you can't just sit there like any whore. I was pretending to carry on a mobile-phone conversation when Pasha came over and asked for my number so I could talk to someone real. Then, from across the bar, he called. I thought, What a big ugly Jew. He was, you know. But he had so much energy, so much charm. He knew everybody, he knew things. He asked about my interests — the usual stuff, you know, but he really listened, and he even knew about design. Then he asked how much I owed my roof — you know, my pimp — because Pasha said he would pay him off, set me up in an apartment and pay for design school. He was serious. I asked him why, and he said because he could see I was a good person. Would you do that? Would you bet on someone like that?"

"I don't think so."

"Well, that was Pasha." She took a long

draw on her cigarette.

"How old are you now?"

"Twenty."

"And you met Pasha . . ."

"Three years ago. When we were talking on the phone at the bar, I asked if he preferred a redhead, because I could be that, too. He said life was too short, I should be whatever I was."

The longer Arkady stared at the screen, at Pasha's hesitation on the threshold of his apartment, the less he looked like a man afraid of a black mood. He seemed to dread something more substantial waiting for him.

"Did Pasha have enemies?"

"Naturally. Maybe hundreds, but nothing serious."

"Death threats?"

"Not from anyone worth worrying about."

"There were attempts in the past."

"That's what Colonel Ozhogin is for. Pasha did say one thing. He said he had once done something long ago that was really bad and that I wouldn't love him if I knew. That was the drunkest I ever saw him. He wouldn't tell me what and he never mentioned it again."

"Who did know?"

"I think Lev Timofeyev knew. He said no, but I could tell. It was their secret."

"How they stripped investors of their money?"

"No." Her voice tightened. "Something awful. He was always worse around May Day. I mean, who cares about May Day anymore?" She wiped her eyes with her sleeve. "Why don't you think he killed himself?"

"I don't think one way or the other; I just haven't come across a good enough reason for him to. Ivanov was clearly not a man who frightened easily."

"See, even you admired him."

"Do you know Leonid Maximov and Nikolai Kuzmitch?"

"Of course. They're two of our best friends. We have good times together."

"They're busy men, I'm sure, but can you think of any way I could talk to them? I could try official channels, but to be honest, they know more officials than I do."

"No problem. Come to the party."

"What party?"

"Every year Pasha threw a party out at the dacha. It's tomorrow. Everyone will be there."

"Pasha is dead and you're still having the party?"

"Pasha founded the Blue Sky Charity for children. It depends financially on the party, so everyone knows that Pasha would want the party to go on."

Arkady had come across Blue Sky during the investigation. Its operating expenses were minute compared to other Ivanov ventures, and he had assumed it was a fraud. "How does this party raise money?"

"You'll see. I'll put you on the list, and tomorrow you'll see everyone who's anyone in Moscow. But you will have to blend in."

"I don't look like a millionaire?"

She shifted, the better to see him. "No, you definitely look like an investigator. I can't have you stalking around, not good for a party mood. But many people will bring their children. Can you bring a child? You must know a child."

"I might."

Arkady turned on the chair's light for her to write directions in. She did it studiously, pressing hard, and, as soon as she was done, turned off the light.

"I think I'll stay here by myself for a while. What's your name again?"

"Renko."

"No, I mean your name."

"Arkady."

She repeated it, seeming to try it out and find it acceptable. As he rose to go, she brushed his hand with hers. "Arkady, I take it back. You do remind me of Pasha a tiny bit."

"Thank you," said Arkady. He didn't ask whether she was referring to the brilliant, gregarious Pasha or the Pasha facedown on the street.

Arkady and Victor had a late dinner at a car-wash café on the highway. Arkady liked the place because it looked like a space station of chrome and glass, with headlights flying by like comets. The food was fast, the beer was German and something worthwhile was being attempted: Victor's car was being washed. Victor drove a forty-year-old Lada with loose wiring underfoot and a radio wired to the dash, but he could repair it himself with spare parts available in any junkyard, and no self-respecting person would steal it. There was something smug and miserly about Victor when he drove, as if he had figured out one bare-bones sexual position. Among the ranks of Mercedeses, Porsches and BMWs being hosed and buffed, Victor's Lada was singular.

Victor drank Armenian brandy to maintain his blood sugar. He liked the café because it was popular with the different Mafias. They were Victor's acquaintances, if not his friends, and he liked to keep track of their comings and goings. "I've arrested three generations of the same family. Grandfather, father, son. I feel like Uncle Victor."

Two identical black Pathfinders showed up and disgorged similar sets of beefy passengers in jogging suits. They glared at each other long enough to maintain dignity before sauntering into the café.

Victor said, "It's neutral ground because nobody wants his car scratched. That's their mentality. Your mentality, on the other hand, is even more warped. Making work out of an open-and-shut suicide? I don't know. Investigators are supposed to just sit on their ass and leave real work to their detectives. They last longer, too."

"I've lasted too long."

"Apparently. Well, cheer up, I have a little gift for you, something I found under Ivanov's bed." Victor placed a mobile phone, a Japanese clamshell model, on the table.

"Why were you under the bed?"

"You have to think like a detective. People place things on the edge of the bed all the time. They drop, and people kick them under the bed and never notice, especially if they're in a hurry or in a sweat."

"How did Ozhogin's crew miss this?"

"Because everything they wanted was in the office."

Arkady suspected that Victor just liked to look under beds. "Thank you. Have you looked at it yet?"

"I took a peek. Go ahead, open it up." Victor sat back as if he'd brought bonbons.

The mobile phone's introductory chime drew no attention from other tables; in a space-age café, a mobile phone was as normal as a knife or fork. Arkady went through the call history to Saturday evening's outgoing calls to Rina and Bobby Hoffman; the incoming calls were from Hoffman, Rina and Timofeyev.

A little phone, and yet so much information: a wireless message concerning an Ivanov tanker foundering off Spain, and a calendar of meetings, most recently with Prosecutor Zurin, of all people. In the directory were phone numbers not only for Rina, Hoffman, Timofeyev and different NoviRus heads, but also for well-known journalists and theater people, for millionaires whose names Arkady recognized from other investigations, and, most interesting, for Zurin, the mayor, senators and ministers, and the Kremlin itself. Such a phone was a plug into a power grid.

Victor copied the names into a notepad. "What a world these people live in. Here's a number that gives you the weather in Saint-Tropez. Very nice." It took two brandies for Victor to finish the list. He looked up and nodded to a truculent circle of people at the next table. In a low voice, he said, "The Medvedev brothers. I've arrested their father *and* mother. But I have to admit, I feel comfortable with them. They're ordinary thugs, not businessmen with investment funds."

Arkady punched "Messages."

There was one at 9:33 p.m. from a Moscow number, and the message did not sound like a businessman's: "You don't know who this is, but I'm trying to do you a favor. I'll call you again. All I'll say now is, if you stick your dick in someone else's soup, sooner or later it's going to get cut off."

"A man of few words. Familiar?" Arkady handed the phone to Victor.

The detective listened and shook his head. "A tough guy. From the South, you can hear the soft O's. But I can't hear well enough. All the people talking here. Glasses tinkling."

"If anyone can do it . . ."

Victor listened again, the mobile phone pressed tight to his ear, until he smiled like a man who had identified one wine from a million. "Anton. Anton Obodovsky."

Arkady knew Anton. He could imagine Anton throwing someone out a window.

The tension was too great for Victor. "Got to pee."

Arkady sat alone, nursing his beer. Another crew in jogging suits pushed into the café, as if the roads were full of surly sportsmen. Arkady's gaze kept returning to the mobile phone. It would be interesting to know whether the phone Anton had called from was within fifteen minutes of Ivanov's apartment. It was a landline number. He knew he should wait for Victor, but the detective could take half an hour just to avoid the bill.

Arkady picked up the mobile phone and pushed "Reply to Message."

Ten rings.

"Guards' room."

Arkady sat up. "Guards' room? Where?"

"Butyrka. Who is this?"

By the time Victor returned, Arkady was outside in the Lada, which proved unredeemed by soap. A wind bent the advertising banners along the highway and snapped the canvas. Each car that buzzed past rocked the Lada.

Victor got behind the wheel. "I'll drive you back to your car. You paid the whole thing? What a friend!"

"You know, with the money you've saved eating with me, you could buy a new car."

"Come on, I'm worth it, getting the mobile phone and sharing my repository of knowledge. My head is a veritable Lenin Library."

Mice and all, Arkady thought. As Victor pulled onto the highway, Arkady told him about the return call to Anton, which amused the detective immensely.

"Butyrka! Now, there's an alibi."

4

The address on Butyrka Street was a five-story building of aluminum windows, busted shades and dead geraniums, ordinary in every way except for the line that snaked along the sidewalk: Gypsies in brilliant scarves, Chechens in black and Russians in thin leather jackets, mutually hostile as groups but alike in their forlorn bearing and the parcels that, one by one, they dutifully submitted at a steel door for the thousands of souls hidden on the other side.

Arkady showed his ID at the door and passed through a barred gate to the underbelly of the building, a tunnel where guards in military fatigues lounged with their dogs, Alsatians that constantly referred to their handlers for orders. Let this one pass. Take this one down. The far end opened onto the morning light and — totally hidden from the street — a fairy-tale fortress with red walls and towers surrounded by a whitewashed courtyard; all that was missing was a moat. Not quite a fairy tale, more a nightmare. Butyrka Prison had been built by Catherine the Great, and for over two hundred years since, every ruler of Russia, every tsar, Party secretary and president had fed it enemies of the state. A guard carrying an elongated sniper rifle watched Arkady from a turret and could have been a fusilier. The satellite dishes lining the battlements could have been heads on pikes. In Stalin's era, black vans delivered fresh victims every night to this same courtyard and these same blood-red walls, and questions about someone's health, whereabouts and fate could be answered in a single whispered word: Butyrka.

Since Butyrka was a pretrial prison, investigators were a common sight. Arkady followed a guard through a receiving hall where new arrivals, boys as pale as plucked chickens, were stripped and thrown their prison clothes. Wide eyes fixed on the hall's ancient coffin cells, barely deep enough to sit in, a good place for a monk's mortification and an excellent way to introduce the horror of being buried alive.

Arkady climbed marble stairs swaybacked from wear. Nets stretched between railings to discourage jumping and passing notes. On the second floor, light crept from low windows and gave the impression of sinking, or eyelids shutting.

The guard led Arkady along a row of ancient black doors with iron patchwork, each with a panel for food and a peephole for observation.

"I'm new here. I think it's this one," the guard said. "I think."

Arkady swung a peephole tag out of the way. On the other side of the door were fifty men in a cell designed for twenty. They were sniffers, lifters, petty thieves. They slept in shifts in the murk of a caged lightbulb and a barred window. There was no circulation, no fresh air, only the stench of sweat, pearl porridge, cigarettes and shit in the single toilet. In the heat they generated, everyone stripped to the waist, young ones virginally white, veterans blue with tattoos. A tubercular cough and a whisper hung in the air. A few heads turned to the blink of the peephole, but most simply waited. A man could wait nine months in Butyrka before he saw a judge.

"No? This one?" The guard motioned Arkady to the next door.

Arkady peeked into the cell. It was the same size as the other but held a single occupant, a bodybuilder with short bleached-blond hair and a taut black T-shirt. He was exercising with elastic bands that were attached to a bunk bed bolted to the wall, and every time he curled a bicep, the bed groaned.

"This is it," Arkady said.

Anton Obodovsky was a Mafia success story. He had been a Master of Sport, a so-so boxer in the Ukraine and then muscle for the local boss. However, Anton had ambition. As soon as he had a gun, he began jacking cars, peeling drivers out of them. From there, he took orders for specific cars, organizing a team of carjackers and then stealing cars off the street in Germany and driving convoys across Poland to Moscow. Once in Moscow, he diversified, offering protection to small firms and restaurants he then took over, cannibalizing the companies and laundering money through the restaurants. The man lived like a prince. Up by eleven a.m. with a protein smoothie. An hour in the gym. A little networking on the phone and a visit to the auto-repair shops where his mechanics chopped cars. He shopped in clothing stores that wouldn't take his money, dined in restaurants for free. He dressed in Armani black, partied with the most beautiful prostitutes, one on each arm, and never paid for sex. A diamond ring in the shape of a horseshoe said he was a lucky man. At a certain level of society, he was royalty, and yet — and yet — he was dissatisfied.

"It's the bankers who are the real thieves. People bring the money to you, you fuck them and no one lays a hand on you. I make a hundred thousand dollars, but bankers and politicians make millions. I'm a worm compared to them."

"You're doing pretty well," Arkady said. The cell had a television, tape player, CDs. A Pizza Hut box lay under the bottom bunk. The top bunk was stacked with car magazines, travel brochures, motivational tapes. "How long have you been here?"

"Three nights. I wish we had satellite. The walls of this place are so thick, the reception is shit."

"Life is tough."

Anton looked Arkady up and down. "Look at your raincoat. Have you been polishing your car with that? You should hit the stores with me sometime. It makes me feel bad that I'm better dressed inside prison than you are out."

"I can't afford to shop with you."

"On me. I can be a generous guy. Everything you see here, I pay for. Everything is legal. They allow you anything but alcohol, cigarettes or mobile phones." Anton had a restless, sharklike quality that made him pace. A man could get a stiff neck just having a conversation with him, Arkady thought.

"What's the worst deprivation?"

"I don't drink or smoke, so for me it's phones." No one consumed phones like the Mafia; they used stolen mobile phones to avoid being tapped, and a careful man like Anton changed phones once a week. "You get dependent. It's kind of a curse."

"It's led to the demise of the written word. You look in the pink."

"I work out. No drugs, no steroids, no hormones."

"Cigarette?"

"No, thanks. I just told you, I keep myself strong and pure. I am a slave to nothing. It's pitiful to see a man like you smoke."

"I'm weak."

"Renko, you've got to take care of yourself. Or other people. Think of the secondary smoke."

"All right." Arkady put away the pack. He hated to see Anton get worked up. There were actually three Antons. There was the violent Anton, who would snap your neck as easily as shake your hand; there was Anton the rational businessman; and there was the Anton whose eyes took an evasive course when anything personal was discussed. Most of all, Arkady didn't like to see the first Anton get excited.

Anton said, "I just think at your age, you shouldn't abuse your body."

"At my age?"

"Look, go fuck yourself, for all I care."

"That's more like it."

A smile crept onto Anton's lips. "See, I can talk to you. We communicate."

Arkady and Anton did communicate. Both understood that Anton's prize cell was available only because of a belated effort to bring Butyrka's ancient chamber of horrors up to modern European prison standards, and both understood that such a cell would obviously go to the highest bidder. Both also understood that while the Mafia ruled the streets, a subcaste of tattooed, geriatric criminals still ruled the prison yards. If Anton were stuck in an ordinary cell, he would be a shark in a tank with a thousand piranhas.

Anton couldn't sit still without twitching a pec here, a deltoid there. "You're a good guy, Renko. We may not see eye to eye, but you always treat a person with respect. You speak English?"

"Yes."

Anton picked up a copy of *Architectural Digest* from the bunk and flipped to a picture of a western lodge set against a mountain range. "Colorado. Beautiful nature and, as an investment, relatively inexpensive. What do you think?"

"Can you ride a horse?"

"Is that necessary?"

"I think so."

"I can learn. I'll give you the money. Cash. You go and negotiate, pay whatever you think is fair. It could be a beautiful partnership. You have an honest face."

"I appreciate the offer. Did you hear that Pasha Ivanov is dead?"

"I saw the news on television. He jumped, right? Ten stories, what a way to go."

"Did you know him?"

"Me know Ivanov? That's like knowing God."

"You left a message on his mobile phone three nights ago about cutting off his dick. That sounds like you knew him fairly well. It might even sound like a threat."

"I'm not allowed a phone here, so how could I call?"

"You bribed a guard and called from the guards' room."

Anton got to his feet and threw punches as if hitting a heavy bag. "Well, like they say, there's a crow in every flock." He stopped and shook out his arms. “Anyway, if I called Pasha Ivanov, what about?”

“Business. Somebody has been jacking NoviRus Oil trucks and draining the tanks. It’s happening in your part of Moscow — in your soup, so to speak.”

Anton circled again, throwing jabs, crosses, uppercuts. He backed, covered up, seemed to dodge a punch and then moved forward, rolling his shoulders and snapping jabs while the cell got smaller and smaller. Anton may not have been a champion, but when he was in motion, he took up a lot of room. Finally he dropped his fists and blew air. “He has this prick in charge of security, a former colonel from the KGB. They caught one of my boys with one of their trucks and broke his legs. That’s overreaction. It put me in a difficult situation. If I didn’t retaliate, my boys would break my legs. But I don’t want a war. I’m sick of that. Instead, I wanted to go straight to the top, and also make a point about the colonel’s bullshit security by calling Ivanov on his personal phone. I said what I said. It was an opening line; maybe a little crude, but it was meant to begin a dialogue. I have body shops, tanning salons, a restaurant. I’m a respectable businessman. I would have loved to work with Pasha Ivanov, to learn at his knee."

"What was the favor? What did you have to offer him?"

"Protection."

"Naturally."

"Anyway, I never got through and never saw him face-to-face. It seems to me, when Pasha died I was right here, and that phone call proves it."

"Pretty lucky."

"I live right." Anton was modest.

"What did they pick you up for?"

"Possession of firearms."

"That's all?"

A firearms charge was nothing. Since Anton always had a lawyer, judge and bail money standing by, there was no good reason for him to spend an hour in jail, unless he was waiting for some bumbling investigator to come along and officially mark how innocent Anton Obodovsky was. Arkady didn't want to provoke the dangerous side of Anton, but he also didn't like being used.

Anton grabbed some travel brochures off the bunk. "Hey, as soon as I'm out, I'm going on holiday. Where would you suggest? Cyprus? Turkey? I don't drink or do drugs, and that leaves out a lot of places. I want a tan, but I burn easily. What do you think?"

"You want creature comforts? Quiet? Gourmet food?"

"Yeah."

"A staff that caters to your every whim?"

"Right!"

"Why not stay in Butyrka?"

Zhenya stared like a manacled prisoner at what most people would have called an escape to the country. The population of Moscow was pouring into the low hills that couched the city, to rustic dachas and crowded beaches and giant discount stores, and though the highway was designed with four lanes, drivers improvised and squeezed out six.

Arkady wasn't clear on what good cause benefited from Pasha Ivanov's Blue Sky Charity picnic, but he did not want to miss the millionaires Nikolai Kuzmitch and Leonid Maximov. Such dear friends were sure to appear. After all, they had vacationed with Pasha in Saint-Tropez when a limpet mine was discovered on his Jet Ski. Tomorrow they would be scattered to the four winds on their corporate jets, behind their ranks of lawyers. Hence, Arkady's use of Zhenya as a disguise. Arkady tried to shrug off his guilt by telling himself that Zhenya could use the sun.

"Maybe there'll be swimming. I brought you a swimsuit just in case," Arkady said, indicating a gift-wrapped box at the boy's feet. Up till now Zhenya had ignored it. Now he began crushing it with his heels. Arkady usually kept a pistol in the glove compartment. He'd had the foresight to remove the magazine; he patted himself on the back for that. "Or maybe you're a dry-land kind of man."

Even with cars weaving over the median and the shoulder of the road, traffic advanced at a snail's pace. "It used to be worse," Arkady said. "There used to be cars broken down by the side of the road all the way. No driver left home without a screwdriver and hammer. We didn't know about cars, but we knew about hammers." Zhenya delivered a last savage kick to the box. "Also, windshields had so many cracks, you had to hold your head out the window like a dog to see. What's your favorite car? Maserati? Moskvich?" A long pause. "My father used to take me down this same road in a big Zil. There were only two lanes then, and hardly any traffic. We played chess as we went, although I was never as good as you. Mostly I did puzzles." A Toyota went by with a backseat full of kids playing scissors-paper-rock like normal, happy children. Zhenya was stone. "Do you like Japanese cars? I was once in Vladivostok, and I saw stacks of bright new Russian cars loaded for Japan." Actually, when the cars got to Japan, they were turned to scrap metal. At least the Japanese had the decency to wait until they received the cars before crushing them like beer cans. "What did your father drive?"

Arkady hoped the boy might mention a car that could somehow be traced, but Zhenya sank into his jacket and pulled his cap low. On the side of the road stretched a memorial of tank traps in the form of giant jacks, marking the closest advance of the Germans into Moscow in the Great Patriotic War. Now the memorial was dwarfed by the vast hangar of an IKEA outlet. Balloons advertising Panasonic, Sony, JVC swayed in the breeze above an audio tent. Garden shops offered birdbaths and ceramic gnomes. That was what Zhenya looked like, Arkady thought, a miserable garden gnome with his flapped cap, book and chess set.

"There'll be other kids," Arkady promised. "Games, music, food."

Every card Arkady played was trumped by scorn. He had seen parents in this sort of quagmire — where every suggestion was a sign of idiocy and no question in the Russian language merited response — and Arkady, for all the sympathy he mustered, had always delivered a sigh of relief that he was not the adult on the cross. So he wasn't quite sure why, now, an unmarried specimen like himself should have to suffer such contempt. Sociologists were concerned about Russia's plunging birthrate. He thought that if couples were forced to spend an hour in a car with Zhenya, there'd be no birthrate at all.

"It'll be fun," Arkady said.

Finally Arkady reached a suburb of fitness clubs, espresso bars, tanning salons. The dachas here were not traditional cabins with weepy roofs and ramshackle gardens but prefabricated mansions with Greek columns and swimming pools and security cameras. Where the road narrowed to a country lane, Ivanov's security guards waved him to the shoulder behind a line of hulking SUVs. Arkady had on the same shabby raincoat, and Zhenya looked like a hostage, but the guards found their names on a list. So as infiltrators, Arkady and Zhenya went through an iron gate to a dead man's lawn party.

The theme was Outer Space. Pink ponies

and blue llamas carried small children around a ring. A juggler juggled moons. A magician twisted balloons into Martian dogs. Artists decorated children's faces with sparkle and paint, while a Venusian, elongated by his planet's weak gravity, strode by on stilts. Toddlers played under an inflated spaceman tethered to the ground by ropes, and larger children lined up for tennis and badminton or low-gravity swings on bungee cables. The guest list was spectacular: broad-shouldered Olympic swimmers, film stars with carefully disarranged hair, television actors with dazzling teeth, rock musicians behind dark glasses, famous writers with wine-sack bellies overhanging their jeans. Arkady's own heart skipped a beat when he recognized former cosmonauts, heroes of his youth, obviously hired for the day just for show. Yet the dominating spirit was Pasha Ivanov. A photograph was set near the entrance gate and hung with a meadow garland of sweet peas and daisies. It was of a buoyant Ivanov mugging between two circus clowns, and it as good as gave his guests orders to play, not grieve. The photograph couldn't have been taken too long before his death, but its subject was so much more impish and alive than the recent man that it served as a warning to enjoy life's every moment. The guards at the gate must have phoned ahead, because Arkady felt a ripple of attention follow his progress through the partygoers, and the repositioning of men with wires in their ears. Children sticky from cotton candy raced back and forth. Men collected at grills that served shashlik of sturgeon and beef in front of Ivanov's dacha, ten times the normal size but at least a Russian design, not a hijacked Parthenon. A DJ played Russian bubble gum on one stage, while karaoke ruled a second. Separate bars served champagne, Johnnie Walker, Courvoisier. The wives were tall, slim women in Italian fashions and cowboy boots of alligator and ostrich. They positioned themselves at tables where they could watch both their children and their husbands and anxiously track a younger generation of even taller, slimmer women filtering through the crowd. Timofeyev was in a food line with Prosecutor Zurin, who expectantly scanned the crowd like a periscope. It was not a positive sign that he looked everywhere but at Arkady. Timofeyev appeared pale and sweaty for a man about to inherit the reins of the entire NoviRus company. Farther on, Bobby

Hoffman, already yesterday's American, stood alone and nibbled a plate overheaped with food. An outdoor casino had been set up, and even from a distance Arkady recognized Nikolai Kuzmitch and Leonid Maximov. They were youngish men in modest jeans, no Mafia black, no ostentatious gold. The croupiers appeared real, and so did the chips, but Kuzmitch and Maximov hunched over the baize like boys at play.

Arkady had to admit that what often distinguished New Russians was youth and brains. An unusual number of them had been the protégés and darlings of prestigious academies that had gone suddenly bankrupt, and rather than starve among the ruins, they rebuilt the world with themselves as millionaires, each a biography of genius and pluck. They saw themselves as the robber barons of the American Wild West, and didn't someone say that every great fortune started with a crime? Russia already had over thirty billionaires, more than any other country. That was a lot of crime.

Kuzmitch, as a student at the Institute of Rare Metals, had sold titanium from an unguarded warehouse and parlayed that coup into a career in nickel and tin. Maximov, a mathematician, had been asked to keep the numbers at a public auction; the Ministry of Exotic Chemistry was selling off a lab, and the bidding promised to be chaotic. Maximov had conceived a better idea: an auction at an undisclosed location. The surprise winners, Maximov and a cousin at the ministry, turned the lab into a distillery, the start of Maximov's fortune in vodka and foreign cars.

The best example of all had been Pasha Ivanov, a physicist, the pet of the Institute of Extremely High Temperatures, who began with nothing but a bogus fund and one day set his sights on Siberian Resources, a huge enterprise of timber, sawmills and a hundred thousand hectares of Mother Russia's straightest trees. It was a minnow swallowing a whale. Ivanov bought some inconsequential Siberian debts and sued in out-of-the-way courts with corrupt judges. Siberian Resources didn't even know about the suits until ownership was awarded to Ivanov. But the management didn't back down. They had their own judges and courts, and a siege developed until Ivanov made a deal with the local army base. The officers and troops hadn't been paid in months, so Pasha Ivanov hired them to break through the sawmill gates. The tanks carried no live rounds, but a tank is a tank, and Ivanov rode the first one through.

This was the closest Arkady had ever come to the magic circle of the super-rich, and he was fascinated in spite of himself. However, Zhenya was miserable. When Arkady looked at the party through Zhenya's eyes, all color drained. Every other child was wealthier in parents and self-assurance; a shelter boy was, by definition, abandoned. The masquerade Arkady had planned was revealing itself as a cruel and stupid trial. No matter how spiteful or uncommunicative Zhenya was, he didn't deserve this.

"Going already?" Timofeyev asked.

"My friend isn't feeling well." Arkady nodded at Zhenya.

"What a shame, to be so young and not to enjoy good health." Timofeyev made a weak effort at a smile. He sniffed and clutched a handkerchief at the ready. Arkady noticed brown spots on his shirt. "I should have started a charity like this. I should have done more. Did you know that Pasha and I grew up together? We went to the same schools, the same scientific institute. But our tastes were entirely different. I was never the ladies' man. More into sports. For example, Pasha had a dachshund, and I had wolfhounds."

"You don't anymore?"

"Unfortunately, no, I couldn't. I . . . What I told the investigation was that we did the best we could, given the information we had."

"What investigation?" Not Arkady's.

"Pasha said that it wasn't a matter of guilt or innocence, that sometimes a man's life was simply a chain reaction."

"Guilt for what?" Arkady liked specifics.

"Do I look like a monster to you?"

"No." Arkady thought that Lev Timofeyev may have helped build a financial giant through corruption and theft, but he was not necessarily a monster. What Timofeyev looked like was a once hale sportsman who seemed to be shrinking in his own clothes. Perhaps it was grief over the death of his best friend, but his pallor and sunken cheeks suggested to Arkady the bloom of disease and, maybe, fear. Pasha had always been the swashbuckler of the two, although Arkady remembered that Rina had mentioned some secret crime in the past. "Does this involve Pasha?"

"We were trying to help. Anyone with the same information would have drawn an identical conclusion."

"Which was?"

"Matters were in hand, things were

under control. We sincerely thought they were."

"What matters?" Arkady was at a loss. Timofeyev seemed to have switched to an entirely different track.

"The letter said apologize personally, face-to-face. Who would that be?"

"Do you have it?"

Rina called out from the casino. She shone in a silver jumpsuit in the spirit of the day. "Arkady, are you missing someone?"

Zhenya had vanished from Arkady's side only to reappear at the gaming tables. There were tables for poker and blackjack, but Rina's friends had opted for classic roulette, and there Zhenya stood, clutching his book and dourly assessing each bet as it was placed. Arkady excused himself to Timofeyev with a promise to return.

"I want you to meet my friends, Nikolai and Leo," Rina whispered. "They are so much fun, and they're losing so much money. At least they were until your little friend arrived."

Nikolai Kuzmitch, who had cornered the nickel market, was a short, rapid-fire type who placed straight-up and corner bets all over the baize. Leonid Maximov, the vodka king, was heavyset, with a cigar. He was more deliberate — a mathematician, after all — and played the simple progression system that had ruined Dostoyevsky: doubling and redoubling on red, red, red, red, red. If the two men lost ten or twenty thousand dollars on a bounce of the roulette ball, it was for charity and only gained respect. In fact, as the chips were raked in, losing itself became feverishly competitive, a sign of panache — that is, until Zhenya had taken a post between the two millionaires. With every flamboyant bet, Zhenya gave Kuzmitch the sort of pitying glance one would bestow upon an idiot, and every unimaginative double on red by Maximov drew from Zhenya a sigh of disdain. Maximov moved his chips to black, and Zhenya smirked at his inconstancy; Maximov repositioned them on black, and Zhenya, with no change in expression, seemed to roll his eyes.

"Unnerving little boy, isn't he?" Rina said. "He's almost brought the game to a standstill."

"He has that power," Arkady admitted. He noticed that, in the meantime, Timofeyev had slipped into the crowd.

Kuzmitch and Maximov quit the table in disgust, but they put on matching smiles for Rina and a welcome for Arkady that said they had nothing to fear from an investigator; they had been buying and selling investigators for years.

Kuzmitch said, “Rina tells us that you’re helping tie up the loose ends about Pasha. That’s good. We want people reassured. Russian business is into a whole new phase. The rough stuff is out.” Maximov agreed. Arkady was put in mind of carnivores swearing off red meat. Not that they were Mafia. A man was expected to know how to defend himself and own a private army if need be. But it was a phase, and now that they had their fortunes, they firmly advocated law and order.

Arkady asked whether Ivanov had mentioned any anxieties or threats or new names, avoided anyone, referred to his health. No, the two said, except that Ivanov had not been himself lately.

“Did he mention salt?”

“No.”

Maximov unplugged his cigar to say, “When I heard about Pasha, I was devastated. We were competitors, but we respected and liked each other.”

Kuzmitch said, “Ask Rina. Pasha and I would fight over business all day and then party like best friends all night.”

“We even vacationed together,” Maximov said.

"Like Saint-Tropez?" Arkady asked. Bomb and all? he wondered.

They winced as if he had added something unpleasant to the punch. Arkady noticed Colonel Ozhogin arrive and whisper into Prosecutor Zurin's ear. Guards started to move in the direction of the roulette table, and Arkady sensed that his time among the elite was limited. Kuzmitch said that he was piloting his plane to Istanbul for a few days of relaxation. Maximov was coming along with six or seven agreeable girls, and Arkady could come, too. Things could be arranged. There was an implicit suggestion that there might be too many girls for two men to handle. Rina, of course, was more than welcome.

"They're like a boys' club," she told Arkady. "Greedy little boys."

"And Pasha?"

"President of the club."

"Rina straightened him out," Kuzmitch said.

"If I could meet a woman like Rina, I would settle down, too," said Maximov. "As it is, all this wine, women and song could be fatal."

"Where were you when you heard about Pasha's death?" Arkady asked.

"I was playing squash. My trainer will

tell you. I sat down on the floor of the court and cried."

Kuzmitch said, "I was in Hong Kong. I immediately flew back out of concern for Rina."

"All these questions. It was suicide, wasn't it?" Maximov said.

"Tragically, yes." Zurin slipped up to the table. He held Zhenya firmly by the shoulder. "My office looked into matters, but there was no reason for an investigation. Just a tragic event."

"Then why . . ." Kuzmitch glanced at Arkady.

"Thoroughness. But I think I can assure you, there will no more questions now. Could you excuse us, please? I need a word with my investigator."

"Istanbul," Kuzmitch reminded Arkady.

"Give this man a day off," Maximov told Zurin. "He's working too hard."

The prosecutor steered Arkady away. "Having a good time? How did you get in?"

"I was invited, me and my friend." Arkady took Zhenya.

"To ask questions and spread rumors?"

"You know what rumor I heard?"

"What would that be?" Zurin kept Arkady and Zhenya moving.

"I heard they made you a company director. They found you a chair in the boardroom, and now you're earning your keep."

Zurin steered Arkady a little faster. "Now you've done it. Now you've gone too far."

Ozhogin caught up and gripped Arkady's shoulder with a wrestler's thumb that pressed to the bone. "Renko, you'll have to learn manners if you ever want to work for NoviRus Security." The colonel patted Zhenya on the head, and Zhenya clenched Arkady's hand in a hard little knot.

"How dare you come here?" Zurin demanded.

"You told me to ask questions."

"Not at a charity event."

"You know the disk that Hoffman was holding out on us?" Ozhogin let Arkady peek at a shiny CD.

"Ah, that must be it," Arkady said. "Are you breaking arms today, or legs?"

"Your investigation is over," Zurin said. "To sneak into a party and drag in some homeless boy is inexcusable."

"Does this mean I will be reassigned?"

"This means disciplinary action," Zurin said wearily, as if setting down a heavy stone. "This means you're done."

Arkady felt done. He also felt he might have gone a little too far with Zurin. Even sellouts had their pride.

Back he and Zhenya went, away from the circle of important men, past the cosmonauts, cotton candy and smoky grills, the telegenic faces and blue llamas and aliens on stilts. A rocket shot up from the tennis court, rose high into the blue sky and exploded into a shower of paper flowers. By the time the last of the petals had drifted down, Arkady and Zhenya were out the gate. Meanwhile, Bobby Hoffman was waiting at Arkady's car, stuffing a bloody nose with a handkerchief, head tilted back to protect the jacket bequeathed him by Ivanov.

On the drive, Zhenya regarded Arkady with a narrow gaze. Arkady had gone with dizzying speed from the heights of New Russia to a boot out the door. This descent was swift enough to get even Zhenya's attention.

"What's going to happen?" Hoffman asked.

"Who knows? A new career. I studied law at Moscow University, maybe I can become a lawyer. Do you see me as a lawyer?"

"Ha!" Hoffman thought for a second. "It's funny, but there's one thing about you that reminds me of Pasha. You're not as smart, God knows, but you share a quality. You couldn't tell whether he found things funny or sad. More like he felt, What the hell? Especially toward the end."

Arkady asked Zhenya, "Is that good, to share qualities with a dead man?" Zhenya pursed his lips. "It depends? I agree."

Zhenya hadn't eaten. They pulled in at a pirozhki stand and found, on the far side of the stand, an inflated fun house of a homely cabin standing on chicken legs. An inflated fence of bones and skulls surrounded the hut, and on the roof stood the witch, Baba Yaga, with the mortar and pestle on which she flew. In Zhenya's fairy tales, Baba Yaga ate children who wandered to her cabin. This cabin was full of children jumping on a trampoline floor covered with balls of colored foam. Boys and girls slid out one door and ran in another while the mechanical witch cackled hideously above. Zhenya left his chess set and walked into the witch's cabin, spellbound.

Hoffman said, "Thanks for the ride. I don't drive in Russia. Driving here is like endlessly circling the Arc de Triomphe."

"I wouldn't know. How is the nose?"

"Ozhogin pinched it. Wasn't even a punch. Showed me the disk, reached up and popped a blood vessel, just for the humiliation."

"It's a day for bloody noses. Timofeyev had one, too." Now that Arkady thought about it, on the videotapes, Ivanov had held a handkerchief the same way.

Hoffman hunched forward. "Did I mention he likes you just as much as me?"

"I don't know why." The prospect of running into Ozhogin again made Arkady want to lift weights and work out regularly. He lit a cigarette. "Where did you hide the disk?"

"I knew Ozhogin would look in my apartment, so I put it in my gym locker. I actually taped it upside down. It was invisible. I don't know how he found it."

"How often do you go to the gym, Bobby?"

"Once a . . ." Hoffman shrugged.

"There you are."

"Oh, and now that they have the disk, the offer is 'Leave the country or go to jail.' I pissed them off. Fuck them, I'll be back."

"And Rina?"

"Let me tell you about Rina." Bobby picked pirozhki crumbs off his jacket. "She is a lovely kid, and Pasha left her well set up, and within a year the most important thing in her life will be fashion shows. And she'll run Pasha's foundation, that'll keep her busy. Everyone wins except you and me. And I'll bounce back."

"Which leaves me."

"At the bottom of the food chain. I'll tell you this much: the company's dead."

"NoviRus?"

"Kaput. All that held it together was Pasha." Bobby gently touched his nose. "Maybe Timofeyev was a good scientist once upon a time, but in business he is a total dud. No nerve, no imagination. I never understood why Pasha kept him on. Not to mention that Timofeyev is falling apart in front of everyone's eyes. Six months, you know who'll run the show at NoviRus? Ozhogin. He's a cop. Only you can't run a complicated business entity like a cop, you have to be a general. Kuzmitch and Maximov can't wait. When they're done with Ozhogin, you won't be able to find his bones. It's the food chain, Renko. Figure out the food chain, and you figure out the world."

Arkady watched Zhenya bounce in and out of sight. He asked Hoffman, "What do you know about Anton Obodovsky?"

"Obodovsky?" Bobby raised his eyebrows. "Tough guy, local Mafia, jacked some of our trucks and drained some oil tanks. He has balls, I'll give him that. Ozhogin pointed him out on the street once. Obodovsky made the colonel nervous. I liked that."

When Zhenya finally emerged from the fun house, they started home. Hoffman and Zhenya played chess without a board, calling out their moves, the boy piping "e4" from the backseat, followed quickly by Hoffman's confident "c5" up front. Arkady could follow through the first ten moves, and then it was like listening to a conversation between robots, so he concentrated more on his own diminishing prospects.

It was virtually impossible to be dismissed for incompetence. Incompetence had become the norm under the old law, when prosecutors faced no courtroom challenges from upstart lawyers, and convenient evidence and confessions were always close at hand. Drinking was indulged: a drunken investigator who curled up in the back of a car was treated as gently as an ailing grandmother. Corruption, however, was tricky. While corruption was the lubrication of Russian life, an investigator accused of corruption always drew public outrage. There was a painting called *The Sleigh Ride*, of a troika driver throwing a horrified girl to a pursuing wolf pack. Zurin was like that driver. He compiled files on his own investigators, and whenever the press got close to him, he tossed them a victim. Arkady had no reason to be horrified or surprised.

He asked Hoffman, "Does Timofeyev have a cold or a bloody nose?"

"He says he has a cold."

"There were spots on his shirt that looked like dried blood."

"Which could have come from blowing his nose."

"Did Pasha have a bloody nose?"

"Sometimes," Hoffman said. He was still engaged in the chess game.

"Did he have a cold?"

"No."

"An allergy?"

"No. Rook takes b3."

Zhenya said, "Queen to d8, check."

"Did he see a doctor?" Arkady asked.

"He wouldn't go."

"He was paranoid?"

"I don't know. I never looked at it that way. It wasn't that obvious, because he was still on top of the business end. King to h7."

"Queen to e7," said Zhenya.

"Queen to d5."

"Checkmate."

Hoffman threw his hands up as if upsetting a board. "Fuck!"

"He's good," Arkady said.

"Who knows, with these distractions?"

Zhenya won two more games before they got to the children's shelter. Arkady walked him to the door, and Zhenya marched through without a backward look, which was both more and less than disdain. Hoffman was closing his mobile phone when Arkady returned to the car.

"He's Jewish," Hoffman said.

"His last name is Lysenko. That's not Jewish."

"I just played chess with him. He's Jewish. Can you let me off at the Mayakovsky metro station? Thanks."

"You like Mayakovsky?"

"The poet? Sure. 'Look at me, world, and envy me. I have a Soviet passport!' Then he blew his brains out. What's not to like?"

As Arkady drove, he glanced at Hoffman, who was not the sobbing wreck he had been the day before. That Hoffman could not have played chess with anyone. This Hoffman went from poetry to boasting lightly, without incriminating detail, about a variety of business scams — front companies and secret auctions — that he and

Ivanov had perpetrated together.

"How are you feeling?" Arkady asked.

"Pretty disappointed."

"You've been humiliated and fired. You should be furious."

"I am."

"And you lost the disk."

"That was the ace up my sleeve."

"You're bearing up well, considering."

"I can't get over that kid. You probably don't appreciate it, Renko, but that was chess at a really high level."

"It certainly sounded like it. Keeping the disk, hiding the disk, using me and my pitiful investigation to make the disk seem important, and finally letting Ozhogin find it at your gym, of all places. What did you put on it? What's going to happen at NoviRus when that disk goes to work?"

"I have no idea what you're talking about."

"You're a computer expert. The disk is poison."

The sky darkened behind illuminated billboards that used to declaim: The Party Is the Vanguard of the Workers! and now advertised cognac aged in the barrel, as if a madman raving on a corner had been smoothly replaced by a salesman. Neon coins rolled across the marquee of a casino and lit a rank of Mercedeses and SUVs.

"How would you know?" Hoffman twisted in his seat. "I'm getting out. Right here is good."

"We're not at the station."

"Hey, asshole, I said this corner was good."

Arkady pulled over, and Bobby heaved himself out of the car. Arkady leaned across the seat and rolled down the window. "Is that your good-bye?"

"Renko, will you fuck off? You wouldn't understand."

"I understand that you made a mess for me."

"You don't get it."

Drivers trapped behind Arkady shouted for him to move. Horns were rarely used when threats would do. A wind chased bits of paper around the street.

"What don't I get?" Arkady asked.

"They killed Pasha."

"Who?"

"I don't know."

"They pushed him?"

"I don't know. What does it matter? You were going to quit."

"There's nothing to quit. There's no investigation."

"Know what Pasha said? 'Everything is

buried, but nothing is buried long enough.' "

"Meaning what?"

"Meaning here's the hot news. Rina is a whore, I'm a shit and you're a loser. That's as much chance as we had. This whole place is fucked. I used you, so what? Everybody uses everybody. That's what Pasha called a chain reaction. What do you expect from me?"

"Help."

"Like you're still on the case?" Bobby looked up at the heavy sky, at the gold coins of the casino, at the split toes of his shoes. "They killed Pasha, that's all I know."

"Who did?"

Bobby whispered, "Keep your fucking country."

"How —" Arkady began, but the lead Mercedes in line slid forward and popped open its rear door. Bobby Hoffman ducked in and shut it, closing himself off behind steel and tinted glass, although not before Arkady saw a suitcase on the seat. So the car hadn't been idly sitting by, it had been arranged. At once the sedan eased away, while Arkady followed in the Zhiguli. In tandem, the two cars passed Mayakovsky Station and continued on Leningrad Prospect, headed north. What was worth heading to? It was too dark for a sunlit stroll on the beach at Serebryaniy Bor, and too late for races at the Hippodrome. But there was the airport. Evening flights from Sheremetyevo headed in all directions, and Hoffman had been in and out of the airport often enough to grease half the staff there. He would have a ticket to Egypt or India or a former-Sovietstan, any place without an extradition treaty with the United States. He would be whisked through security, ushered to first class and offered champagne. Bobby Hoffman, veteran fugitive, was stealing the march again, and once he was through security, he would be beyond Arkady's reach.

Not that Arkady had any authority to stop Hoffman. He simply wanted to ask him what was buried. And what he had meant when he said that Pasha had somehow been killed? Was Pasha Ivanov pushed or not? Hoffman's driver reached up to place a blue light on the car roof and plowed ahead in the express lane. Arkady slapped on his own official light and swung from lane to lane to stay close. No one slowed. Russian drivers took an oath at birth to never slow, Arkady thought, just as Russian pilots took off no matter what the weather.

But traffic did brake and squeeze around a bonfire in the middle of the road. Arkady thought it was an accident until he saw figures dancing around the fire, executing Hitler salutes and smashing the windshields and headlights of passing cars with rocks and steel rods. As he drew closer, he saw not wood but a blackened car shifting in the flames and spewing the acrid smoke of burning plastic. Fifty or more figures rocked a bus. A woman jumped from the bus door and went down screaming. A three-wheeled Zaporozhets hardly larger than a motorcycle cut in front of Arkady and rammed his fender. Inside were a man and woman, perhaps Arabs. Four men with shaved heads and a red-and-white banner swarmed the car. The largest lifted the car so that its front wheel spun in the air, while another stove in the passenger window with the banner pole. Arkady lifted his eyes to the light towers of Dynamo Stadium blazing ahead and understood what was happening.

Dynamo was playing Spartak. The Dynamo soccer club was sponsored by the militia, and Spartak was the favorite of skinhead groups like the Mad Butchers and the Clockwork Oranges. Skinheads supported their team by stomping any Dynamo fans they found on the street. Sometimes they went a little further. The skinhead holding the front of the Zaporozhets had ripped off his shirt to show a broad chest tattooed with a wolf's head, and arms ringed with swastikas. His friend with the pole beat in the last of the windshield and dragged the woman out by her hair, shouting, "Get your black ass out of that Russian car!" She emerged with her cheek cut and her hair and sari sparkling with safety glass. Arkady recognized Mrs. Rajapakse. The other two skinheads beat in Mr. Rajapakse's window with steel rods.

Arkady was not aware of getting out of the Zhiguli. He found himself holding a gun to the head of the skinhead clutching the bumper. "Let go of the car."

"You love niggers?" The strongman spat on Arkady's raincoat.

Arkady kicked the man's knee from the side. He didn't know whether it broke, but it gave way with a satisfying snap. As the man hit the ground and howled, Arkady moved to the Spartak supporter who was pinning Mrs. Rajapakse to the hood. Since skinheads filled the street and the clip of Arkady's pistol held only thirteen rounds, he chose a middle course. "If you —" the man had begun when Arkady clubbed him with the gun.

As Arkady moved around the car, the skinheads with the rods gave themselves some swinging room. They were tall lads with construction boots and bloody knuckles. One said, "You may get one of us, but you won't get both."

Arkady noticed something. There was no clip in his gun at all. He'd removed it for the drive with Zhenya. And he never kept a round in the breech.

"Then which one will it be?" he asked and aimed first at one man and then the other. "Which one doesn't have a mother?" Sometimes mothers were monsters, but usually they cared whether their sons died on the street. And sons knew this fact. After a long pause, the two boys' grip on the bars went slack. They were disgusted with Arkady for such a low tactic, but they backed off and dragged away their wounded comrades.

Meanwhile, the general melee spread. Militia piled out of vans, and skinheads smashed bus-stop displays as they ran. The Rajapakses brushed glass from their seats. Arkady offered to drive them to a hospital, but they nearly ran over him in their haste to make a U-turn and leave the scene.

Rajapakse shouted out his broken window, "Thank you, now go away, please.

You are a crazy man, as crazy as they are."

Holding his ID high, Arkady walked up to the burning car. Victims of the skinheads sprawled on the road and sidewalk, sobbing amid broken side mirrors, torn shirts, shoes. He went as far as a line of militia barricades being rapidly, belatedly erected at the stadium grounds. Hoffman was nowhere in sight, but everywhere was shining glass, in coarse grains and small.

The elevator operator was the former Kremlin guard Arkady had interviewed before. As the floors passed, he looked Arkady up and down. "You need a code."

"I have you. You know the code." Arkady pulled on latex gloves.

The operator shifted, exhibiting the training of an old watchdog. At the tenth floor, he was still uncertain enough to take a mobile phone from his pocket. "I have to call Colonel Ozhogin first."

"When you call, tell the colonel about the breakdown in building security the day Ivanov died, how you shut down the elevator at eleven in the morning and checked each apartment floor by floor. Explain why you didn't report the breakdown then."

The elevator whined softly and came to a stop at the tenth floor. The operator swayed unhappily. Finally he said, "In Soviet days we had guards on every floor. Now we have cameras. It's not the same."

"Did you check the Ivanov apartment?"

"I didn't have the code then."

"And you didn't want to call NoviRus Security and tell them why you needed it."

"We checked the rest of the building. I don't know why the receptionist was worried. He thought maybe he'd seen a shadow, something. I told him if he missed anything, the man watching the screen at NoviRus would catch it. In my opinion, nothing happened. There was no breakdown."

"Well, you know the code now. After you let me in, you can do whatever you want."

The elevator doors slid open, and Arkady stepped into Ivanov's apartment for the fourth time. As soon as the doors closed, he pressed the lock-out button on the foyer panel. Now the operator could call anyone, because the apartment was, as Zurin had said, sealed from the rest of the world.

With its white walls and marble floors, the apartment was a beautiful shell. Arkady removed his shoes rather than track dirt across the foyer. He turned on the lights room by room and saw that other visitors had preceded him. Someone had cleaned up the evidence of Hoffman's vigil on the sofa; the snifter was washed and the cushions were plumped. The photo gallery of Pasha Ivanov still graced the living room wall, although now it seemed sadly beside the point. The only missing photographs were the ones of Rina with Pasha from the bedroom nightstand. And no doubt Ozhogin had been to the scene, because the office was stripped clean of anything that, encrypted or not, possibly held any NoviRus data: computer, Zip drive, books, CDs, files, phone and message machine. All the videotapes and disks were gone from the screening room. The medicine cabinet was empty. Arkady appreciated professional thoroughness.

He didn't know exactly what he was looking for, but this was the last chance he would have to look at all. He remembered the Icelandic fairy, the imp with nothing but a head and foot, who could be seen only out the corner of the eye. Look directly, and he disappeared. Since all the obvious items had been removed, Arkady had to settle for glimpsed revelations. Or the lingering shadow of something removed.

Of course, the home of a New Russian should be shadow-free. No history, no questions, no awkward legalities, just a clear shot to the future. Arkady opened the window that Ivanov had fallen from. The curtains rushed out. Arkady's eyes watered from the briskness of the air.

Colonel Ozhogin had removed everything related to business; but what Arkady had seen of Pasha Ivanov's last night among the living had nothing to do with business. NoviRus was hardly on the point of collapse. It might be soon, with Timofeyev at the helm, but up to Ivanov's last breath, NoviRus was a thriving, ravenous entity, gobbling up companies at an undiminished rate and defending itself from giant competitors and small-time predators alike. Perhaps a ninja had climbed down the roof like a spider, or Anton had slipped through the bars at Butyrka; either was a professional homicide that Arkady had little realistic hope of solving. But Arkady had the sense that Pasha Ivanov was running from something more personal. He had banned virtually everyone, including Rina, from the apartment. Arkady remembered how Ivanov had arrived at the apartment, one hand holding a handkerchief and the other clutching an attaché case that seemed light in his hand, not laden with financial reports. What was in the case when Arkady saw it on the bed? A shoe sack and a mobile phone recharger. Ivanov might have headed to the apartment office and learned about some disastrous investment? In that case, Arkady pictured a maudlin Ivanov assuaging himself with a Scotch or two before working up the nerve to open the window. What Arkady recalled from the videotape was an Ivanov who emerged reluctantly from his car, entered the building in a rush, bantered with another tenant about dogs, rode the elevator with grim determination and added a valedictory glance at the security camera as he stepped out the door. Was he rushing to meet someone? In his attaché case, why a single shoe sack? Because it wasn't being used for shoes. Ivanov had gone to the bathroom, maybe, but he hadn't swilled pills in any suicidal amount. He was the decisive type, not the sort to wait passively for a sedative's effect. He had talked to Dr. Novotny enough to concern her, then skipped his last four sessions. All Arkady really knew about Ivanov's last night was that he had entered his apartment by the door and left by the window and that the floor of his closet was covered with salt. And there had been salt in Pasha's stomach. Pasha had eaten salt.

The bedroom phone rang. It was Colonel Ozhogin.

"Renko, I'm driving over. I want you to leave the Ivanov apartment now and go down to the lobby. I'll meet you there."

"Why? I don't work for you."

"Zurin dismissed you."

"So?"

"Renko, I —"

Arkady hung up.

Ivanov had gone to the bedroom and laid his attaché case on the bed. Set his mobile phone on the edge of the bed. Opened the attaché case, so intent on the contents that he did not notice having knocked the phone onto the carpet or kicked it under the bed, for Victor to find later. What did Ivanov slip from the shoe sack: a brick, a gun, a bar of gold? Arkady walked through every move, trying to align himself on an invisible track. Pasha had opened the walk-in closet and found the floor covered in salt. Did he know about a coming worldwide shortage of salt? Good men were the salt of the earth. Smart men salted away money. Pasha had rushed home to eat salt, and all he took with him on his ten-story exit was a shaker of salt. Arkady inverted the shoe sack. No salt.

This *thing* from the sack, was it still in

the apartment? Ivanov had not taken it with him. As Arkady remembered, everyone focused on company matters, and a shoe sack was the wrong size and shape for either computer disks or a spreadsheet.

The phone rang again.

Ozhogin said, "Renko, don't hang —"

Arkady hung up and left the receiver off the hook. The colonel's problem was that he had no leverage. Had Arkady been a man with a promising career, threats might have worked. But since he was dismissed from the prosecutor's office, he felt liberated.

Back a step. Sometimes a person thought too much. Arkady returned to the bed, mimed opening the attaché case, slipping something from the shoe sack and moving to the closet. As the closet opened, its lights lent a milky glow to the bed of salt still covering the floor. The top of the mound showed the same signs of activity that Arkady had seen before: a scooping here, a setting something down there. Arkady saw confirmation in a brown dot of blood tunneled through the salt, from Ivanov leaning over. Ivanov had removed the *thing* from the shoe sack, set it on the salt and then . . . what? The saltshaker might have fit nicely into the depression in the middle of the salt. Arkady pulled open a drawer of monogrammed long-sleeved shirts in a range of pastels. He flipped through them and felt nothing, shut the drawer and heard something shift.

Arkady opened the drawer again and, in the back, beneath the shirts, found a bloody handkerchief wrapped around a radiation dosimeter the size of a calculator. Salt was embedded in the seam of its red plastic shell. Arkady held the dosimeter by the corners to avoid latent fingerprints, turned it on and watched the numbers of the digital display fly to 10,000 counts per minute. Arkady remembered from army drills that an average reading of background radioactivity was around 100. The closer he held the meter to the salt, the higher the reading. At 50,000 cpm the display froze.

Arkady backed out of the closet. His skin was prickly, his mouth was dry. He remembered Ivanov hugging the attaché case in the elevator, and his backward glance to the elevator camera. Arkady understood that hesitation now. Pasha was bracing himself at the threshold. Arkady turned the meter off and on, off and on, until it reset. He made a circuit of Pasha's beautiful white apartment. The numbers dramatically shuffled and reshuffled with every step as he picked his way like a blind man with a cane around flames he sensed only through the meter. The bedroom burned, the office burned, the living room burned, and at the open window, curtains dragged by the night wind desperately whipped and snapped to point the fastest way out of an invisible fire.

5

Pripyat had been a city of science built on straight lines for technicians, and it shimmered in the light of a rising moon. From the top floor of the municipal office, Arkady overlooked a central plaza wide enough to hold the city's entire population on May Day, Revolution Day, International Women's Day. There would have been speeches, national songs and dances, flowers in cellophane presented by neatly pressed children. Around the plaza were the broad horizontals of a hotel, restaurant and theater. Tree-lined boulevards spread to apartment blocks, wooded parks, schools and, a mere three kilometers away, the constant red beacon of the reactor.

Arkady sank back into the shadows of the office. He had never thought his night vision was particularly good, but he saw calendars and papers strewn on the floor, fluorescent tubes crushed, file cabinets facedown around a nest of blankets and the glint of empty vodka bottles. A poster on the wall proclaimed something lost in faded letters: CONFIDENT OF THE FUTURE was all Arkady could make out. In camouflage fatigues, he himself was fairly hard to see.

The pinprick of a match being struck drew him closer to the window. He'd missed where. The buildings were blank, streetlamps broken. The forests pressed increasingly closer, and when the wind died, the city was utterly still, without a single light, without the progress of a car or the sound of a footstep. Around the city there was not one human intrusion until the orange bud of a cigarette stirred directly across the plaza in the dark mass of the hotel.

Arkady had to use a flashlight in the stairway because of the debris — bookcases, chairs, drapes and bottles, always bottles, and everything covered by a chalky residue of disintegrating plaster that formed a cavern's worth of stalactites and stalagmites. Even if there had been power, the elevators were rusted shut. From outside, a building might seem intact. Inside, this one resembled a target of artillery, with walls exploded, pipes ruptured and floors heaved by ice.

On the ground floor, Arkady turned off the light and went at a lope around the plaza. The hotel entrance doors were chained together. No matter; he walked through missing panes of glass, turned on the flashlight, crossed the lobby and maneuvered as silently as possible around service trolleys piled on the steps. On the fourth floor, the doors were open. Beds and bureaus materialized. In one room, the wallpaper had curled off in enormous scrolls; in another, the ivory torso of a toilet lay on the carpet. By now he smelled the sourness of a doused fire. In a third room, the window was covered by a blanket that Arkady pulled aside to let moonlight creep in. A box spring had been stripped to the coils and set over a hubcap as a makeshift grill and pan that was filled with coals and water and a ghostly hint of smoke. An open suitcase showed a toothbrush, cigarettes, fishing line, a can of beef and a plastic bottle of mineral water, a plumber's pipe cutter and a wrench wrapped in rags. If their owner had been able to resist a peek out of the blanket, Arkady never would have seen him. He spotted him now, moving at the edge of the plaza.

Arkady went down the stairs two at a time, sliding over an overturned desk, stumbling on the crushed maroon of hotel drapes. Sometimes he felt like a diver plunging through the depths of a sunken ship, his vision and hearing magnified in such faint light. As he hit the ground, he heard a screen door slap shut at the far end of the plaza. The school.

Between the school's two front doors was a blackboard that read APRIL 29, 1986. Arkady ran through a cloakroom painted with a princess and a hippo sailing a ship. The lower rooms were for early grades, with blackboard examples of penmanship, bright prints of farm children with happy cows that smiled amid blown-in windows and desks overturned like barricades. Footsteps pounded the floor above. As Arkady climbed the stairs, a display of children's art fluttered in his wake. Pictures of students sitting neatly in a music room led to a music room with a shattered piano and half-size chairs around broken drums and marimbas. Dust exploded with every step; Arkady swallowed a fine powder with every breath. In a nap room, bed frames stood at odd angles, as if caught in a wild dance. Picture books lay open: Uncle Ilyich visiting a snowy village, *Swan Lake*, May Day in Moscow. Arkady heard another door shut. He ran down a second stairway to the school's other exit and slowed to navigate a heap of child-size gas masks. Crates had been delivered and tipped over in a panic. The masks were shaped like sheep heads, with round eyes and rubbery tubes. Arkady burst out the door, too late. He played the flashlight around the plaza and saw nothing.

Although it was wrong to think "nothing" when the place was so alive with cesium, strontium, plutonium or pixies of a hundred different isotopes no larger than a microdot hiding here and there. A hot spot was just that: a spot. Very close, very dangerous. One step back made a great difference. The problem with, say, cesium was that it was microscopic — a flyspeck — and it was water-soluble and adhered to anything, especially the soles of shoes. Grass that grew chest-high from seams in the road earned another tick from the dosimeter. At the opposite end of the plaza from the school was a small amusement park, with crazy chairs, a rink of bumper cars and a Ferris wheel that stood against the night like a rotting decoration. The reading at the rink shot the needle off the dial and made the dosimeter sing.

Arkady made his way back to the hotel, to the room with the box-spring grill. He weighted, with the can of beef, a note with his mobile-phone number and the universal sign for dollars.

Arkady had left a motorcycle in a stand of alders. He wasn't a skilled rider, but a Uralmoto bike, unlike some fancier makes, relished punishment. He fishtailed to the highway and, headlights off, rode out of the city.

This quarter of the Ukraine was steppe, flatland edged by trees, and the moon was bright enough to show pines on either side of the road. The trees had turned red — dead where they stood — the day after the accident. Otherwise, the fields swept all the way to the reactors.

Death had been so generous here that there was a graveyard even for vehicles. Arkady coasted to a halt at a fence of wooden stakes and barbed wire and a loosely tied gate with the warnings EXTREME DANGER and REMOVE NOTHING FROM THIS SITE. He untied the rope and rode in.

Trucks were lined up by the thousands. Heavy trucks, tankers, tow trucks, flatbeds, decontamination trucks, fire engines, mess trucks, buses, caravans, bulldozers, earthmovers, cement trucks and row after row of army trucks and personnel carriers. The yard was as long as an Egyptian necropolis, although it was for the remains of machinery, not men. In the headlight of the motorcycle, they were a labyrinth of metal cadavers. A giant spread its arms overhead, and Arkady realized that he had passed under the rotors of a crane helicopter. There were more helicopters, each marked in paint with its individual level of radiation. It was here, tucked in the center of this yard, that Timofeyev's BMW, covered with the dust of the long trip from Moscow, had been found.

A fountain of sparks led Arkady to a pair of scavengers cutting up an armored car with an arc welder. Radioactive parts from the yard were sold illegally in car shops in Kiev, Minsk, Moscow. The men were hidden in coveralls and surgical masks, but they were familiar to Arkady because they had sold him his motorcycle. The yard manager, Bela, a round Hungarian, used a voluminous handkerchief to wipe his brow free of the dust that kicked off the raw earth. Bela's office was a trailer a few meters away. Dust infiltrated the trailer's windows and lined the maps on his worktable. Each map corresponded to a section of the yard, locating every vehicle. Bela culled the yard judiciously, leaving the impression of a full row here, a complete car there. The trailer itself was going nowhere; at this point it was as radioactive as the surrounding vehicles. Bela didn't care that he was king of a poisoned realm; with his canned food, bottled water, television and VCR, he considered himself hermetically sealed where it counted. He waved to Arkady, who rode past, looped around a mountain of tires and went out the gate.

By this point the eye was always pulled to the reactors. Chain link and razor wire surrounded what had been a massive enterprise of cooling towers, water tanks, fuel storage, cooling ponds, the messenger ranks of transmission towers. Here four reactors had produced half the power of the Ukraine, and now sipped power to stay lit. Three reactors looked like windowless factories. Reactor Four, however, was buttressed and encased by ten stories of lead-and-steel shielding called a sarcophagus, a tomb, but it always struck Arkady, especially at night, as the steel mask of a steel giant buried to the neck. St. Petersburg had its statue of the Bronze Horseman. Chernobyl had Reactor Four. If its eyes had lit and its shoulders begun shifting free of the earth, Arkady would not have been totally surprised.

Ten kilometers from the plant was a checkpoint, its gate a crude bar counterweighted by a cinder block. As

Arkady was Russian and the guards were Ukrainian, they walked the bar out of his way at half speed.

Past the checkpoint were a dozen "black villages" and fields where scarecrows had been replaced by diamond-shaped warning signs on tall stakes. Arkady swung the bike onto the crusted ruts of a dirt road and rode a jaw-shaking hundred meters around a tangle of scrub and trees into a gathering of one-story houses. All the houses were supposed to be evacuated, and most looked collapsed from sheer emptiness, but others, even in the moonlight, betrayed a certain briskness: a mended picket fence, a sledge for gathering firewood, a haze of chimney smoke. A scarf and candle turned a window red or blue.

Arkady rode through the village and up a footpath through the trees another hundred meters to a clearing surrounded by a low fence. He swung his headlamp, and up jumped a score of grave markers fashioned from iron tubing painted white and decorated with plastic flowers, improbable roses and orchids. No burials had been allowed since the accident; the soil was too radioactive to be disturbed. It was at the cemetery gate that Lev Timofeyev — one week after the suicide of Pasha Ivanov — had been found dead.

The initial militia report was minimal: no papers, no money, no wristwatch on a body discovered by a local squatter otherwise unidentified, cause of death listed as cardiac arrest. Days later, the cause of death was revised to "a five-centimeter slice across the neck with a sharp unserrated blade, opening the windpipe and jugular vein." The militia later explained the confusion with a note that said the body had been disturbed by wolves. Arkady wondered whether the excuse had wandered in from a previous century.

He lifted his ear to the muffled flight of an owl and the soft explosion that marked the likely demise of a mouse. Leaves swirled around the bike. All of Chernobyl was reverting to nature. Sometimes it crept in while he watched.

One way to look at Chernobyl was as a bull's-eye target, with the reactors at the center and circles at ten and thirty kilometers. The dead city of Pripyat fit within the inner circle, and the old town of Chernobyl, for which the reactors were named, was actually farther away, in the outer circle. Together the two circles composed the Zone of Exclusion.

Checkpoints blocked the roads at ten and

thirty kilometers, and though the houses of Chernobyl were ostensibly abandoned, dormitories and housing had been found for security troops, and the town's café contained the Zone's social life. The café looked as if it had been slapped together over a weekend. Twenty people fit comfortably, but fifty had pushed their way in, and what was more comforting than the press of other bodies, what tastier than dried fish and candy bars, nuts and chips? Arkady bought peanuts and beer and slipped into a corner to watch couples dance to what was either hip-hop or polka. All the men were in camouflage uniforms they called camos, and the women wore sweats, except for a few younger secretaries who couldn't stand to be drab, even next door to disaster. One of the researchers was having a birthday that required repeated toasts with champagne and brandy. Cigarette smoke was so thick that Arkady felt as if he were on the bottom of a swimming pool.

A researcher named Alex brought Arkady a brandy. "Cheers! How long have you been with us, Renko?"

"Thanks." Arkady downed the glass in a swallow and didn't breathe for fear of detonation.

"That's it. People around you are trying

to get drunk. Don't be a prig. How long?"

"Three weeks."

"Three weeks and you're so unfriendly. It's Eva's birthday, and you have yet to give her so much as a kiss."

Eva Kazka was a young woman with black hair that put Arkady in mind of a wet cat. Even she was in camos.

"I've met Dr. Kazka. We shook hands."

"She was unfriendly? That's because your colleagues from Moscow were cretins. First they stepped on everything, and then they were afraid to step on anything. By the time you came, fraternal relations were in the toilet." Alex was a tall man with a swimmer's broad shoulders and a cynic's long nose. He brightened up as a captain in militia blues entered with two corporals in camos and knit caps. "Your fan club. They just love the way you've complicated their lives. Do you ever feel like the most unpopular man in the Zone?"

"Am I?"

"By acclamation. You have to pull your head out of your investigation and enjoy life. Wherever you are, that's where you are, as they say in California."

"Except that they're in California."

"Good point. Check out Captain Marchenko. With his mustache and uniform, he looks like an actor abandoned in a provincial theater. The rest of the troupe has moved on and left him nothing but the costumes. And the corporals, the Woropay brothers, Dymtrus and Taras, I see them as the boys most likely to have sexual congress with barnyard animals."

Arkady had to agree that the captain had a classic profile. The Woropays had pasty faces speckled with a late bloom of acne, and their shoulders were broad as barrels. They turned away from Arkady to share a laugh with the captain.

"Why does Marchenko spend his time with them?" Arkady asked.

"The sport here is hockey. Captain Marchenko fields a team, and the Woropays are two of his stars. Get used to it. You're a sitting duck. People say you've been exiled and your boss in Moscow wants to keep you here forever."

"It would help if I solved the case."

"But you won't. Wait, I want to hear this."

The other table started serenading Eva Kazka, and she let her face go blissfully stupid. Researchers were variously described to Arkady as the scientific crème de la crème or washouts, but always as fools because they were volunteers; they didn't have to be here. Alex returned to his friends briefly to bay like a wolf and steal a bottle of brandy before returning to Arkady.

"Because people think you're crazy," Alex said. "You go to Pripyat. Nobody gives a damn about Pripyat anymore. You ride through the woods on a bike that glows in the dark. Do you know anything about radioactivity?"

"I went over the bike with a dosimeter. It's clean, and it doesn't glow."

"No one is going to steal it, let me put it that way. So, Investigator Renko, on this most blighted part of the planet, what are you looking for?"

"I'm looking for squatters. In particular, the squatter who found Timofeyev. Since I don't have a name, I'm questioning all the squatters I can find."

"You're not serious. You are serious? You're crazy. Over the course of a year, we get all sorts: poachers, scavengers, squatters."

"The police report said the body was found by a local squatter. That suggests a sort of permanency, someone the militia officer had seen before."

"What kind of officers can you get at Chernobyl? Look at the Woropays. They can barely write their names, let alone a report. You're married? You have children at home waiting for you?"

"No." Arkady thought fleetingly of Zhenya, but the boy could hardly have been called family. For Zhenya, Arkady had been nothing but transportation to the park. Besides, Victor was looking in on the boy.

"So, you've given yourself an impossible task in a radioactive wasteland. You're either a compulsive-obsessive or a dedicated investigator."

"Right the first time."

"We'll drink to that." Alex refilled their glasses. "Do you know that alcohol protects against radiation? It removes oxygen that might be ionized. Of course, deprivation of oxygen is even worse, but then every Ukrainian knows that alcohol is good for you. Red wine is best, then brandy, vodka, et cetera."

"But you're Russian."

Alex put his finger to his lips. "Shhh. I am provisionally accepted as a madman. Besides, Russians also drink precautionary vodka. The real question is, are you a madman, too? My friends and I serve science. There are interesting things to be learned here about the effects of radiation on nature, but I don't think the death of some Moscow businessman is worth spending a minute here, let alone almost a month."

Arkady had told himself as much many

times over the days he'd spent searching the apartments of Pripyat or farmhouses hidden in the woods. He didn't have an answer. He had other questions. "Whose is?" he asked.

"What do you mean?"

"Whose death is worth it? Only good people? Only saints? How do we decide whose murder is worth investigating? How do we decide which murderers to let go?"

"You're going to catch every killer?"

"No. Hardly any, as a matter of fact."

Alex regarded Arkady with mournful eyes. "You are totally lunatic. I am awed. I don't say that lightly."

"Alex, are you going to dance with me or not?" Eva Kazka pulled him by his arm. "For old times' sake."

Arkady envied them. There was a desperate quality to the scene. In general, the troops were not getting healthier for having been posted to Chernobyl. The Ukraine was even poorer than Russia, and hazard pay meant little if it was constantly late or missed entirely, but considering the circumstances, it could hardly be spent better than on getting drunk. The researchers were a different matter. There were several teams carrying out various studies, but as a group the men had long hair, the women were disheveled, and they shared the esprit of scientists on an asteroid hurtling toward Earth. The work had its drawbacks, but it seemed definitely unique.

Kazka laid her head on Alex's shoulder for a slow dance. Although Ukrainian women were said to be beautiful in a soulful, doe-eyed way, Kazka looked like she would bite the head off anyone who flattered her. She was too pale, too dark, too sharp. The way she and Alex moved suggested a past involvement, a momentary truce in a war. Arkady was surprised at himself for even speculating, which he took to be a result of his own social isolation.

Why was he at Chernobyl? Because of Timofeyev? Because of Ivanov? Arkady had finally been convinced of Pasha's suicide. Suicide of an aggravated nature. A radiation team in leaded suits found that the heap of salt in Ivanov's closet was minutely tainted with cesium-137 in salt form, maybe one grain to a million, but that was enough. It was a needle in a haystack. By appearances, sodium chloride and cesium chloride were indistinguishable. The effect was something else. Handling a gram of pure cesium-137 for three seconds could be fatal, and while a grain of cesium chloride was a smaller, dilute version, it still had a punch. Pasha's stomach was so radioactive that the second autopsy had to be halted and the morgue evacuated. He was buried in a lead-lined coffin. The saltshaker that Victor had found on the pavement under Ivanov was the hottest item of all, a bomb spraying gamma rays so hot they turned the glass gray. Fortunately the shaker had been stored in an unoccupied evidence room, from which it was moved by a team using tongs and placed in a double container of lead ten centimeters thick. Arkady and the team went to the residences that Pasha had left so abruptly and found his mansion and town house baited in the same deadly way. Had Ivanov known? He had ordered the town house and estate left vacant, he let no one into his apartment and he carried a dosimeter. He knew. Arkady thought about the salt he had licked off his fingers at the apartment and felt a chill.

Timofeyev's prerevolutionary palace was the same. He hadn't barred visitors because he didn't have Pasha's strength of character, but the halls and rooms of his gilded abode were a radioactive warren. No wonder about the man's nervousness and loss of weight. After waltzing with dosimeters through Timofeyev's palace, Arkady and Victor took the precaution of visiting the militia doctor, who gave them iodine tablets and assured them that they had suffered no more exposure to radiation than an airline passenger flying from St. Petersburg to San Francisco, although they might want to shower, dispose of their clothes and look out for nausea, loss of hair and, especially, nosebleeds, because cesium affected bone marrow where platelets were formed. Victor asked what to do about nosebleeds. The doctor said to carry a handkerchief.

Ivanov and Timofeyev had lived with this sort of anxiety? Why hadn't either reported to the militia that someone was trying to kill them? Why hadn't they alerted NoviRus Security? Finally, why had Timofeyev driven a thousand kilometers from Moscow to Chernobyl? If it was to save his life, it hadn't worked.

The investigation of Timofeyev's body, once it was found at the village cemetery, had been a farce. The cemetery grounds were radioactive — family members were supposed to visit grave sites only one day a year — and the first thing the lads from the militia did was drag Timofeyev a safe distance away to turn him this way and that. Since the dead man's billfold and wristwatch were missing, they had no idea of his identity or importance. Because of the rain, they wanted to toss the body in a van and go. Their surmise was that a businessman with, say, an uncle or auntie buried in the cemetery had made a clandestine visit, had a heart attack and dropped. No one asked where his car was or whether his shoes were muddy from walking. Chernobyl had neither detectives nor pathologists, and Kiev showed no interest in a death from natural causes in the provinces. Timofeyev was kept in a refrigerator, and the idea that he was Russian and not Ukrainian hadn't crossed anyone's mind until a BMW with Moscow plates was found in the truck yard two days later. By then someone who had seen Timofeyev in the cooler had the sense to notice that his throat was cut.

There was a great flurry from Moscow. Prosecutor Zurin came personally to Chernobyl with ten investigators — not including Arkady — who joined with their counterparts from Kiev to uncover the truth. They discovered nothing. The scene at the cemetery had been defiled first by wolves and then by the hurried removal of Timofeyev's body. If there had been blood on the ground, it was washed away by rain, so there was no way of telling even if the cemetery was where his throat had been cut. No photographs had been taken of the body in situ. The body itself, declared too hot to autopsy or even burn, was buried in a sealed coffin. The militia officer who made the initial report had disappeared, presumably with Timofeyev's billfold and watch. The longer the investigators from Moscow and Kiev stayed, the unhappier they became about tramping from one radioactive village to another. The old people who had surreptitiously returned to their homes knew they weren't supposed to be there, and since an encounter with officialdom was sure to gain them a one-way bus ticket to some dismal basement in the city, they went to ground like rabbits, to other cabins in other black villages, and after a few weeks the investigators threw in their cards and left, with much less fanfare than when they had arrived. Another prosecutor might have admitted defeat, but here Zurin showed his brilliance, his ability to survive any calamity. He retrieved the situation by volunteering Arkady to the Chernobyl militia, a move that, in one stroke, signified cooperation between fraternal countries, satisfied the demand for further investigation and, incidentally, put a comfortable distance between the prosecutor and his most difficult investigator.

At the same time, Zurin made it impossible for Arkady to succeed. On his own, without detectives or access to any friends of Timofeyev, or a sympathetic priest or a masseuse that Timofeyev might have shared his anxiety with, exiled as far from Moscow as Pluto from the sun, Arkady was left chasing ghosts. Faced with Zurin's legerdemain, he was dazzled.

"Renko! Last dance!" Alex dragged Arkady from the corner and pushed him into the arms of a burly researcher. "Don't be such a stick! Vanko needs a partner."

With his pallor and stringy hair, Vanko looked more like a crazed monk than an ecologist. "Are you gay?" he asked Arkady. "I don't dance with gays. A straight man is permissible under the circumstances."

"It's okay."

"You're not so bad. Everyone said you'd be gone in a week, like the others. You stuck it out; I have to respect that. Do you want to lead?"

"Whichever."

"Doesn't matter, I agree. Not here. This is the café at the end of the world. If you want to know what the end of the world will be like, this is it. Not so bad."

6

Captain Marchenko steered with one finger and waved a radio microphone in his other hand like a tank commander. "This is good. We will prove there is law and order in the Zone. Even here! These vultures go into the village churches and steal the church icons, or go into the houses of simple people and take the icons there. Well, we have him now. The fields are too boggy to cross, and there isn't much traffic on this road. Aha, there he is! The vulture is in sight!"

A dot on the horizon was developing into a motorcycle and sidecar, not a powerful bike, more what a farmer might use to transport chickens. Gray sky swept by. Red firs lined the road, and markers showed where houses and barns too hot to truck away or burn were buried.

Captain Marchenko had swung by in a militia car and invited Arkady to help pursue a thief who had escaped a checkpoint with an icon in the sidecar of his motorcycle. From exchanges on the radio, Arkady gathered that another car was posted ahead. It was clear that it gave the captain pleasure to turn an investigator from Moscow into a captive audience. "We may not have investigators like in Moscow, but we know what we're about."

"I'm sure that Chernobyl holds its own."

"Ch'o'rnobyl. The Ukrainian pronunciation is Ch'o'rnobyl."

Much of the topsoil had been buried under sand; up to the woods the ground was bulldozed flat, a chute for a headwind that made the motorcycle skitter from one side of the road to the other, not over a hundred meters ahead, and although the rider hunched down, the car was gaining. Arkady could see that the bike was small, maybe 75cc, blue, the license plate taped over.

"They're criminals, Renko. This is the way you have to treat them, not like you do, making friends, leaving food and money like it's everybody's birthday. You think you're going to find informants? You think that one dead Russian is more important than regular policing? Maybe he was a big man in Moscow, but he was nothing here. His office called. A Colonel Ozhogin said to keep an eye on you. I told him you were getting nowhere."

To locate the local squatter, Arkady had,

over three weeks, created a registry of Zone illegals: old folks, squatters, scavengers, poachers and thieves. The old people were hidden but stationary. Scavengers operated out of cars and trucks. Poachers were usually restaurant employees from Kiev or Minsk, looking for venison or boar. Icon thieves were hit-and-run and harder to net.

Arkady said, "Then why was Timofeyev here? What was the connection between him and Chornobyl? What was the connection between him and Ivanov and Chornobyl? How many murders do you have here?"

"None. Only your Timofeyev, only a Russian. I would have a perfect record otherwise. I might be out of here with a clean record. How do we know he was killed by someone from here? How do we know he was even here before in his life?"

"We ask. We find local people and ask, although I'll grant you, it isn't easy when officially no one *is* here."

"That's the Zone."

Sometimes Arkady thought of the Zone as an amusement-park mirror. Things were different in the Zone. He said, "I still wonder about the body. An Officer Katamay turned in the first report. I haven't been able to interview him, because he quit the militia. Do you have any idea where Katamay is?"

"Try the Woropay brothers. He was close to them."

"The Woropays were not responsive." The brothers Woropay knew that Arkady had no authority. They had been both dull and sly, smirking to each other, going heavy-lidded and silent. "I'd like to find Katamay, and I'd like to know who led him to the body."

"What does it matter? The body was a mess."

"How so?"

"Wolves."

"Specifically what did the wolves do?"

"They ate his eye."

"Ate his eye?" No one had mentioned that before.

"The left eye."

"Wolves do that?"

"Why not? And they tugged on his face a bit. That's why we missed the knife wound on the throat."

"He was dead when the wolves arrived. He wouldn't have bled that much."

"There wasn't that much blood. That's one reason we thought heart attack. Except for his eye and his nose, his face was clean."

"What was in his nose?"

"Blood."

"And his clothes?"

"Pretty clean, considering how the rain and how the wolves messed up the scene."

Hardly more than the militia, Arkady thought, but bit his tongue. "Who examined the body the second time? Who noticed that his throat was cut? They left no name or official report, only a one-line description of the neck wound."

"I'd like to get my hands on them, too. If it hadn't been for someone mucking around where they shouldn't have been, the Russian would still be a heart attack, you wouldn't be here and my slate would be clean."

"Now, there's a new approach to militia work. If they don't have a pickax in the head, call it cardiac arrest." Arkady had meant to sound lighthearted, but Marchenko didn't seem to take it that way. Maybe it came out wrong, Arkady thought. "Anyway, the second examiner knew what he was doing. I'd just like to know who it was."

"You always want to know. The man from Moscow and his hundred thousand questions."

"I'd also like to take another look at Timofeyev's car."

"See what I mean? I don't have the time or the manpower for a homicide investigation. Especially of a dead Russian. Do you know what the official attitude is? 'There's nothing in the Zone but spent uranium, dead reactors and the suckers stationed there. Fuck them. Let them live on berries.' You saw yourself how all those other investigators didn't want to stay around too long. Nevertheless, we still carry out our functions, like now." Marchenko squinted ahead. "Ah, here we come."

Ahead, where dead firs gave way to potato fields, a white militia Lada and a pair of officers blocked the road. The fields were wet from the previous week's rain: no escape there. No problem. The motorcycle rider slowed to size up the blockade, sped up, leaned to his left and steered down and up the right shoulder of the road as neatly as plucking a blade of grass.

Marchenko picked up the radio. "Get out of the way."

The officers desperately pushed the Lada onto the shoulder as Marchenko barreled through. Arkady was glad he hadn't quit smoking. If he was going to die in the Zone, why deny himself a simple pleasure?

"Do you work out?" Marchenko asked.

Arkady hung on to a strap. "Not really."

"Middle of Moscow, it can't be easy. You can have Moscow. Do you like the Ukraine?"

"I haven't seen much besides the Zone. Kiev is a beautiful city." Arkady hoped that was diplomatic enough.

"Ukrainian girls?"

"Very beautiful."

"The most beautiful in the world, people say. Big eyes, big . . ." Marchenko cupped his chest. "Jews come once a year. They talk Ukrainian girls into going to America to be au pairs and keep them as slaves and whores. The Italians are as bad."

"Really?" There was a free-floating quality to the captain's anger that Arkady found disturbing.

"A bus goes daily to Milan, full of Ukrainian girls who end up as prostitutes."

"But not to Russia," Arkady said.

"No, who would go to Russia?" The captain shifted and dug out of a pocket a large knife in a leather sheath. "Go ahead, take it out."

Arkady unsnapped the guard and drew out a heavy blade with a blood groove and a two-edged tip. "Like a sword."

"For wild boar. You can't do that in Moscow, right?" Marchenko said.

"Hunting with a knife?"

"If you have the nerve."

"I am sure I do not have the nerve to catch a wild boar and stab it to death."

"Just remember, it's essentially a pig."

"And then you eat them?"

"No, they're radioactive. It's sport. We'll try it sometime, you and I."

The motorcycle swerved onto a side road, but Marchenko would not be shaken. The road dove down along a black mire of ragged cattails and then up by an apple orchard carpeted with rotting fruit. Two hovels seemed to rise from the ground, and the motorcycle went in between, followed by Marchenko, at the cost of a wing mirror. Suddenly they were in the middle of a village that was a quagmire of houses so cannibalized from the bottom up for firewood that every roof and window was at a slant. Washtubs sat in the front yards, and chairs sat at the street, as if there had been a final parade out of town and people to watch. Arkady heard the dosimeter raise its voice. The motorcycle shot through a barn, in the front and out the back. Marchenko followed only ten meters behind, close enough for Arkady to see an icon and blanket stuffed in the sidecar. The road dropped again toward a stand of sickly willows, a stream and, rising on the far side, a field of grain tangled by wind and gone to seed. The road narrowed at the willows, the perfect point to cut off the motorcycle — just like in the movies, Arkady thought, when Marchenko swerved to a stop and the motorcycle slipped into the trees and out of sight behind a screen of leaves.

Arkady said, "We can go on foot. A path like that, we'll catch up."

The captain shook his head and pointed to a radiation marker rusting among the trees. "Too hot. This is as far as we can go."

Arkady got out. The trees didn't quite reach the creek, and although the grass was high, the slope was downhill, and his boots were heavy with mud, Arkady managed to push through. Marchenko shouted for Arkady to stop. He saw the thief emerge from the trees. Despite the fact that the rider had gotten off to push, the motorcycle stayed virtually in place, spewing smoke and spraying mud. The rider was short, in a leather jacket and cap, with a scarf wrapped around his face. The icon, a Madonna with a starry cowl, peered from the sidecar. Arkady nearly had his hand on it when the bike gained traction and lurched forward on a road so overgrown it was barely a fold in the grass. He was close enough to read the logo on the engine cover. Suzuki. The bike bounced down from rut to rut, Arkady a step behind and Marchenko a step behind him. Arkady tripped over a radiation sign but was still almost within reach when the bike spurted across the streambed, kicking back rocks. From one step to the next, he was about to reach for the sidecar, but the climb from the stream on the other side was steeper, the wheat sleeker, and the motorcycle had more space to maneuver. Arkady dove for the rear fender and held it until a reflector snapped off in his hand and the bike pulled away by one meter, then five, then ten. It drew off while Arkady leaned on his knees and gave up. Blowing like a whale, Marchenko joined him.

The hillside was a yellow knoll topped by a silhouette of bare trees dead where they stood. The biker climbed to the trees, stopped and looked back. Marchenko pulled out his gun, a Walther PP, and aimed. It would take a real marksman at this range, Arkady thought. The pistol swayed with the captain's breathing. The biker didn't move.

Finally Marchenko replaced the gun in its holster. "We're over the border. The stream is the border. We're in Byelorussia. I can't go shooting people in other countries. Brush off the wheat. It's hot. Everything is hot."

Horseflies spun around the two men as they trudged back to the car. For humiliation, the day was already quite full, Arkady thought. Out of curiosity, he turned on his dosimeter when they crossed the stream, then shut off the angry ticking as soon as he heard it. "Can you take me back to Chernobyl?" he asked.

The captain slipped in the mud. As he rose, he bellowed, "It's Chornobyl. In Ukrainian, it's Chornobyl!"

Arkady's room in Chernobyl was in a metal dormitory perched on the edge of a parking lot. He had a bed and a quilt, a desk trimmed in cigarette burns, a dim lamp and a stack of files.

The team of investigators from Moscow had not completely wasted their time. They had searched for any possible connection among Timofeyev, Ivanov and Chernobyl. After all, before finding a second vocation in business, the two men had been physicists. They had grown up in the same Moscow neighborhood and, from the playground, had become good friends,

Ivanov a natural leader, Timofeyev an ardent follower and both gifted enough in science to be sent to special schools and the Institute for Extremely High Temperatures under the tutelage of its director, Academician Gerasimov himself. For them the operation of a nuclear power plant would have been as dull as driving a bus. As far as detectives had been able to ascertain, Ivanov and Timofeyev had no relatives or friends at Chernobyl. None of their teachers or fellow students came from the Chernobyl area. They had never visited Chernobyl before the accident. There was no connection to Chernobyl at all.

Who was connected to Chernobyl?

Not Colonel Georgi Jovanovich Ozhogin, the head of NoviRus Security. His file was stuffed with encomiums to his first career as a Master of Sport, and adulatory references to his second career as a "selfless agent of the Committee for State Security." The authors of the report did not detail what this selflessness involved beyond citing his efforts for "international amity and athletic competition in Turkey, Algeria and France." Age: fifty-two. Married: Sonya Andreevna Ozhogin. Children: George, fourteen, and Vanessa, twelve. Arkady had not been part of the investigation team. Had he been, he might have pursued the idea that the only person with access to all the contaminated residences was the chief of NoviRus Security. However, the colonel volunteered to be interviewed under truth serum and hypnosis and passed both tests. From that point on, the investigators tiptoed around Ozhogin.

The investigators hadn't known what to make of Rina Shevchenko. Pasha Ivanov had given his lover excellent but thoroughly fictitious papers: birth certificate, school record, union card and residency permit. At the same time, it was clear from police reports that an underage Rina had run away from a cooperative farm outside St. Petersburg, moved illegally to Moscow and survived initially as a prostitute. The investigators' dilemma was whether the protection of such a powerful benefactor extended posthumously. On the advice of lawyers retained for her by her two friends Kuzmitch and Maximov, she refused to meet with investigators a second time. Would they have asked her about her Ukrainian surname? Well, millions of Russians had a Ukrainian surname. Arkady couldn't see her walking around Ivanov's apartment broadcasting salt and cesium. What he had seen in the apartment was

Rina unable to do anything other than watch a video of Pasha over and over again.

The investigators loathed Robert Aaron Hoffman. Age: thirty-seven. Nationality: U.S.A. and Israel. Occupation: business consultant. A visa photograph of Hoffman accentuated his small eyes and round jowls. According to the report, Hoffman had stolen a computer disk from the Ivanov apartment, and although the disk was retrieved, there was reason to believe that he had altered the contents to compromise the entire NoviRus computer network. Hoffman might have stolen other items from the apartment as well. However, all Arkady had seen Hoffman take was the gift of a suede jacket. And Arkady remembered Bobby's drunken vigil. Would a man who had spread toxic cesium linger at all?

On the other hand, in June of the previous year, Hoffman had taken a NoviRus jet from Moscow to Kiev's Boryspil Airport, and a bus from Boryspil to Chernobyl to, in the opinion of the investigators, "meet fellow Jews and possibly transfer diamonds." He had returned to Moscow that night. Arkady sometimes avoided raising the subject of Jews because people who appeared quite decent and sane one moment would start ranting about Jewish cabals the next. Arkady found anti-Semitism depressing and endemic, like scabies or lice. Captain Marchenko, however, had been correct about one thing: according to the investigators Jews did sometimes visit Chernobyl's Jewish cemetery. Bobby Hoffman, who hadn't struck Arkady as the religious sort, had come with them. He hadn't noticed any Jews in Chernobyl, so why would they visit?

Who else had the investigators turned their attention to?

The muscleman Anton Obodovsky proved a disappointment. He may have threatened Ivanov, but he was in Butyrka Prison the night of Pasha's suicide and very publicly in Moscow casinos at the time of Timofeyev's disappearance.

The elevator operator at Pasha's building, the Kremlin veteran, had access to the tenth floor, but not to Ivanov's two previous homes or Timofeyev's. A sweep of his wardrobe and apartment showed not a trace of radioactivity.

Timofeyev's household staff was under treatment for exposure to radioactive materials. They had no information to offer, and their loss of hair seemed sincere.

Day by day Moscow lost interest. After all, Ivanov was a suicide, half crazed from radiation or not. Timofeyev had been murdered, but not in Moscow, not even in Russia. In short, any homicide investigation was properly a Ukrainian responsibility, with Russian assistance limited to a single investigator. It was fair to say that there was no real investigation anymore. Arkady occasionally felt like a man underwater breathing through a reed, the reed being his mobile phone. For a while Victor ran down leads in Moscow, an example being laboratories that produced cesium chloride. Although there was no commercial use of anything so toxic, grains were used in scientific research. Victor tracked down labs and researchers until, on Zurin's orders, he stopped taking Arkady's calls. Arkady was on his own. Meanwhile, NoviRus stock plunged, and the world moved on.

Although the Chernobyl cafeteria offered borsch, buns, tomato salad, meat and potatoes, pudding, lemonade and tea, it struck Arkady that the delegation from the British Friends of the Ecology seemed unsure, less than famished, shy of their food.

They also seemed intimidated by a constantly moving corps of heavily rouged waitresses who might have once been a sister trapeze act.

Alex stood and played host. “We welcome all our British Friends and, in particular, Professor Ian Campbell, who will be staying on with us for a week.” He indicated a bearded, ginger-haired man who looked like he had drawn the short straw. “Professor, perhaps you’d like to say a few words?”

“Is the food locally grown?”

“Is the food locally grown?” Alex repeated. He savored the question like the blue smoke of his cigarette. “Although we are not quite ready to label it ‘Product of Chernobyl,’ yes, much of the food was grown and harvested in the neighboring environs.” He took an extravagant inhale. “Chernobyl is not the Black Earth region of the Ukraine, famous for its wheat. We have a more sandy soil given to potatoes and beets. The greens are local, the lemons in the lemonade are not and the tea, I believe, is from China. Bon appétit.”

Another question passed the length of the table before Alex could sit.

“Ah, is the food radioactive? The answer to that depends on how hungry you are.

For example, this copious meal makes up in part for the low pay of the staff. They are paid in calories as well as cash. The waitresses are overage but extremely coquettish, practically a floor show in and of themselves. The food? Milk is dangerous; cheese is not, because radionuclides stay in the water and albumin. Shellfish are bad, and mushrooms are very, very bad. Did they serve mushrooms today?"

While the Friends glumly regarded their lunch, Alex sat and vigorously carved his meat. Vanko put a soup bowl next to Arkady and sat down. The researcher looked like he had been following an earthworm down a hole.

"Did you understand any of that?" he asked Arkady.

"Enough. Is Alex trying to be dismissed?"

"They wouldn't dare." Vanko ladled the soup slowly. "This is my grandmother's remedy for a hangover. You don't even have to chew."

"Why wouldn't they?"

"He's too famous."

"Oh." Arkady felt suddenly ignorant.

"He is Alex Gerasimov, son of Felix Gerasimov, the academician. With Alex, the Russians will fund the study; without him, they won't."

"Why doesn't he just leave?"

"The work is too interesting. He says he'd rather leave with his head off than on. Last night was fun. You shouldn't have left."

"They closed the café."

"The party continued. It was a birthday. You know who can really drink?"

"Who can really drink?" Coming from Vanko, this sounded like high praise.

"Dr. Kazka. She's tough. She was in Chechnya, a volunteer. She saw real action." Vanko mopped up the soup with bread. Alex seemed to be having a grand time at the long table, urging his guests to dig in.

"You mentioned something last night about poachers," Arkady said.

"No, *you* mentioned poachers," Vanko said. "I thought you were looking for the squatter who found that millionaire from Moscow."

"Maybe. The note said squatter, but squatters tend to stay in Pripyat. They like apartments. I get the impression that black villages are more for old folks."

A salad swimming in oil replaced Vanko's soup. He didn't raise his head again until he had wiped the last piece of lettuce from his chin. "Depends on the squatter."

"I don't think squatters spend much time at cemeteries. There's nowhere to sleep and nothing to steal."

"Are you going to eat your potatoes? They're locally grown."

"Help yourself." Arkady pushed his plate over. "Tell me about poachers."

Vanko talked between mouthfuls. The good poachers were local. They had to know their way around, or they could walk into some very hot spots. They might be adding some meat to their diet, or they might be called by a restaurant so a chef could put game on the menu.

"A restaurant in Kiev."

"Maybe Moscow. Gourmets love wild boar. The problem is that wild boars love to root for big fat radioactive mushrooms. Stick to pigs that eat slops, and you'll be fine."

"I'll keep that in mind. You study wild boar?"

"Boar, elk, mice, kestrels, catfish and shellfish, tomatoes and wheat, to name a few."

"You must know some poachers," Arkady said.

"Why me?"

"You set traps."

"Of course."

"Poachers set traps. Maybe they even rob your traps from time to time."

"Yeah." Vanko's eating slowed to a ruminative pace.

"I don't want to arrest anyone. I only want to ask about Timofeyev, exactly when he was found, his position and condition, whether his car was ever nearby."

"I thought his car was found in Bela's yard. A BMW."

"Timofeyev got there somehow."

"The path to the village cemetery is too narrow for a car."

"See, that's exactly the kind of information I need."

Meanwhile, Alex got to his feet again. "To vodka, the first line of radiation defense."

Everyone drank to that.

Pripyat was worse in the light of day, when a breeze stirred the trees and lent a semblance of animation. Arkady could almost see the long lines of people and the way they must have looked over their shoulders at their apartments and all their possessions, their clothes, televisions, Oriental rugs, the cat at the window. Families must have pulled the reluctant young and pushed the confused elderly and shielded babies from the sun. Ears had to close to the question "Why?" Patience must have been an asset as the doctors handed iodine tablets to every child, too late. Too late because, at the beginning, although everyone saw the fire at Reactor Four, only two kilometers away, the official word was that the radioactive core was undamaged. Children went to school, though they were drawn to the spectacle of helicopters circling the black tower of smoke and fascinated by the green foam covering the streets. Adults recognized the foam as the plant's protection against an accidental release of radioactive materials. Children waded though the foam, kicked it, packed it into balls. The more suspicious parents called friends outside Pripyat for news that might have been withheld, but no, they were told that May Day preparations were in full swing in Kiev, Minsk, Moscow. Costumes and banners were finished. Nothing was canceled. Still, those people with binoculars went to the roofs of their apartment blocks and watched firemen scramble off giant ladders onto the reactor and carry back blocks of indeterminate material, no fireman staying longer than sixty seconds. No one was allowed out of Pripyat except to fight the fire, and those who returned from the plant were dizzy, nauseated, mysteriously tanned. Supermarket stocks of iodine tablets sold out. Children were sent home from school with instructions to shower and ask Mommy to wash their clothes, even though all the city's water had been diverted to the fire. The news broadcast from Moscow said that there had been an incident at Chernobyl, but measures were being taken and the fire was contained. Finally, no one in Pripyat was allowed outside. Three days passed between the accident and the sudden evacuation of the city. Eleven hundred buses took away the fifty thousand inhabitants. They were told they were going to a resort, to bring casual clothes, documents, family pictures. As the buses departed, loose pictures scattered, and children waved at the dogs running behind.

So any stir of the trees or tall grass created a false sense of resurrection, until Arkady noticed the stillness at doors and windows and recognized that the sound traveling from block to block was the moving echo of his motorcycle. Sometimes he imagined Pripyat not so much as a city under siege but as a no-man's-land between two armies, an arena for snipers and patrols. From the central plaza he rode up one avenue to the town stadium and back on another, amid headless streetlamps, over a black crust of roads undergoing a slow upheaval. Outdoor murals of Science, Labor and the Future peeled off office fronts.

A movement at a corner window made Arkady swing the motorcycle to an apartment block, park and climb the stairs to the third floor, a living room with tapestries on the wall, a reclining chair, a collection of decanters. A bedroom was heaped with clothes. A little girl's room had a pink theme, school awards and a pair of ice skates hanging from the wall. In a boy's room an intricate skeleton curled in a glass tank under posters of Ferraris and Mercedeses. Photographs were everywhere, color pictures of the family caravanning in Italy, and older black-and-white portraits of a previous generation of mustached men and tightly buttoned women. The photos seemed trampled, suggesting violent disagreement or grief. A doll dangling from a cord tapped the sash of a broken window — the movement Arkady had seen. Scavengers had come and gone, punching in walls to rip out electrical wiring. Every time he left an apartment like this, he felt he was stepping from a tomb, in a city of tombs.

He rode back to the main plaza and to the office where he had spotted the scavenger the night before. The suitcase and makeshift grill were gone. So was the note with Arkady's mobile-phone number and the dollar sign. He didn't know whether he was hunting or fishing, but he was doing what he could, and that, he had to admit, was where Zurin was so brilliant. The prosecutor knew that where another, more balanced individual would say that if the Chernobyl nuclear accident had caused forty or four million deaths — depending on who was counting — who would care what had happened to a single man? So what if Arkady found a connection between Timofeyev and Chernobyl? Russians, Byelorussians, Ukrainians, Danes, Eskimos, Italians, Mexicans and Africans touched by the poison as it spread around the world had no connection to Chernobyl, and they would die, too. The first ones, Pripyat's firemen, irradiated inside and out, died in a day. The rest would die obliquely over generations. On that scale, what did Timofeyev or Ivanov matter? Yet Arkady couldn't stop himself. In fact, riding a motorcycle through the abandoned streets of Pripyat, he found himself more and more at home.

The Chernobyl militia station was a brick building with a linden tree sprouting from a corner like a feather in a cap.

Marchenko joined Arkady in the parking lot where Timofeyev's impounded BMW had disappeared.

The captain wore clean camos and bitter satisfaction. "You wanted to take another look? Too late. Bela took it to Kiev while you and I were out chasing the icon thief. So someone in my own station house told Bela I was gone." He tilted his head. "Listen: the first cricket of the evening. An idiot, obviously. Anyway, I should apologize for my outburst this morning. Chernobyl, Chornobyl, what difference does it make?"

"No, you were right, I should say Chornobyl."

"Let me give you some advice. Say, 'Farewell, Chornobyl.' "

"But something occurred to me."

"Something always occurs to you."

"When you originally found Timofeyev's car in the truck graveyard, it had no keys?"

"No keys."

"You towed it here from the truck graveyard?"

"Yes. We went over this."

"Remind me, please."

"Before we towed the car here, we looked for keys, looked for blood on the car seats, forced open the trunk to look for blood or any other evidence. We didn't find anything."

"Nothing to suggest that Timofeyev had been killed somewhere else and taken in the car to the cemetery?"

"No."

"Did you take casts of any tire treads at the cemetery?"

"No. Anyway, our cars rolled over any tracks there."

"Right."

"It's a black village. Radioactive. Everyone moved fast. And it rained on and off, don't forget."

"And there were wolf tracks?" Arkady still found that hard to believe.

"Big as a plate."

"Who did the towing?"

"We did."

"Who drove?"

"Officer Katamay."

"Katamay is the officer who found Timofeyev's body and then disappeared?"

"Yes."

"He does a lot around here."

"He knows his way around. He's a local boy."

"And he's still missing?"

"Yes. It's not necessarily a crime. If he quits, he quits. Though we would like the uniform and gun."

"I looked at his file. He had disciplinary problems. Did you ask him about Timofeyev's wallet and watch?"

"Naturally. He denied it, and the matter was dropped. You have to meet his grandfather to understand."

"Is he from around here?"

"From a Pripyat family. Look, Renko, we're not detectives, and this is not the normal world. This is the Zone. We are as forgotten as any police can be. The country is collapsing, so we work for half pay, and everyone steals to make ends meet. What's missing? What's not missing? Medicine, morphine, a tank of oxygen, gone. We were given night-vision goggles from the army? Disappeared. I was with Bela when we discovered Timofeyev's BMW, and I remember his look, as if he would kill me for that car. If that's the truck graveyard manager, what kind of officers do you think I'm going to have? I know what he's doing, I see the sparks at night. Everyone else is suffering, and he's making his fortune, but I'm not allowed to conduct the sort of raid I would like, because he has a 'roof,' understand, he's protected from above."

"I didn't mean to criticize."

"Fire away. Like my wife says, anyone intelligent steals. The thieves understand. Most of the time they just pay off the guards at the checkpoints; this morning was an exception. Usually they slip from one black village to the next, and if we get too close, they just dive into a hot spot we can't go into. I'm not going to risk the lives of my men, even the worst of them, and there are maybe a thousand hot spots, a thousand black holes for thieves to dive into and come out who knows where. If you know anyone else who is willing to come here, ask them." While they talked, the afternoon had turned to dusk. Marchenko lit a cigarette and smiled like the happy captain of a sinking ship. "Invite all your friends to Chornobyl."

Since the ecologists and British Friends had been absent from the cafeteria, Arkady had eaten a quiet dinner and gone to bed with case notes when a phone call came from Olga Andreevna at the children's shelter in Moscow. "I am sorry to report that we have had problems with Zhenya since you left. Behavioral problems and refusal to eat or communicate with other children or with staff. Twice we caught him leaving the shelter at night — so dangerous for a boy his age. I cannot help but associate this increase in social dysfunction with your absence, and I must ask when you plan to return."

"I wish I could say. I don't know." Arkady reached automatically for a cigarette to help him think.

"Some estimate would be helpful. The situation here is deteriorating."

"Has my friend Victor visited Zhenya?"

"Apparently they went to a beer garden. Your friend Victor fell asleep, and the militia returned Zhenya to the shelter. When are you coming back?"

"I am working. I am not on vacation."

"Can you come next weekend?"

"No."

"The weekend after?"

"No. I'm not around the corner, and I'm not his father or an uncle. I am not responsible for Zhenya."

"Talk to him. Wait."

There was silence on the other end of the line. Arkady asked, "Zhenya, are you there? Is anyone there?"

Olga Andreevna came on. "Go ahead, he's here."

"Talk about what?"

"Your work. What it's like where you are. Whatever comes to mind."

All that came to Arkady's mind was an image of Zhenya grimly clutching his chess set and book of fairy tales.

"Zhenya, this is Investigator Renko. This is Arkady. I hope you are well." This sounds like a form letter, Arkady thought. "It seems you've been giving the good people at the shelter problems. Please don't do that. Have you been playing chess?"

Silence.

"The man you played chess with in the car said you were very good."

Maybe there was a boy at the other end, Arkady thought. Maybe the telephone was dangling down a well.

"I'm in the Ukraine, a long drive from Moscow, but I will be back in a while, and I won't know where to find you if you run away from the shelter."

Talk about what else, a man with his throat cut? Arkady searched. "It's like Russia here, but wilder, overgrown. Not many people, but real elk and wild boar. I haven't seen any wolves, but maybe I'll hear them. People say that's a sound you don't forget. It makes you think of wolf packs chasing sleds across the snow, doesn't it? My parents and I used to drive to a dacha. I didn't play chess like you."

Arkady remembered the disassembled pistol in his hands and wondered how he'd gotten on this topic. "It was dark when we arrived. There were other dachas, but the people in them had been warned away. When we pulled up to the house, the younger officers who had gone ahead would greet my father by baying like wolves. He would lead them like a conductor. He tried to teach me, but I was never any good."

7

Chernobyl Ecological Station Three was a run-down garden nursery. A filmy light penetrated a plastic roof that had been torn and patched and torn again. Rows of potted plants sat on tables, suffering the music of a radio hanging on a post. Ukrainian hip-hop. Bent over a microscope, Vanko shifted with the beat.

Alex explained to Arkady, "Actually, the most important instrument for an ecologist is a shovel. Vanko is very good with a shovel."

"What are you digging for?"

"The usual villains: cesium, plutonium, strontium. We sample soil and groundwater, test which mushroom soaks up more radionuclides, check the DNA of mammals. We study the mutation rate of *Clethrionomys glareolus*, whom you'll meet, and sample the dose rates of cesium and strontium from a variety of mammals. We kill as few as possible, but you have to be 'Merciless for the Common Good,' as my father used to say." Alex led Arkady outside. "This, however, is our Garden of Eden."

Eden was a five-by-five-meter plot of melons sprawled lazily on the ground, red tomatoes fat on the vine and sunflowers blazing in the morning sun. Beet greens grew down one row and cabbage down another, a veritable borsch on the hoof. In the corners were orange crates propped on sticks.

Alex had a gardener's pride. "The old topsoil had to be scraped away. This new soil is sandy, but I think it's doing well."

"Is that the old soil?" Arkady pointed to an isolated bin of dark earth fifty meters off. The bin was half covered by a tarpaulin and surrounded by warning signs.

"Our particularly dirty dirt. It's worse than finding a needle in a haystack. A speck of cesium is too small to see without a microscope, so we dig everything up. Ah, another visitor."

One of the orange crates had fallen. As Alex lifted the trap, a ball of quills tipped in white rolled out, a pointed nose appeared and two beady eyes squinted up.

"Hedgehogs are serious sleepers, Renko. Even trapped, they don't like to be awakened quite so rudely."

The hedgehog got to its feet, twitched its

nose and, with sudden attention, dug up a worm. An elastic tug-of-war ended in a compromise; the hedgehog ate half the worm while half escaped. More alert, the hedgehog considered going one way, then another.

"All he can think of is a new nest with soft, cool rotting leaves. Let me show you something." Alex reached down with a gloved hand, picked up the hedgehog and set it in front of Arkady.

"I'm in his way."

"That's the idea."

The hedgehog marched forward until it encountered Arkady. It butted his foot two, three, four times until Arkady let it through, spines bristling, the exit of a hero.

"He wasn't afraid."

"He's not. There have been generations of hedgehogs since the accident, and they're not afraid of people anymore." Alex pulled off his gloves to light a cigarette. "I can't tell you what a pleasure it is to work with animals that aren't afraid. This is paradise."

Some paradise, Arkady thought. All that separated the plot from the reactor was four kilometers of red forest. Even at that distance, the sarcophagus of Reactor Four and the red-and-white-striped chimney loomed above the trees. Arkady had assumed the garden was only a test site, but no, Alex said, Vanko sold the produce. "People will eat it, it's nearly impossible to stop them. I used to have a big dog, a rottweiler, to guard the place. One night I was working late, and he was outside barking in the snow. He wouldn't stop. Then he stopped. I went out ten minutes later with a lamp, and there was a ring of wolves eating my dog."

"What happened then?"

"Nothing. I chased them and fired a couple of shots."

A Moskvich with a bad muffler went by on the way to Pripyat. Eva Kazka shot Arkady and Alex a glance without slowing down.

"Mother Teresa," Alex said. "Patron saint of useless good works. She's off to the villages to tend the lame and the halt, who shouldn't be here in the first place." Black smoke poured out the tailpipe of the Moskvich like a bad temper.

"She likes you," Alex said.

"Really? I couldn't tell."

"Very much. You're the poetic type. So was I once. Cigarette?" Alex unwrapped a pack.

"Thank you."

"I had stopped smoking before I came to

the Zone. The Zone puts everything in perspective."

"But the radioactivity is fading."

"Some. Cesium is the biggest worry now. It's a bone seeker; it heads to the marrow and stops the production of platelets. And you've got a radiation-sensitive lining in your intestines that cesium just fries. That's if everything goes well and the reactor doesn't blow again."

"It might?"

"Could. No one really knows what's going on inside the sarcophagus, except that we believe there's over a hundred tons of uranium fuel keeping itself very warm."

"But the sarcophagus will protect any new explosion?"

"No, the sarcophagus is a rust bucket, a sieve. Every time it rains the sarcophagus leaks and more radioactive water joins the groundwater, which joins the Pripyat River, which joins the Dnieper River, which is the water that Kiev drinks. Maybe then people will notice." From his camos, Alex produced two miniature bottles of vodka, the kind that airlines sold. "I know you drink."

"Not usually this early in the day."

"Well, this is the Zone." Alex unscrewed the caps and threw them away. "Cheers!"

Arkady hesitated, but etiquette was etiquette, so he took the bottle and tossed it down in a swallow.

Alex was pleased. "I find that a cigarette and a little vodka lends a perspective to a day in the Zone."

Although Alex said, "The general rule for moving around the Zone is to stay on the asphalt," he seemed to despise the road. His preferred route was across the mounds and hollows of a buried village in a light truck, a Toyota with extra clearance, which he steered like a boat.

"Turn off your dosimeter."

"What?" That was the last thing Arkady had in mind.

"If you want the tour, you'll get the tour, but on my terms. Turn off the dosimeter. I'm not going to listen to that chattering all day." Alex grinned. "Go ahead, you have questions. What are they?"

"You were a physicist," Arkady said.

"The first time I came to Chernobyl, I was a physicist. Then I switched to radioecology. I am divorced. Parents dead. Political party: anarchist. Favorite sport: water polo, a form of anarchy. No pets. Except for disorderly conduct, virtually no arrests. I am very impressed that I have drawn the attention of a senior investigator from Moscow, and I have to confess that you have my assistant Vanko almost soiling his pants about this poacher you're looking for. He thinks you suspect him."

"I don't know enough to suspect anyone."

"That's what I told Vanko. Oh, I should add, favorite writer: Shakespeare."

"Why Shakespeare?" Arkady held on as the truck climbed a slope of chimney bricks.

"He has my favorite character, Yorick."

"The skull in Hamlet?"

"Exactly. No lines but a wonderful role. 'Alas, poor Yorick, I knew him well . . . a man of infinite jest . . .' Isn't that the best you can say about anyone? I wouldn't mind being dug up every hundred years so someone could say, 'Alas, poor Alexander Gerasimov, I knew him well.' "

"A man of infinite jest?"

"I do the best I can." Alex accelerated as if crossing a minefield. "But Vanko and I don't know much about poachers. We're only ecologists. We check our traps, tag this animal or that, take blood samples, scrape some cells for DNA. We rarely kill an animal, at least a mammal, and we don't have barbecues in the woods. I can't even tell you the last time I ran into a poacher or a squatter."

"You trap in the Zone, and poachers hunt in the Zone. You might have run into each other."

"I honestly don't remember."

"I talked to a poacher who was caught with his crossbow. He said another man whom he took to be a hunter had put a rifle to his head and warned him off. He described the man as about two meters tall; lean; gray eyes; short dark hair." That pretty much described Alex Gerasimov. Arkady leaned back for a better view of the rifle bouncing in the van's rear seat. "He said the rifle was a Protecta twelve-millimeter with a barrel clip."

"A good all-purpose rifle. These characters use crossbows so they can hunt without making a lot of noise, but they're hardly the marksmen they imagine they are. Usually they botch the job, the animal escapes and takes days of agony to bleed to death. To put the barrel of a rifle to someone's head, though — that is a little extreme. This poacher, will he prosecute?"

"How can he, without admitting he was breaking the law himself?"

"A real dilemma. You know, Renko, I'm beginning to see why Vanko is afraid of you."

"Not at all. I appreciate the ride. Sometimes activity prompts a memory. You might empty a trap today and remember that you ran into such-and-such a man right there."

"I might?"

"Or perhaps a person came to you with a moose he accidentally hit with his car, to ask whether it was safe to eat, the moose already being dead and food a shame to waste."

"You think so? There wouldn't be much car left after hitting a moose."

"Just a possibility."

"And I wouldn't advise going in those woods at all."

A wall of rusting pines stretched as far as Arkady could see, from left to right. Being dead, the branches held no cones and no squirrels; except for the flit of a bird, the trees were as still as posts. *Alas, poor Yorick, I knew him well.* Arkady could picture a skull on each post. Something ghostly did a pirouette in front of the trees. It fluttered like a handkerchief and darted away.

"A white swallow," Alex said. "You won't see many of those outside of Chernobyl."

"Do poachers come here?"

"No, they know better."

"Do we?"

"Yes, but it's irresistible, and we do it anyway. In the wintertime you should see it, the ground covered with snow, like a belly dimpled with mysterious scars, and the trees bright as blood. People call it the red forest or the magic forest. Sounds like a fairy tale, doesn't it? And not to worry — as the authorities always say, 'Appropriate measures will be taken, and the situation is under control.' "

They moved along the face of the red forest to an area replanted with new pine trees, where Alex hopped out of the truck and brought back the end of a bough.

"See how stunted and deformed the tip is. It will never grow into a tree, only scrub. But it's a step in the right direction. The administration is pleased with our new pines." Alex spread his arms and announced, "In two hundred and fifty years, all this will be clean. Except for the plutonium; that will take twenty-five thousand years."

"Something to hope for."

"I believe so."

Still, Arkady found himself breathing easier when the red pines gave way to a mix of ash and birch. At the base of a tree, Alex brushed back high grass to reveal a tunnel leading to a cage of what looked to

Arkady like squirming field mice.

"Clethrionomys glareolus," said Alex. "Voles. Or maybe super voles. The rate of mutation among our little friends here has accelerated by a factor of thirty. Maybe they'll be doing calculus next year. One reason voles have such a fast rate of mutation is that they reproduce so quickly, and radiation affects organisms when they are growing much more than it does when they're adult. A cocoon is affected by radiation, a butterfly is not. So the question is, How does radiation affect this fellow?" Alex opened the top of the cage to lift out a vole by its tail. "The answer is that he does not worry about radionuclides. He worries about owls, foxes, hawks. He worries about finding food and a warm nest. He thinks that radiation is by far the smallest factor in his survival, and he's right."

"And you, what is the largest factor in your survival?" Arkady asked.

"Let me tell you a story. My father was a physicist. He worked at one of those secret installations in the Urals where spent nuclear fuel was stored. Spent fuel is still hot. Insufficient attention was paid, and the fuel exploded, not a nuclear explosion but very dirty and hot. Everything was done secretly, even the cleanup, which was fast and messy. Thousands of soldiers, firemen, technicians waded through debris, including physicists led by my father. After the accident here, I called my father and said, 'Papa, I want you to tell me the truth. Your colleagues from the Urals accident, how are they?' My father took a moment to answer. He said, 'They're all dead, son, every one. Of vodka.' "

"So you drink and smoke and ride around a radioactive forest."

Alex let the vole drop into the cage and switched the full cage with an empty. "Statistically, I admit that none of these are healthy occupations. Individually, statistics mean nothing at all. I think I will probably be hit by a hawk of some kind. And I think, Renko, that you're a lot like me. I think you are waiting for your own hawk."

"Maybe a hedgehog."

"No, trust me on this, definitely a hawk. From here we walk a little."

Alex carried the rifle, and Arkady carried a cage that had a one-way gate baited with greens. Step by step, the woods around them changed from stunted trees to taller, sturdier beeches and oaks that produced a dappling of birdcalls and light.

Arkady asked, "Did you ever met Pasha Ivanov or Nikolai Timofeyev?"

"You know, Renko, some people leave their problems behind them when they go into the woods. They commune with nature. No, I never met either man."

"You were a physicist. You all went to the Institute of Extremely High Temperatures."

"They were older, ahead of me. Why this focus on physicists?"

"This case is more interesting than the usual domestic quarrel. Cesium chloride is not a carving knife."

"You can get cesium chloride at a number of labs. Considering the economic health of the country, you can probably persuade a scientist to siphon off a little extra for either terrorism or murder. People steal warheads, don't they?"

"To transport cesium chloride would take professional skill, wouldn't it?"

"Any decent technician could do that. The power plant still employs hundreds of technicians for maintenance. Far too many for you to question."

"If the person who used cesium in Moscow is the same person who killed Timofeyev here, wouldn't that narrow the field?"

"To those hundreds of technicians."

"Not really. The technicians live an hour away. They commute by train to the plant, work their shift and go directly home. They don't wander around the Zone. No, the person who cut Timofeyev's throat is part of the security staff, or a squatter or poacher."

"Or a scientist living in the Zone?" Alex said.

"That's a possibility, too." There weren't many of those, Arkady thought. There was no scientific glory work being done at Chernobyl. Everything was cleanup or observation.

"Cesium is a complicated way to kill someone or drive them crazy."

"I agree," said Arkady. "And hardly worth the effort, unless you're sending a message. The fact that neither Ivanov nor Timofeyev complained to the militia or their own security, in spite of a threat to their lives, suggests that some sort of message was understood."

"Timofeyev had his throat cut. Where's the subtle message in that?"

"Maybe it was in where he was found — at the threshold of a village cemetery. Either he drove all the way from Moscow just to go to that graveyard, or someone went to a great deal of trouble to put him there. Who noticed his throat was cut?"

"I suppose someone who went into the freezer. I can tell you that people were very unhappy there was a body inside. They had to clean everything else out."

"Then why go into the freezer except to look at the body?"

"Renko, I had never appreciated before how much detection work was groundless speculation."

"Well, now you know."

Trees continued to grow taller, shadows deeper, roots more ancient and interlaced. Arkady waded through fronds of bracken and had the illusion of spiders, salamanders, snakes scurrying ahead, a subtle ripple of life. Finally Alex stopped Arkady at the edge of blinding light, an arching meadow of wide-open daisies and, here and there, the red flags of poppies. Alex motioned him to crouch and be quiet, then pointed to the top of the meadow, where two deer stared back with dark liquid eyes. Arkady had never been so close to deer in the wild. One was a doe; the other had a wide rack of antlers, a hunter's prize. The tension in their gaze was different from the placid observation of zoo deer.

Alex whispered, "They are fat from grazing at the orchards."

"Are we still in the Zone?" Arkady found it hard to believe.

"Yes. What you can see from the road is a horror show — Pripyat, the buried villages, the red woods — but much of the Zone is like this. Now slowly stand."

Both deer went still as Arkady rose. They balanced more particularly but held their ground.

Alex said, "Like the hedgehog, they're losing their fear."

"Are they radioactive?"

"Of course they're radioactive, everything here is. Everything on earth is. This field is about as radioactive as a beach in Rio. There's a lot of sun in Rio. That's why I wanted you to turn off your Geiger counter, so you would hear more than that little ticking. Use your eyes and ears. What do you hear?"

For a minute Arkady heard nothing more than the mass drone of field life or his hand slapping a bug on his neck. By concentrating on the deer, however, he started to pick up their thoughtful chewing, the individual transit of dragonflies amid a sunlit cross fire of insects, and in the background, a squirrel scolding from a tree.

Alex said, "The Zone has deer, bison,

eagles, swans. The Chernobyl Zone of Exclusion is the best wild-animal refuge in Europe because the towns and villages have been abandoned, fields abandoned, roads abandoned. Because normal human activity is worse for nature than the greatest nuclear accident in history. The next greenie I meet who tells me how he wants to save the animals, I'll tell him that if he's sincere, he should hope for nuclear accidents everywhere. And the next poacher I find here, I will do more than break his toy crossbow. If you do find any poachers, will you please tell them that? Don't move. Be absolutely still. Look over your left shoulder, between the two pretty birches."

Arkady turned his head as slowly as possible and saw a row of yellow eyes behind the trees. The air grew heavy. Insects slowed in their spirals. Sweat ringed Arkady's neck and ran down his chest and spine. The next moment the deer bolted in an explosion of dust and flower heads, took the measure of the field in two bounds and crashed into the woods on the far side. Arkady looked back at the birches. The wolves had gone so silently that he thought he might have imagined them.

Alex unslung his rifle and ran to the

birches. From a lower branch, he freed a tuft of gray fur that he carefully placed inside a plastic bag. When he had put the bag in a pocket and given the pocket a loving pat, he tore a strip of bark off the birch, placed the strip between his palms and blew a long, piercing whistle. "Yes!" he said. "Life is good!"

Eva Kazka had set up a card table and folding chairs in the middle of the village's only paved road. Her white coat said she was a doctor; otherwise, her manner suggested a weary mechanic, and she didn't tame her black hair back as much as subdue it.

On either side of this outdoor office, the village slumped in resignation. Window trim hung loose around broken panes, the memory of blue and green walls faded under the black advance of mildew. The yards were full of bikes, sawhorses and tubs pillowed in tall grass and bordered by picket fences that leaned in an infinitely slow collapse. All the same, set farther back from the main street were, here and there, repainted houses with windows and intricate trim intact, with a haze of wood smoke around the chimney and a goat cropping the yard.

A benchful of elderly women in versions of shawl-and-coat-and-rubber-boots waited while Eva looked down the throat of a round little woman with steel teeth.

"Alex Gerasimov is crazy, this is a well-known fact," Eva said as an aside to Arkady. "Him and his precious nature. He's a perfectionist. He is a man who would drive a car into a pole again and again until it was a perfect wreck. Close."

The old woman closed her jaw firmly to signify nothing less then complete cooperation. Arkady doubted that, from the shawl tied tight around her head to her boots hanging clear of the ground, she was over a meter and a half tall. Her eyes were bright and dazzling, a true Ukrainian blue.

"Maria Fedorovna, you have the blood pressure and heart rate of a woman twenty years younger. However, I am concerned about the polyp in your throat. I would like to take it out."

"I will discuss it with Roman."

"Yes, where is Roman Romanovich? I expected to see your husband, too."

Maria lifted her eyes to the top of the lane, where a gate swung open for a bent man in a cap and sweater, leading a black-and-white cow by a rope. Arkady didn't know which looked more exhausted.

"He's airing the cow," Maria said.

The cow trudged dutifully behind. A milk cow was an asset precious enough to be displayed for visitors, Arkady thought. All attention was fixed on the animal's plodding circuit up and down the street. Its hooves made a sucking sound in the wet earth.

Eva's fingers played with a scarf tucked into the collar of her lab coat. She wasn't pretty in an orthodox way; the contrast of such white skin and black hair was too exotic and her eyes had, at least for Arkady, an unforgiving gaze.

"There's no house here you could use for more privacy?" Arkady asked.

"Privacy? This is their entertainment, their television, and this way they can all discuss their medical problems like experts. These people are in their seventies and eighties. I'm not going to operate on them except for something like a broken leg. The state doesn't have the money, instruments or clean blood to waste on people their age. I'm not even supposed to be making calls, and Maria would never go to a city, for fear they wouldn't let her return here."

Arkady said, "She's not supposed to be here anyway. This is the Zone."

Eva turned toward the ladies on the bench. "Only someone from Moscow could say something as stupid as that." To judge by their expressions, they seemed to agree. "The state turns a blind eye to the return of old people. It has given up trying to stop them," Eva informed Arkady. "It has also stopped sending doctors to see them. It demands they go to a clinic."

Maria said, "At our age, you go into the hospital, you don't come out."

Eva asked Arkady, "You've seen those television shows with the bathing beauties dropped off on a tropical island to see if they can survive?" She nodded to Maria and to her friends on the bench. "These are the real survivors."

The doctor introduced them: Olga had a corrugated face and filmy glasses; Nina leaned on a crutch; Klara had the angular features of a Viking, braids and all. Their leader was Maria.

"An investigator of what?" Maria asked.

Arkady said, "A body of a man was found at the entrance of your village cemetery in the middle of May. I was hoping that one of you might have seen or heard someone, or noticed something odd or maybe a car."

"May was rainy," Maria said.

"Was it at night?" Olga asked. "If it was at night and it was raining, who would even go outside?"

"Do any of you have dogs?"

"No dogs," Klara said.

"Wolves eat dogs," said Nina.

"So I hear. Do you know a family called Katamay? The son was in the militia here."

The women shook their heads.

"Is the name Timofeyev familiar to you?" Arkady asked.

"I don't believe you," Eva said. "You act like a real detective, like you're in Moscow. This is a black village, and the people here are ghosts. Someone from Moscow died here? Good riddance. We owe Moscow nothing, they've done nothing for us."

"Is the name Pasha Ivanov familiar to you?" Arkady asked the women.

Eva said, "You're worse than Alex. He values animals above people, but you're worse. You're just a bureaucrat with a list of questions. These women have had their whole world taken away. Their children and grandchildren are allowed to visit one day a year. The Russians promised money, medicine, doctors. What do we get? Alex Gerasimov and you. At least he's doing research. Why did Moscow send you?"

"To get rid of me."

"I can see why. And what have you found?"

"Not much."

"How can that be? The death rate here is twice normal. How many people died from the accident? Some say eighty, some say eight thousand, some say half a million. Did you know that the cancer rate around Chornobyl is sixty-five times normal? Oh, you don't want to hear this. This is so tedious and depressing."

Was he in a staring contest with her? This had to be like a falconer's dilemma, holding a not completely trained bird of prey on the wrist.

"I did want to ask you a few questions, maybe someplace else."

"No, Maria and the other women can use a little amusement. We will all concentrate on one Russian stiff." Eva opened a pack of cigarettes and shared them with her patients. "Go on."

"You do have drugs?" Arkady asked.

"Yes, we do have some medicine, not much, but some."

"Some has to be refrigerated?"

"Yes."

"And some frozen?"

"One or two."

"Where?"

Eva Kazka took a deep draw on her cigarette. "In a freezer, obviously."

"Do you have one, or do you use the freezer at the cafeteria?"

"I have to admit, you have a single-mindedness that must be very useful in your profession."

"Do you store medicine in the cafeteria freezer?"

"Yes."

"You saw the body in the freezer?"

"I see a lot of bodies. We have more deaths than live births. Why not ask about that?"

"You saw the body of Lev Timofeyev."

"What if I did? I certainly didn't know who he was."

"And you left a note that he hadn't died of a heart attack."

Maria and the women on the bench looked to Eva, Arkady and back as if a tennis match had come to the village. Olga removed her glasses and wiped them. "Details."

Eva said, "There was a body dressed in a suit and wrapped in plastic. I'd never seen him before. That's all."

"People told you that he had had a heart attack?"

"I don't remember."

Arkady said nothing. Sometimes it was better to wait, especially with such an eager audience as Maria and her friends.

"I suppose the kitchen staff said he had a heart attack," Eva said.

"Who signed the death certificate?"

"Nobody. No one knew who he was or how he died or how long he had been dead."

"But you're fairly expert in that. I hear you spent time in Chechnya. That's unusual for a Ukrainian doctor, to serve with the Russian army on the battlefront."

Eva's eyes lit. "You have it backward. I was with a group of doctors documenting Russian atrocities against the Chechen population."

"Like slit throats?"

"Exactly. The body in the freezer had its throat cut with one stroke of a long sharp knife from behind. From the angle of the cut, his head was pulled back, and he was kneeling or seated, or the killer was at least two meters tall. Since his windpipe was cut, he couldn't have uttered a sound before dying, and if he was killed at the cemetery here, no one would have heard a thing."

"The description said he had been 'disturbed by wolves.' Meaning his face?"

"It happens. It's the Zone. Anyway, I do not want to be involved in your investigation."

"So he was lying on his back?"

"I don't know."

"Wouldn't someone whose throat was cut from behind be more likely to fall forward?"

"I suppose so. All I saw was the body in the freezer. This is like talking to a monomaniac. All you can focus on in this enormous tragedy, where hundreds of thousands died and continue to suffer, is one dead Russian."

The old man turned the cow in the direction of the card table. Despite the heat, Roman Romanovich was buttoned into not one but two sweaters. His pink, well-fed face and white bristles and the anxious smile he cast at Maria as he approached suggested a man who had long ago learned that a good wife was worth obeying.

Eva asked Arkady, "Do you know how Russia resolved the crisis of radioactive milk after the accident? They mixed radioactive milk with clean milk. Then they raised the permissible level of radioactivity in milk to the norm of nuclear waste and in this way saved the state nearly two billion rubles. Wasn't that clever?"

Roman tugged on Arkady's sleeve. "Milk?"

"He wants to know if you would like to buy some milk," Eva said. She twisted her scarf with her fingers. "Would you like some milk from Roman's cow?"

"This cow?"

"Yes. Absolutely fresh."

"After you."

Eva smiled. To Roman she said, "Investigator Renko thanks you but must decline. He's allergic to milk."

"Thank you," Arkady said.

"Think nothing of it," said Eva.

"He must come to dinner," Maria said. "We'll give him decent food, not like they serve at the cafeteria. He seems a nice man."

"No, I'm afraid the investigator is going back to Moscow soon. Maybe they'll send medicine or money in his place, something useful. Maybe they'll surprise us."

8

Each commuter on the six p.m. train from the Chernobyl Nuclear Power Station began his trip by standing in the booth of a radiation detector and placing his feet and hands on metal plates until a green light signaled that he could continue to the platform. The train itself was an express that passed through Byelorussian territory without stopping, bypassing border checks. It was a cozy ride through pine forests on a summer evening.

Men rode at one end, women at the other. Men played cards, drank tea from thermoses or napped in rumpled clothes, whereas the women held conversations or knit sweaters and were painstakingly well dressed, with not a gray hair among them, not while henna grew on earth.

Halfway, the car became more subdued. Halfway, eyes wandered to the window, more and more a mirror. Halfway, thoughts turned to home, to coping with dinner, children, private lives.

Arkady, too, nodded from the rhythm of the train. One thought dissolved into another.

He gave Eva Kazka credit for bringing medical service, however minimal, to people in villages no one else dared visit. But she had played him like a thief before a jury in front of the old women. Eva had that knack of making a person draw too little air or speak too loud. In front of such an individual, a man could become so aware his weight was on his left foot that he might fall over on his right, and the village women had practically cackled while watching the show. She had called them survivors. What kind of appearance did he present, an intrepid investigator following clues to the end of the earth, or a man lost by the wayside? At a dead end, at least. A signal flashed by the window, and Arkady thought of Pasha Ivanov flying through the air. Arkady didn't approve or disapprove. The problem was that once people landed, other people had to clean up the mess.

And what had he learned on his excursion with Alex? Not much. On the other hand, he'd seen at least three wolves behind the white trunks of the birches, eyes shining like pans of gold, weighing the deer, he and Alex and the deer much the same. He remembered how the hairs had stiffened down the back of his neck. The word "predator" meant more when you were potential prey. He laughed at himself, imagining that he was on his motorcycle being chased by wolves.

Slavutych had been built for people evacuated from Pripyat. It was a successor city, with spacious squares and white municipal buildings that looked like a child's building blocks — arches, cubes, columns — on a giant scale. It was a city with modern amenities. A sunken football field was serviced by espresso bars. The Palace of Culture offered feng shui and origami. Even better, the apartment blocks themselves were designed with architectural themes like fanciful Lithuanian trim or the grace notes of Uzbeki brickwork.

Oleksander Katamay lived on the fifth floor of an "Uzbeki" building. A young woman in a jogging suit and top-heavy blond hair let Arkady in and immediately left him in a living room arranged around a taxidermy worktable with lamps and a stand-up magnifying glass aimed at a badger skin rolled up with the head inside. Another badger, farther along, bathed in a bucket of degreaser. Shelves held plastic sacks of clay and papier-mâché and a menagerie of stuffed and mounted animals: a lynx with bared fangs, an owl looking over its shoulder, a slinking fox. A pair of hunting rifles resided in a glass cabinet with a Soviet flag: small-bore, single-shot, bolt-action rifles polished as lovingly as a brace of violins. Hung on the walls had to be twenty framed photos of men in hard hats studying plans, setting pilings or working the levers of a crane, and in the middle or taking the lead in each was the same tall vigorous figure of Oleksander Katamay. Arkady was studying a photograph of workers in front of a power plant and realized that it was the first photo he had seen of the intact Chernobyl Reactor Four, a massive white wall next to its twin, Reactor Three. The men in the picture were as relaxed and confident as if they stood on the prow of a mighty ship.

A deep voice called, "Is that the investigator? I'm coming."

While Arkady waited, he noticed a framed plaque that displayed civilian medals, including Veteran of Labor, Winner of Socialist Competition and Honored Builder of the U.S.S.R., plus rows of military ribbons. Arkady was standing by them when Oleksander Katamay rolled into the room in a wheelchair. Though a pensioner in his late seventies, he still had a laborer's chest and shoulders, with a broad, pushed-in face and a mane of white hair. He gripped Arkady's hand firmly enough to squeeze the blood out.

"From Moscow?"

"That's right."

"But Renko is a good Ukrainian name." Katamay leaned close, as if to peer into Arkady's soul, then abruptly spun and shouted, "Oksana!" He brought his gaze back to Arkady and the taxidermy in progress. "You were admiring my hobby? Did you see the ribbons?" Katamay rolled to the plaque of medals and pointed out one with writing in Arabic. " 'Friendship of the Afghan People.' The friendship of niggers, I guess that's worth my son's life. Oksana!"

The woman who had let Arkady into the apartment brought a tray of vodka and pickles, which she set on a coffee table. Although there was something negligent about her, her hair was a golden beehive. She sat on the floor by Katamay's wheelchair while he drew close a stand-up ashtray on the other side. Arkady settled on an ottoman and had the sense of being in a scene both posed and askew. It was the table with the two badgers, one in the stew, one out. It was Oksana. Her stiff hair was a wig. But it was more than that.

Katamay pointed to the stuffed animals

and asked Arkady, "Which do you like most?"

"Oh. They're all lifelike." Which was the best Arkady could come up with, considering his first instinct had been to say, There's a dead cat on your shelf.

"The trick is suppleness."

"Suppleness?"

"Getting off all the flesh and then shaving the inside of the skin until it's blue. Timing, temperature, the right glue are all important, too."

"I wanted to ask about your grandson, Karel."

"Karel is a good boy. Oksana, am I right?"

Oksana said nothing.

Katamay half-filled the glasses with vodka and passed one to Arkady.

"To Karel," Katamay said. "Wherever he is." The old man put his head back, took the vodka in one continuous swallow and watched out of the corner of his eye to make sure Arkady and Oksana did the same. Maybe he was in a wheelchair, but he was still the man in charge. Arkady wondered what it was like to have been chief of construction of such a huge enterprise and now to be restricted to such a small arena. Katamay refilled the glasses. "Renko, you came to the right part of the Ukraine. People of the western Ukraine say the hell with Russia. They pretend they can't speak Russian. They think they're Poles. People in the eastern Ukraine, we remember." Katamay raised his glass. "To —"

Arkady said, "I'd like to ask some questions first."

"To fucking Russians," Katamay said and downed his glass.

Arkady opened the file he carried and passed around a photograph of a young man with half-finished, impatient features: a pinched nose, a thin mouth, a gaze that challenged the camera.

Oksana said, "That's my brother."

"Karel Oleksandrovich Katamay, twenty-six, born Pripyat, Ukrainian Republic." Arkady skipped to the salient points. "Two years' service in the army, trained as a sniper. He's a marksman?"

"He can shoot and leave something worth stuffing, if that's a marksman," Katamay said.

"Twice demoted for physical abuse of newer recruits."

"That's hazing. It's a tradition in the army."

True enough, Arkady thought. Some kids were hazed enough that they hanged themselves. Karel must have stood out among the tormentors.

"Disciplinary action once for theft."

"Suspicion of theft. If they had been able to prove anything, they would have put him in the brig. He has a wild side, but he's a good boy. He couldn't have joined the militia here without a clean record."

"In the militia, Karel was frequently late or absent from his post."

"Sometimes he was hunting for me. We always got things straightened out with his chief."

"That would be Captain Marchenko?"

"Yes."

"Hunting for what? Another fox or lynx? A wolf?"

"A wolf would be the best." Katamay rubbed his hands at the thought. "Do you know how much money a properly mounted wolf would bring?"

"Karel's father died in Afghanistan. Who taught Karel how to hunt?"

"I did. That was when I still had functioning legs."

"Karel's mother?"

"Who knows? She believed all that propaganda about the accident. I've talked to the top scientists. The problem at Chornobyl isn't radiation, it's fear of radiation. There's a word for it: radiophobia. Karel's mother was radiophobic. So she left. The fact of the matter is, these people are lucky. The state built them Pripyat and then Slavutych, gave them the best salary, the best living conditions, schools and medicine, but the Ukrainian people are all radiophobic. Anyway, Karel's mother disappeared years ago. I raised him."

"Dressed him, fed him, sent him to school?"

"School was a waste of time. He was meant to be a hunter; he was wasted indoors."

"When did you lose the use of your legs?"

"Two years ago, but it was a result of the explosion. I was operating a crane for the firemen when a piece of the roof came down. It came down like a meteor and crushed my back. The vertebra finally gave in. There's a citation on the wall; you can read all about it."

"Had Karel ever been to Moscow?"

"He'd been to Kiev. That's enough."

"You haven't seen him since he found that body in the Zone?"

"No."

"Heard from him?"

Arkady noticed Oksana's glance at yet

another hide lolling in a bucket of degreaser in a corner. For a man who hadn't seen or spoken to his marksman grandson in months, Katamay seemed to have no lack of fresh material for his craft.

Katamay said, "Nothing, not a word."

"You don't seem worried."

"It's not like he did anything wrong. He resigned from the militia — so what? Karel's a big boy. He can take care of himself."

"Did you ever hear of two physicists named Pasha Ivanov or Lev Timofeyev?"

"No."

"They never visited Chernobyl?"

"How would I know?"

Arkady asked for the names of family or friends whom Karel might have visited or contacted, and Katamay dispatched Oksana to make up a list. While they waited, Katamay's gaze drifted back to the photographs on the wall. One had probably been taken on International Women's Day, because a younger version of Katamay was surrounded by women in hard hats. In another photograph he strode ahead of technicians in lab coats, who struggled to keep up.

"That must have been a great responsibility, being head of construction," Arkady said.

Katamay said nothing while Oksana rustled through papers in the other room. Then he refilled his glass. "It's all political, you know, shutting down the other reactors. Totally unnecessary. The other three could have run for another twenty years, and we could have built Five and Six, Seven and Eight. Chornobyl was and is the best power-plant site anywhere. The charities got in and blew up statistics. What's easier, to milk foreign aid or run a power plant? So we went from a world power to a third-class nation. Do you know how many died because of Chornobyl, the real figures? Forty-one. Not millions, not hundreds of thousands. Forty-one. The wonderful thing we have discovered is that the human organism can live with much higher levels of radiation than we once thought. But radiophobia has taken over. Forty-one. You have that many dying of lung cancer in the hospitals of Kiev every day of the week, but people don't abandon Kiev." The mention of lung cancer prompted Katamay to find a cigarette. "There are always those who fan hysteria and undermine efforts at normalization, the same elements who always profit from chaos. Except we used to be able to control them. This time they overthrew the entire Soviet Union. Together we were a respected power, now we're a pack of beggars. Can I show you something? Come with me."

Katamay energetically swung his chair around and propelled himself into the next room, a study where his granddaughter had been gathering names and phone numbers at a desk. The desk and all the furniture had been pushed against the wall to make space for a draftsman's table holding an architectural model of the Chernobyl power plant, with stylized green trees and a broad blue Pripyat River cut from blue plastic. All six reactors were there, suggesting a moment in time — past, present or future — that never existed. The panorama was complete with cardboard cooling towers, turbine halls, fuel storage, the domes of water tanks and a parade of transmission towers. On the access roads were miniature trucks and human figures for scale. Here the accident had never happened. Here the Soviet Union was intact.

Arkady was aware of being followed by Oksana from the apartment. She was in her jogging suit but had replaced her wig with a knit cap and darted like a mouse from doorway to doorway. Arkady had an hour until the next train. He stopped at a café called Colombino and took two coffees to an outside table where he had a view of the shallow pools of light cast by the plaza lamps. The structures of civilization — city hall, football stadium, cinema, supermarket — were apparent, just not the activity. He watched Oksana buy an apple from a farmer outside the supermarket, then start to eat the apple as she crossed the plaza and act surprised to find him.

"You were expecting someone?" She looked at the second cup.

"As a matter of fact, you."

She looked cautiously around. Her cheeks were flushed. Now that she was close, it was obvious that under her cap, Oksana's head was shaved. She tucked in her ears. "I must seem pretty ridiculous to you."

"Not a bit. I was hoping you would join me."

She inched into the chair without taking her eyes off Arkady. He waited until she was settled before pushing the second cup in her direction. They sat for a minute quietly. Shoppers weighted with bags came out of the supermarket and lurched from side to side under archways decorated with symbols of a peaceful atom.

Oksana sipped her coffee. "It's cold."

"I'm sorry."

"No, I like coffee cold. I usually have it cold after serving my grandfather."

"He is a strong personality."

"He's the boss."

"He's close to Karel?"

"Yes."

"Are you?"

"Karel is my little brother."

"Have you seen him or talked to him?"

Oksana turned a wide smile toward Arkady. "Did you really like my grandfather's stuffed animals?"

"I'm not a great fan of taxidermy." Perhaps because of my line of work, he thought.

"I could tell. 'Lifelike.' Like us at Slavutych."

"Do you work at the station?"

"Yes."

"Why is that amusing?"

"The pay was good, a fifty percent bonus to live here and work at Chornobyl. We called it coffin money. My grandfather gets an added pension for his disability. But there's a catch."

"Because you're just cleaning up Chernobyl and you'll have to find a new job in a few years?"

"At the rate we're going? It will take a hundred. That's not the catch."

"What is the catch?"

"They cut our pay seventy-five percent. After rent and utilities and school, we end up paying to work at Chornobyl. But it's a job, and that's saying something in the Ukraine. Anyway, that's still not the catch."

"What is the catch?"

Oksana adjusted her cap so her ears showed. "Quiet, isn't it?"

"Yes." Arkady saw a customer leaving the illumination of the market, a couple of schoolgirls with backpacks, a man with a cigarette stuck in a weathered face, no more than ten people, in all, along the square and its promenades.

"Everyone is leaving. They built the town for fifty thousand people, and there are fewer than twenty thousand now. Over half the town is empty. The catch is, they built on contaminated land. Cesium from Chornobyl was waiting for us here. Pripyat to Slavutych, we didn't escape at all." Oksana smiled, as at a joke that never grew stale, and she rolled her cap down. "I wear the wig because it makes women here unhappy to see me shaved. I feel a little like a stuffed animal with it on, though. What do you think?"

"The shaved look is very popular."

"Want to see?" She pulled off the cap, revealing an almost perfectly round skull with blue tones. The nakedness made her eyes seem large and luminous. "You can feel." She took his hand and moved it around her head, which felt almost polished. "Now what do you think?"

"Smooth."

"Yes." As she pulled the cap back on, she wore the smile of someone who had divulged a secret.

"You miss Pripyat."

"Yes." She recited her old address there: street, block and flat. "We had the best view, right on the water. In the fall we would watch the ducks follow the river south, and in the spring follow the river north."

"Oksana, have you seen your brother?"

"Who?"

"Have you seen Karel?"

Arkady's mobile phone rang. He tried to ignore it, but Oksana seized the interruption to bolt down the rest of her coffee and get up from her chair. "I have to go. I have to cook for my grandfather."

"Please. This will just take a second." A local number on the caller ID. Arkady answered, "Hello."

A man said, "This is your friend from the Pripyat Hotel."

The scavenger with the plumber's tools and bedspring grill whom Arkady had chased through the school. A Ukrainian speaking Russian, so he knew who Arkady was. A penetrating voice husky from years of smoking. No identifiable background noise. A landline, no breaking up. Arkady looked at Oksana, who was disengaging step by step.

"Yes," Arkady said into the phone.

"You wanted to talk, and you're willing to pay money?"

"That's right."

As Oksana slipped away onto the plaza, she whispered, "You're very nice, very nice. Just . . . don't stay too long."

"What about?"

"The body of a Moscow businessman was found in a village near Chernobyl two months ago. I'm looking into it."

"Can you pay in American dollars?"

"Yes."

"Then you're a lucky man, because I can help you."

"What do you know?"

"More than you do, I bet, because you've been here a month, and you don't know anything."

The longer they spoke, the more Arkady heard a sibilant S and the scratchiness of an unshaved chin. Arkady gave him a name: the Plumber.

"Like what?"

"Like your businessman was really rich, so there's a lot of money involved."

"Maybe. What do you know?"

Arkady saw Oksana run past the supermarket and vanish around a corner.

"Oh no, not over the phone," the Plumber said.

"We should meet," Arkady said. "But you have to give me some idea of what you know so that I'll know how much money to bring."

"Everything."

"That sounds like nothing." And that was Arkady's impression of the Plumber. A blowhard.

"A hundred dollars."

"For what?"

The Plumber hurried. "I'll call you in the morning and tell you how we'll meet."

"Do that," Arkady said, although the Plumber had already hung up.

On the ride back, the train carried the smaller crew of the night shift, all men and most napping, chins on their chests. What was there to see? The moon was obscured by clouds, and the coach moved in a black terrain of evacuated farms and villages, only a rattling of the rails to indicate forward motion. Then a signal light would plunge by like a face at the window, and Arkady would be thoroughly awake.

Pasha's death was complicated because he had been dying already. He had a dosimeter. He knew that he was dying and what he was dying from. That was part of the ordeal. Arkady tried to imagine the first time Pasha became aware of what was happening. He had been a social animal, the sort who took off his jacket and rolled up his sleeves, as Rina put it, to have a good time. How did it start? In the blurred confusion of a party, had someone slipped a saltshaker and a dosimeter into his jacket pocket? The meter's sound would have been turned off. Arkady pictured Pasha's face when he read the meter, and the fast, tactful exit away from everyone else. The dose wouldn't have been too high, more like the first probe of artillery. "We flushed the radioactive water right into the Moscow River," Timofeyev had said, so there was a precedent for tossing the shaker overboard. But from then on, Ivanov was vulnerable. There was no way to tell cesium chloride from salt without a meter, and salt came in his food or sprinkled on top, sat in a plastic shaker in the lowest dive or in crystal in the most elegant restaurant. How did he dare eat? Or have any contact with the outside world, when a barely visible grain could arrive in a letter or be transferred onto clothing as someone brushed by in the street? Finally, what to do when he found a gleaming mound of salt in his closet? How to find one grain of poison among a million pure?

And it would go on. Timofeyev was also under attack. So, by sheer proximity, was Rina. Ivanov and Timofeyev had both had cesium pallor. Their bloody noses were signs of platelet failure. They couldn't eat or drink. Each day they were weaker and more isolated. And in the sanctuary of Ivanov's apartment, in the closet of his bedroom was this shining floor of salt. With a saltshaker. It hadn't matched any pepper shaker in the apartment, and Arkady guessed that it had sat on top of the pile like a tiny lighthouse, pulsating gamma rays. Suicides had a pattern, first fatigue and then a manic energy. Here's the chair, where's the rope? Here's the razor, where's the bath? How to dispose of radioactive salt? Eat it. Eat it with wads of bread. Choke it down with sparkling water. The dosimeter screams? Turn it off. The nosebleeds? Wipe it off, wrap the handkerchief around the meter and place them in the shirt drawer. Neatness counts, but hurry. Momentum is important. The stomach wants to throw back what you've fed it. Open the window. Now grasp the saltshaker, climb high above the world, curtains flapping, and fix your eye on the bright horizon. It's easier to die if you're already dead.

9

Morning rain fell on the Chernobyl Yacht Club, a gap-toothed dock on the Pripyat River. Planks had dropped through, leaving a slippery checkerboard for Arkady and Vanko to cross with the aluminum rowboat that Arkady was renting for the day from Vanko. Vanko had offered for an extra bottle of vodka to come along and point out this place or that to fish, but Arkady had no intention of fishing. He had borrowed a rod and reel for form's sake only.

Vanko said, "That's all you've got? No bait?"

"No bait."

"A light rain like this can be good fishing."

Arkady changed the subject. "There really used to be a yacht club here?"

"Sailboats. They sailed away after the accident. Now they're all sold to rich people on the Black Sea." The idea seemed to delight Vanko.

Vapors drifted around a fleet of commercial and excursion boats scuttled or run aground, rusting from white to red. An explosion seemed to have lifted ferries, dredgers and scows, coal barges and river freighters out of the water and set them haphazardly along the river's edge. The dock's end was guarded by a padlocked gate and signs that read HIGH RADIATION! and NO SWIMMING and NO DIVING. Taken together, the signs were, it seemed to Arkady, redundant.

"Eva lives up there in a cabin." Vanko pointed across the bridge toward a brick apartment block. "Way back. You'd never find it."

"I'll take your word for it."

Vanko had a key for the boat's padlock and helped Arkady portage the boat over a floodgate and bridge to the north arm of the river. Arkady had noticed before that Vanko, with his stolid manner and calflike fringe of hair, seemed to have keys to everything, as if he were the town custodian. "Chornobyl was a busy port once. A lot of business went up and down the river when we had Jews."

Arkady thought that conversations with Vanko sometimes skipped a groove. "So you haven't had Jews here since the war? Since the Germans?"

They scrambled down to the water.

Vanko slid the rowboat in and gripped it by the stern. "Something like that."

As Arkady got in with the oars, he gave a last glance at the posted warnings. "How radioactive is the river?"

Vanko shrugged. "Water accumulates radiation a thousand times more than soil."

"Oh."

"But it settles to the bottom."

"Ah."

"So avoid the shellfish." Vanko still held the boat. "That reminds me. You're invited to the old folks' tonight for dinner. Remember Roman and Maria from the village?"

"Yes." The old woman with the bright blue eyes and the old man with the cow.

"Can you come?"

"Of course." Dinner in a black village. Who could pass that up?

Vanko was pleased. He gave a push. Arkady slipped the oars into the oarlocks and pulled a first long stroke, then another, and the boat eased into the sluggish current of the Pripyat.

He was here because the Plumber had kept his promise and called in the morning with instructions: Arkady was to come alone in a rowboat to the middle of the cooling pond behind the Chernobyl power plant and bring the money.

Arkady's camos and cap were reasonably water-resistant, and as he settled into even strokes, he soon had the rowboat clear of shipwrecks and decaying piers. He dipped his hand in. The water was glassy, brown from peat bogs far upstream and dimpled with light rain. The land ahead was low-lying, riddled by the myriad channels of an ancient river and softened by pines and willows. It was four kilometers against the current from the yacht-club dock to even reach the cooling pond. Arkady checked his watch. He had two hours to cover the full distance, and if he was a little late, he figured the Plumber would probably wait for a hundred dollars.

Arkady didn't have the money, but he couldn't miss the chance to make contact. In fact, he thought his lack of money might be his safe passage out if the Plumber's only interest was robbery.

Mist steamed from the riverbanks, snagged on birches, drifted free. Frogs plopped for cover. Arkady found that the discipline of rowing led to a trancelike state that left whirlpools of oar strokes behind. A swan cruised by, a white apparition that deigned to turn its head in Arkady's direction. There were, as Vanko might have said, worse ways to spend a day.

Sometimes the river silted and broadened, sometimes narrowed to a tunnel of trees, and much of the time Arkady wondered what he was doing. He wasn't in Moscow, he wasn't even in Russia. He was in a land where Russians were not missed. Where a dead Russian was kept for weeks on ice. Where a black village was a perfect place for dinner.

An hour later, Arkady had fallen into such a rhythm that it took him a moment to react to a crowd of radiation signs on a sandy beach. His target. He gathered speed, drove the boat onto the beach and jumped out, dragging the boat over the sand and up to the crown of a causeway that separated the river from the man-made reservoir of the cooling pond. The pond was twelve kilometers long and three wide; it took a lot of water to cool four nuclear reactors. When the plant had been active — when Chernobyl had four reactors online and two more under construction — water had constantly circulated from the pond, around the power plants in a grid of channels and out a discharge main back to the pond. Now it was a block of granite-black water wreathed in fog.

A causeway road was blocked by a

chain-link fence, bent on one side as if to say, "Come this way." Saplings had uprooted the cement slabs that were the walls of the pond; at one point a red shirt tied to a tree marked where slabs had shifted and, in their disrepair, become stairs down to the water. Arkady checked his meter, which ticked with increasing interest; then he lowered the rowboat onto the surface and pushed off as he stepped in.

In fair weather, the cooling pond might have been a clever rendezvous. With binoculars, the Plumber could have made sure Arkady was alone, in a rowboat and far from help. No doubt the Plumber would have the advantage of an outboard engine. Whatever the plan, Arkady didn't like approaching with his back turned, bent over oars. And it was raining harder; visibility was down to a hundred meters and closing in. People made mistakes when they couldn't see clearly. They misconstrued what they did see, or saw what wasn't there. What did he know about the Plumber? The brief phone conversation suggested that he was hardly an experienced professional, more a slovenly middle-aged Ukrainian male with bad dental work. He had probably lived in Pripyat and, to judge from his choice of rendezvous, had probably worked at the power plant. A scavenger rather than a poacher, a man likely to carry a hammer rather than a gun, if that was a comfort.

Arkady stayed in sight of the causeway to keep his bearings and checked his watch to determine how far he had come. For a moment he thought he'd caught the throb of an outboard engine ahead in the rain, but he couldn't honestly say which way it came from, or whether he'd really heard it. All he heard for certain was his own oars ladling water.

He had rowed for half an hour along the causeway when he glimpsed, over his shoulder, two red-and-white chimneys hanging in the fog. Mist closed in, but not before he had a new bearing, directly toward the reactor stacks. He rowed and coasted until he got a new sighting, rowed and coasted again. Perhaps it was going to work out after all. The Plumber would putt-putt into view, and they would talk.

Arkady rowed to what he guessed was halfway across the pond and waited, turning the boat every minute or two for a different view. He was aware of boats far off on the periphery, but not a single one approached. Ten minutes passed. Twenty. Thirty. By then he wished he had a cigarette, damp or otherwise.

He was about to quit when he heard a metallic rattle and an empty boat drifted sideways out of the rain. It was an aluminum tub like his, with a small outboard engine clamped to the stern and a chain swinging at the bow. The engine was off. An empty vodka bottle rolled forward as Arkady stopped the boat. Nothing else was in it, not a cigarette butt, not a fishing rod, not a paddle.

Arkady tied the empty boat to the back of his and started rowing to another boat he saw on the reactor side of the pond. He couldn't imagine why anyone besides the Plumber or Vanko would be out in such weather, but maybe the other boat's occupant had seen someone or knew whose boat this was. Towing the boat was awkward; with every pull, it snapped against Arkady's boat and produced the sound of a bass drum lightly kicked, the perfect acclaim for a day wasted.

There were two men in the boat, fifty meters off, and every ten meters the rain got worse, veiling the boat even as Arkady approached. The Woropays. Dymtrus stood and Taras sat, all their attention on the water directly by their boat until Dymtrus knelt and hauled a body out of the water. It was a woman with long black hair. Her gray skin suggested a long immersion, but she was slim and sleek, her face secretively turned away, a dress adhering to her arms and the smoothness of her back. She was still one moment, and the next she thrashed and nearly capsized the boat.

Taras leaned on a gunwale to keep the boat steady. He noticed Arkady through the rain and shouted, "She likes to fight."

Arkady had stopped rowing. The woman was gone, replaced by a catfish weighing at least sixty kilos, a slippery, scaleless monster that thrashed this way and that and turned its blunt face and jelly eyes to Arkady. Oriental whiskers spread from its lips, and what looked like sopping embroidery fell into the water.

"You netted it?" Arkady asked.

"They're too heavy to pull up otherwise," said Dymtrus.

"Chornobyl giants," said Taras. "Mutants. Glow in the dark."

"Then don't catch them." Arkady noticed that the Woropays had sidearms. He supposed he was lucky they weren't fishing with grenades. "Let it go."

Dymtrus opened his arms. The fish dropped with a great splash into the water, swirled to the surface and then sank ponderously out of sight. "Relax, it's just for fun. There are bigger fish down there."

Taras said, "Twice as big."

The brothers wore slack, calculating smiles.

"We wouldn't eat one," Dymtrus said. "They're loaded with all sorts of radioactive shit."

"We're not crazy."

Arkady felt his heart rate start to slow. He pointed to the empty boat. "I'm looking for the man who came in that."

The Woropays shrugged and asked how Arkady knew there had been someone in it. People hid boats around the cooling pond. The wind could have blown the boat in. And since when did they take orders from fucking Russians? And maybe they could use a fucking outboard engine of their own. They made the last comment too late, after Arkady had switched boats and retied the lines and was towing Vanko's boat away, under power, into the face of a squall that drenched any idea of pursuit.

Arkady switched boats again at the causeway to take Vanko's back downstream. At least this time he would have the current working with him. A stork with a red beak as sharp as a bayonet and white wings trimmed in black sailed by and passed over another stork that waded in slow motion along the edge of the river, painstakingly stalking a victim. The streets of Chernobyl were empty, but the river was full of life. Or murder, which was sometimes the same thing.

As he began to row, however, the mist cleared enough for the apartment blocks of Pripyat to loom like giant headstones. Hadn't Oksana Katamay described her block in Pripyat as overlooking the river? He swung the boat around.

The Katamay apartment wasn't difficult to find. Oksana had given him the address, and although the flat was on the eighth floor, the stairs were clear of the usual debris. The door was open and the view from the living room took in the power station, the river, the dark wormholes of former river tracks and banks of steamy mist. Arkady could imagine Oleksander Katamay, Chief of Construction, standing like a colossus before such a panorama.

The family must have returned on the sly to remove items they hadn't been able to carry with them at the evacuation. This bare wall had been covered by a tapestry.

Those empty shelves had held books or a stuffed menagerie. Overall, however, the family had been selective and Arkady had the impression that squatters and scavengers knew to give the Katamay flat a pass. Sofa and chairs still sat in the parlor; wiring and plumbing still seemed intact. Someone had cleaned out the refrigerator, taped a broken window, made the beds, scrubbed the tub. The place was practically in move-in condition, disregarding radiation.

One bedroom was, Arkady guessed, the grandfather's; it was stripped clean but for a few pails of taxidermy degreaser and crusted glue. A second bedroom was decorated with Happy Faces, pictures of pop stars and posters of girl gymnasts tumbling with manic energy on a mat. Names swam back from the past: Abba, Korbut, Comaneci. Stuffed toys sat on the bed. Arkady ran a dosimeter over a lion and produced a little roar.

Karel's room was at the end of the hall. He must have been about eight at the time of the accident, but he was already a marksman. Paper targets punched in the middle were taped to the wall, along with a boy's selection of posters of heavy metal musicians with painted faces. The shelves were lined with Red Army tanks, fighter planes, shark's teeth and dinosaurs. A broken ski leaned in a corner. A bedpost was hung with ribbons and medals for a variety of sports: hockey, soccer, swimming. Taped over the bed was a photograph of Karel at a fun fair with his big sister Oksana; she was no more than thirteen, with straight dark hair that hung to her waist. Also pictures of Karel fishing with his grandfather and posing with a soccer ball and two surly teammates, the proto-Woropays. Squares of peeled paint were left where tape had peeled off. Under the bed Arkady found pictures that had fallen: a team picture of the Kiev Dynamo soccer team, the ice hockey great Fetisov, Muhammad Ali and, finally, a snapshot of Karel posed with his fists up with a boxer. Karel was in trunks just like a real fighter. The boxer wore trunks and gloves. He was maybe eighteen, a skinny, slope-shouldered boy as white as soap, and his autograph was scrawled across the photograph: "To My Good Friend Karel. May we always be pals. Anton Obodovsky."

Roman introduced Arkady to a pig that rubbed with exquisite pleasure against the slats of its sty as Roman poured in slops.

"Oink, oink," said Roman, "oink, oink," his cheeks apple red from the rays of the setting sun and pride of ownership. It was possible that Roman had had a nip before Arkady arrived. Alex and Vanko followed in Arkady's footsteps; the rain had stopped but left the farmyard ankle-deep in mud. The scene reminded Arkady of the official inspections that had once been Soviet fare: "Party Secretary Visits Collective Farm and Vows More Fertilizer." "Oink, oink," said Roman, the soul of wit. He seemed delighted to be leading the tour without his wife's assistance. "Russians raise pigs for meat, we raise pigs for fat. But we're saving Sumo. Aren't we, Sumo?"

"For what?" asked Arkady.

Roman placed a finger to his lips and winked. A secret. Which struck Arkady as appropriate for an illegal resident of the Zone. Roman led the way to a chicken coop. In the cool after the rain, Arkady felt the heat of the sitting hens. The old man showed Arkady how he tied the bar of the door shut with a twist of wire. "Foxes are very clever."

"Perhaps you should have a dog," Arkady suggested.

"Wolves eat dogs." That did seem to be the consensus of the village, Arkady thought. Roman shook his head as if he'd given the matter a lot of consideration. "Wolves hate dogs. Wolves hunt down dogs because they regard them as traitors. If you think about it, dogs are dogs only because of humans; otherwise they'd all be wolves, right? And where will we be when all the dogs are gone? It will be the end of civilization." He opened a barn with an array of shovels and hoes, rakes and scythes, a grindstone, a pulley hanging from a crossbeam and bins of potatoes and beets. "Did you meet Lydia?"

"The cow? Yes, thank you."

A pair of huge eyes in the depths of a stall beseeched the tour to leave her alone to masticate her hay. Which reminded Arkady of Captain Marchenko when Arkady alerted him to the possibility of a body floating in the cooling pond. The captain had suggested that a loose boat was not sufficient reason to leave a dry office, and the pond was a large body of water to go pounding around in the rain or the dark. The empty vodka bottle aside, had there been blood in the boat? Signs of struggle? Professional to professional, didn't this sound like a wild goose chase?

Roman led his guests out by a half-shed packed so tight with firewood that not another piece could have been inserted. Arkady suspected that when Roman was too drunk to stand, he could still stack wood with lapidary care. Roman waved to an orchard and identified cherries, pears, plums and apples.

Arkady asked Alex, "Have you gone around the yard with a dosimeter?"

"What's the use? This is a couple in their eighties, and their own food tastes better to them than starving in the city. This is heaven."

Maybe, Arkady thought. Roman and Maria's house was a weathered blue, windows trimmed with carving, one corner resting country-style on a tree stump. It shone amid abandoned houses that were as black as if they'd been burned, with tumbledown barns and fruit trees wrapped in brambles. One dirt path led from the house to the village center; another climbed toward the wrought-iron fence and crosses of the cemetery, within a few steps a compass of peasant life and death.

The interior was a single room: a combination kitchen, bedroom and parlor centered around a whitewashed brick stove that heated the house, cooked the food, baked the bread and — peasant genius! — on especially cold nights provided a second sleeping bench directly over the oven. Lamps and candles lit walls covered with embroidered cloths, tapestries with forest scenes, family photos and picture calendars collected from various years. Photos framed a younger Roman and Maria, he in a rubber apron, she holding an enormous braid of garlic, together with an urbanized group that must have been their son and his family, a timorous wife and a skinny girl about four years of age. A separate picture of the girl showed her maybe a year older, in a sun hat by a rust-pocked sign that said HAVANA CLUB.

Maria glowed so, she could have been polished for the occasion. She wore an embroidered shirt and apron, a tasseled shawl and, of course, her brilliant blue eyes and steel smile. Despite the crowded quarters, she was everywhere at once, setting out bowls of cucumbers, pickled mushrooms, pickles in honey, thin and fat sausages, apple salad, cabbage in sour cream, dark bread and home-churned butter and a center plate of salted fat with an alabaster glow.

"Don't even think about your dosimeter," Alex whispered to Arkady.

"How often do you eat here?"

"When I feel lucky."

The rattle of a car muffler drew up outside, and a moment later, Eva Kazka appeared with flowers. She also wore a scarf. It seemed to be her style.

"Renko, I didn't know you were going to be here," Eva said. "Is this part of your investigation?"

"No. Purely social."

"Social is as social does." Roman arranged a row of small glasses around a bottle of vodka. The party had gone a long time without vodka, Arkady thought; Vanko looked as if he had crawled on his knees to a water hole. The host poured every glass to the trembling brim, and Maria watched proudly as he distributed each without the loss of a drop. "Wait!" Roman magisterially struck a match and lit his glassful like a candle, a yellow flame dancing on the surface of the liquid. "Good. It's ready." He blew out the flame and raised his glass. "To Russia and Ukraine. May we lie in the same ditch."

Arkady took a swallow and gasped, "Not vodka."

"Samogon." Alex wiped his eyes. "Moonshine from fermented sugar, yeast and maybe a potato. It doesn't get much purer than that."

"How pure?"

"Maybe eighty percent."

The samogon had its effect: Eva looked more dangerous, Vanko more dignified, Roman's ears went red and Maria glistened. There was a solemn dipping into the food while Roman poured another round. Arkady found the pickles crisp and sour, with perhaps a hint of strontium. Roman asked him, "You went fishing in Vanko's boat? Did you catch anything?"

"No, although I did see a very large fish. A Chernobyl Giant, people said." He noticed Vanko smirking at Alex. "You know about this fish?"

Eva said, "The catfish? It's Alex's joke."

"A catfish is a catfish," Vanko said.

"Not quite," said Alex. "People here are accustomed to channel catfish that grow to a paltry meter or two. Someone — I couldn't say who — seems to have imported Danube catfish, which grow to the size of a truck. That's a respectable fish."

"It's a sick joke," Eva said. "Alex would like a plague to sweep across Europe and kill all the people to make room for his stupid animals."

"Present company excluded, of course," Alex said. Maria smiled. The party seemed to be off to a nice start.

"What shall we drink to?" Roman asked.

"Oblivion," Alex suggested.

Arkady was better prepared for his second samogon, but he still had to step back from the impact. Eva declared herself warm. She loosened her scarf but didn't remove it.

Maria advised Arkady to eat a slice of fat. "It will grease the stomach."

"Actually, I'm feeling fairly well greased. This picture of the girl by the Havana Club sign was taken in Cuba?"

"Their granddaughter," Vanko said.

"Maria, after me," Maria said.

Alex said, "Every year Cuba takes Chernobyl kids for therapy. It's very nice, all palm trees and beaches, except the last thing those kids need is solar radiation."

Arkady was aware of having introduced an element of unease. Roman cleared his throat and said, "We're not sitting. This is irregular. We should be sitting."

In such a small cabin, there were only two chairs and room for only two on the bench. Alex pulled Eva down on his lap, and Arkady stood.

"Truly, how is the investigation going?" Alex asked.

Arkady said, "It's not going anywhere. I've never made less progress."

"You told me that you weren't a good

investigator," Eva said.

"So when I tell you that I've never made less progress, that's saying something."

"And we hope you never make any progress," said Alex. "That way you can stay with us forever."

"I'll drink to that," Vanko said hopefully.

Eva said, "None of us makes progress, that's the nature of this place. I will never cure people who live in radioactive houses. I will never cure children whose tumors appear ten years after exposure. This is not a medical program, this is an experiment."

"Well, that's a downer," Alex said. "Let's go back to the dead Russian."

"Of course," said Eva, and she filled her own glass.

Alex said, "I can understand why a Russian business tycoon would have his throat slit. I just don't understand why he would come all the way to this little village to have it done."

"I've wondered the same thing," Arkady said.

"There must have been plenty of people in Moscow willing to accommodate him," Alex said.

"I'm sure there were."

"He was protected by bodyguards, which means he had to escape his own security to be killed. He must have been coming here for protection. From whom? But death was inevitable. It was like an appointment in Samarra. Wherever he went, death was waiting."

"Alex, you should be an actor," Vanko said.

Eva said, "He *is* an actor."

"You were a physicist before you became an ecologist," Arkady said to Alex. "Why did you change?"

"What a dull question. Vanko is a singer." Alex poured for everyone. "This is the entertainment section of the evening. We are on a night train, samogon is our fuel and Vanko is our engineer. Vanko, the floor is yours."

Vanko sang a long song about a Cossack off to the wars, his chaste wife and the hawk that carried their letters back and forth until it was shot down by an envious nobleman. When Vanko was done, everyone applauded so hard they sweated.

"I found the story absolutely believable," Alex said. "Especially the part about how love can turn to suspicion, suspicion to jealousy and jealousy to hate."

"Sometimes love can go right to hate," said Eva. "Investigator Renko, are you married?"

"No."

"Been married?"

"Yes."

"But no more. We often hear how difficult it is for investigators and militia detectives to maintain a successful marriage. The men supposedly become emotionally cold and silent. Was that your problem, that you were cold and silent?"

"No, my wife was allergic to penicillin. A nurse gave her the wrong injection, and she died of anaphylactic shock."

"Eva," Alex whispered. "Eva, that was a bad mistake."

"I'm sorry," she told Arkady.

"So am I," said Arkady.

He left the party for a while. Physically he was present and smiled at the appropriate times, but his mind was elsewhere. The first time he'd met Irina was at the Mosfilm studio, during an outdoor shoot. She was a wardrobe mistress, not an actress, and yet once the sun lit her huge deep-set eyes, everyone else seemed made of cardboard. It was not a placid relationship, but it was not cold. He could not be cold around Irina; that was like trying to be cold beside a bonfire. When he saw her on the gurney, dead, her eyes so blank, he thought his life had ended, too, yet here he was years later, in the Zone of Exclusion, lost and stumbling but alive. He looked around the room to clear his head and happened to light on the icons high in their corner, Christ on the left wall, the Madonna on the right, the two framed by richly embroidered cloths and lit by votive candles on a shelf. The Christ was actually a postcard, but the Mother was the genuine article, a Byzantine painting on wood of the Madonna in an unusual blue cowl with gold stars, her fingertips lightly pressed together in prayer. She looked like the stolen icon he had seen in the motorcycle sidecar. That icon had been taken over the border to Byelorussia. What was it doing here?

Vanko said, "The Jews are here."

"Where?" Arkady asked.

"In Chernobyl. Everywhere, walking up and down the streets."

Alex said, "Thank you, Vanko, we've been warned." He added to Arkady, "Hasidic Jews. There's a famous rabbi buried here. They visit and pray. Maria's turn."

After the formalities of modesty and protest, Maria sat up in her chair, closed her eyes and broke into a song that transformed her from an old woman into a girl looking for her lover at a midnight tryst, and singing in a register so high the windowpanes seemed to vibrate like crystals. When Maria finished, she opened her eyes, spread a smile of steel teeth and swung her feet with pleasure. Roman tried to follow with selections on a violin, but a string broke, and he went hors de combat.

"Arkady?" Alex asked.

"Sorry, I'm low in entertainment skills."

"Then it's your turn," Alex told Eva.

"All right." She ran her hands through her hair as if that combed it, fixed her eyes on Alex and began:

We're all drunkards here and harlots:
How wretched we are together . . .

The poetry was coarse and blunt, Akhmatova's words, familiar to Arkady, familiar to any literate man or woman over the age of thirty, before the new poetry of "Billions Served" and "Snickers for Energy!"

I have put on a narrow skirt
to show my lines are trim.
The windows are tightly sealed,
What brews? Thunder or sleet?
How well I know your look,
Your eyes like a cautious cat.

She swung her own gaze from Alex to Arkady and hesitated so long that Alex took over the last line:

O heavy heart, how long
before the tolling bell?
But that one dancing there,
will surely rot in hell!

Alex pulled Eva's face to his and collected a deep kiss until she pulled away and slapped him hard enough to make even Arkady smart. She stood and plunged out the door. It was like a Russian party, Arkady thought. People got drunk, recklessly confessed their love, spilled their festering dislike, had hysterics, marched out, were dragged back in and revived with brandy. It wasn't a French salon.

Arkady's mobile phone rang. It was Olga Andreevna, from the children's shelter in Moscow.

"Investigator Renko, you have to come back."

"A second, please." Arkady gestured apologies to Maria and went outside. Eva was nowhere in sight, although her car hadn't left.

Olga Andreevna asked, "Investigator, what are you still doing in the Ukraine?

"I am assigned here. I am working on a case."

"You should be here. Zhenya needs you."

"I don't think so. I can't think of anyone he needs less."

"He goes and stands by the street, waiting for you and looking for your car."

"Maybe he's waiting for the bus."

"Last week he was gone for two days. We found him sleeping in the park. Talk to him."

She put Zhenya on the line before Arkady could get off. At least he assumed Zhenya was on; all Arkady heard at his end was silence.

"Hello, Zhenya. How are you doing? I hear you've been causing people at the shelter some anxiety. Please don't do that." Arkady paused in case Zhenya wanted to offer any response. "So I suppose that's all, Zhenya."

He was in no mood and no condition to have another one-sided conversation with the garden gnome. He leaned back to take a breath of cool air and watched clouds cover the moon, slipping the house in and out of shadow. He heard the cow shuffle in her stall and a twig snap and wondered whether it was a night for wolves to be abroad.

"Still there?" Arkady asked. There was no answer; there never was an answer. "I met Baba Yaga. In fact, I'm outside her house right now. I can't say whether her fence is made of bones, but she definitely has steel teeth." Arkady heard, or thought he heard, a focusing of attention at the other end. "I haven't seen her dog or cat yet, but she does have an invisible cow, who has to be invisible because of the wolves. Maybe the wolves wandered in from a different story, but they're here. And a sea serpent. In her pond she has a sea serpent as big as a whale, with long whiskers. I saw the sea serpent swallow a man whole." There was unmistakable rustling on the other end now. Arkady tried to remember other details of the fairy tale. "The house is very strange. It is absolutely on chicken legs. Right now the house is slowly turning. I'll lower my voice in case it hears me. I didn't see her magic comb, the one that can turn into a forest, but I did see an orchard of poisonous fruit. All the houses around are burned and full of ghosts. I will call in two more days. In the meantime, it's important that you stay at the shelter and study and maybe make a friend in case we need help. I have to go now, before they see that I'm missing. Let me say a word to the director."

There was a passing of the phone, and

Olga Andreevna came back on. "What did you tell him? He seems much better."

"I told him that he is a citizen of a proud new Russia and should behave like one."

"I'm sure. Well, whatever you said, it worked. Are you coming to Moscow now? Your work there surely must be done."

"Not quite yet. I'll call in two days."

"The Ukraine is sucking us dry."

"Good night, Olga Andreevna."

As Arkady put the mobile phone away, Eva stepped out of the orchard, silently applauding. "Your son?" she asked.

"No."

"A nephew?"

"No, just a boy."

She shifted like a cat getting comfortable. "Baba Yaga! Quite a story. You are an entertainer after all."

"I thought you were going."

"Not quite yet. So you're not with anybody now? A woman?"

"No. And you, are you and Alex married, separated or divorced?"

"Divorced. It's that obvious?"

"I thought I detected something."

"The residue of an ancient disaster, the crater of a bomb, is what you detect." The window light on her was watery, the stamp of linen making her eyes darker. "I still love him. Not the way you loved your wife. I can tell you had one of those great faithful romances. We didn't. We were more . . . melodramatic, let's say. Neither of us was undamaged goods. You can't be in the Zone without a little damage. How much longer do you plan to stay?"

"I have no idea. I think the prosecutor would like to leave me here forever."

"Until you're damaged?"

"At least."

What was disturbing about Eva Kazka was her combination of ferocity and, as she said, damage. She had been to Chernobyl *and* Chechnya? Maybe disaster was her milieu. Her smile suggested that she was giving him a second chance to say something interesting or profound, but Arkady thought of nothing. He had spent his imagination on Baba Yaga.

The door opened. Alex leaned out to say, "My turn."

"Our new friend Arkady may not know all the facts. Facts are important. Facts should not be swept aside."

"You're drunk," Eva said.

"It goes without saying. Arkady, do you enjoy comedy?"

"If it's funny."

"Guaranteed. This is Russian stand-up comedy," Alex said. "Comedy with samogon."

Maria opened a new bottle, releasing the sickeningly sweet smell of fermented sugar, and toddled from guest to guest refilling glasses.

"April twenty-sixth, 1986. The setting: the control room of Reactor Four. The actors: a night shift of fifteen technicians and engineers conducting an experiment — to see whether the reactor can restart itself if all external power for the machinery is cut off. The experiment has been performed before with safety systems on. This time they want to be more realistic. To defeat the safety system of a nuclear reactor, however, is no simple matter. It involves application. You have to disconnect the emergency core cooling system and close and lock the gate valves." Alex walked rapidly back and forth, attending to imaginary switches. "Turn off the automatic control, block the steam control, disable the pre-sets, switch off design protection and neutralize the emergency generators. Then start pulling graphite rods from the core by remote control. This is like riding a tiger, this is fun. There are a hundred and twenty rods in all, a minimum of thirty to be inserted at all times, because this was a Soviet reactor, a military model that was a little unstable at low efficiency, a fact that was, unfortunately, a state secret. Alas, the power plunged."

"When does this start to become funny?" Eva asked.

"It's already funny. It just gets funnier. Imagine the confusion of the technicians. The reactor efficiency is dropping through the floor, and the core is flooding with radioactive xenon and iodine and combustible hydrogen. And somehow they have lost count — they have lost count! — and pulled all but eighteen control rods from the core, twelve below the limit. All the same, there is one last disastrous step to take. They can replace the rods, turn on the safety systems and shut down the reactor. They have not yet turned off the turbine valves and started the actual experiment. They have not pushed the final button."

Alex mimicked hesitation.

"Let's pause and consider what is at stake. There is a monthly bonus. There is a May Day bonus. If they run the test successfully they will likely win promotions and awards. On the other hand, if they shut down the reactor, there would certainly be embarrassing questions asked and consequences felt. There it is, bonuses versus disaster. So, like good Soviets, they marched forward, hands over their balls."

Alex pushed the button.

"In a second the reactor coolant began to boil. The reactor hall started to pound. An engineer hit the panic switch for the control rods, but the rod channels in the reactor melted, the rods jammed, and superheated hydrogen blew off the roof, carrying reactor core, graphite and burning tar into the sky. A black fireball stood over the building, and a blue beam of ionized light shot from the open core. Fifty tons of radioactive fuel flew up, equal to fifty Hiroshima bombs. But the farce continued. Cool heads in the control room refused to believe that they had done anything wrong. They sent a man down to check the core. He returned, his skin black from radiation, like a man who had seen the sun, to report that there was no core. Since this was not an acceptable report, they sacrificed a second man, who returned in the same fatal condition. Now, of course, the men in the control room faced their greatest test of all: the call to Moscow."

Alex picked up his glass of samogon.

"And what did our heroes say when

Moscow asked, 'How is the reactor core?' They answered, 'The core is fine, not to worry, the core is completely intact.' Moscow is relieved. That's the punch line. 'Don't worry.' And here is my toast: 'To the Zone! Sooner or later, it will be everywhere!' Nobody's drinking?"

Roman and Maria sat numb and deflated, feet hanging free of the floor. Vanko looked away. Eva pressed her fist to her mouth, then stood and applied the fist to Alex, not slapping him as she had before but hitting him solidly in the chest until Arkady pulled her away. For a moment no one moved, like marionettes gone limp, until Eva bolted again for the door. This time Arkady heard her car start.

Alex's glass spilled. He refilled and raised it a second time. "Well, it seemed hilarious to me."

10

As a rule, fresh bodies hang facedown underwater, with their arms and legs dangling in a shallow dive. This one was suspended against the bars of the inlet that fed water from the cooling pond to the smaller holding ponds of the station. Emergency water was still needed; the reactors were full of fuel, and in some ways they weren't so much dead as in hibernation.

Two men with gaffs were trying to pull the body closer without falling in themselves. Captain Marchenko watched from the wall of the pond with a group of useless but curious militia officers, the Woropay brothers in front. Eva Kazka stood by her car, as far from the proceedings as possible. Arkady noticed that she looked, if possible, wilder and more unkempt than usual. Probably she had just gone home and dropped, in a samogon stupor. She seemed to be drawing the same conclusion about him.

As Marchenko joined Arkady, a shadow broke the surface of the water to display a slick gray head with rubbery lips, then slid back toward the bottom to stir with even larger catfish in the murk.

The captain said, "Taking into account the bad weather yesterday and the dimensions of the cooling pond, I think you'll agree that it was wise to wait before looking for a body. The way the ponds circulate, everything ends up here at the inlet. Now it's right in our hands."

"And now it's ten in the morning a day later."

"A fisherman falls off his boat and drowns, it really doesn't matter whether you find him one day or the next."

"Like the tree that falls in the forest, does it make a noise?"

"Lots of trees fall in the forest. They're called accidental deaths."

Arkady asked, "Is Dr. Kazka the only doctor available?"

"We can't pull the station doctors. All Dr. Kazka has to do is sign a death certificate."

"You couldn't call for a pathologist?"

"They say Kazka was in Chechnya. If that's the case, she's seen plenty of dead bodies."

Eva Kazka tapped out a cigarette. Arkady had never seen such a nervous individual.

"By the way, I meant to ask you, Captain, did you ever find out whose icon we saw stolen the other day?"

"Yes. It belonged to an old couple named Panasenko. Returnees. The militia keeps a record. I understand it was a beautiful icon."

"Yes."

So a thief on a motorcycle had stolen the icon of Roman and Maria Panasenko's, a crime officially recorded, and yet the icon had returned to its corner perch in the Panasenko cabin. Which was, to Arkady, the opposite of a tree falling without a sound.

From the inlet Arkady had a view of half-completed cooling towers that resembled, with the brush that flourished under and around them, temples half-built. The towers had been meant for the planned Reactors Five and Six. Now power went the other direction, at a trickle, to keep lightbulbs and gauges alive.

An ironic cheer went up when the body was finally grappled. As it was lifted, water drained from its pants and sleeves.

"Don't you have a tarp or plastic to lay the body on?" Arkady asked Marchenko.

"This is not a murder investigation in Moscow. This is a dead drunk in Chornobyl. There's a difference." Marchenko cocked his head. "Don't be shy, take a look."

The captain's men moved truculently

out of Arkady's way; the Woropays snickered at the recorder in Arkady's hand.

"Speak up," Marchenko said. "We can all learn."

"Pulled from the water at the inlet of Chernobyl Nuclear Power Plant at 1015 hours on July 15, a male apparently in his sixties, two meters tall, dressed in a leather jacket, blue work pants and construction boots." An ugly man, in fact, his thick features bleached by immersion, brown teeth badly sorted, clothes sodden as a wet sheet. "Extremities are rigid, exhibiting rigor mortis. No wedding ring." Arms and legs yearned for the sky, fingers open. "Hair brown." Arkady peeled an eyelid back. "Eyes brown. Left eye dilated. Fully clothed, the body presents no tattoos, moles or other identifying marks. No immediately evident abrasions or contusions. We'll continue at the autopsy."

"No autopsy," Marchenko said.

"We know him," Dymtrus Woropay said.

Taras said, "He's Boris Hulak. He scavenges and fishes. He squats in apartments in Pripyat, always moving around."

"Do you have latex gloves?" Arkady asked.

Marchenko said, "Afraid of getting your hands wet?"

At a nod from the captain, the Woropays

unzipped the dead man's jacket and dug out his booklet of identification papers.

Marchenko read them: "Boris Petrovich Hulak, born 1949, residence Kiev, occupation machinist. With his picture." The same ugly face with a living glower. This was the Plumber, Arkady was sure of it. Marchenko threw the ID at Arkady. "That's all you need to know. A social parasite fell off his boat and drowned."

"We'll check his lungs for water," Arkady said.

"He was fishing."

"Where's the rod?"

"He caught a catfish. He had consumed an entire bottle of vodka, he was standing in his boat, a catfish bigger than him pulled the rod out of his hands, and he lost his balance and fell in. No autopsy."

"Maybe the bottle was empty to begin with. We can't assume he was drunk."

"Yes, we can. He was a well-known drunk, he was alone, he fished, he fell in." From his tunic Marchenko pulled the hunting knife he had shown Arkady before, the boar knife. "You want an autopsy? Here's your autopsy." He drove the knife into Boris Hulak's stomach, spewing the sweet gas of digested alcohol. The samogon in Arkady's own stomach rose to his throat. "That's drunk."

Even the Woropays took a step back from the hanging mist. Marchenko wiped his blade on the dead man's jacket.

Arkady said between shallow breaths, "There's still the eye."

"What eye?" the captain asked, his satisfaction interrupted.

"The right eye is normal, but the left eye is fully dilated, which indicates a blow to the head."

"He's decomposing. The muscles relax. His eyes could go different directions. Hulak hit his head on the boat as he went over, what does it matter?"

"He's not a pig. We have to see."

"The investigator is right," Eva Kazka said. She had wandered over from her car. "If you want me to sign a death certificate, there should be a cause of death."

"You need an autopsy for that?"

"Before you stick the body again, I think so," Eva said.

She wasn't talkative. Boris Hulak was laid out naked on a steel table with his head propped against a wooden block, and he said about as much as Eva did while she opened his body, first with an incision from his collar to his groin and then in handfuls, moving organs into separate bedpans, all with the brisk dispatch of someone washing dishes. The room was meanly furnished, with little more than the essentials of scales and pails, and she had already spent an hour washing the body and examining it for bruises, tattoos and needle tracks. Arkady had checked Hulak's clothes at a sink, finding nothing more remarkable in the dead man's pockets than a purse of loose change and a door key, and nothing in his billfold except a damp twenty-hryvnia note, a photo-booth picture of a boy about six years old and an expired video-club card. Arkady had cut off Hulak's boots and found hidden under the sole almost two hundred American dollars — not bad for a scavenger of radioactive electrical wiring. While Eva Kazka worked on one side of the table, Arkady worked on the other, drying out fingers wrinkled by immersion and then plumping them with injections of saline to lift the ridges and produce usable prints to compare with those he had lifted from the bottle found in the boat.

Fluorescent lights turned cadavers green, and Boris Hulak was greener than most, a fleshy body wrapped in fat through the middle, hard through the legs and shoulders, exuding a bouquet of ethanol. Eva wore her lab coat, cap and professional demeanor, and she and Arkady smoked as they worked to mask the smell. There were few enough benefits to smoking; this was one.

"Ever wish you hadn't asked for something?" Eva said. She saw through him, which didn't make him feel any better. She consulted her autopsy chart. "All I can tell you so far is that between cirrhosis of the liver and necrosis of the kidney, Boris had perhaps two more years to live. Otherwise, he was a hardy specimen. And no, there was virtually no water in the lungs."

"I think I chased Hulak through Pripyat a few nights ago."

"Did you catch him?"

"No."

"And you never would have. Scavengers know the Zone like a magician knows his trapdoors and top hats and radioactive bunnies." She tapped the scalpel on the table. "Captain Marchenko doesn't like you. I thought you were great friends."

"No. I've ruined his perfect record. A militia station commander wants no problems, no homicides and, most of all, no unsolved homicides. He certainly doesn't want two of them."

"The captain is a bitter man. The story

is that he got in trouble in Kiev by turning down a bribe, which embarrassed his superiors, who had taken their share of the money in good faith. He's been stationed here to give him a glimpse of hell in case he ever thinks of making that mistake again. Then you arrive from Moscow, and he feels more trapped than ever. You were comparing Hulak's fingerprints to some on a card."

"From the vodka bottle I found in the boat."

"And?"

"They're all Hulak's."

"Wouldn't you say that was fairly strong evidence Hulak was alone? Have you ever known a Russian or a Ukrainian to not share a bottle? He didn't drown, but I have to tell you that apart from being posthumously stabbed by the captain, I see no signs of recent violence. Maybe he did hook a big fish and hit his head on the boat as he went over. Either way, you made the wrong enemy in Captain Marchenko. It might make him happy if we stopped right here."

Arkady leaned over the body. Boris Hulak had a pugnacious head with heavy brows, a broad nose mapped in erupted veins, brown hair thick as otter fur and cheeks covered in stubble, no bruising or swelling, no ligature marks around the neck, no defensive wounds on the hands, not a scratch in the scalp. However, there was that dilated iris of the left eye, as open as the stuck shutter of a camera. Also, Arkady had worked his way out of his samogon stupor.

Arkady said, "Then it will make the captain even happier if we prove I'm wrong."

Most doctors never encountered a cadaver after anatomy class, and forgot the reeking totality of death. But Eva coolly repositioned the block farther down under Hulak's neck.

He said, "You've seen men shot in the head before."

"Shot in the head with a pistol and shot in the back with a rifle, supposedly in the middle of combat. Either way, there's usually an entry wound, which your man appears to lack. Last chance to stop."

"You're probably right, but let's see."

Eva sliced the back of Hulak's scalp from ear to ear. She folded the flap of skin and hair forward over the eyes to work with a circular saw. A power saw was always heavy and, what with the cloud of white dust it produced, hard to manage in delicate work. She popped the top of his skull with a chisel, reached in with a scalpel to free the brain from the spinal cord and laid the soft pink mass in its glistening sac beside the empty head.

"The captain is not going to like this," Eva said.

A red line ran across the top, the trail of a bullet that had traversed the brain and then, bouncing off angles, scoured the cranium. Hulak must have gone down instantly.

"Small-caliber?" Eva asked.

"I think so."

She turned the brain in every direction before choosing one pomegranate-red clot to attack. She cut the sac, sliced into gray matter and squeezed out a bullet like a pip. It pinged as it dropped onto the table. She wasn't done. She shone a penlight around the inside of the skull until a beam came out the left ear.

"Who is this good a shot?" she asked.

"A sniper, a sable hunter, a taxidermist. I would guess the bullet is five-point-six-millimeter, which is what marksmen use in competitive shooting."

"From a boat?"

"The water was still."

"And the sound?"

"A silencer, maybe. A small-caliber doesn't make that much noise to begin with."

"So, now, two murders. Congratulations, Chornobyl has killed a million people, and you have added two more. I would say that at death, you're very good."

While she was impressed Arkady asked, "What about the first body, the one from the cemetery? Besides the nature of the wound on the throat, was there anything else you could have added to your note?"

"I didn't examine him. I simply saw the wound and wrote something. Wolves tear and yank, they don't slice."

"How bloody was his shirt?"

"From what I saw, very little."

"Hair?"

"Clean. His nose was bloody."

"He suffered from nosebleeds," Arkady said.

"This would have been quite a nosebleed. It was packed."

"How do you explain that?"

"I don't. You're the magician — only you pull up the dead instead of rabbits."

Arkady was wondering how to respond when there was a knock at the door and Vanko stuck in his head.

"The Jews are here!"

"What Jews?" Arkady asked. "Where?"

"In the middle of town, and they're asking for you!"

* * *

The afternoon sun detailed Chernobyl's drab center: café, cafeteria, statue of Lenin amid candy wrappers. A pair of militia stepped out of the cafeteria to look up the road; they stared so hard, they leaned. Vanko ran off, to what purpose Arkady didn't know. All he saw was a man walking with familiar flat-footed arrogance ahead of a car. He was dressed in a Hasidic Jew's black suit, white shirt and fedora, although in place of a full beard was red stubble.

"Bobby Hoffman."

Hoffman looked over his shoulder. "I knew I'd find you if I just kept walking. This is the second day I've been marching up and down."

"You should have asked people where I was."

"Jews do not ask Ukrainian cannibals. I asked one, and he disappeared."

"He said the Jews were coming. It's just you?"

"Just me. Did I scare them? I wish I could fry the whole fucking lot of them. Let's keep walking. My advice to Jews in the Ukraine is, always present a moving target."

"You've been here before."

"Last year. Pasha wanted me to look into

the spent-fuel situation."

"There's a profit in spent radioactive fuel?"

"It's the coming thing."

The car was a mud-spattered Nissan, a comedown from the Mercedes Arkady had last seen Hoffman in. Hoffman's clothes, too, were a change.

"Is this a new you?"

"The Hasidic gear? Hasidim are the only Jews they see around here. The idea is, this way I draw less attention." Hoffman looked at Arkady's camos. "Join the army?"

"Standard wear for a citizen of the Zone. Does Colonel Ozhogin know you're here?"

"Not yet. You remember that disk the colonel was so proud of finding? It was more than just a list of foreign accounts. It was an order to reroute them to a little bank of my own. I could have stayed in Moscow, but when Pasha died and Ozhogin locked me out of NoviRus, out of my own office, I said, 'Fuck them! Them or me!' But I had to get the asshole to want the disk and feed it into the system. Remember how the colonel pinched my nose until he got blood? Well, I'm doing the pinching now, buddy, and it's not by the nose."

"So you should be on the run. Why are you here?"

"You need help. Renko, you've been here

over a month. I talked to your detective Victor."

"You talked to Victor?"

"Victor does e-mail."

"He hasn't communicated with me. I call and he's out of the office, I call his mobile phone and there's no answer at all."

"Caller ID. You're not paying him, and I am. And Victor says you didn't send any reports to Moscow worth shit. Have you made any progress?"

"No."

"No progress at all?"

"Nothing."

"You're drowning here. You're on dream time."

They had walked past the café to a neighborhood of acacias and two-story wooden houses where once lived Chernobyl's socialist gentry: mayor and militia commander, local Party secretary and assistants, prosecutor and judge, port and factory managers. Some walls rotted and dragged down the roof; some roofs collapsed and buckled the walls. Trees groped into one window and pushed open the shutters of the next. A doll with a bleached-out face stood in the yard.

"How are you going to help?" Arkady asked.

"We'll help each other."

Hoffman motioned for the car to draw forward and pushed Arkady inside. The driver offered a glance of indifference. He had sunken eyes and a skullcap pinned to a wisp of hair. He rested busted knuckles on the steering wheel.

Hoffman said, "Don't worry about Yakov. I selected him because he's the oldest Jew in the Ukraine, and he doesn't speak a word of English." The space in back was tight and became more cramped when Hoffman opened a laptop computer. "I'm going to give you a chance to shine, Renko. I'm not saying you're a complete incompetent."

"Thanks."

"I'm just saying you need a little assistance. For example, you had an idea about collecting surveillance videotapes not only from Pasha's apartment building but also from the buildings on either side. In fact, Victor did what you told him. The problem was that you caved. You called Pasha's death a suicide."

"It was a suicide."

"Driven to killing himself is not what I call suicide. Don't get me started. Okay, Pasha was called a suicide, and no more investigation, and Victor had read somewhere about vodka protecting against radiation. He got real protected. By the time he got sober, he had forgotten all about the tapes. Then Timofeyev got his throat cut, and Prosecutor Zurin sent you here." Bobby looked out the car window at the houses. "Eskimos are kinder: they just set you on a fucking ice floe."

"The tapes?"

"I reached Victor. Know what his e-mail address is? You can buy it on the Internet; it's illegal, but you can do it. Apparently, like all Russians, he once had a dog named Laika. So I reached 'Laika 1223' and offered Victor a reward for any notes or evidence left over. I caught him at a sober moment, because he even transferred the tapes to a disk for me."

"You and Victor, what a pair."

"Hey, I feel bad about the way I left you in Moscow, I do. Maybe this will make up for it." Hoffman's fingers played the laptop keyboard, and on the screen appeared a daytime view of a driveway and Dumpsters. A clock in the corner of the tape read 1042:25. "Do you recognize this?"

"The service alley behind Pasha Ivanov's apartment house. But this is taken from the apartment house on the right."

"You saw the tape from Pasha's building?"

"It was taped over; it was on a short loop. We saw Pasha arrive and fall, and we saw about two hours before that, but nothing from before."

"Watch," Hoffman said.

The camera froze images with a five-second lag to stretch tape time. Also, it was on a motorized pivot that swung 180 degrees. The result was a curious collage: a cat was caught in the act of entering from the street; seen next balanced on the rim of a Dumpster; and then, in a sideways view, approaching the Dumpster next door, at Ivanov's building.

Hoffman said, "According to Victor, you thought there was a security breach about now."

"We know that the staff went up and down the building knocking on doors. There was some sort of event."

At 1045:15 the cat was caught in acrobatic midleap from the Dumpster as a white van entered the left side of the alley.

"When you're right, you're right," Hoffman said.

At 1045:30 the van had stopped beside Ivanov's Dumpster. At fifteen-second gaps, the camera returned to the Dumpster, and the screen showed what were essentially poor-quality black-and-white photographs of:

The van with the driver's door open and a dark figure at the wheel.

The van with the door shut and the driver's seat empty.

The same scene for one minute.

A bulky man in coveralls, gas mask and cowl that completely covered his head, shouldering a tank and hose and rolling a suitcase on casters from the van to Ivanov's building.

The van in the driveway.

The same scene for five minutes.

An encore by the cat.

The van.

For one more minute, the van.

The same man with the same gear returning to the rear of the van.

The van.

A figure in coveralls and mask climbing into the driver's seat.

The van moving away as the driver removed the mask, his face a blur.

The empty alley.

The cat.

The building's doorman, fists on his hips.

The empty alley.

The cat.

Time 1056:30. Time elapsed, eleven minutes. Seven minutes of risk for the driver.

"When you interrogated the staff, they never mentioned an exterminator, did they?" Hoffman said. "A fumigator? Bugs?"

"No. Can you enlarge the image of the man moving from the van to the building?"

Hoffman did. How he fit such fat fingers onto the keyboard, Arkady didn't know, but Bobby was quick.

"The head?" Arkady asked.

Hoffman circled the head and magnified a gas mask with goggles and two shiny filters.

"Can you enlarge it more?"

"I can enlarge it all you want, but it's a grainy picture. All you'll get is bigger grains. A fucking exterminator."

"That's not an exterminator's mask. That's radiation gear. Can you enlarge the tank?"

The tank bore what appeared to be fumigation warnings.

"The suitcase?"

The suitcase was covered with cartoon decals of dead rats and roaches. On the way in the suitcase was rolled. Arkady remembered that on the way out it had been carried.

"It's a delivery. The suitcase arrived heavy, it left light."

"How heavy?"

"I would guess — fifty or sixty kilos of salt, a grain of cesium and lead-lined suitcase — maybe seventy-five kilos in all. Quite a load."

"See, this is fun. Working together. This is a breakthrough, right?"

"Can you bring out the license plate?"

It was a Moscow plate. Hoffman said, "Victor checked it out. This van is from the motor pool of Dynamo Electronics. They install cable TV. Dynamo Electronics is owned by Dynamo Avionics, which is owned by Leonid Maximov. They reported it missing."

"Victor is on your payroll now?"

"Hey, I'm doing your work for you *and* paying for it. I'm giving you Maximov on a platter. While you've been stumbling around here, there's been a war in Moscow between Maximov and Nikolai Kuzmitch over NoviRus."

"I have been out of touch," Arkady granted.

"They both always wanted NoviRus."

Arkady remembered them at the roulette table. Kuzmitch was a risk taker who stacked chips on a number; Maximov, a mathematician, was a methodical, cautious player.

"The Ivanov case is closed," Arkady

said. "Ivanov jumped. If Kuzmitch drove him to it, then Kuzmitch succeeded. I'm working on the Timofeyev case. Someone cut his throat. That's murder. And the evidence has not been paid for."

"How much do you want?"

"Much what?"

"Money. How much to drop Timofeyev and concentrate on Pasha? What's your number?"

"I don't have a number."

Hoffman closed the laptop. "Let me put it another way. If you won't help, Yakov will kill you."

Yakov turned and aimed a gun at Arkady. The gun was an American Colt, an antique with a silencer but nicely greased and cared for.

"You'd shoot me here?"

"Nobody would hear a thing. A little messy, that's why the old car. Yakov thinks of everything. Are you in or are you out?"

"I'd have to think about it."

"Fuck thinking. Yes or no?"

But Arkady was distracted by the sight of Vanko's face pressed against Hoffman's window. Hoffman recoiled. Up front, Yakov was swinging the gun toward Vanko when Arkady raised his hands to reassure him and told Hoffman to open his window.

Bobby demanded, "Who is this nut?"

"It's okay," Arkady said.

As the window slid down, Vanko shook a massive ring of keys. "We can start now. I'll let you in."

Hoffman and Arkady followed Vanko on foot back the way they had come as Yakov trailed behind. Away from the car, he was a small man dressed like a librarian, in a mended sweater and jacket, but his crushed brow and flattened nose gave him the look of a man who had been run over by a steamroller and not totally reassembled.

"Yakov's not afraid," Bobby said. "He was a partisan in the Ukraine during the war and in the Stern Gang in Israel. He's been tortured by Germans, British and Arabs."

"A walking history lesson."

"So where is our happy friend with the keys taking us?"

"He seems to think you know," Arkady said.

Vanko veered toward a solid building in municipal yellow that stood alone, and Arkady wondered whether they were headed to some sort of historical archive. Short of the building, Vanko stopped at a windowless bunker that Arkady had passed a hundred times before and always assumed housed an electrical substation or mechanics of some sort. Vanko unlocked a metal door with a flourish and ushered Hoffman and Arkady in.

The bunker sheltered two open cement boxes, each about two meters long and one wide. There was no electricity; the only light came through the open door, and there was barely enough overhead clearance for Bobby's hat. There were no chairs, no icon or pictures, instructions or decoration of any kind, although the rims of the two boxes were lined with votive candles burned down to tin cups, and the inside of each box was stuffed with papers and letters.

"Who is it?" Arkady asked.

Hoffman took so long to answer that Vanko, the tour guide, did. "Rabbi Nahum of Chornobyl and his grandson."

Hoffman looked around. "Cold."

Vanko said, "Holy places are often cold."

"A religious expert here." Hoffman asked Arkady, "What am I supposed to do now?"

"You're the Hasidic Jew. Do what a Hasidic Jew does."

"I'm just dressed like a Hasidic Jew. I don't do this stuff."

Vanko said, "One day a year the Jews all come in a bus. Not alone like this."

"What stuff?" Arkady asked.

Hoffman picked up a couple of papers from a tomb and held them to the light to read them. "In Hebrew. Prayers to the rabbi."

"Oh, yes." Vanko was emphatic.

"Do that many Jews live here?" Arkady asked.

"Just visitors," Vanko said.

"All the way from Israel." Hoffman looked at a third letter. "Crazy Jews. Somebody else wins the Super Bowl, and he says, 'I'm going to Disneyland!' A Jew wins, he says, 'I'm going to Chernobyl!' "

"They're pilgrims," Arkady said.

"I get the idea. Now what?"

"Do something."

Vanko had been following the conversation more with his eyes than his ears. He dug into his pockets and came up with a fresh votive candle.

Hoffman said, "You happen to have a tallith, too? Never mind. Thank you, thanks a ton. What do I owe you?"

"Ten dollars."

"For a candle worth a dime? So the tomb is your concession?" Hoffman found the money. "It's a business?"

"Yes." Vanko was eager for that to be understood. "Do you need paper or a pen to write a prayer?"

"At ten dollars a page? No, thanks."

"I'll be right outside if you need anything. Food or a place to stay?"

"I bet." Hoffman watched Vanko escape. "This is beautiful. Left in a crypt by a Ukrainian Igor."

There were hundreds of prayers in each box. Arkady showed two to Hoffman. "What do these say?"

"The usual: cancer, divorce, suicide bombers. Let's get out of here."

Arkady nodded to the candle. "Do you have a match?"

"I told you, I don't do that stuff."

Arkady lit the candle and set it on the edge of the tomb. A flame hovered on the wick.

Bobby rubbed the back of his head as if it didn't fit right. "For ten dollars, that's not much light."

Arkady found used candles with wax left and relit them until he had a dozen flames that guttered and smoked but together were a floating ring of light that made the papers seem to shift and glow. The light also made Arkady aware of Yakov standing at the open door. He was thin enough for Arkady to think of a stick that had been burned, whittled and burned again.

"Is something wrong?" Vanko asked from outside.

Yakov removed his shoes and stepped inside. He kissed the tomb, prayed in a whisper as he rocked back and forth, kissed the tomb a second time and produced his own piece of paper, which he laid on the others.

Bobby bolted out and waited for Arkady. "The visit to the rabbi is over. Happy?"

"It was interesting."

"Interesting?" Bobby laughed. "Okay, here's the deal. The deaths of Pasha and Timofeyev are related. It doesn't matter that one died in Moscow and one died here, or that one was an apparent suicide and the other was obviously murder."

"Probably." Arkady watched Yakov emerge from the tomb and Vanko lock it up.

Bobby said, "So, maybe you should concentrate on Timofeyev, and I'll concentrate on Pasha. But we'll coordinate and share information."

"Does this mean that Yakov isn't going to shoot me?" Arkady asked.

"Forget about that. That's inoperative."

"Does Yakov know it's inoperative? He might be hard of hearing."

"Don't worry about that," Bobby said.

"The point is, I'm not leaving, so I'll either be in your way, or we'll work together."

"How? You're not a detective or an investigator."

"The tape we just looked at? It's yours."

"I've seen it."

"What are you offering in return? Nothing?"

Vanko had been hanging back out of earshot but reluctant to leave a scene where more dollars might appear. Sensing a gap in the conversation, he sidled up to Arkady and asked, as if helpfully suggesting another local attraction, "Did you tell them about the new body?"

Bobby's head swiveled from Vanko to Arkady. "No, he hasn't. Investigator Renko, tell us about the new body. Share."

Yakov rested his hand in his jacket.

"Trade," Arkady said.

"What?"

"Give me your mobile phone."

Bobby yielded the phone. Arkady turned it on, scrolled through stored numbers to the one he wanted and hit "Dial."

A laconic voice answered, "Victor here."

"Where?"

There was a long pause. Victor would be staring at the caller ID.

"Arkady?"

"Where are you, Victor?"
"In Kiev."
"What are you doing there?"
Another pause.
"Is it really you, Arkady?"
"What are you doing?"
"I'm on sick leave. Private business."
"What are you doing in Kiev?"
A sigh. "Okay, right now I'm sitting in Independence Square eating a Big Mac and watching Anton Obodovsky sip a smoothie only twenty meters away. Our friend is out of prison, and he just spent two hours with a dentist."
"A Moscow dentist wasn't good enough? He had to go all the way to Kiev?"
"If you were here, you'd know why. You've got to see it to believe it."
"Stay with him. I'll call you when I get there."
Arkady turned off the mobile phone and returned it to Bobby, who clutched Arkady's arm and said, "Before you go. A new body? That sounds like progress to me."

11

Kiev was two hours by car from Chernobyl. Arkady made it in ninety minutes on the motorcycle by riding between lanes and, when necessary, swerving onto the shoulder of the road and dodging old women selling buckets of fruit and braids of golden onions. Traffic came to a halt for geese crossing the road, but it plowed over chickens. A horse in a ditch, men throwing sand on a burning car, stork nests on telephone poles, everything passed in a blur.

As soon as Arkady saw the gilded domes of Kiev resting in summer smog, he pulled to the side of the road, called Victor and resumed his ride at a saner pace. Anton Obodovsky was back in the dentist's chair and looked like he would be there for a while. Arkady rolled along the Dnieper and endured the shock of returning to a great city that spilled over both banks of the river. He climbed the arty neighborhood of Podil, rode around the Dumpsters of urban renovation and coasted to a halt at the head of Independence Square, where five streets radiated, fountains played and somehow, more than Moscow, Kiev said Europe.

Victor was at a sidewalk café reading a newspaper. Arkady dropped into the chair beside him and waved for a waiter.

"Oh, no," Victor said. "You can't afford the prices here. Be my guest."

Arkady settled back and took in the square's leafy trees and sidewalk entertainers and children chasing fountain water carried by the breeze. Soviet-classical buildings framed the long sides of the square, but at its head the architecture was white and airy and capped with colorful billboards.

Victor ordered two Turkish coffees and a cigar. Such largesse from him was unknown.

"Look at you," Arkady said. An Italian suit and silk tie softened Victor's scarecrow aspect.

"On an expense account from Bobby. Look at *you*. Military camos. You look like a commando. You look good. Radiation is good for you."

The coffees arrived. Victor took exquisite pleasure in lighting the cigar and releasing its blue smoke and leathery scent. "Havana. The good thing about Bobby is that he expects you to steal. The bad thing about Bobby is Yakov. Yakov is old and he's scary. He's scary because he's so old he's got nothing to lose. I mean, if Bobby thinks we're working together, he'll be pissed on one level but half expect it on another level. If Yakov thinks so, we're dead."

"That is the question, isn't it? Who are you working for?"

"Arkady, you're so black and white. Modern life is more complicated. Prosecutor Zurin told me that I wasn't supposed to communicate with you under any circumstances. That it would insult the Ukrainians. Now the Ukrainians have a president who was caught on tape ordering the murder of a newspaper reporter, but he's still their president, so I don't know how you insult the Ukrainians. Such is modern life."

"You're on sick leave?"

"As long as Bobby is willing to pay. Did I tell you that Lyuba and I got back together?"

"Who is Lyuba?"

"My wife."

Arkady suspected that he had committed a gaffe. The struggle for Victor's soul was like catching a greased pig, and any mistake could be costly. "Did you ever mention her?"

"Maybe I didn't. It was thanks to you. I sort of screwed up with your little friend Zhenya the Silent, and I ran into Lyuba when I was coming out of the drunk tank, and I told her everything. It was wonderful. She saw a tenderness in me that I thought I had lost years ago. We started up again, and I took stock. I could carry on the same old life with the same crowd, mostly people I put in jail, or start fresh with Lyuba, make some real money and have a home."

"That was when Bobby e-mailed you?"

"At that very moment."

"At Laika 1223."

"Laika was a great dog."

"It's a touching story."

"See what I mean? Always black and white."

"And you're dry now, too?"

"Relatively. A brandy now and then."

"And Anton?"

"This is an ethical dilemma."

"Why?"

"Because you haven't paid. I'm not just thinking about me anymore, I have to consider Lyuba. And remember, Zurin said no contact. Not to mention Colonel Ozhogin.

He said absolutely no contact with you. No one wants me to talk to you."

"Did Bobby Hoffman call you while I was coming here? What did he say?"

"To talk to you but keep my mouth shut."

"How are the new shoes?" Arkady caught sight of Victor's footwear.

"Beginning to pinch."

From time to time Arkady saw Victor glance two doors over at a building with an Italian leather-goods shop on the ground floor and professional offices above. Victor had an ice-cream sundae. Arkady picked at a crepe. Somehow, the Zone dampened hunger. Afternoon faded into evening, and the square only became more charming as spotlights turned fountains into spires of light. Victor pointed out a floodlit theater on the hill above the square. "The opera house. For a while the KGB used it, and they say you could hear the screams from here. Ozhogin was stationed here for a while."

"Tell me about Anton."

"He's having dental work done, that's all I can say."

"All day? That's a lot of dental work."

Arkady got up and walked to the Italian leather store, admired the handbags and jackets and read the plaques for the businesses upstairs: two cardiologists, a lawyer, a jeweler. The top floor was shared by a Global Travel agency and a dentist named R. L. Levinson, and Arkady remembered the vacation brochures on Anton's bunk at Butyrka Prison. On the way back to Victor's table, Arkady noticed a girl, about six years old, with dark hair and luminous eyes, dancing to the music of a street fiddler dressed as a Gypsy. The girl wasn't part of the act, just a spontaneous participant making up her own steps and spins.

Arkady sat. "How do you know he's visiting the dentist and not getting tickets to go around the world?"

"When he arrived, all the offices but the dentist were shut for lunch. I'm a detective."

"Are you?"

"Fuck you."

"I've heard that before."

Victor sank into a bitter smile. "Yeah, it's like old times." He loosened his tie and stood to observe himself in the plate glass of the café window. He sat and waved for a waiter. "Two more coffees, with just a touch of vodka."

Anton Obodovsky, as Victor told it, was

a bonus. Victor had been flying to Kiev two days before to meet Hoffman and only happened to see Anton on the same plane. Anton had traveled light, not even a carry-on, and on landing, Victor thought he had lost Anton for good, assuming that he would vanish into the nether regions of Kiev, where he still had a slice of some chop shops and convenience stores. He was like any businessman who maintained domiciles in two different cities, except no one knew where those domiciles were; in Anton's business, a safe night's rest required secrecy. But dentists couldn't pick up their drills and make house calls, and Victor had spied Anton crossing the square on the way to his appointment.

Victor said, "Now that you and Bobby looked at the surveillance tapes, he's convinced Obodovsky was the guy with the suitcase in the exterminator van. Anton was strong enough, he'd threatened Ivanov on the phone and he wasn't put in Butyrka until the afternoon. Motive, means and opportunity. Besides which, he's a killer. There he is."

Anton stepped out of the door and felt his jaw as if to say that all the muscles in the world were no protection from an abscessed tooth. As usual, he was in Armani black and, with his bleached hair, not a difficult man to spot. He was followed by a short, dark woman in her mid-thirties, wearing a trim, sensible jacket.

"The dentist is a woman? She's so good, he comes all the way from Moscow?"

"That's not the whole package. Wait until you see this," Victor said. Last out of the door was a tall woman in her twenties with swirls of honey-colored hair and a brief outfit in denim and silver buttons. She took a firm grip on Anton's arm. "The dental hygienist."

After the dentist had locked the door, she was joined by the dancing girl, who by every feature was her daughter. The girl gestured toward a figure on stilts farther up the square, where a public promenade of sorts had developed, drawing sketch artists and street acts. She appealed to Anton, who shrugged expansively and led the way, he and the hygienist striding ahead, the girl skipping around her mother a step behind. Arkady and Victor fell in thirty meters back, relying on that fact that Anton would not be looking for a Moscow investigator in Ukrainian camos and certainly would not expect to see Victor in an elegant suit and puffing a cigar.

Victor said, "Bobby thinks that Anton

was paid by Nikolai Kuzmitch. The van came from a Kuzmitch company, so that much makes sense."

"Kuzmitch has an exterminator company? I thought he was into nickel and tin."

"Also fumigation, cable television and airlines. He buys a company a month. I think the airline and fumigation came together, one of those Asian routes."

"Well, Anton is a carjacker. He doesn't need help getting a van."

"You think the Kuzmitch van was a setup?"

"I think it's unlikely a smart man would use a vehicle that could be easily traced to him, and Kuzmitch is a very smart man."

The stilt walker was flamboyant in a Cossack's red coat and conical hat; he blew up balloons that he twisted into animals. Anton bought a tubular blue dog for the girl. As soon as the gift was presented, the dentist gave Anton a polite good-bye handshake and pulled her daughter away. Victor and Arkady watched from a table selling CDs, and Arkady wondered whether it would be a lifelong trait of the little girl to be attracted to dangerous men. The hygienist obviously was.

"The hygienist wears a diamond pin

with her name, Galina," Victor said. "She walked by with that bouncing pin and my erection nearly knocked over the table."

The dentist and daughter turned toward the metro stop while Anton and Galina continued into a brilliantly lit glass dome where an elevator carried passengers down to an underground shopping mall, a borehole of boutiques selling French fashion, Polish crystal, Spanish ceramics, Russian furs, Japanese computer games, aromatherapy. Victor and Arkady followed on the stairs.

Victor said, "Anytime I think Russia's fucked up, I think about the Ukraine, and I feel better. While they were digging the mall, they ran into part of the Golden Gate, the ancient wall of the city, an archaeological treasure, and the city knew if it announced what it had found that work would stop. So they kept mum and buried it. They lost a little identity, but they got McDonald's. Of course, it's not as good as the McDonald's in Moscow."

A bow wave of fear preceded Anton in each store, and mall guards greeted him with such deference that Arkady considered the possibility that Anton might be a silent partner in a store or two. The beautiful Galina traded in her denim top for a mohair sweater. She and Anton slipped into the changing room at a lingerie shop while Arkady and Victor watched from a rack of cookware in the opposite store. The plate-glass transparency of the modern mall was a gift to surveillance.

"A whole day in the dentist's chair, and all Obodovsky can think of is sex. You've got to give him credit," Victor said.

Arkady thought that Anton's shopping spree had more the aspect of a public tour, a prince of the streets demanding respect. Or a dog marking his old territory.

"Anton was originally Ukrainian. I need to know from where. Let me know if he stays around. I'm going back to Chernobyl."

"Don't do it, Arkady. Fuck Timofeyev, fuck Bobby, it's not worth it. Since I got together with Lyuba again, I've been thinking: nobody misses Timofeyev. He was a millionaire, so what? He was a stack of money that blew away. No family. After Ivanov was dead, no friends. Really, I think what happened to him and Ivanov must have been a curse."

The ride back from Kiev was an obstacle course of potholes on an unlit highway and all he had looked forward to was sleep or oblivion; what he had not expected was Eva Kazka waiting at his door, as if he were late for an appointment. She drew sharply on her cigarette. Everything about her was sharp, the cutting attitude of her eyes, the edge of her mouth. She wore her usual camos and scarf.

"Your friend Timofeyev was dead white. You ask so many questions I thought you'd like to know."

"Would you like to come in?" Arkady asked.

"No, the hall is fine. You don't seem to have any neighbors."

"One. Maybe this is the low season for the Zone."

"Maybe," she said. "It's after midnight, and you're not drunk."

"I've been busy," Arkady said.

"You're out of step. You have to keep up with the people of Chornobyl. Vanko was looking for you at the café."

They were interrupted by Campbell, the British ecologist, who came out into the hall in an undershirt and drawers. He swayed and scratched. Eva had stepped aside, and he didn't appear to see her at all.

"Tovarich! Comrade!"

"People don't actually say that anymore," Arkady said. In fact, they rarely had. "In any case, good evening. How are you feeling?"

"Tip-top."

"I haven't seen you around."

"And you won't. I brought a lovely pair of nonradioactive balls here, and I will leave with the same number. Stocked for the duration. Whiskey, mainly. Pop in anytime, although I apologize in advance for the quality of Ukrainian television. Will fix that soon enough. You do speak English?"

"That's what we're speaking." Although Campbell's Scottish burr was so thick that he was barely intelligible.

"You're so right. The joke's on me. A standing invite, any hour. We're Scots, not Brits, no formalities with us."

"You're very generous."

"Seriously. I'll be badly disappointed if you don't." Campbell seemed to count to ten before adding, "Then it's settled," and disappearing back into his room.

Eva let the air clear for a moment. "Your new friend? What did he say?"

"I think he said that whiskey was better than vodka for protection against radioactivity."

"You can't help some people."

"What do you mean, he was white?"

"It was only an impression I had because Timofeyev was clothed and refrigerated. Even so, he seemed bloodless, drained. I didn't think about it at the time. I've seen wounds like his among the dead in Chechnya. Cut the major arteries of the throat, and there's an effusion of blood. Not your dead friend, though. His shirt was clean, taking into account the mud and rain. His hair was clean, too. However, his nostrils were plugged with clotted blood."

"He had nosebleeds."

"This would have been more than a nosebleed."

"A broken nose?"

"There was no bruising. Of course, the local wolf pack had tugged him this way and that, so I couldn't be sure."

"Throat slit and an appearance of bloodlessness, but no bloodstains on the shirt or hair, only in the nose. Everything is contradictory."

"Yes. Also, I should apologize again for the comment about your wife. That was stupid of me. I'm afraid I've lost all sensitivity. It was unforgivable."

"No, her dying was unforgivable."

"You blame the doctors."

"No."

"I see. You're the self-elected captain of the lifeboat; you think you're responsible for everyone." She sighed. "I'm sorry, I must be drunk. On one glass, even. I usually don't get obnoxious quite so fast."

"I'm afraid there's no one left in the lifeboat, so I didn't do a very good job."

"I think I should be going." She didn't, though. "Who was the boy you were talking to on the phone? Just a friend, you said?"

"For reasons beyond my comprehension, I seem to have become responsible for an eleven-year-old boy named Zhenya who lives in a children's shelter in Moscow. It's a ridiculous relationship. I know nothing about him because he refuses to speak to me."

"It's a normal relationship. I refused to speak to my parents from the age of eleven on. Is he slow?"

"No, he's very bright. A chess player, and I suspect he might have a mathematical mind. And courage." Arkady remembered the times Zhenya had run away.

"Spoken like a parent."

"No. His real father is out there, and that's who Zhenya needs."

"You like helping people."

"Actually, when people get to me,

they're generally beyond help."

"You're laughing."

"But it's true."

"No, I think you help. In Chechnya they always tried to drag the bodies back, even under fire. It was more important not to be abandoned. Did you feel abandoned when your wife died?"

"What does Chechnya have to do with my wife?"

"Did you?"

"Yes."

"That's how I am with Alex, except that he hasn't died, he just changed."

"How did we get on this subject?"

"We were being honest. Now you ask a question."

Arkady gently tugged her scarf so that it hung free. The hallway light was poor but when he raised her chin he saw a lateral scar like a minus sign at the base of her neck. "What's that?"

"My Chornobyl souvenir."

He realized that his hand hadn't moved, that it lingered on the warmth of her skin, and that she hadn't objected.

The door downstairs opened, and a voice called up, "Renko, is that you? I have something for you. I'm coming up."

"It's Vanko." Eva retied her scarf in a rush.

"I'll show you." Vanko started up.

"Wait, I'm coming down," Arkady said.

Eva whispered, "I wasn't here."

The café was Chernobyl's evening social club and senate, and Arkady's stature had risen since the discovery of Boris Hulak in the cooling pond. He was afforded elbow room and a table while Vanko bought him a beer. The music was Pink Floyd, which some people thought they could dance to.

"Alex says you attract murders the way a magnet attracts iron filings."

"Alex says the nicest things."

"He'll be by. He's looking for Eva."

Arkady did not say that he had just left her. Interesting, he thought. Our first collusion. "You said you had something for me?"

"For the Jews." Vanko opened up a backpack and handed Arkady a videotape, unlabeled except for a price of fifty dollars.

"How did you come up with that price?"

"It's a valuable keepsake. We could sell this to your American friend and share the profit. What do you think?"

"A videotape of a tomb? This is the gravesite we saw yesterday? You really *have* made a business out of it."

"I can be a guide, too. I know where

everything is. I was here during the accident, you know, just a boy."

"Considering the exposure you had then, isn't the Zone the last place you should be?"

"The Zone is the last place for anyone to be. Anyway, we rotate, as many days off as on."

"What do people do in their free time?"

"I don't do much. Alex makes good money; he says he works in the belly of the beast. That's what he calls Moscow. Eva works in a clinic in Kiev." Vanko nudged the tape closer to Arkady. "What do you think?"

Arkady turned the cassette over. "A Jewish tomb? I haven't noticed many Jews here."

"Because of the Germans and the war. Although many people suffered from the Germans during the war, not just Jews. You always hear about the Jews."

Arkady nodded. "The genocide and all."

"Yes."

"But you seem to be the unofficial welcoming party for visiting Jews."

"I try to help. I found accommodations for your friend and his driver in a decontaminated house."

"Sounds charming." Arkady knew that

this was against Zone regulations; he also knew that dollars worked miracles. "So do you have a tape player? I can't sell the tape to the American unless I know what's on it."

"Mine is broken. Some of the militia had personal machines in their rooms, but they got stolen. But no problem, this can be organized. Hold on to the tape."

"You can count on Vanko." Alex pulled a chair up to the table. "He can organize anything. And congratulations to you, Senior Investigator. Another dead body, I understand. You bring out the murder in people. I suppose in your line of endeavor that is a talent. Where is Eva?"

Vanko shrugged and Arkady said he didn't know, even as he asked himself why he had now lied twice about her.

"You're sure you haven't seen her?" Alex asked Arkady.

"I just returned from Kiev."

"That's right," Vanko said. "His bike was warm."

"Maybe we should issue a missing-persons bulletin for her," Alex said. "What do you think, Renko?"

"Why are you worried?"

"A husband worries."

"You're divorced."

"That doesn't matter, not if you still care. Vanko, can you get us a round of beers?"

"Sure." Vanko, happy to attend, pushed his way through dancers toward the crowd at the counter.

Arkady didn't want to talk about Eva with Alex. He said, "So, your father was a famous physicist, and you were a physicist. Why did you change to ecology?"

"You keep asking."

"It's an interesting switch."

"No, what's interesting is that there are two hundred nuclear power plants and ten thousand nuclear warheads around the world and all in the hands of incompetents."

"That's a sweeping statement."

"It only takes one. I think we can count on it." Alex lowered his voice to a confidential level. "The thing is, Renko, that Eva and I are not really divorced. On paper, yes. However, in my heart, no. And of course it's so much worse if you've been married. That kind of intimacy never ends."

"A former husband doesn't have claims."

"Outside the Zone, maybe. The Zone is different, more intimate. You're an educated man: do you know what smell is?"

"A sense."

"More than that. Smell is the essence, the attachment of free molecules of the thing itself. If we could really see each other, we would see clouds of loose molecules and atoms. We're dripping with them. Every person you meet, you exchange some with. That's why lovers reek of each other, because they've joined so completely that they're virtually the same person. No court, no piece of paper can ever separate you." Alex took Arkady's hand in his and began to squeeze. Alex's hand was broad and strong from setting traps. "Who knows how many thousands of molecules we're exchanging right now?"

"This is something you learned in ecology?"

Alex squeezed harder; his hand was a vise with five fingers. "From nature. Smell, taste, touch. You have pictures in your mind of her with another man. You know every inch of her body, inside and out. Every single feature. The combination of experience and imagination is what drives you crazy. Because you've slept with her, you even know what gives her pleasure. You hear her. To picture someone physically with her is too much. A wolf wouldn't put up with it. Would you say you are a wolf or a dog?"

Arkady pulled his hand into a fist for self-protection. "I'd say I'm a hedgehog."

"See, that's exactly the sort of answer Eva would enjoy. I know the kind of man she's attracted to. I knew when she said she disliked you."

"It was that obvious?"

"You even look alike, the same dark hair and soulful pallor, like brother and sister."

"I hadn't noticed."

"I'm just saying that even if the opportunity presents itself, for Eva's sake you shouldn't take advantage. I ask as a friend, your first friend in the Zone, is anything going on between you and Eva?"

"No."

"That's good. We don't want to get territorial, do we?"

"No."

"Because all you came to the Zone for was your investigation. Stay focused on that." Alex let go. Arkady's hand looked like wadded clay, the blood driven out, and he resisted the temptation to flex it to see what worked. "Go ahead, did you have any questions?"

"I understand that for safety's sake, you only do research in the Zone every other month. What do you do during your month in Moscow?"

"That kind of question: good."

"What do you do?"

"I visit various ecological institutes, pull together research I did here, lecture, write."

"Is that lucrative?"

"Obviously you have never written for a scientific journal. It's for the honor."

Alex described amusingly a scientific conference on the tapeworm where hungry scientists stayed near the canapés, and he and Arkady went on talking in a normal fashion about everyday subjects — films, money, Moscow — but on another, silent level Arkady had the feeling that he had been knocked down and straddled.

On his way back to the dormitory, Arkady heard the muffled flight of a nightjar scooping up moths. He had retreated from the café when he became aware that Alex was watching for Eva's arrival and realized that Alex was waiting only to see how she and Arkady would act, to look for social uneasiness, to discover the telltale clues a former husband couldn't miss. The clinging molecules and atoms.

The streetlamp had gone out since Arkady had crossed under it with Vanko. The only light at the dormitory was a weak bulb at the front step, and where trees crowded out the moon, the street disappeared in the dark. Arkady didn't mind darkness. The problem was that he didn't feel alone. Not another bird or a cat slinking for cover but something else glided by him, first on one side and then the other. When he stopped, it circled him. When he walked, it kept pace. Then it stopped, and he felt ridiculous even as his neck grew cool.

"Alex? Vanko?"

There was no answer but the sifting of leaves overhead, until he heard a laugh in the dark. Arkady clutched Vanko's videotape under his arm and started to trot. The dormitory light was a mere fifty meters off. He wasn't afraid; he was just a man taking midnight exercise. Something flew by, scooped up his leg in midstride and planted him on his back. Something from the other side speared him in the stomach and knocked the air out of him. Oxygen floated over him just out of reach, and his chest made the sound of a dry pump. The best he could do was roll to the side as a blade dug into the street by his ear, which earned him a slap on the head from the other direction. The gliding sound went on. Face on the pavement, he sucked his first breath and saw, silhouetted against the distant light of the café, a figure in camos on inline skates and carrying a hockey stick. It rolled forward, stick poised for a winning goal. Arkady tried to get to his feet and immediately went down on a numb leg, his reward a blow across the back. Facedown again, he noticed that what made them such excellent shots were night-vision goggles strapped to their heads. Since he was going nowhere, they circled, darting in and out, letting him twist one way and then the other. When he kicked back, they slashed his legs. When he tried to grab a stick, they feinted and hit him from the other side. The last thing he was prepared for was a man stepping in between with a flashlight that he shone directly into the eyes of the nearest skater. While the skater blindly staggered back, the man put a large gun under the skater's chin and directed the light on it so that the second skater could see the relationship of gun barrel to head.

A voice croaked, "Fascists! I will shoot, and your friend will blow up like a grapefruit. Get back, go home or I'll shoot both of you *goyischer* boot shit. Go on, go!"

It was Yakov, and although he was half the size of the skater in his grasp, Yakov gave him a kick to send him on his way to the other skater. They huddled for a moment, but the click of the gun hammer being cocked discouraged them, and they rolled off into the shadows on the far side of the street.

Arkady got to his feet and located, in order, his head, shins and the videotape.

"If you're standing, you're okay," Yakov said.

"What are you doing here?"

"Following you."

"Thank you."

"Forget it. Let me see again." Yakov played the flashlight beam around Arkady's head. "You look fine."

Yakov is now the arbiter of damage? Arkady thought. This was trouble.

12

Yakov set up a camp stove on the dock of the Chernobyl Yacht Club and made a breakfast of smoked fish and black coffee for Hoffman and Arkady. The gunman cooked in shirt-sleeves, his shoulder holster showing, and he seemed to take pleasure in the vista of rusted ships heaped against a gray sky.

Hoffman beat his chest like Tarzan. "This is like going down the Zambezi River. Like *The African Queen*. Except all the cannibals here are blond, blue-eyed Ukrainians."

"You're not prejudiced?" Arkady asked.

"Just saying that the house your pal Vanko got us was as cold and dark as a cave. Forget kosher kitchen."

"Is the house radioactive?"

"Not particularly. I know, I know, in Chernobyl that's four-star accommodations."

Arkady looked Hoffman over. The red stubble on the American's jowls was filling in. "You stopped shaving?"

"They want Hasidim, I'll give them

Hasidim. You, on the other hand, look like you've been fucked by a bear."

"Yakov says I'll be fine." Arkady had checked himself when he woke. He was crosshatched with bruises from his shins to his ribs, and his head throbbed every time he turned it.

Hoffman was amused. "With Yakov, unless broken bones are sticking through the skin, you're fine. Don't ask for any sympathy from him."

"He's fine," Yakov said. He picked crust off the pan to throw in the water. Fish rose to take it in gulps. "He's a mensch."

"Which means?" Arkady asked.

"Schmuck," Hoffman said. "Get close to people, help them, trust them, it just makes you vulnerable. Do you know who jumped you?"

"I'm pretty sure they were two brothers named Woropay. Militia. Yakov scared them off."

"Yakov can do that."

Yakov squatted by the stove and — except for the cannon hanging from his shoulder — resembled any pensioner at peace with the slow-moving water, the array of wrecks going nowhere, the mounting thunderheads. Arkady couldn't tell how much Yakov understood or cared to understand. Sometimes he responded in Ukrainian, sometimes Hebrew, sometimes nothing, like an ancient radio with a varying signal.

Hoffman said, "Yakov did the right thing by letting the creeps go. Ukrainians are not going to take the word of a Russian and a Jew over two of their own police. Besides, I don't want Yakov tied up. I'm paying him to protect me, not you. If they really start digging around, they've got warrants out for Yakov that go back to the Crimean War. You notice he wears a yarmulke. He puts the goyim on notice enough."

"Have you been here before?" Arkady asked, but Yakov busied himself turning the fish, which was smoked, grilled and charred. What more could be done to it? Arkady wondered.

"So you saw our friend Victor in Kiev yesterday," Hoffman said. "Didn't he look prosperous?"

"Transformed."

"Better, let's leave it at that. The main thing is, the two of you saw that ape Obodovsky with his dentist."

"And dental hygienist."

"Dental hygienist. Why don't you and Victor steal a page from the Woropay brothers and take a couple of hockey sticks to Obodovsky? Get him to tell you where he was when that van showed up in the alley behind Pasha's apartment house. If you don't know how, Yakov can help you. This happens to fall into his field of expertise. You must have questions."

"I do. You said you were here last year, on instructions from Pasha Ivanov, to look into a commercial transaction involving spent nuclear fuel."

"They're stuffed to the gills here. No working reactor, but tons of dirty fuel. Insane."

"It didn't make business sense?"

"Right. What does this have to do with Obodovsky?"

"Who did you talk to here? What officials?" Arkady asked.

"I don't know. I don't remember."

"That would have involved an investment of millions of dollars. You talked to the plant manager, the engineers, the ministry in Kiev?"

"People like that, yes."

"You had to come disguised for that?"

Hoffman's eyes got smaller as he got angry. "What are these questions? You're supposed to be on my side. The fuel deal never happened. It had nothing to do with Pasha or Timofeyev dying. Or Obodovsky, for that matter."

"Eat, eat." Yakov handed out camp plates of grilled fish.

Hoffman asked, "How about Yakov and I just go back to Kiev, have Victor lead us to Obodovsky and blow his head off?"

"Coffee." Yakov passed metal cups of something black and syrupy. "Before it rains."

The fish had the texture of underwater cable. Arkady sipped the coffee and, now that he had time, admired Yakov's American gun, a .45 with bluing worn to bare steel.

"Reliable?"

"For fifty years," Yakov said.

"A little slower than a modern gun."

"Slow can be good. Take your time and aim, is what I say."

"Wise words."

"Why not beat on Obodovsky?" Hoffman insisted.

"Because Anton Obodovsky is very much an outside person, and whoever arranged the delivery of cesium chloride to Pasha's apartment was inside. They didn't break in; they had the codes and somehow got around the cameras."

"Colonel Ozhogin?"

"He certainly is inside NoviRus Security."

"I can have him killed. He killed

Timofeyev and Pasha."

"Only, Ozhogin has never been here. You are the one who has been, and you won't tell me why. How long are you going to stay?"

"I don't know. We're enjoying ourselves, camping out, what's the rush?"

There didn't seem to be one for Hoffman. He sat on the car fender and picked his teeth with a fish bone. He looked like a man with a sudden abundance of patience.

"Thank you for the coffee." Arkady started off the dock.

"My father was here," Yakov said.

"Oh?" Arkady stopped.

Yakov felt in his shirt pocket and lit half of a cigarette he had saved. He spoke in an offhand way, as if a detail had come to mind. "Chernobyl was a port town, a Jewish center. When the Reds were taking over Russia, the Ukraine was independent. So what did they do? The Ukrainians put all the Jews in Chernobyl into boats and sank them, drowned them and machine-gunned anyone who tried to swim for shore."

"Like I told you," Hoffman told Arkady, "don't ask for any sympathy from Yakov."

As soon as Arkady rode to the street above the river he called Victor, who admitted that he had lost Anton Obodovsky at a casino the night before.

"You have to buy a hundred-dollar membership before they let you in. And they really liked sticking it to a Russian. Anton games all night while I'm jerking off in front. He's up to something. I just feel sorry for Galina."

"Galina?"

"The hygienist. Miss Universe? She seems like a sweet kid. Maybe a tad materialistic."

"How was Anton's tooth?" Arkady asked.

"He seemed normal."

"Where are you now?"

"Back at the café, in case Anton returns. It's pouring here. You know what Europeans do in the rain? They spend all day over a cup of coffee. It's very chic."

"You sound like you're having a wonderful vacation. Go to the travel agency across from the dentist and see whether Anton bought tickets anywhere. Also, I know we checked before to see what Ivanov and Timofeyev were doing during the accident here at Chernobyl, but I want you to do it again."

"We already know. Nothing. They were two prodigies in Moscow doing research."

"On what, for whom?"

"Ancient history."

"I'd appreciate it if you would do it anyway." Through the trees Arkady could make out Hoffman and Yakov on the dock. Yakov meditated by the water and Hoffman was on a mobile phone. "How much of this information are you passing to Bobby?"

After momentary embarrassment, Victor said, "Lyuba called. I explained the situation to her, and then she explained the situation to me. As she says, Hoffman is paying me."

"You're giving him everything?"

"Pretty much. But I'm giving the same to you, and I'm not charging you a kopek."

"Bobby is using me as a hunting dog. He's going to sit around and wait until I flush something into the open."

"You do the work and he cashes in? I think that's called capitalism."

"One more thing. Vanko admires the way Alex Gerasimov makes money during his off-time from Chernobyl by interpreting and translating at a Moscow hotel. No shame in that. But Alex says he does nothing but academic work that pays little or nothing at all. A small discrepancy, and probably none of my business."

"That's what I was thinking."

Arkady caught a raindrop in his palm. "Start by calling Moscow hotels that cater to Western businessmen — the Aerostar, Kempinski, Marriott — and work your way down. This will be expensive. Call from your hotel on Bobby's account."

"Magic words."

Before the rain hit, Arkady rode to the black village where Timofeyev had been found. He had visited the site twenty times before, and each time he had tried to imagine how a Russian millionaire could have arrived at the gate of a cemetery in the Zone. Arkady also tried to picture how Timofeyev's body had been discovered by Militia Officer Katamay and a local squatter. Did that description fit the scavenger hauled from the cooling pond? Now all three were gone, Timofeyev and Hulak dead and Katamay vanished. The facts made no sense. The atmospherics, on the other hand, were perfect, a spatter of raindrops from an ominous sky and an approaching fanfare of thunder, the same as Timofeyev's last day.

Arkady got off the bike in the clearing where Eva Kazka had held her outdoor medical clinic. In a way, there were two cemeteries. One was the village itself, with its punched-in windows and falling roofs. The other was the graveyard of simple crosses of metal tubing painted blue or white, some with a plaque, some with a photograph sealed in an oval frame, some decorated with bright bouquets of plastic flowers. Keep your eternal flame, Arkady thought, bring me plastic flowers.

Maria Panasenko popped up from a corner of the cemetery. Arkady was surprised, because a diamond marker by the gate indicated that the cemetery was too hot to trespass on, and visits were limited to one a year. Maria wore a heavy shawl in case of rain; otherwise, she was the same ancient cherub who had provided the drunken samogon party two nights before. Maria held a short scythe and, over her shoulder, a burlap sack of brambles and weeds she refused to let Arkady relieve her of. Her hands were small and tough, and her blue eyes shone even in the shadows of heavy clouds.

"Our neighbors." She looked around the graveyard. "I'm sure they'd do the same for us."

"It's nicely kept," Arkady said. A cozy anteroom to heaven, he thought.

She smiled and showed her steel teeth. "Roman and I were always afraid there wouldn't be a good cemetery plot for us. Now we have our choice."

"Yes." The silver lining.

She cocked her head. "It's sad, all the

same. A village dies, it's like the end of a book. That's it, no more. Roman and I may be the last page."

"Not for many years."

"It's long enough already, but thank you."

"I was wondering, what are the militia like around here?"

"Oh, we don't see much of them."

"Squatters?"

"No."

"There don't happen to be any Obodovskys in the cemetery?"

Maria shook her head and said she knew all the families from the surrounding villages. No Obodovskys. She glanced up at the sack. "Excuse me, I should get these in before they get wet. You should stop for a drink."

"No, no, thank you." The very threat of samogon made him sweat.

"You're sure?"

"Yes. Another day, if I may."

He waited until she was gone before he brought his mind back to Lev Timofeyev's death. Arkady was sure of so little: basically that the body had been found faceup in the mud at the cemetery gate, his throat slit, his left eye a cavity, neither his hair nor his shirt bloody but blood packed in his nose. Arkady was nowhere near to asking why; it was all he could do to ask how. Had Timofeyev driven himself to the village or been brought by someone else? Searched out the cemetery or been led to it? Dragged to it dead or alive? If there had been a competent detective at the scene, would he have found tire tracks, a trail of blood, the twin shoe marks of a dragged body or mud inside the dead man's shoes? Or at least footprints; the report cited wolf prints, why not shoes? If it came to why, was Timofeyev the target of a conspiracy, or a plum that happened to fall into the hands of Officer Katamay?

Arkady started again in the village clearing as the most likely place for a car to stop. From there, the way to the cemetery narrowed to a footpath. A curtain shifted at one of the few occupied houses, and before the curtain closed, he caught a glimpse of Maria's neighbor Nina, on a crutch. How could anything have occurred within eyesight of these wary survivors and not be spied? Yet they had all sworn they'd seen nothing.

Walking up the path, Arkady stopped every few feet to brush aside leaves and look for prints or signs of blood, as he had done a dozen times before and with no more success. He paused at the cemetery gate and imagined Timofeyev standing, kneeling, lying on his back. Photographs really would have been helpful. Or a diagram or sketch. At this point Arkady was no better than a dog trying to uncover a stale scent. Yet there was always something. Visitors to the rolling hills of Borodino still felt the breath of French and Russian fusiliers underneath the grass. Why not an echo of Timofeyev's last living moment? And why not the spirits of those buried in this village plot? If ever there were simple lives, there were these, passed within the circuit of a few fields and orchards, almost as far from the rest of the world as another century.

Arkady opened the gate. The cemetery was a second village of plots and crosses separated by wrought-iron fences. A few plots had barely enough room to stand in, while one or two offered the comfort of a table and bench, but there were no impressive crypts or stones; wealth played little part in the life or death of such a community. Maria had industriously cleared around the crosses on one entire side, and on their own, without crosses, stood four glass jars of pansies, purple, blue and white, each at the head of a faintly discernible mound. The light was so thin that Arkady couldn't be sure. He knelt and spread his arms. Four child-size graves hidden by their lack of crosses. Illegal graves. How great a crime was that?

Eva had said that Timofeyev was white, he seemed drained. Frozen bodies could fool, but Arkady was willing to believe that she had seen more violence than most physicians, and Timofeyev's one-eyed stare through a mask of hoarfrost must have reminded her more of Chechnya than of cardiac arrest. Only, when Timofeyev's throat was cut, the blood went where? Right side up, blood should have soaked his shirt. Upside down, his hair. That only his nose was filled with blood suggested that he was inverted and, afterward, his face and hair rinsed. And the eye? Was that a delicacy for wolves?

Unless he was hung by his feet and, afterward, had his hair washed. Despite the draining there still would have been some lividity of settled blood around the head, but that could have been confused with freezer burn.

Arkady stood with his hand on the gate and for a moment caught the glint of something revealed, something lying in front of him and then gone, chased by a patter of raindrops, the light preparation of a hard rain.

* * *

The next black village had no inhabitants at all, and its cemetery lay deep in the embrace of brambles and weeds. Arkady had hoped the comparison would lead to some sort of realization, but what he found as he dismounted from the motorcycle and walked around was a deepening gloom of rotting cottages. A loamy toadstool smell vied with the oversweet scent of decaying apples. Where wild boar had dug for mushrooms, the dosimeter in Arkady's pocket spoke up. He heard something shifting in the house ahead and asked himself which was faster to the motorcycle, man or boar? Suddenly he wished he had Captain Marchenko's hunting knife or, better, Yakov's cannon.

The house gave a single-cylinder whine, and a rider in a helmet and camos on a small motorbike came out the front door. The rider pushed through the debris in the yard and over a prostrate picket fence, where he momentarily came to a halt to lower his helmet visor. The bike had no sidecar to stuff an icon in, and it did have a license plate, but it was a blue Suzuki, and the reflector was missing from the rear fender. Arkady had that reflector in his pocket.

"Are you looking for more icons to

steal?" Arkady asked.

The thief returned Arkady's gaze as if to say, "You again?" and started off. By the time Arkady had reached his own motorcycle, the thief was halfway out of the village.

Arkady had the bigger, faster bike, but he simply wasn't as good a rider. The thief left the village on a narrow trail made for gathering firewood. Where branches had half-fallen, he ducked, and where the path was blocked, he deftly slipped by. Arkady crashed through the smaller branches and was swept clean off his saddle by the out-stretched arm of an oak. The bike was all right, that was the main thing. He climbed back on and listened for the voice of the Suzuki. Rain pinged the leaves. Birches swayed in the arriving breeze. There was no hint of the thief.

Arkady pushed ahead with his engine off and, at this more deliberate speed, found motorbike tracks in the damp leaves underfoot; moisture made footprints and tire treads easier to read. Where the path forked, he consciously took the wrong trail for fifty meters before cutting through the woods to the right trail, where he saw the thief waiting behind a glistening screen of firs. The forest floor of damp needles was soft, and the thief's attention was fixed entirely on the trail until the steel jaws of a trap sprang from the ground and snapped shut next to Arkady's foot. The thief turned to regard the tableau of Arkady, bike and trap, and in a second was riding back down the trail the way he had come.

The thief kept ahead of Arkady but didn't completely lose him; as long as Arkady kept the smaller bike in sight, he could anticipate obstacles. Also, Arkady took chances he wouldn't have in a saner mood, following a far more expert rider leap for leap, fishtailing on leaves to swing off the path and weave through a stand of pines until they broke back into the village. On the far side was a forestry road with chest-high seedlings of second-growth trees. The thief took them like a slalom skier, leaning one way and then the other. Arkady rode straight over the seedlings, gaining all the time.

As Arkady drew close, the thief veered off the forestry road into a line of rust-colored pines, the outer reach of the Red Forest, then through onto an undulating field with radiation markers of buried houses, cars and trucks. Arkady plunged into hollows, churned his way out and plunged again, while the thief flew in and out with acrobatic ease. Every way Arkady turned, the thief appeared farther out of reach until a hidden ditch twisted the front wheel of Arkady's bike and sent him over the handlebars. He hauled himself up, but the chase was over. The thief disappeared toward Chernobyl as the horizon went white and shuddered, followed by a thunderclap that announced a storm finally delivered.

As the clouds unloaded, the lights of the town seemed to drown. Arkady rode in at a limp, wet hair wrapped across his brow. He passed the inviting glow of the café and heard the splash of people running for its door. The windows were steamed. No one saw him go by. He rode past the dormitory, the parking lot sizzling with rain. He rode under bending branches. He pictured Victor sitting out the storm at a café in Kiev, sharing the space with pigeons. Arkady's camos took a clammy grip on his chest and shoulders. A truck went by with windshield wipers thrashing, and he doubted it had noticed him at all.

He turned at the road that led down to the river, where he had a panorama of the storm. Steam rose from the water as rain fell, but Arkady could see that Hoffman, Yakov and their car had deserted the yacht-club dock. Scuttled ships levitated from fog with each lightning strike. The far bank was a hazy sketch of aspens and reeds, but farther upstream the bridge led to the forlorn lights of staff quarters still occupied. Arkady could see well enough by the lightning to keep his own headlight off. He crossed the bridge and passed between the solid brick buildings on spongy soil that came to an end, except for a car track that led along what might once have been a sports field but had sunk under cattails and ferns.

Arkady killed his engine and pushed, following the track around a shadowy stand of trees to a garage fashioned from sheets of corrugated steel. The doors were held shut with a loose padlock. They creaked as he swung them open, but with thunder in every direction, he doubted anyone would hear less than a bomb. Arkady scanned the interior with his penlight. The garage was crammed but orderly: hardware in jars on shelves, hand tools in rows along the walls. In the middle was Eva Kazka's white Moskvich. On one side of the car was a Suzuki bike with the engine still warm; under a tarp on the other side, a disengaged sidecar. From his pocket Arkady took the reflector he had snapped off the rear fender of the icon thief's bike and mated it to the metal stub on Eva's fender. They fit.

Wood smoke led to a cabin set among a blue mass of lilacs. A porch had been converted to a parlor. Through a window Arkady glimpsed an upright piano and bright chinks of fire in a woodstove. He rapped on the door, but thunder had opened up like siege guns, flattening all other sounds. He opened the door as lightning flashed behind him, strobe-lighting a glassed-in porch's assortment of a rug, wicker table and chairs, bookshelves and paintings. The room sank back into the dark. He had taken a step in when the sky above cracked open and filled the room like a searchlight. Eva moved to the middle of the rug with a gun. She was barefoot, in a robe. The gun was a 9mm, and she seemed familiar with it.

Eva said, "Get out or I'll shoot."

The door slammed shut in the wind, and for a moment Arkady thought she had fired. She gathered the robe together with her free hand.

"It's me," he said.

"I know who it is."

In a momentary dark he moved closer and pushed aside the collar of the robe to kiss her neck on the same fine scar he had found before. She pressed the muzzle of the pistol against his head as he slid open the robe. Her breasts were cold as marble.

He heard a mechanism of the gun at work, easing the hammer down. He felt a tremor run through her legs. She pressed the flat of the gun against his head, holding him.

Her bed was in a room with its own woodstove, which whistled softly with heat. How they had arrived there, he wasn't quite sure. Sometimes the body took over. Two bodies, in this case. Eva rolled on top as he entered until her head rocked back, sweat like kohl around her eyes, her body straining as if she were about to leap, as if all the frenzy he had detected in her before had become a voracious need. No different from him. They were two starving people feeding from the same spoon.

Chaos turned to steady rain. Eva and Arkady sat at opposite ends of the bed. The light of an oil lamp brought out the black of her eyes, hair, curls at the base of her stomach, the gun by her hand.

"Are you going to shoot me?" he asked.

"No. Punishment only encourages you." She gave his scratches and bruises a professional glance.

"Some of these are thanks to you," he said.

"You'll live."

"That's what I thought."

She gestured vaguely to the bed, as if to a battlefield. "This didn't mean anything."

"It meant a great deal to me."

"You took me by surprise."

He thought about it. "No. I took you by inevitability."

"A magnetic attraction?"

"Something like that."

"Have you ever seen little toy magnetic dogs? How they attract each other? That doesn't mean they want to. It was a mistake."

The lamp threw as much shadow as light, but he could see an agreeable mess: an overlap of pillows, books and rugs. A framed photo showing an older couple in front of a different house; Arkady had to look twice to recognize the ruin where Eva had hidden with her bike. A poster for a Stones concert in Paris. A teapot and cups with bread, jams, knife, cutting board and crumbs. All in all, an intimate cabin.

Arkady nodded to the gun. "I could field-strip that for you. I could field-strip it blindfolded by the age of six. It's about the only thing my father ever taught me."

"A handy ability."

"He thought so."

"You and Alex have more in common than you imagine."

One item they had in common was obvious, but Arkady felt that Eva had meant more than herself. "How is that?"

Eva shook her head. She dismissed that line of conversation. Instead, she said, "Alex said this would happen."

"Alex is a smart man," Arkady said.

"Alex is a crazy man."

"Did you drive him crazy?"

"By sleeping with other men? Not that many. I desperately need a cigarette."

Arkady found two and an ashtray he put in no-man's-land at the center of the bed.

Eva said, "What do you know about suicide? Besides cutting down the bodies, I mean?"

"Oh, I come from a long line of suicides. Mother and father. You'd think it would be a short line, but no, they get their procreation done early, and then they kill themselves."

"Have you . . ."

"Not successfully. Anyway, here we are in Chernobyl. I think we're making effort enough. And you?"

She balked again, not ready to let him lead. "So how is your investigation going?"

"Moments of clarity. Millionaires are generally murdered for money. I'm not sure that's the case here."

"Anything else?"

"Yes. When I first came, I assumed that the deaths of Ivanov and Timofeyev were connected. I still think so, but in a different way. Perhaps more parallel."

"Whatever that means. What were you doing in the village today?"

"I was at the cemetery at Roman and Maria's, and I began wondering if any of the official fatalities from the accident came from the villages in the Zone. Whether I would recognize names on the crosses. I didn't, but I found four unmarked graves of children."

"Grandchildren. Of different causes supposedly unrelated to Chornobyl. What happens is the family breaks up, and no one is left to bury the dead but the grandparents, who take them home. No one keeps track. There were forty-one official deaths from the accident and half a million unofficial. An honest list would reach to the moon."

"Then I went to the next village, where I found you. What were you doing on a motorcycle in a house? Let me guess. You take icons so they can be reported as stolen to the militia. That way scavengers and the corrupt officers they work with have no reason to bother old folks like Roman and Maria. Then you return the icons. But there were no occupied houses or icons in that village, so why were you there? Whose house was it?"

"No one's."

"I recognized the bike by the broken reflector and recognized you by the scarf. You should get rid of your scarves." He leaned across the bed to kiss her neck. That she didn't shoot him he took as a good omen.

Eva said, "Every once in a while I remember this thirteen-year-old girl parading on May Day with her idiotic smile. She's moved out of the village to Kiev to live with her aunt and uncle so she can go to a special school for dance; their standards are rigid, but she's been measured and weighed and has the right build. She has been selected to hold a banner that says, 'Marching into the Radiant Future!' She is so pleased the day is warm enough not to wear a coat. The young body is a wonder of growth, the division of cells produces virtually a new person. And on this day she *will* be a new person, because a haze comes over the sun, a breeze from Chornobyl. And so ends her days of dancing and begins her acquaintanceship with Soviet surgery." She touched the scar. "First the thyroid and then the tumors. That's how you know a true citizen of the Zone. We fuck without worries. I am a hollow woman; you can beat me like a drum. Still, once in a while, I remember this fatuous girl and am so ashamed of her stupidity that if I could go back in time with a gun, I would shoot her myself. When this feeling overcomes me, I go to the nearest hole or black house and hide. There are enough black houses that this is never a problem. Otherwise I have nothing to fear. Were you ambitious as a boy? What did you want to be?"

"When I was a boy, I wanted to be an astronomer and study the stars. Then someone informed me that I wasn't seeing the actual stars, I was seeing starlight generated thousands of years before. What I thought I was seeing was long since over, which rendered the exercise rather pointless. Of course, the same can be said about my profession now. I can't bring back the dead."

"And the injured?"

"Everybody's injured."

"Is that a promise?"

"It's the only thing I'm sure of."

13

In the morning the rain had passed and the cabin felt like a boat safely landed. Eva was gone but had left him brown bread and jam on a cutting board. While Arkady dressed he noticed more photographs: a ballet mistress, a tabby cat, friends skiing, someone shielding their eyes on a beach. None of Alex, which, he confessed, reassured him.

As he stepped out the screen door he couldn't help but notice how the willows, like timid girls, stood with one foot in the water and that the river, swollen with runoff, bore an earthy smell and a new full-throated voice. Arkady hadn't slept with a woman for a while and he felt warm and alive. Blow on cold ashes, he thought, you never know.

"Hello." Oksana Katamay slipped into view around the corner of the house. She was in her blue jogging suit and knit cap; a wig, maybe, or lunch for her brother Karel was in her backpack. She ducked her head with every step forward and pulled her hands into her sleeves. "Is everyone up?"

"Yes."

"The lilacs smell so sweet. This is the doctor's house?"

"Yes. What are you doing here?"

"I saw your motorbike. That's my friend's Vespa next to it. I borrowed it."

"A friend's?"

"Yes."

Arkady saw the bike and scooter in the yard but they were hardly visible from the road. Oksana smiled and looked around in a goose-necked way.

Arkady asked, "Have you been here long?"

"A while."

"You're very quiet."

She smiled and nodded. She must have rolled the scooter the last fifty meters with the engine off to arrive so silently, and she obviously didn't find anything odd about waiting for him outside another woman's door.

"You're not at work today?" Arkady asked.

"I'm home, sick." She pointed at her shaved head. "They let me take time off whenever I want. There's not much to do, anyway."

"Can I give you some coffee, hot or cold?"

"You remembered. No, thank you."

He looked at the scooter. "You can travel around here? What about checkpoints?"

"Well, I know where to go."

"So does your brother Karel. That's the problem."

Oksana shifted uncomfortably. "I just wanted to see how you were. If you're with the doctor, I suppose you're okay. I was worried because of Hulak."

"You knew Boris Hulak?"

"He and my grandfather would rant on the telephone for hours about traitors who shut down the plant. But my grandfather would never really hurt anyone."

"That's good to know."

Oksana seemed relieved. If a man in a wheelchair a train ride away was not going to attack him, Arkady was happy, too.

"Look." She pointed out a stork skimming over its mirror image on the surface of the river.

"Like you. You simply come and go."

She shrugged and smiled. For inscrutability, the *Mona Lisa* had nothing on Oksana Katamay.

He asked, "Do you remember Anton Obodovsky? A big man in his mid-thirties. He used to box."

Her smile spread.

Arkady tried an easier question. "Where

would I find the Woropays?"

Dymtrus Woropay skated on a street of empty houses, gliding backward, sideways, forward, handling a hockey stick and rubber ball around potholes and grass. His yellow hair lifted and his eyes were intent on the rolling ball. He didn't notice Arkady until they were a few steps apart, at which point Dymtrus pushed forward and cocked his stick, and Arkady threw the trash-bin cover he had carried behind his back. The cover cut off Dymtrus at the ankles. He went down on his face, and Arkady put a foot on the back of his neck and kept him splayed.

"I want to talk to Katamay," Arkady said.

"Maybe you want a stick up your ass, too."

Arkady leaned. He was afraid of the burly Dymtrus Woropay, and sometimes fear could be exorcised only one way. "Where is Katamay?"

"Get stuffed."

"Do you enjoy breathing?" Arkady dug his heel into Woropay.

"Do you have a gun?" Woropay twisted his eyes up to see.

Arkady unclipped Woropay's pistol, a

Makarov, militia issue. "Now I do."

"You won't shoot."

"Dymtrus, look around. How many witnesses do you see?"

"Fuck off."

"I bet your brother is tired of being your brother. I think it's time he stood on his own two feet." Arkady pushed off the pistol's safety and, to be convincing, put the muzzle to Dymtrus's head.

"Wait. Fuck. Katamay who?"

"Your friend and teammate, your fellow militia officer Karel Katamay. He found the Russian at the cemetery. I want to talk to him."

"He's missing."

"Not to everyone. I talked to his grandfather, and soon two thugs, you and your brother, begin playing hockey with my head."

"What do you want to talk about?"

"The Russian, pure and simple."

"Let me up."

"Give me a reason." Arkady applied more weight to the decision making.

"Okay! I'll see."

"I want you to take me to him."

"He'll call you."

"No, face-to-face."

"I can't breathe."

"Face-to-face. Arrange it, or I will find you and shoot off your knee. Then we'll see how you skate." Arkady applied one last squeeze before getting up.

Dymtrus sat up and rubbed his neck. He had a sloped face like a shovel and small eyes. "Shit."

Arkady gave Dymtrus his mobile-phone number and, since he felt Dymtrus tensing for a fight, threw in as an afterthought, "You're not a bad skater."

"How the fuck would you know?"

"I saw you practice. You prefer ice?"

"So?"

"I bet you're wasted on the league down here."

"So?"

"Just an observation."

Dymtrus pushed his hair back. "So what? What do you know about ice hockey?"

"Not much. I know people."

"Like who?"

"Wayne Gretzky." Arkady had heard of Wayne Gretzky.

"You know him? Fuck! Do you think he'd ever come down here?"

"To Chernobyl? No. You'd have to go to Moscow."

"He could see me there?"

"Maybe. I don't know."

"But he might? I'm big and I'm fast and I'm willing to kill."

"That's an unbeatable combination."

"So he might?"

"We'll see."

A Dymtrus with a more positive frame of mind got to his feet. "Okay, we'll see. Could I have my gun back?"

"No. That's my guarantee that I will meet Katamay. You get your gun back after."

"What if I need it?"

"Stay out of trouble."

Feeling in a better frame of mind himself, Arkady rode to the café, where he found Bobby Hoffman and Yakov working on black coffee in the absence of a kosher kitchen.

"I figured it out," Bobby told Arkady. "If Yakov's father was here when they sank the ferry full of Jews, and that was 1919, 1920, that makes Yakov over eighty. I didn't know he was that old."

"He seems to know his business."

"He wrote the book. But you look at him and think, All this guy wants is to sit in a beach chair in Tel Aviv, take a nap and quietly expire. How are you feeling, Renko?"

Yakov raised a basilisk's gaze. "He's fine."

"I'm fine," Arkady said. Despite the accumulation of bruises, he was.

Yakov was tidy, like a pensioner dressed to feed the birds, but Bobby's face and clothes were corrugated from lack of sleep, and his hand was swollen.

"What happened?"

"Bees." Bobby shrugged it off. "I don't mind bees. So what about Obodovsky, what's he doing in Kiev?"

"Anton is doing what you'd expect someone of his stature to do when he's visiting his hometown. He's showing off money and a girl."

"The dental hygienist?"

"That's right. We're not in Russia. Neither Victor nor I have any authority to pick him up or question him."

Bobby whispered, "I don't want him questioned, I want him dead. You can do that anywhere. I'm out on a very long limb here. And nothing is happening. My two Russian cops are taking tea, visiting the malls. I give you Kuzmitch, you don't want him. You see Obodovsky, you can't touch him. This is why you don't get paid, because you don't produce."

"Coffee." Yakov brought Arkady a cup. There was no waiter.

"And Yakov, here, he prays all night. Oils his gun and prays. You two are a pair."

Arkady said, "Yesterday you were patient."

"Today I'm shitting a brick."

"Then tell me what you were doing here last year."

"It's none of your business." Bobby leaned to look out the window. "Rain, radiation, leaky roofs. It's getting to me."

A militia car swung into the space beside Yakov's battered Nissan, and Captain Marchenko emerged slowly, perhaps posing for a painting called *The Cossack at Dawn*, Arkady thought. A lot of things had escaped Marchenko's notice — a slit throat, tire treads and footprints at a murder scene — but the Zone's two newest residents had caught the captain's eye. The captain entered the café and affected friendly surprise at the sight of Bobby and company, like a man who sees a lamb and the possibility of lamb chops. He came immediately to the table.

"Do I see visitors? Renko, please introduce me to your friends."

Arkady looked at Bobby, asking in a silent way what name he would care to offer.

Yakov stepped in. "I am Yitschak Brodsky, and my colleague is Chaim

Weitzman. Please, Mr. Weitzman speaks only Hebrew and English."

"No Ukrainian? Not even Russian?"

"I interpret."

"And you, Renko, do you speak Hebrew or English?"

"A little English."

"You would," the captain said, as if it were a black mark. "Friends of yours?"

Arkady improvised. "Weitzman is a friend of a friend. He knew I was here, but he came to see the Jewish grave."

"And stayed overnight not one night but two, without informing the militia. I talked to Vanko." Marchenko turned to Yakov. "May I see your passports, please?" The captain studied them closely, to underline his authority. He cleared his throat. "Excellent. You know, I often say we should make our Jewish visitors especially welcome."

"Are there other visitors?" Arkady asked.

There was an answer — specialists in toxic sites — but Marchenko maintained a smile, and when he handed back the passports he added a business card.

"Mr. Brodsky, please take my card, which has my office phone and fax. If you call me first, I can organize much better accommodations, and perhaps a day visit for a much larger group, strictly supervised because of radiation, naturally. Late summer is good. Strawberry season." If the captain expected an effusive response from Yakov, he didn't get it. "Anyway, let's hope the rain is over. Let's hope we don't need Noah and his ark, right? Well, gentlemen, a pleasure. Renko, you weren't going anywhere, were you?"

"No."

"I didn't think so."

As the captain climbed into his car, Bobby waved and muttered, "Asshole."

Arkady asked, "Bobby, how many passports do you have?"

"Enough."

"Good, because the captain's brain is like a closet light that sometimes lights and sometimes doesn't. This time it didn't; the next time it might, and he'll connect Timofeyev and me and you. He'll check on your papers or call Ozhogin. He has the colonel's number. It might be wise to go now."

"We'll wait. By the way, Noah was an asshole, too."

"Why Noah?" Arkady asked. This was a new indictment.

"He didn't argue."

"Noah should have argued?"

Yakov explained, "Abraham argues with

God not to kill everyone in Sodom and Gomorrah. Moses pleads with God not to kill worshippers of the golden calf. But God tells Noah to build a boat because He's going to flood the entire world, and what does Noah say? Not a word."

"Not a word," said Bobby, "and saves the minimum. What a bastard."

Perhaps Eva had gone to the Panasenkos' to give Roman a physical examination, but the cow had gotten out during the storm and trampled the vegetable garden, and Maria and Eva were in the middle of trying to resurrect what they could when Arkady arrived and joined in. The air was hot and humid, the ground damp and baked and oozing humors, and each step produced a sharp scent of crushed mint or chamomile.

The old couple had laid out their garden in straight-as-a-string rows of beets, potatoes, cabbage, onion, garlic and dill, the necessities of life; celery, parsley, mustard and horseradish, the savor of life; buffalo grass for vodka and poppies for bread, everything chopped by the cow into muck. The root vegetables had to be rebedded and the greens salvaged. Where water pooled, Roman shaped drainage with a hoe.

Maria wore a shawl around her head and around her waist a second shawl to hold what she picked. Eva had laid aside her lab coat and shoes to work barefoot in a T-shirt and shorts, no scarf.

They worked separate rows, digging their hands into the mud and freeing the greens or replanting root vegetables tops up. The women were faster and more efficient. Arkady hadn't worked in a garden since he was a boy, and that was just at the dacha to keep him out of the way. The neighbors — Nina on her crutch, Olga squinting through her glasses, Klara with Viking braids — came to witness. From the general interest and the size of the lot, it became clear that Roman and Maria fed the entire population of the village. Maria could have pulled a small train behind her, the way she leaned in to the work and smiled with satisfaction in it, except when she looked up from strangling red-veined greens of beets to gaze on Roman.

"You're sure you latched the cow's stall? She could have been eaten by wolves. The wolves could have gotten her."

Roman acted deaf, while Lydia, the cow, peeked through an open slat of her stall; the two put Arkady in mind of a pair of drunks who remembered nothing.

Eva had ignored him since his arrival, and the more he thought about it, the more he realized that the night with her had been a mistake. He had gotten too involved. He had lost his sacred objectivity. He was like one of those telescopes launched into space with lenses so distorted it could be seeing either headlights or the Milky Way.

When the garden was done, Maria brought cold water for Arkady and Eva and kvass for Roman. Kvass was a beer made from fermented bread, and a summons to life for Roman. Eva managed to keep one of the old couple between her and Arkady at all times: a dance of avoidance.

Arkady's mobile phone rang. It was the director of the Moscow children's shelter.

"Investigator Renko, this is impossible. You must return at once. Zhenya waits every day."

"The last time I saw Zhenya, he didn't as much as wave good-bye. I doubt very much that he's upset."

"He's not demonstrative. Explain to Zhenya."

Again the void on the phone, from either the bottom of a waste bin or an undemonstrative boy.

"Zhenya? Are you there? Zhenya?"

Arkady heard nothing, but he could feel the boy pressing a receiver close to his ear and pursing his lips in a disagreeable way.

"How are you doing, Zhenya? Driving the director insane, it sounds like."

Silence and perhaps a nervous shift of the phone from one ear to the other.

Arkady said, "No news about Baba Yaga. Nothing to report."

He could see Zhenya gripping the phone tight with one hand and chewing the nails of the other. Arkady tried to outwait him, which was impossible, because Zhenya just hung on.

"We had a storm during the night. A dragon got loose and went on a rampage, tearing up the fields and knocking over fences. Bones everywhere. We chased him over the fields to the river, where he escaped because the bridge was guarded by a monster that had to be defeated in a game of chess. None of us was good enough, so the dragon got away. Next time we should take along a better chess player. Other than that, nothing happened in the Ukraine. We'll talk again soon. In the meantime, behave."

Arkady folded the phone and discovered Roman and Maria regarding him with astonishment. Eva seemed unamused.

Nevertheless, they carried scythes into

the field behind the cow barn to cut grass and barley bent by the rain. The scythes were long two-handled affairs with blades so sharp they whistled. Eva and Maria bundled cut grass into sheaves with binding twine, while Arkady and Roman waded ahead. Arkady had cut grass in the all-purpose Red Army, and he remembered that the rhythm of scything was like swimming; the smoother the motion, the longer the stroke. Straws flew and insects spiraled in a golden dust. It was the most mindless labor he had performed for years and he gave himself over to it completely. At the end of the field, he dropped the scythe and lay down in high grass, in the warm stalks and cool ground, and stared numbly at the sky slightly spinning above.

How could they do it? he wondered. Work this field so happily when a short walk up the path, four grandchildren lay in unmarked graves. He imagined each funeral and the rage. Could he have stood it? Yet Roman and Maria and the other women seemed to approach every task as God's allotment. Work is holy, he remembered one of Tolstoy's heroes saying.

A body dropped nearby, and though he couldn't see her, he heard Eva's breathing. It was so normal, Arkady thought. Although it wasn't in the least normal. Did he normally perform farm labor? Through closed eyes, he felt the dull pulsation of the sun. What a relief to think of nothing, to be a rock in the field and never move again. Even better, he thought: two rocks in the field.

Unseen behind the grass, Eva asked, "Why did you come here?"

"Yesterday Maria said you would be here."

"But why?"

"To see you."

"Now that you've seen me, why don't you go?"

"I want more."

"Of what?"

"You."

Directness was not a language he generally spoke, and he expected her to leap to her feet and walk away.

There was a stir, and Eva's hand grazed his.

She said, "Your friend Zhenya plays chess."

"Yes."

"And he's very good?"

"Apparently."

He heard a murmur of satisfaction in a guess confirmed.

"You didn't ask," Eva said.

"Ask what?"

"Whether the garden was radioactive. You're becoming a real citizen of the Zone."

"Is that good or bad?"

"I don't know."

"For you," he asked, "is it good or bad?"

She uncurled his fingers and laid her head on them. "Disaster. The worst."

Arkady's mobile phone rang as he coasted into town, and he turned onto the side street of beech trees to take the call. It was Victor phoning from the state library in Kiev. "Encyclopedia entry 'Felix Mikhailovich Gerasimov, 1925 to 2002, director of the Institute of Extremely High Temperatures, Moscow.' Blah, blah. National prizes for physics, esteemed this and that, theoretician, patents for fuck-all, different state councils on science, international atomic controls, 'nuclear prophylaxis,' whatever the hell that is, papers on waste management. An all-around guy. Why are you interested? He died two years ago."

Arkady leaned the motor bike on its stand. The sun danced through the trees, belying the fact that the street was dead and the houses empty. "Something someone said. Any connection to Chernobyl?"

Sounds of paper flipping. "Not much. A delegation six months after the accident. I bet every scientist in Russia was there by then."

"Anything personal?"

Eva had told Arkady that he and Alex Gerasimov had more in common than he knew. He had a suspicion of what, but he wanted to be sure. While he talked, he paced by houses, each in its individual state of decay. At one window stood a doll, at least the third or fourth he'd seen at windows in Chernobyl.

Victor said, "These are scientific books and journals, not fan magazines. Lyuba called last night. I told her about the lingerie shop here. She said to pick out anything I wanted. My choice."

"Look for Chelyabinsk."

"Okay, here's an article translated from the French about an explosion of nuclear waste in Chelyabinsk in '57. Which was a secret site, so we kept the lid on that. Gerasimov must have been a kid at the time, but he's mentioned as helping run the cleanup. I don't think they cleaned it up much. Okay, here's more nuclear pollution on Novaya Zemlya test grounds. Gerasimov again. For a theoretician, he did weird shit. A peace prize for military research. Very astute. This is how you climb the academic ladder. What is the Institute for Extremely High Temperatures, anyway? Could build warheads, could cure cancer."

Could dump radioactive water into the Moscow River when the pipes at the institute froze. Arkady remembered Timofeyev's confession.

"More recent stuff," Victor said. "Newspaper clippings. London *Times* portrait from ten years ago, 'Physics in a Russian family: Academician Felix Gerasimov and his son, Alexander.' Genius in the genes, blah, blah. Friendly debate between generations over safety of reactors. 'Found dead.' Sorry, I skipped to another piece. From *Izvestya*, 'Institute director found dead at home by his own hand.' A gun. In good health but declining spirits after the death of his wife six months earlier. Last one, an appreciation in *Pravda*. 'Career that touched the highs and lows of Soviet science.' Here's the wife again. 'Tragic death.' "

A family tradition of suicide, that was the connection between Alex and Arkady.

Eva had spotted the merry bond right away. "What is the date on the *Izvestya* piece?"

"May second. He was found on May Day."

Imagine, Arkady thought. One day Felix Gerasimov is the respected and honored director of a scientific institute well enough funded to have its own research reactor in the middle of Moscow, a reactor he's earned not only through his groundbreaking work in theoretical physics but also through his willingness to engage in the down-to-earth problems of nuclear this and that (test-site pollution and spontaneous explosions in the hinterland), all the signs of a politically shrewd careerist. And then the political system collapses. The Communist Party lies as gutted as Reactor Four. Bankrupt. The director and his faculty (including Ivanov and Timofeyev) have to walk around the institute in blankets and dump "hot water" on the sly. That did, indeed, seem like twists enough for one career.

"Arkady, are you there?"

"Yes. Call Petrovka —"

"In Moscow?"

"Yes. Call headquarters and see if there's any record of a suicide attempt by the son, Alexander."

"What makes you think there will be?"

"Because there will. Did you get anywhere with his off-time work in Moscow?"

"Sorry. I called, at Bobby's expense, every major hotel in Moscow. Nine have business centers offering interpreting, translation, PCs and fax. But none round the clock, and none employed an Alex Gerasimov. To put not too fine a point on it, a dead end. Lyuba says you're exploiting me."

"Yes, that's why you're in Kiev and I'm in Chernobyl. Any sight of Anton?"

"I have my notes right here." There was a rush of papers falling. "Shit! Fuck your mother! I have to call you back."

Victor really wasn't meant for the hushed confines of a library, Arkady decided. He looked at the doll in the window. Her face was bleached off, but the contours and a ponytail of golden filaments remained, and he glimpsed a shelf of more dolls, as if the house had been entrusted to a second, smaller family. The doorway lured him to the threshold. Close up, the doll's arms bore a gauze of spiderwebs that he untangled, and when his mobile phone rang, he almost saw her flinch.

Arkady answered, "Hello, Victor, go ahead."

A raspy voice asked, "Who is Victor?"

"A friend," Arkady said.

"I bet you don't have many. I hear you got someone shot at the cooling pond."

Arkady started again. "Hello, Karel."

It was Katamay, the missing militia officer. Dust motes eddied around the doll as if she were breathing.

"I want to talk to you about the Russian that you found. That's all, nothing else," Arkady said and waited. The gaps were so long it was almost like talking to Zhenya.

"I want you to leave my family alone."

"I will, but I have to talk to you."

"We're talking."

"In person. Just about the Russian, that's all I'm here for, and then I can go home."

"With your friend Wayne Gretzky?"

"Yes."

A seizure of coughing, followed by "When I heard that, I almost split my side."

"Then I won't bother your grandfather and sister anymore, and Dymtrus can have his gun back."

A long silence.

"Pripyat, the center of the main square, ten tonight. Alone."

"Agreed," Arkady said, but to a dial tone.

Victor rang the next instant. "Okay, Anton was at a couple of casinos by the river."

"Why is he spending so much time here?"

"I don't know. Galina wore this tight outfit."

"Spare me." Arkady was still trying to switch gears from the Katamay call.

"Hey, thank God for our little hygienist, or I'd never see Anton. He picks her up after work every day. Goes up to the office like a real gentleman. Took her to a Porsche showroom, churches and a graveyard."

"A graveyard?"

"Very prestigious. Poets, writers, composers all laid out. He put a pile of roses at a gravestone. I looked at it later. Sure enough, the stone said 'Obodovsky'. His mother died this year."

"I'm interested in where he was born. See if you find any record that he lived in Pripyat."

"Bobby is going to be very interested in this."

"Wonderful. Is Anton doing any business?"

"Not that I can see."

"Then why is he hanging around Kiev? What is he waiting for, going to cemeteries and showrooms?"

"I don't know, but you should see the Porsches."

Arkady rode down an avenue not of Porsches but of fire engines on one side and army trucks on the other. Few visitors came to the yard except dealers in auto parts. From row to row, the variety changed from cars to armored personnel carriers, from tanks to bulldozers, all too hot to bury but sinking in the mud. Arkady followed the single power line to the trailer office of Bela, the manager.

Bela had few visitors and he was eager to roll up yard maps and share with Arkady the living comforts engineered into his trailer: microwave, minibar, flat-screen TV and videotape collection. A pornographic tape was already playing, pneumatic sex with the sound down, like background music.

Bela picked a hair off his shoulder. In his dirty white suit he looked like a lily beginning to rot.

"I'm seriously thinking of retiring. The demands of this job are too much."

"What demands?"

"Demands. Customers can't just drive into the Zone to shop for auto parts. This is not a showroom. On the other hand, they want to see what they're buying. So I bring them."

"Bring them here?"

"In the back of my van. I have an understanding with the boys at the checkpoint. They have to eat, too. Everyone eats, that's the golden rule."

"And Captain Marchenko?"

"A mass of envy. However, the Zone administrators in their wisdom have given me control of the yard with no interference from the captain because they understand how unreliable the militia is. I am up before dawn every day to make sure things run smoothly. I am, if nothing else, reliable. Hence, this multitude of vehicles outside is all mine."

Now that Arkady thought about it, there was something Napoleonic in the pride Bela took in his army of radioactive vehicles, in his splendid isolation.

"And with every car a free dosimeter?"

"Don't even joke about such things. You should enjoy life's more beautiful things." The manager held up a box that said *Moscow Escort Girls.* "I can show you Russian porn, Japanese, American. Dubbed, undubbed, not that it makes a great deal of difference. You're a sports enthusiast? Hockey? Football?" Another shelf of tapes.

"Classic films, cartoons, natural history. Whatever tickles your fancy. I'll open a tin of biscuits, pour some liqueur and we'll relax." The manager made it sound like the end of a day on a tropical island.

"Actually, I brought one." Arkady handed over Vanko's tape.

"No label. Some amateur action? A little hanky-panky? Bathroom camera?"

"I somehow doubt it."

"But it could be?"

Bela eagerly switched tapes. As he watched Vanko's tape, the yard manager's face expressed first surprise and then disappointment, as if sugar he had shoved into his mouth proved to be salt.

14

The steppe was soft. The steppe was a vast plain that shone with ponds and corkscrew rivers and evoked a wistful sadness. The poetry was stentorian, to rouse a patriotic fervor, but the bread was as plump as pillows, and bread always won over poetry. Ukrainian beauty was the child of history: the luminous doe eyes and fair skin of the Slav set on Tartar cheeks. At least that was the ordinary beauty. Galina was probably like that, Arkady thought.

Eva was not soft. Her pale skin and black hair — black as a cormorant's, liquid to the hand — set a theme of contradiction. Her eyes were dark mirrors. Her body looked slight but was strong as a bow, and Arkady thought she would have made an excellent imp in hell, goading slow and doughy sinners with a pitchfork. She should have come from a landscape of flames and spewing lava. Then he remembered that, in part, she did.

They had kicked the sheet off the bed and lay, skin on skin, enjoying the cool evaporation of the sweat they had produced. Dusk hung outside the window.

She asked, "Why do you have to go?"

"I have to meet a missing man."

"That sounds like a children's rhyme, but it's not, is it? You're still investigating."

"From time to time. I'll be back in a few hours."

"That's up to you." She turned her face to him. Her eyes were too dark to distinguish an iris and they seemed huge. "If you do return, you should know the risks."

"Such as?"

She moved his hand with hers to the scar on her neck. "Cancer of the thyroid, but you knew that." To her breast. "Chornobyl heart, literally a hole in the heart." She played his fingers along her ribs. "Leukemia in the bone marrow." Below the ribs. "Cancer of the pancreas and liver." Across a ruff of pubic hair. "Cancer of the reproductive organs, not to mention tumors, mutations, missing limbs, anemia, rigidity. Not that any of this necessarily matters. Alex says, in the future our main concern will be predators."

"What kinds?"

"All kinds."

"People aren't like that."

"You don't know. When people in Kiev

learned about the accident they didn't act with great nobility. Trains were mobbed. Iodine tablets were hoarded. Everyone was drunk and everyone fucked everyone. There were no morals. If you want to know how people will react at the end of the world, this was it. Later, the populations of Pripyat and Chornobyl were farmed out across the country, which didn't want them. Who would want someone radioactive in his home, then or now? They got very good at spotting us, at asking our age and where we were from. I don't blame them a bit. Now do you want me?"

"Yes."

She sighed and stroked his cheek. "Well, you may come back or not, but you've been warned."

In Pripyat light slowed to a drifting mist. Arkady had arrived on his motorbike on time at ten, and another twenty minutes passed while he heard the occasional whir or glimpsed a moving shadow that meant the Woropay brothers were making sure he had come alone.

The square was fronted by the city hall, hotel, restaurant, school, all shells. The moon made figures out of streetlamps, turned the amusement park Ferris wheel into a huge antenna. Other civilizations, when they vanished, at least left awesome monuments. The buildings of Pripyat were, one after the other, prefabricated ruins.

Dymtrus Woropay popped up like a large sprite at Arkady's side and said, "Leave the bike. Follow me."

Easier said than done. The Woropays wore night-vision goggles and glided on inline skates, clicking over cement and sweeping through the grass. On foot they might be clumsy, but on wheels they swung in graceful arcs. Arkady walked briskly while the brothers circled in and out of shadows to shepherd him along an arcade to a footpath through what had once been a tended garden and now was a maze of branches. Nothing stopped the Woropays; they splashed through standing water and shouldered aside brush to a two-story building with stone columns that supported a mural of organ pipes and atoms: Pripyat's cultural theater. Taras, the younger brother, punched the doors open and whooped as he rolled into a lobby. Dymtrus elbowed his way in and thrust his arms over his head as if he'd scored a goal.

By the time Arkady entered, the Woropays were gone. He heard them, but in the dark it was difficult to see which way they had gone, and the path was obstructed by stage flats stacked in the lobby. What dramas had been left behind, to rest cheek to cheek for eternity? "Uncle Vanya, meet Anna Karenina." Of course, there would have been children's productions, too. "Mouse King, meet Raskolnikov."

A crashing of piano keys came from deep inside the theater, and Arkady pushed through the flats and the clatter of cloakroom racks into a passageway of near-total darkness. He used his cigarette lighter to see along a wall defaced with curses, threats and crude anatomy. He had been in the theater before, but in the daytime. The dark gave no warning of the broken glass that slid underfoot or of the ripped wires that dangled in the face.

Finally Arkady groped his way to a drawn curtain and ropes and the light of a kerosene lamp. A piano with broken and missing keys was onstage, and Taras Woropay played as he sang, " 'You can't always get what you want, but you get what you need!' " while Dymtrus, night goggles flipped up, skated and danced wildly from one side of the stage to the other.

The audience seats were tiers of red benches strewn with broken chairs and tables, bottles and mattresses, like furniture thrown down the steps of a house, while Dymtrus's shadow stamped around the walls. A couch had been dragged to the other side of the piano, where Karel Katamay lay propped by pillows and covered with shawls. Arkady barely recognized the virtual skinhead he had seen in photographs at the grandfather's house. This Karel Katamay wore his hair long and beaded around a chalky face with pink eyes. A hockey shirt — the Detroit Red Wings — swam over him. Small, thoughtful pansies sat in jars of water around the couch, and a liter of Evian was tucked between his legs. Arkady didn't know what he had expected, but not this. He'd read descriptions of the court of Queen Elizabeth. That was what Karel Katamay looked like, a powdered Virgin Queen with two oafish courtiers. A satin pillow cushioned his head; a corner of the pillow was embroidered *"Je ne regrette rien."* "I regret nothing." When Karel smiled, tickled by the sight of Dymtrus whirling like a dervish, he showed pulpy gums.

" 'Get what you need! need! need!' "

Taras collapsed over the keys while his big brother weaved dizzily on the stage, and

Katamay made more a gesture of clapping than actually bringing his hands together.

Dymtrus steadied himself and pointed in Arkady's direction. "Brought him."

"A chair." Katamay's voice was not much more than a whisper, but Dymtrus immediately jumped off the stage to bring a chair from the benches and set it in front of the couch so that Arkady and Karel Katamay would be at the same eye level. Close up, Katamay looked crayoned by a child.

Arkady said, "You don't look well."

"I'm fucked."

Katamay's nose sprang a leak. He pressed a towel against the blood in an off-hand, nearly elegant way. The towel, to judge by its blotches of brown, had been used before.

"Summer cold," Katamay said. "So you wanted to know about the dead Russian I found?"

"Yes."

"There's not much to say. Some old fart I found in a village."

The hoarseness of Katamay's voice brought the volume down to a level of intimacy, as if they were theatrical types discussing a production to be presented on this very stage. Katamay said he had never seen the Russian before, and couldn't know the dead man was Russian, since his papers were missing. He was found in the morning lying on his back, his head at the cemetery gate, bloody but not too bloody, stiff from full rigor mortis, disorganized because of wolves. Katamay found the body coincidentally with a squatter he had seen before, a guy called Seva, about forty years old, missing a little finger on his left hand. Arkady took notes in case the Woropays wanted to stomp on anything afterward. Notes were a good target. But around Katamay, they were like dogs under voice command, and he had obviously told them to be still.

"Just a few questions. How was the dead man dressed?"

"He was rich. Expensive gear."

"Nice shoes?"

"Beautiful shoes."

"Well cared for?"

"Beautifully."

"Not muddy?"

"No."

"His shirt was damp. Was it clean or dirty?"

"A few leaves, I think."

"So he had been turned over?"

"What do you mean?"

"A man who drops dead to the ground doesn't roll around much."

"Maybe he wasn't dead yet."

"More likely someone turned him over to relieve him of his money and threw away the ID later. Did you find anything else on the body? Directions, matches, keys?"

"Nothing."

"No car keys? He left them in the car?"

"I don't know."

"You didn't notice that his throat had been cut?"

"It was under his collar, and there wasn't that much blood. Anyway, wolves had been messing with him."

"Moved him? Torn him up?"

"Didn't move him. Yanked on his nose and face a bit, enough to get an eye."

Lovely picture, Arkady thought. "Do wolves go for eyes?"

"They'll eat anything."

"You saw their tracks?"

"Huge."

"Did you see a car or any tire tracks?"

"No."

"Where were the people in the village, the Panasenkos and their neighbors?"

"I don't know."

"People in black villages don't get a

great deal of entertainment. They're pretty nosy about visitors."

"I don't know."

"Why were you there that day?"

Dymtrus said, "That's enough. He's got a million questions."

"It's all right, Dyma," Katamay said. "On the captain's orders, we were taking a count of villagers in the Zone, and items of value."

"Like icons?"

"Yes."

"Would you like to stop for a minute and drink something?"

"Yes." Katamay sipped French water and laughed into his handkerchief. In case he spits up blood, Arkady thought. "I still can't get over Wayne Gretzky. Tell the truth, do you know Gretzky?"

"No," Arkady whispered, "no more than you know a squatter named Seva missing a little finger."

"How could you tell?"

"The bizarre detail. Keep lies simple."

"Yeah?"

"It's always worked for me. Give me your hands."

The Woropays shifted anxiously, but Katamay put out his hands, palms up. Arkady turned them over to look at purpled fingernails. He motioned Katamay to lean forward, and held up the lantern to observe tendrils of bleeding capillaries in the whites of Katamay's eyes.

"So tell me the truth," said Katamay. "Am I fucked or am I fucked?"

"Cesium?"

"Fucked as they come."

"Is there a treatment?"

"You can take Prussian blue; it picks up cesium as it passes through the body. But it has to be administered early. It wasn't. There's no point going to the hospital now."

"What happened? How did you get exposed?"

"Ah, that's a different story."

"Maybe not. Three men suffered from cesium poisoning: your Russian, his business partner and you. You don't think they're related?"

"I don't know. It depends how you look at it. History moves in funny ways, right? We've gone through evolution, now we're going through de-evolution. Everything is breaking down. No borders, no boundaries. No limits, no treaties. Suicide bombers, kids with guns. AIDS, Ebola, mad cow. It's all breaking down, and I'm breaking down with it. I'm bleeding internally. No platelets. No stomach lining. Infected. The reason I agreed to see you was to say that my family had nothing to do with this. Dymtrus and Taras had nothing to do with any of this, either." Katamay stopped for a spasm of wet coughs. The Woropays were solicitous as nurses, wiping blood from his lips. He raised his head and smiled. "Much better than a hospital. I had my theater debut here in *Peter and the Wolf*. I played the wolf. I thought I was a wolf until I met a real one."

"Who is that?"

"You'll know when you know. Anyway, we stray. Just the Russian I found, we agreed."

"His car. You towed it. Was there anything inside? Papers, maps, directions?"

"No."

Arkady reviewed his notes. "His watch, you said it was a Rolex?"

"Yes. Oh, that was sneaky. You caught me." Katamay held up an arm to show a gold Rolex like a bauble.

Dymtrus punched Arkady in the back of the head. He obviously did not appreciate lèse-majesté.

Katamay said, "No, no, fair is fair. He caught me. It doesn't matter, anyway."

"It doesn't, does it?" Arkady said.

"Give Dymtrus back his gun. He's embarrassed."

"Sure."

Arkady returned the pistol to Dymtrus, who muttered, "Gretzky."

"Okay, there was a checkpoint pass and directions," Katamay said.

"To where, exactly?"

"The cemetery."

"Where are the directions now?"

"I don't know."

"Typewritten?"

"Hardly." Katamay was amused.

"But the pass was signed by Captain Marchenko?"

"Maybe."

"It's just a form that could be snatched off a desk?"

"Pretty much."

"You saw the pass and directions when you found the body or when you towed the car?"

"When we found the body."

"You said you found the body while you were canvassing houses about theft. The cemetery gate is fifty meters from the nearest occupied house. Why were you at the gate?"

"I don't remember."

"That was cute, towing the car and

hiding it at Bela's yard."

"Right under Bela's nose and where Marchenko couldn't go. I hear Bela walks the whole yard every day now." Karel's laugh turned into a cough; every word seemed to cost him.

"You disappeared at the same time. Were you sick then?"

"A little."

"But you still wanted money from a stolen car?"

"I thought I could leave something . . . to someone."

"Who?" Arkady asked, but Katamay stopped for breath. "Leave me something. Who was the 'squatter' who led you to the gate?"

"Hulak," Katamay got out.

"Boris Hulak? The body pulled out of the cooling pond?"

"That's the only reason I'm telling you." Karel sank out of sight against the cushions with a laugh no more than a sigh. "There's nothing you can do about it anyway."

As Arkady rode by the sarcophagus, he felt the monster shift within its steel plates and razor wire. But the monster wasn't only there. It was riding a Ferris wheel here, swirling though a bloodstream there, seeping into the river, rooting in a million bones. What leitmotif for this kind of beast? An ominous cello. One note. Sustained. For fifty thousand years.

The closer Arkady got to the turnoff to Eva's cabin, the more each passing radiation marker sounded like the stroke of an ax. He didn't have to go back. She wouldn't answer any questions. She was a complication. The truth was that, after such close contact with Karel Katamay, part of Arkady craved nothing more than a chance to burn his own clothes, to scrub himself with a stiff brush and ride as far away as he could.

By itself, the motorbike seemed to turn her way. He rode over the rattle of the bridge and along nodding catkins to the house among the birches, where he found her sitting in bed in her bathrobe, smoking, cradling a glass and an ashtray between her legs. She looked as if she had stared a hole through the door since he'd left.

Arkady asked, "Are we drinking?"

"We're drinking."

There was a sharpness in the air that said it wasn't water.

"Do you think we drink too much?"

"It depends on the circumstances. I used to go over patient files in the evening, but since you arrived, I have been trying to understand who you are. When I get the answer, I may not want to be sober."

"Ask me." He tried to take the bottle, but she held on.

"No, no, you're the Question Man. Alex says most people get over asking why by the age of ten, only you never did."

"Was Alex here?"

"See? The problem is, I hate questions and poking into other people's lives. I don't see much of a future for us."

He pulled a chair up to the bed and sat. Being with her was like watching a bird beat against a pane of glass. Anything he did could be disastrous. "Well, I had a question."

"No questions."

"What's your opinion of Noah?" Arkady asked.

"From the Bible?"

"The Bible, the Flood, the ark."

"You are a strange man." He felt her tease around the question, searching for his angle. Eva said, "My opinion of Noah is low, my opinion of God is lower. Why on earth do you ask?"

"I was wondering 'Why Noah?' Was he a

carpenter or a sailor?"

"A carpenter. All he had to do was float, and muck the stupid animals. It wasn't as if he was going anywhere."

"How do you know?"

"God would have given him directions."

"You're right." If Timofeyev had driven from Moscow to the Ukraine, to a small village he had never seen before, he would have needed directions. "Do you think the ark could have settled here?"

"Why not? It's a nice place," Eva said. "Full of murdered Poles, Jews, Reds and Whites, not to mention the victims starved to death by Stalin or hung by the Germans, but still nice. The best milk, best apples, best pears. We used to spend the summer on the river, in boats or on the beach. We fished. The Pripyat was famous for pike in those days. I would lie down on a towel on the beach and watch fluffy clouds and dream of dancing and traveling to foreign countries where I would meet a famous pianist, a passionate genius, and marry him and have six or seven children. We would live in London, but we would always spend our summers here. I'll let you guess: what part of that have I not accomplished?"

"Is this a trick question?"

"Definitely not. A trick question is, how

long will you be here? When will you suddenly disappear? People do that. They're here for a week or two, and poof, they're gone, taking with them their fascinating tales of living with the exotic natives of the Zone."

"Let's dance." Arkady took the glass.

"Are you a good dancer?"

"Awful, but I remember you dancing with Alex."

"You were dancing with Vanko, after all."

"It wasn't the same thing."

"Slow?"

"Please."

"I didn't think you were coming back."

"But I did."

She slipped out of bed over to a cassette player. "A waltz at midnight. This is romantic. You're surprising. You can cut wheat like a farmer, you can dance."

"I surprise myself."

"A midnight waltz in Chornobyl, that's kicking death in the teeth."

"Exactly."

He took her in his arms and executed a practice dip. She was incredibly light for being so much trouble.

Arkady's mobile phone rang.

"Ignore it," Eva said.

"I'll just see who it is."

He assumed the caller was Victor or Olga Andreevna, but it was Zurin the prosecutor, calling from Moscow.

"Good news, Renko. Sorry to ring you in the middle of the night. We're bringing you home."

It took Arkady a moment to absorb the news. "What are you talking about?"

"You're coming back to Moscow. We've booked you on the six a.m. Aeroflot. There'll be a ticket waiting for you at the airport counter. How do you feel about that?"

"I'm not done."

"It's not a failure, not a bit. You've been working hard, I'm sure. However, we've decided to wrap up things at Chernobyl, at least on the Russian side. I thought you'd be delighted."

Arkady turned with the phone away from Eva. "There is no Ukrainian side to this investigation."

"So be it. This matter should have been shouldered by the Ukrainians from the start. They can't always depend on us to wipe up their spilled milk."

"The victim was Russian."

"Killed in the Ukraine. If he'd been killed in France or Germany, would we have investigated? Of course not. Why should the Ukraine be any different?"

"Because it is."

"They wanted to be independent, now they are. There's also a manpower issue. I can't have a senior investigator staying indefinitely in Chernobyl. At a risk to his health, let me add."

"I need more time," Arkady said.

"Which will become more time and more time. No, it's been decided. Get to the airport, catch the early flight and I'll expect to see you in my office by noon tomorrow."

"What about Timofeyev?"

"Unfortunately, he died at the wrong place."

"And Ivanov?"

"Wrong way. We're not reopening a suicide."

"I'm not finished."

"One last thing. Before you come into the office, take a shower and burn your clothes," Zurin said and hung up.

Eva refilled two glasses like a good barmaid. "Marching orders? And where are you going from here? You must be going someplace."

"I don't know."

"Don't look so sad. You can't be stuck

here forever. Someone must be getting killed in Moscow."

"I'm sure."

"How long can you sleep with a radioactive woman? I'd say the odds against that are not very good."

"You're not radioactive."

"Don't quibble with me, I'm the doctor. I simply need to understand the situation. The prognosis. It sounds as if you're leaving soon."

"That's not up to me."

"Oh, it isn't? I had taken you for a different kind of man."

"What kind?"

"Imaginary." Eva delivered a smile. "I'm sorry, that's unfair. You were enjoying yourself so much, and I was enjoying you. 'Never pop a bubble' is a good rule. But you should be happy to go. Out of exile, back among the living."

"That's what I'm told." He felt his mind race in ten directions.

"Secretly, aren't you a wee bit happy, a little relieved to have the decision taken out of your hands? I'm happy for you, if that helps."

"It doesn't."

"Just as well, because I don't think we really made the ideal couple. You obviously hate histrionics, and I am completely histrionic. Not to mention damaged goods. When, exactly, are you going?"

"I have to go now."

"Oh." Her smile began to sink. "That was fast. Hardly more than a one-night stand." She drank half her glass in a swallow and set it down. "Not samogon. We will always have our samogon party. Well, they say short farewells are the best."

"I will be back in a day. Two at the most."

"Don't even —" She pulled her robe tight and picked up the gun when he approached. Shining streaks ran down her face. "The Zone is an exclusive club, a very exclusive club, and you have just been voted out. So get out."

15

Arkady found Bobby Hoffman sitting with a lantern in a backyard that was wild with roses and thorny canes that reached into the dark. Someone had once put beehives in the garden, and a colony still thrived; a dozen had been lured out by Bobby's light, in spite of the hour. Bobby let a bee crawl over the back of one hand to another and around his fingers like a coin trick. Other bees wandered on his hat.

"My father kept hives on Long Island. It was his hobby. Sometimes he wore a beekeeper's mask, but usually not. In cold winters he'd drive the hives down to Florida. I loved that drive. Cold cigar in the corner of his mouth. He never lit up around the bees. The neighbors would complain, 'Mr. Hoffman, what if they sting?' My father would say, 'You like flowers, you like apples, you like peaches? Then you put up with the fucking bees.' One year, just to make his point, he sent me around the neighborhood to collect money from people, depending on how many flowers and fruit trees they had, like we should get a cut. I made some change, too. When I was thirteen, I was bar-mitzvahed, and he took me to the Copa. A club. Everyone knew him: big guy, big voice. He had one of the chorus girls sit on my lap, and he gave her a pin in the shape of a bee with diamond eyes. He did everything to the hilt. If he liked you, you were in. If he didn't, forget it. One of our drives down south, a couple of crackers saw our license plate and asked if I was a New York Jewboy. He beat them half to death. Motel manager had to pull him off. That was loyalty. The first time I met Pasha, I said, 'Jesus, it's the old man.' "

"We've got to go," Arkady said.

"The old man was tight with the Irish. They thought he was Irish because he could drink and sing and fight. Women? They were like bees. My mother would say, 'So you've been with your shiksa ho'ahs?' She was very religious. The funny thing is, he was just as strict about me going to a yeshiva. He'd say, 'Bobby, what makes the Jews special is that we don't just worship God, we have a contract with Him in writing. It's the Torah. Figure out the fine print in that, and you can figure out the fine print in anything.' "

"Tell him again," Yakov said. He was watching the street.

Arkady said, "I got a call from Prosecutor Zurin ordering me back to Moscow. He was happy to keep me here on ice forever, so there's only one reason I can think of for him to pull me out in such a rush: Colonel Ozhogin is on his way."

"Remember the nice police?" said Yakov.

"Captain Marchenko at the café?" Arkady reminded Bobby. "The one who wanted your business? I think that little lightbulb in his head went on. I think he called Ozhogin, and to judge by the urgency in Zurin's voice, Ozhogin is commandeering a company jet to come and get you. Not to arrest you; they would have kept me here for that."

"He wants to give Bobby a beating?" Yakov asked. "We could let him have Bobby for ten minutes. A little pain . . ."

Bobby laughed gently, so as not to disturb the bees browsing on his hat. "He's not flying in from Moscow just for ten minutes of 'Pound the Jew.' "

Arkady said, "It won't just be punishment — there's also the threat to NoviRus as long as you're around."

Bobby shrugged, and it struck Arkady that, day by day, Bobby had been getting more inert.

"This is just guesswork on your part," Bobby said. "You have no proof that the colonel is coming."

"Do you want to wait and find out? If I'm wrong, you leave the Zone a day early. If I'm right and you stay, you won't last the day."

Bobby shrugged.

Arkady asked, "What happened to the old elusive Bobby Hoffman?"

"He got tired."

Yakov asked, "What happened to your father?"

"Prison killed him. The feds tossed him in just to make him name his associates. He was a stand-up individual, and he named no one, so they kept handing him more years. Six years in, he got diabetes and bad circulation. But decent medical treatment? Not a chance. They started whittling him down, one leg and then the other. They took a big man like my father and turned him into a dwarf. His last words to me were 'Don't ever let them put you inside, or I will come back from the grave to beat the living shit out of you.' When I think of him, I remember how he was before they put him inside, and whenever I see a bee, I know what the old man would be thinking: Where's this little guy going? To an apple blossom? A pear tree? Or is he just buzzing around in the sun?"

"But not just waiting to be stepped on," Arkady said.

Bobby blinked. "Touché."

"Time to go, Bobby."

"In more ways than one?" A wan smile, but awake.

"The dormitory. It's a short walk and it's dark."

"We're not taking the car?"

"No. I don't think your car can get through a checkpoint now."

"Why are you doing this? What's in this for you?"

"A little help."

"A quid pro quo. Something for you, too."

"That's right. There's something I want you to see."

Bobby nodded. He gently blew the bee off his fingers, got to his feet and shook the bees from his jacket, removed his hat and, with soft puffs, blew the bees off the brim.

Arkady led Bobby and Yakov to the room next to his, heard the vague tumult of a cheering stadium and knocked.

When no one answered Arkady used the phone card Victor had given him and popped the latch. Professor Campbell sat in a chair, his eyes shut and his head tucked into his chest, as stiff as a mummy, an empty bottle at his feet. Empties on the desk reflected the dim light of the television, where a soccer match surged back and forth, and the home crowd swayed and sang its fight song.

Arkady listened to Campbell's breath, which was deep and smelled nearly combustible.

"Dead or drunk?" Bobby asked.

"He looks fine," Yakov said.

Bobby settled into a chair next to Campbell to watch the game. It was a tape of two British teams playing a trench-warfare style of soccer devoid of Latin frills. Arkady doubted very much that Bobby Hoffman was a soccer fan; it was more as if he knew what was coming. Arkady ejected the game.

"Got any baseball?" Bobby asked.

"I have this." Arkady fed Vanko's tape into the player and pushed Play.

Chernobyl, day, exterior: the crossroad of the café, commissary and dormitory established in a handheld shot. For atmosphere, a monument to firefighters, a statue of Lenin pushing out his chest, trees dressed in the bright green of early spring.

A telephoto shot of an approaching bus that sinuously dipped up and down and spread into a long line of buses as they neared. Jump to buses parked in the dormitory lot and hundreds of bearded men, at first sight identical in black suits and hats, disembarking and milling around. At second sight all ages, including boys with side curls. And a separate bus of women wearing head scarves. A pair of militia with the sullen expression of the dispossessed. A close-up of Captain Marchenko shaking hands and welcoming a man whose expression was hidden in his beard.

"This was taped last year by Vanko," Arkady said.

A disorganized march — carrying a murmur in Hebrew and English — filled the road and spilled over onto the sidewalk, trying not to get too far ahead of patriarchs with beards that spread like unraveling silk. They had come from New York and Israel, Yakov said, that was where Chernobyl's Jews were now. A brief rinse cycle as Vanko ran ahead with his camera on. Cut to the bunker of the rabbi's tomb. Rabbi Nahum of Chernobyl, Yakov said. A great man, the sort who saw God everywhere. The visitors watched an elder arthritically remove his shoes, then enter. Yakov said that one grave in the tomb was for Rabbi Nahum, the other for his grandson, also a rabbi. Arkady remembered how tight the space was in the tomb, yet it appeared to swallow man after man, each shoeless and with an expression of walking on air. A pan of the ecstatic crowd, and there he was on the fringe, Bobby Hoffman in his suit and hat, but no beard to obscure his expression of agony.

Arkady asked himself whether any rabbi, dead or alive, could meet the expectations of the people waiting their turn to enter. Many carried letters, and he knew what they asked: health for the ill, ease for the dying, safety from the suicide bomber. Arkady set the tape on slow motion to catch Bobby, about to take his turn, dropping out of line. For everyone else, there was a curious relaxation, as if they were all playing on grandfather's lap. Men sang and danced, hands on the shoulders of the man in front, and snaked back and forth across the street. Bobby stayed apart and moved only to shun the camera. When people unwrapped sandwiches and ate, Bobby disappeared. Vanko cut to more dancing, continuous visits to the tomb, then finally a prayer said by a long line of men facing the river.

As Yakov sang along, his croak of a voice became sonorous: *"Y'hay sh'may raho m'vorah, l'olam ulolmay olmayo.*" He translated: "Blessed and praised, glorified and exalted, extolled and honored, adored and lauded be the name of the Holy One, blessed be he." He added, "Kaddish, the prayer for the dead."

The camera glimpsed Bobby with his lips sealed. Then the buses reloaded and formed their convoy and started the drive back to Kiev. In the room, Bobby's head dropped into his hands.

"Why did you come last year, Bobby?" Arkady asked. "You didn't visit the grave or sing or dance or pray. You told me that you came to look into processing reactor fuel, and you certainly didn't do that. You arrived on the bus, and you left on the bus, but you didn't do anything, so why were you here?"

Bobby looked up, his eyes hot and wet. "Pasha asked me."

"To visit the tomb?" Arkady said.

"No. All he wanted was that I prayed, that I said the Kaddish. I told him I didn't do that stuff. Pasha said, 'Go, you'll do it.' He insisted so much I couldn't say no. But I got here and it didn't matter. I couldn't."

"Why not?"

"I didn't pray for my father. He died in prison, but he wanted a Kaddish, from me especially, only I was already on the run over some stock swap. Unimportant. The thing is, I blew it. And what the hell kind of deal did God give my father, anyway? Half his life in jail, a disease that took half his body, my mother for a wife and me for a son. So I signed off on all this stuff. I just don't do it."

"What did you tell Pasha when you got back to Moscow?"

"I lied. The only favor he ever asked of me, and I let him down. And he knew it."

"Why did he choose you?"

"Who else would he? I was his guy. Besides, I told him once I was a yeshiva kid. Me, Bobby Hoffman. Can you believe it?"

Before Bobby went completely down the emotional drain, Arkady wanted to get the facts straight. "The men facing the river were saying Kaddish for Jews killed in the pogrom eighty years ago?" A listless nod. "And that's what Pasha Ivanov sent you from Moscow to join?"

"It had to be Chernobyl."

"To say a prayer for victims of the pogrom here." That, at least, seemed understood.

Bobby had to laugh. "You don't get it. Pasha wanted a Kaddish for Chernobyl, for victims of the accident."

"Why?"

"He wouldn't say. I asked. And after I went back to Moscow, he never mentioned it again. Months went by, and apparently no harm done, and then Pasha dives out a window and Timofeyev comes here to get his throat cut."

Well, there had been a few signs of trouble brewing, Arkady thought. Isolation, paranoia, nosebleeds.

Bobby said, "Somehow I can't help but believe that if I had only prayed when Pasha asked, he and Timofeyev would be alive today."

"Was someone watching you?" Arkady asked.

"Who would watch?"

"The camera watched."

"Do you think it would have made any difference?" Bobby asked.

"I don't know."

Out of mercy, Arkady switched tapes and stepped into the hall with Yakov.

"Clever," Yakov said. The eye under the crushed brow shone in the light of the moon.

"Not really. I think Bobby has been trying to tell us this since he arrived. That's probably why he came."

"Now that he has, do you have a way to take us out?"

"I have an individual in mind."

"Trustworthy?"

Arkady weighed Bela's character. "Reliable but greedy. How much money do you have?"

"Whatever he wants, if we get to Kiev. On us now, maybe two hundred fifty dollars."

"Not much."

"It's what we have left."

Not enough, Arkady thought. "That will have to do, then. Keep Bobby as quiet as possible and take off his shoes. And keep the television on; as long as the housekeeper thinks the Englishman's here, she won't go in."

"You know Ozhogin?"

"A little. He'll watch your car and the house first. Then he'll strike into the field. He's more a spy than military; he likes to operate alone. He might bring two or three men. All he'll want from Marchenko is to keep the checkpoints closed. When you leave, I'll follow you out."

"No, I operate alone, too."

"You don't know Colonel Ozhogin."

"I've known a hundred Ozhogins." Yakov took a deep breath. Outside, the taller trees were starting to separate from the night. The first birdsong rang out.

"Such a day. Rabbi Nahum said no man was beyond redemption. He said redemption was established before the creation of the world itself, that's how important redemption is. No one can take it away."

Arkady went into his own room and packed, if for no other reason than to give the impression that he was leaving and following orders. His life — case notes and clothing — fit into a small suitcase and duffel bag with room to spare. There were flights all day to Moscow. He had options. He could change from camos, bungee-cord the suitcase and bag to the rear fender of the motorcycle and look like any other office worker making an early commute to the city. If he raced, he might still catch a plane and get to the prosecutor's office by noon. Where would Zurin assign him next? Was there a position for a senior investigator out on the permafrost? The people of the Arctic Circle were said to be full of life. He was ready for a laugh.

He noticed, at the top of his file, the employment application for NoviRus. He was surprised to find he still had it. He scanned the opportunities. Banking? Brokerage? Security or combat skills? It did nothing for his confidence to realize he had not one marketable talent. Certainly not communication skills. He wished he could start the night over again, beginning with Zurin's call, and clarify to Eva what he was doing. Not going, only helping a criminal flee the Zone. Was that better?

Bela was already up, having a daybreak coffee in front of CNN, when Arkady arrived.

"I always like to hear the weather in Thailand. I picture listening to the soft rain as Thai girls walk up and down my back, kneading it with their little toes."

"Not Russian girls in boots?"

"A different picture altogether. Not necessarily a bad one. I judge no one. In fact, I always liked those Soviet statues of women with powerful biceps and tiny tits."

"You've been here too long, Bela."

"I take time off. I see the doctor. I walk around the whole yard every day. That's a 10K walk."

"Let's walk," Arkady said.

The scale of the yard was best appreciated on foot. As it broke the horizon the sun turned shadowy canyons into the neat ranks of a necropolis. The endless rows of poisoned vehicles evoked the hundreds of thousands of soldiers who had dug, bulldozed and loaded radioactive debris. The trucks were here. Where were the men? Arkady wondered. No one had kept track.

"Two passengers," Arkady said. "You take them out like your usual customers."

"But they're not regular customers. Things out of the ordinary make me nervous."

"Selling radioactive auto parts is ordinary?"

"*Mildly* radioactive."

"Get out while you're ahead."

"I could. I should be reaping the benefits of my labor, not living in a graveyard. The situation with Captain Marchenko has become intolerable, the bastard's always trying to get me dismissed."

"Does he ever stop your van?"

"He wouldn't dare. I have more friends upstairs than he does, because I'm generous and spread the money around. When you think about it, I have a good thing going here. I'm the only one in the Zone with a good thing going. I'm sitting pretty."

"You're sitting in the middle of a radioactive dump."

Bela shrugged. "Why should I jeopardize that for two men I don't know?"

"For five hundred dollars that you don't have to spread around."

"Five hundred? If you called a taxi from Kiev, he'd charge you for both ways, two people, luggage. A hundred dollars, easy. And then he couldn't get past the checkpoint."

"What are you moving today?"

"An engine block. I got a van specially outfitted, with jump seats for the customers."

"Then they'll just be two customers riding along, as usual."

"But I sense desperation. Desperation means risk, and risk means money. A thousand each."

"Five hundred for both. You're going anyway. The real question is why you would come back."

Bela spread his arms. His chains and medals jingled. "Look around. I've got thousands of auto parts to sell."

"Because you're losing your hair. Look in a mirror."

Bela touched his hairline. "What a joker. You had me for a second."

Arkady shrugged. "And the virility is normal?"

"Yes!"

"Five hundred for transportation for two to Kiev, for a service that you usually provide for free. Half to start and half on arrival, to start immediately."

"Immediately? We're pulling the engine

now, but it's not ready." Bela glanced in the wing mirror of a car.

"Any dryness of the mouth?"

"It's the dust, the wind always kicking it up."

"You'd know better than I. It's just that everyone rotates time here except you. I don't want to see you holding on to a sack of money with one hand and an IV tube with the other."

"Don't lecture me. I was here for years before you showed up, my friend." Bela slapped dust off his sleeves.

"My point exactly."

"Change of subject!"

They turned the corner onto an avenue of heavy trucks. Halfway down the row was a shower of sparks.

"Fifteen hundred." Bela touched his hair again.

"I hate haggling," Arkady said. "Why don't we do this? Clean your hairbrush and brush your hair. We'll start at five thousand. No, we'll start at ten thousand, and for every new hair in the brush, we deduct a thousand."

"I wouldn't have any money left."

"And we haven't mentioned yet that you're illegally selling state goods."

"They're radioactive."

"Bela, that's not a mitigating factor."

"What do you care? They're Ukrainian goods. You're Russian."

"I'll shut you down."

"I trusted you."

"Nothing personal."

"Five hundred."

"Done."

To prevent the removal of the hotter engines, the hoods of some trucks had been welded shut. Bela's welder, in a mask and greasy coveralls, was cutting one open with an acetylene torch. A lifting sling and a crane stood by to pull the engine out; then the welder would seal the hood again. It was a perfect system. Arkady checked his dosimeter. The count was twice normal. Well, what was normal?

Feeling high from a successful negotiation and the euphoria of a sleepless night, Arkady detoured. Instead of returning directly to the dormitory, he went to Eva's cabin to explain to her that while he had to report to Moscow, he could return in a day or two on his own. Even if he wasn't allowed back in the Zone, they could meet in Kiev. She was difficult. He was difficult. They could be difficult together. They could try to "forge the glorious future," as the banners used to say.

Or fight and break up, like everyone else. He imagined the entire conversation in advance.

As Arkady rode the motorcycle up to the cabin, he saw Alex's Toyota truck parked at the garage, and as he walked to the screen door of the house, he heard a scuffle within. There was something about the sound that prevented him from rushing in immediately. No one was in the front room; no one played the piano or sorted through the papers on the desk. He heard no real conversation: instead, a groan and a noise like shuffling feet.

Arkady moved to the bedroom window, and there, through the lilacs, he had a view of Alex and Eva. They stood together. Her bathrobe was open, and he was pressing her against a bureau, his pants down, his buttocks flexing in and out. She clung limp as a rag doll, arms around his neck, as he pounded his flesh into hers, covered her mouth with his. Was this the magical dance floor from the night before? Arkady wondered. A change of partners, obviously. As Alex pulled Eva's head back by her hair to kiss her she saw Arkady at the window. She freed a hand to motion him to leave. The bureau, jostled, spilled brushes, pictures, perfume bottles. Alex saw Arkady in the bureau mirror and more vigorously lifted her with his strokes. As she rocked, Eva listlessly watched Arkady. He waited for some signal from her, but she closed her eyes and laid her head on Alex's shoulder.

Arkady backtracked to the bike, staggering as if he'd lost his sense of balance. It was a little early in the day to cope with this. Apparently, Eva hadn't expected him back. All the same, it was, he felt, a little sudden. And it seemed to spell farewell. He felt a rage take over, although he wasn't sure at whom. This was, he understood, why domestic quarrels ended so badly.

Alex came out of the cabin's screen door, tucking his shirt in, buckling his belt, the man of the house encountering an unexpected visitor. "Alas, poor Renko, I knew him well. Sorry you caught us like that. I know it's painful."

"I didn't know you would be here."

"I thought you were gone. Anyway, why not? She's still my wife."

"Did you rape her?"

"No."

"Was there resistance?"

"No. Since you ask." Alex looked back at the cabin as Eva appeared through the haze of the screen door. "It was very good. Felt like home."

Arkady walked to the cabin door. As he reached the front step Eva bolted the screen door and backed up to the middle of the little parlor clutching her robe tight. "She'll get over it," Alex said. "Eva is tougher than she looks."

Arkady rattled the door. He considered ripping it out, but she shook her head and said in a hoarse voice, "This is none of your business."

"You're upsetting her," Alex said.

"Are you bruised?" Arkady asked.

Eva said, "No."

"I need to talk to you."

"Go away, please!" Eva said.

"I need to —"

This was exactly the sort of scene that police the world over hated. Two men starting to wrestle on the ground, a motorcycle kicked over, a woman sobbing inside the house. The gun in Alex's hand was the next escalation. He pushed it against Arkady's temple and said, "We had an understanding, you and I. You came here for an investigation. Fine, investigate. Any questions you want. But leave Eva alone. I take care of Eva. She needs someone reliable who will be here tomorrow and the day after. Go back to Moscow now, and no one's the worse."

"I was lonely," Eva said. She came to the screen. "I phoned Alex and asked him over. It was my idea."

"All of it?"

But she retreated from sight.

"Is that good enough for you?" asked Alex. "So, you're finished here, right? We can be friends again. We'll run into each other on the street in Moscow, remember our drunken samogon party and pretend to wish each other well. Agreed?"

Alex was first to his feet. He tucked the gun, a 9mm, into the back of his belt. Arkady rose more slowly.

"One question."

"The investigator is back on the case. Excellent."

"Who did they call?"

"Who called who?"

"At the samogon party, you did a hilarious impersonation of the control-room technicians, how they blew up the reactor and had to report to Moscow. Who in Moscow did they call?"

"You're serious? What does it matter?"

"Who?"

"It was a chain. The minister of energy, the director of power-plant construction, the minister of health, Gorbachev, the Politburo."

"And who did *they* call? Someone respected, with firsthand experience in nuclear disasters. I think they called Felix Gerasimov. They called your father."

"That's a guess."

"It can be checked."

Alex seemed to consider a wide range of responses. With self-control, he picked up Arkady's motorcycle and dusted off the saddle. "A good trip home, Renko. Be careful."

A thought struck Arkady. "You said you had an understanding with me. Do you have an understanding with Eva?"

Alex smiled, caught out. "I said I wouldn't hurt you."

16

Bela tucked Bobby and Yakov into jump seats behind a washed and brushed Kamaz V8 in a wooden cradle and security straps.

"Not hidden but not seen," Bela said. "It's going to go down like cream. I've done this a hundred times. As soon as we get going, I'll turn on the air conditioner. I guarantee a good time."

Yakov kept one hand on the gun inside his jacket and smiled like a grandpa. Bobby held onto his laptop.

Arkady glanced at Bela's CDs. "Your Tom Jones collection?"

"It's a long drive."

Bobby rallied enough to say, "Renko, you remind me of a dog I once had. With one eye, three legs, no tail. Answered to the name Lucky. That's you. You never know when to stop."

"Probably not." Arkady wasn't sure it was a compliment.

"Ozhogin is really coming?"

"I think so."

Yakov nodded. Wonderful, Arkady

thought, the paranoids agree.

Bobby said, "One thing, Renko. Tell me you're staying because you know who killed Pasha. Tell me you're close."

Arkady let his fingers lie: he held his thumb and forefinger a centimeter apart and slid the van door shut.

"Where are you?" Zurin demanded. "I expected you here in this office an hour ago."

"I'm sorry. That flight was overbooked," Arkady said.

"To Moscow?"

"Yes."

"Where are you right now? I hear shouts."

"On the plane." Arkady was in Campbell's dormitory room. The professor himself was curled up in the bottom of the shower stall, and a tape of a soccer game between Liverpool and Arsenal was on the television.

"What flight number?" the prosecutor asked. "When are you landing in Moscow?"

"Can Colonel Ozhogin meet me?"

"No."

"How do you know? You haven't asked him."

"I'm sure he's busy. When are you landing?"

"They're telling us to turn off our mobile phones."

"How could you —"

Arkady ended the call. That was the problem with long leashes, he thought. You couldn't tell whether the dog was at the other end or not.

He hoped he had done one thing right and gotten Bobby and Yakov safely out of Chernobyl. It wasn't like rescuing babes from a fire, but Arkady was willing to celebrate small accomplishments. Yakov's expression at the end might have been the ghost of a smile.

He cleared Campbell's desk enough to write a list of what he knew about Timofeyev: the pivotal relationship with Pasha Ivanov, their paired careers, their similar poor health and poisoning, the letter that Timofeyev had mentioned at Pasha's charity party, the discovery of Timofeyev's body in the Zone by what Militia Officer Karel Katamay had reported as a local squatter. Everything parallel to Ivanov except his death; that was different. The only person as ill as they were, in the same extraordinary fashion, was Karel Katamay. Katamay was the key, and he was a wraith in the woods. Or hidden in Pripyat near the theater, at least during the day, while the Woropay brothers were on duty.

Arkady's task was to avoid Ozhogin. The colonel would consider him the most likely lead to Bobby, and Arkady suspected that he enjoyed gathering information. Arkady had taken the precaution of hiding his motorbike in back of a woodpile behind the dormitory. Of course, Ozhogin's arrival might be a figment of Arkady's imagination, and the urgency in Zurin's commands merely revealed excitement at having Arkady near.

In the meantime, Arkady hydrated the wilted Campbell with a glass of water and a lukewarm shower; any decent guest would have.

Victor called. "You were right about the travel office. Anton and Galina picked up tickets for Morocco."

"For when?" Arkady felt apologetic: he had completely forgotten about Anton. He paced, negotiating empty bottles on the floor. On the television Liverpool still played Arsenal.

"Two days. I caught the travel agent on the way down and bought her a coffee."

"You chatted up the agent?" The newly attired Victor must be much less frightening than the old one, Arkady thought.

"I chatted up an agent. Did you know that it's often cheaper for two people to travel than one?"

"You're getting very sophisticated."

"But there's more to it than that. We were having our coffees, the travel agent and I, when Anton and Galina came out of the building. See, after the agent. So, they must have gone into the dentist's office. That just struck me as odd. Where was the dentist?"

"Dr. Levinson?" No inspiration in Liverpool. Arkady switched to England versus Holland. From the 1990s. A classic.

"That's right. There was a phone number on her office sign. I called it and a voice said she was going on a month's vacation starting tomorrow. It was a sweet voice, but not a well-educated voice, and my bet is it was our lovely Galina. I worry about the dentist."

"Why?"

"You know where Anton went from there? A bank. I ask you, since when does Anton Obodovsky use a legitimate bank? He launders money or he buys diamonds. He does not stand in line like a normal person at an ordinary bank. Something is going on."

"What?"

"I don't know. Whatever it is, I have a feeling that when he and Galina take off to Morocco they're not going to leave any loose ends behind. If so, I am very disappointed in Galina."

"Where is Anton now?" It was the end of the soccer match. Arkady could tell because the British fans were ripping out grandstand railings and hurling them at police.

"The last I saw, he and Galina were tearing along the river in a new Porsche convertible. Real lovebirds."

Klaxon wailing, a bus pulled onto the field and disgorged Dutch police with helmets and shields.

Victor said, "By the way, you may be right about Alex Gerasimov. He either fell or jumped off a four-story building a week after his father blew his head off. But the son lived. Is he crazy or strong?"

"Good question."

"Where's Bobby?" Victor asked. "His phone's off. What's going on up there? Do I hear soccer?"

Only Victor would rightly interpret a riot as a soccer match, Arkady thought.

"Kind of. Get a home number for the dentist, just to hear her voice. And if Zurin calls . . ."

"Yes?"

"You haven't talked to me in weeks."

"I wish."

Arkady closed the mobile phone and rewound the video to the point where police buses rolled into view. The phone rang. The caller ID showed a local number.

"Arkady?" It was Eva.

There was a pause while British fans threw seat cushions, bottles, coins.

"Eva, I think I misunderstood your relationship with Alex."

"Arkady . . ."

Thugs, stripped to Union Jack tattoos, dragged down local fans and stomped them with boots.

Eva said, "Alex said you went to Moscow."

"So?"

Once down, a victim could be kicked in any number of vital spots. Some hooligans, British or Russian, were virtuosos with steel-toed boots. Meanwhile, the police ducked from the rain of hard objects.

"I thought you'd left."

"You were wrong."

A crowd surged onto the field, broke through the police line and rocked a bus.

"I hear shouts. Where are you, Arkady?"

"I can't tell you."

"You don't trust me?"

He let the question stand. The bus driver had locked the doors but trapped himself inside. The bus windows burst into crystal.

Eva asked, "What can I do?"

Rioters put their shoulders to the bus and rocked it from side to side. The lights were on. Running back and forth, the driver looked like a moth in a swinging lamp.

"If you want to help," Arkady said, "you can tell me what Alex does in Moscow in his off-time. You're close to him."

"Is that what you want to talk about?"

"Can you help or not? What does a radioecologist do in Moscow to earn money?"

Police formed a wedge in an effort to rescue the bus. However, a number of hooligans had appropriated helmets and batons and put up a stiff resistance. One policeman, taken hostage, spun comically between blows.

"Can you help or not?" Arkady repeated.

Oopah! The bus went over with a cheer. Figures swarmed it, kicking in the windshield and dragging the driver out.

"Please don't," she said.

"Can you help or not?"

Too late, a water cannon arrived to clear the field. As the jet drove the crowd back, the stampede in the exits gained the strength of desperation. A second wave of bodies rushed the camera and sucked it under.

"No? Too bad." Arkady ended the call.

The next images were taped later, of police picking over clothes on the field and the empty stands, photographing the scene, maneuvering a tractor crane to lift the toppled bus back on its wheels. An ambulance stood by in case anyone was underneath. There was a special, mutual pain to the conversation, he thought. Hurting her, of course. Also — by ending the call and demonstrating who was in control — denying himself the chance to listen. This way he could enjoy the deep satisfaction of twisting the knife in two people at the same time. It was the sort of pain a man could suck on forever. The bus lurched onto its wheels. No bodies. The final shot was of the score: 0–0. As if nothing had happened at all.

Great minds compartmentalized. Arkady put on Vanko's tape and fast-forwarded, then rewound. The question, he decided, was why the camera had found Bobby, among all the Hasidim. On repeated viewings, it was a little more obvious, and not as a matter of editing. If Vanko had edited, he would have excised the clumsy shot of his run to the tomb. And the virtual close-up of Bobby at the prayer was not hidden well enough. Toward the end of the tape, at the leave-taking of the buses, Arkady could almost feel the camera search for Bobby. He went frame by frame until he saw a reflection in the bus's folded glass door of Vanko handing out business cards. If Vanko hadn't been taping, who had? When had the handover taken place? Before the Kaddish? Or even earlier, before the visit to the tomb?

Arkady heard a car brake hard in the dormitory parking lot and bodies rush into the downstairs hall. A rapid conversation included the bewildered tones of the housekeeper. A moment later, heavy feet ran up the stairs and stopped next door, at the room Arkady had occupied. A key jiggled and they were in. It sounded like they tossed the mattress and drawers, then collected again in the hall.

Arkady slid a chain bolt into the doorplate a moment before someone rapped on the other side.

"Renko? Renko, if you're in there, open up." It was Ozhogin, which gave Arkady the perverse satisfaction of knowing he had been right. At the same time, the door seemed flimsy. Arkady moved back. He heard the housekeeper waddle up the hall and mention the Scotsman, maybe adding a gesture of drinking. She scratched the door and called Campbell's name. A fist knocked less politely.

"Renko," Ozhogin said, "you should have filled out the form. We would have found some kind of job for you. Now it's come to this."

The housekeeper tried the wrong key and apologized. A key was a formality; Arkady knew how simple it was to pop the lock. Anyway, she had the key; it was only a matter of finding her glasses.

"Here we are," she said.

Arkady became aware of someone behind him. Campbell had wandered in from the bathroom in his undershirt and drawers, wet as a duck. The professor punched Vanko's tape out of the machine, replaced it with one marked Liverpool-Chelsea and raised the volume. On his way back to the bathroom, he picked up a bottle that was not completely empty. When the door suddenly opened the length of the chain he paused to shout through the space, "Shut yer fookin' gobs!"

Arkady didn't know how well Ozhogin spoke English but he seemed to get the message. There was a long moment while the colonel decided whether to break in on the drunken Scot. The moment passed. Arkady heard Ozhogin and his men retreat down the hall, confer, then move with dispatch down the stairs and out to their car. Doors slammed and they drove away.

Hours slipped around the window shade. Arkady knew he should sleep; he also knew that as soon as he closed his eyes he would be back on the ground outside Eva's cabin.

Arkady called the children's shelter and asked for Zhenya. Olga Andreevna came on the line. "Are you finally here in Moscow?" she asked.

"No."

"You're impossible. But at least you called *him* this time, and that's an improvement. His group is in music class now, although Zhenya doesn't actually sing. Wait."

Arkady sat with the phone for ten minutes.

The director came back on and said, "Here he is." Zhenya, naturally, said nothing.

"Do you like music?" Arkady asked. "Any special group? Have you been playing chess? Eating well?" Arkady remembered films of pioneers of flight, the unsuccessful ones with man-made wings who ran and flapped, ran and flapped, and never got off the ground. That was like trying to talk to Zhenya.

"My case here is winding up soon. I'll be back, and if you like, we can go to a soccer game. Or Gorky Park." If Arkady had not met Zhenya, he would have no good reason to believe the boy actually existed. Just for a test, he said, "Baba Yaga has a wolf."

There was a perceptible quickening of the breath on the other end.

"The wolf lives in a red forest with his wife, a human who wants to escape. He doesn't know whether he wants to eat her or keep her, but he does know he'll eat anyone who tries to help her. In fact, the forest is littered with the bones of those who have tried and failed. I wanted your advice on whether I should try. What do you think? Take your time. Consider every possibility, like a chess game. When you know, call me. In the meantime, be good."

He hung up.

Liverpool wore red uniforms, Chelsea white. Zurin called and Arkady didn't answer. Something was right in front of him, dangling and shining like a mirror ball, but every time he reached out, it disappeared. Or skipped along like that Icelandic sprite you could see only from the corner of your eye.

Vanko had said Alex made lots of money.

In the belly of the beast, Alex had said. Exactly what beast? Arkady wondered.

Arkady opened his file. On the NoviRus employment application were an Internet site, e-mail address, phone and fax numbers.

Arkady called the phone number, and a woman's musical voice said, "Welcome to NoviRus. How may I direct your call?"

"Interpreting and translation."

"Legal, international or security?"

"Security." He never would have guessed.

"Hold, please."

Arkady held until a brusque male voice answered, "Security."

"I'm calling Alex Gerasimov."

A pause to punch in the name. "You want the accident section."

"That's right."

"Hold."

A Liverpool forward scored on a breakaway, the gift of a bad pass that left the Chelsea goalie naked. Soccer had been Arkady's sport, and goalie had been his position. A goalie's life balanced between anxiety and agony. Once in a while, though, there was the unexpected, undeserved save.

"Accident." A second male voice was not nearly so military.

"Alex Gerasimov?"

"No. He's not on duty for another two weeks."

"Doing interpreting and translation?"

"That's right."

"For the accident section?"

"Yes."

"He was going to explain everything to me."

"Sorry, Alex is not here. I'm Yegor."

A good sign; a man who offered his name invited conversation.

"I apologize for bothering you, Yegor, but Alex was going to tell me about the job."

Arkady heard a rustle like a newspaper being put down.

"You're interested?"

"Very."

"You talked to the people in Employment?"

"Yes, but you know how it is with them, they never give you an honest picture. Alex was going to."

"I can do that."

Yegor explained that NoviRus offered physical security to Russian and foreign clients in the usual form of bodyguards and cars. For foreign clients, they provided standby interpreters who could go to the scene of a traffic accident or an incident involving police or any emergency where their presence could alleviate a dangerous or costly misunderstanding, often with prostitutes, for which there was a discretionary fund. Interpreters were expected to be university-educated, well dressed and fluent in two foreign languages. They worked a twenty-four-hour shift every three days and were paid a handsome ten dollars an hour, perfect for part-time work. What the people in Employment didn't tell applicants was that the twenty-four-hour shift was spent either racing around Moscow, from one scene of confusion to the next, or going nowhere at all, which meant a day and a night in a basement room not much larger than a closet, with three cots, a coatrack and a minibar. The interpreters had been promised real quarters, but they were still stuck like an afterthought behind Surveillance, which, by virtue of all the screens it monitored, had a quarter of the floor.

"Alex made it sound better than that," Arkady said.

"Alex has the run of the place. He's been here awhile. He knows everyone, and he's in and out of everywhere."

"Ten dollars an hour?" Arkady figured this was about five times what a senior investigator made. "That covers a lot of sins. Were you on duty the day Pasha Ivanov died?"

"No."

"But Alex was, wasn't he?"

"Yeah. Who did you say you were?"

Arkady hung up. The game was getting interesting. With a minute to go, Chelsea was a man down but pressing for a tie and getting corner kick after corner kick to try for a header. The goalie tugged on his gloves and stationed himself one long diagonal step in front of the goalmouth. Campbell had come out of the bathroom to watch. Red and white uniforms elbowed for position as the ball rose from the corner and curled toward the goal. Players milled, thrust themselves up by their elbows and achingly stretched. The goalie committed, diving into the mass, hands high to intercept. Moving swiftly for a drunk, the professor crossed to the videotape and pressed Stop. The players hung in midair.

"I can't see it. I won't watch it one more time. It's agony aforesaid, the turning of the thumbscrews, the inevitable lop. They can freeze for fookin' eternity for all I care. Who cares? Do y'know what happens? Do y'know?" Exhausted, Campbell dropped on his bed and passed out.

No, Arkady thought, he didn't know. By now Bobby Hoffman could be halfway to Cyprus or Malta. Anton was either menacing someone or buying matching luggage with Galina. It was even getting dark enough for Arkady to stir.

Arkady's mobile phone rang. Eva. He was about to answer when an image of her and Alex came flooding back. The sight of Eva pressed against the bureau. The sound of perfume bottles rolling to the floor. Arkady remembered her eyes, the look of a drowning woman who embraces the whirlpool. He still couldn't answer.

Another call. From Bela. Arkady took this one because he could use good news, but Bela said, "We're at the power station, at the sarcophagus. We were headed to the checkpoint when the fat one changed his mind."

"Why did you go to the power station? Why did you agree?"

Bela's voice got small. "He offered so much money."

Arkady covered the first few kilometers on dirt roads through black villages to see whether anyone was following him before taking the motorcycle onto the highway. Ozhogin would focus on the route south to

Kiev, not to the center of the Zone. There was no avoiding the checkpoint outside the power station, but Arkady was waved through. He had become a familiar figure, the eccentric investigator who haunted Pripyat. Usually he rode by the station entrance. This time, he killed his headlight and swung in. In the twilight were faint indications of towers and high-tension wires. The power station's main office was a four-story building as white as a ghost. Arkady remembered that the complex had been designed for a total of eight reactors, the largest in the world. A digital clock over the main door read 20:48.

A Uralmoto motorcycle was not a quiet machine, and Arkady half expected to see a flashlight's beam or hear the challenge of a guard. Buses he saw, but no cars or vans. He crossed the parking lot to a row of what might have been laboratories and saw enough radiation posters and advisory signs to persuade him to turn on his headlight again. He U-turned at a dead end of dump bins overflowing with bags marked TOXIC WASTE, ignored a sign that said AUTHORIZED PERSONNEL ONLY, as any Russian would anywhere, and followed a wire fence crowned with razor wire. More fences and wire led him right and left up to a sign that said DO NOT ENTER — REPORT TO GUARD BEFORE PROCEEDING — ARE YOU WEARING YOUR RADIATION PIN? Arkady coasted through and found a service road where Bela's van was parked at a gate, not a simple counterweighted pole but a steel gate that was rolled shut. A sign in English said STOP. Bela was in the van. Bobby Hoffman and Yakov stood in the middle of the road facing a security wall decked with shiny coils of wire. Each man wore a yarmulke and a tasseled shawl. Arkady couldn't make out what they were saying, though they rocked back and forth to its rhythm.

Beyond the wall was another wire-draped wall and, fifty meters farther on, the sarcophagus, as stained and massive as a windowless cathedral. Dim security lamps glowed here and there. A crane and a chimney stack towered over the sarcophagus, but compared to it, they were insignificant. Connected to the sarcophagus was the more presentable Reactor Two, which was invisible. The sarcophagus was apart, alone, alive.

Bela crept out of the van. "This is as close as we could get."

Arkady didn't need to use his dosimeter; he felt his hair rise.

"It's close enough. Why are you here?"

"The fat one insisted."

"The old guy didn't try to talk him out of it?"

"Yakov? He seemed to expect it. They just waited until dark so it was safer. They seem to have a lot of names. You didn't tell me they were on the run."

"Does it matter?"

"It drives up the price."

Arkady looked around. "Where are the guards?"

Bela pointed to a pair of legs sticking out from the shadow of the gate. "Just a watchman. I gave him some vodka."

"You're always prepared."

"I am."

It was the night shift, Arkady thought. There were no office or construction workers. A skeleton crew could maintain the three reactors that were shut down, and no one entered the sarcophagus. On the power grid, the Chernobyl station was a black hole, a repository of spent fuel in a bankrupt country. How many guards would there be?

The chanting wasn't loud enough to carry far. Bobby's voice was whispery. Yakov's was deep and worn, and Arkady recognized the Kaddish, the prayer for the dead. Their voices overlapped, separated, joined again.

"How long have they been doing this?"

"Half an hour, at least. When I called you."

"The rest of the time, what did you do all day?"

"Drove into the woods. I found them a hill with nice mobile-phone reception. The fat one called and arranged things."

"What things?"

"Belarus is just a few kilometers north. Your friends have got visas and a car waiting. They've got every move figured out."

"Like a game of chess."

"Exactly like chess."

Except if they were doing it for Pasha, it was too late, Arkady thought. Arkady was aware of having been manipulated by Bobby and Yakov, but he didn't feel angry. They were escape artists, what else would they do?

"But they let you call me?"

"Yakov suggested it."

So they should have been on the run to Minsk, gateway to the world, instead of standing outside the corrupted shell of a nuclear disaster, rocking back and forth like human metronomes and intoning the same verses over and over, *"Ose sholom himromov hu yaase sholom."* When they finished the prayer, they simply began again. Arkady told himself he should have known this was coming. Would Bobby have come all this way to repeat his failure? Wasn't this the logical, inevitable outcome, whether Bobby knew it consciously or not? Or was Yakov, like a black angel, forcibly keeping Bobby out of hell?

Arkady moved into their line of vision. Each step brought the sarcophagus closer, too, as if it had been waiting for the right hour to leap the wall, a hard sight to face without a prayer. Yakov acknowledged Arkady with the briefest nod, to say not to worry, that he and Bobby were fine. Bobby clutched a list of names that Arkady could see because of a rising moon that spilled over the station yard. Maybe Bobby and Yakov had planned well and had some luck, but every minute spent at the power plant was a chance taken, and the list looked long. Arkady remembered Eva saying that a complete list would reach the moon. The thought of his cold-blooded rejection of her made him wince. It occurred to him that when she needed him most he had abandoned her, and that he had made an irretrievable mistake.

17

The way to see Pripyat, like the Taj Mahal, was by moonlight. The broad avenues and stately chestnuts. The confident plan of greenery, office towers and residential blocks. The way the central plaza admired the Soviet wreath that topped the city hall. Never mind the empty sockets of the windows or the grass that grew between the pavers.

Arkady left his motorcycle in the plaza. He went to the theater where he had met Karel Katamay, feeling his way again through the flats stacked in the lobby, shining his flashlight on the stage, around the piano, up the tiers of benches. Karel Katamay and the couch were gone, leaving only a few dried drops of blood in the dust.

Arkady couldn't search a city built for fifty thousand people. However, a dying man and his couch could not have gone far, even with the Woropay brothers bearing him on a royal litter. His nosebleeds were small leaks. He was bleeding internally from the lungs, intestinal tract, cerebellum. Faced with that prospect, Pasha Ivanov had chosen the quicker alternative of a ten-story jump.

Back on the plaza, Arkady turned off the chatter of his dosimeter. He had a mental map of the city now: the hot buildings, the alleys to be taken only on the run.

Arkady called out, "Karel! We should talk." While we can, he thought.

Something slipped through the grass and disappeared like smoke in the beam of Arkady's flashlight. He swung the light around the front of offices. Where plate glass was still intact, the beam winked back. He swung the light up but decided the Woropay brothers wouldn't have tried to carry Katamay above the ground floor. Anyway, why would Karel want to be in a dark room littered with plaster, sour with squatter's piss, when outside in the balmy air he could touch the moon?

Arkady returned to the center of the plaza and kept going when he saw the amusement park. It had three rides: a Ferris wheel, bumper cars and crazy chairs. In the crazy chairs, children sat in a circle of flower petals that spun until the children were dizzy or nauseated. Half the bumper cars were on their side; the rest were still entangled in traffic. The Ferris wheel was big enough for forty gondolas. Everything was edged and pitted with corrosion; the wheel looked like it had rolled, stopped and rusted in place.

Karel Katamay lay on his couch in front of the crazy chairs. Arkady turned off his flashlight; he didn't need it. Karel was in the same hockey shirt and propped up with cushions, as before. His face was luminously pale, but his hair seemed brushed and freshly beaded. On the ground in front of the couch were plastic flowers, a plastic liter of Evian and a porcelain teacup, no doubt filched from an apartment. Also, a tank of oxygen, a breathing tube and a harness. So the Woropay brothers had made him as comfortable as possible. He did seem a prince of the netherworld.

However, Karel was dead. The eyes, red as wounds, stared through Arkady. The hockey shirt seemed voluminous, twice Karel's size. His hands lay with their palms up on either side of the white satin pillow embroidered *Je ne regrette rien.* One foot wore a Chinese slipper, the other was bare. There were worse ways to die than peacefully outside on a summer night, Arkady thought.

Arkady found the other slipper two meters away on the other side of the crazy-chairs fence and, honoring the professional rule of "touch nothing," left it where it was. He returned to Katamay. Purple bruises consistent with tissue breakdown and lack of clotting spotted Karel's skin. Blood smeared his chin and rouged his cheeks. When had he died? He was still warm, but he had mentioned infections, and a fever could burn in a body for an hour or more. He had probably lived on nothing but water and morphine for weeks. Actually, Arkady thought he might have lived a minute ago.

Why would a peacefully expiring man kick off a slipper? Katamay's mouth relaxed a little and let the tongue peek out. The satin pillow between his hands was spotless. Arkady broke his rule and turned the pillow over. The opposite side was soaked with blood only starting to brown. Blood from two sources, it seemed, mouth and nose, and what a brief struggle that must have been.

Arkady became aware of Dymtrus Woropay standing on the other side of the crazy chairs. Woropay held a cardboard box that looked heavy with bottles and flowers and trailed the sort of tinsel used to decorate at the holidays. Arkady also saw what the scene looked like to Dymtrus: Arkady standing over Karel Katamay with a bloody pillow.

"What the fuck are you doing?"

"I found him like this."

"What the fuck did you do?"

Dymtrus dropped the box and let the bottles explode. He swung himself directly over the fence on the other side and bulled through the crazy seats. Arkady put the pillow between Katamay's hands and moved away.

Dymtrus snapped the gate chain. He knelt by the couch, touched the dead man's face, picked up the pillow.

"No! No!" He got to his feet and bellowed, "Taras!" His voice went around the plaza. "Taras!"

Arkady ran.

He ran for his motorbike, but another figure closed fast from the side, parting the grass with his arms, striding from paver to paver: Taras Woropay on skates. Arkady jumped on the bike and started it. He told himself that if he reached the highway, he would be safe. Dymtrus threw something shiny. A shopping cart. Arkady outraced it and was back on the plaza, headed for the road, when his rear tire popped and took

Arkady to the ground. He rolled free and looked back at Taras on one knee with a gun. A good shot.

Arkady was on foot. When he was a boy and his father took him hunting, the general would shout, "Run, rabbit!," because shooting a standing rabbit was so little fun. "Wave," he'd tell Arkady. "Damn it, wave." Arkady would wave, the rabbit would bolt and the old man would drill it.

Dymtrus followed Arkady into the school, by the hanging chalkboard. Arkady tripped in the dark over gas masks on the lobby floor. They flopped out of the crate like rubber fish. He moved by memory as much as sight, heading for the kitchen in the back of the building. White tiles lined the kitchen walls. A dough bowl the size of a wheelbarrow stood on its legs. All the oven doors were open or broken off. The back door, however, had been boarded up in the last week. We should have rehearsed, the comic in him said. He looked out a window at chairs set on the ground for staff to use while smoking. He considered breaking the window with a loose oven door, until he saw Dymtrus waiting behind a birch. Arkady returned to the lobby and looked out the front window. Skates off, Taras was stepping up to the door.

Arkady went up the stairs two at a time, kicking bottles and debris aside. Taras was inside, at the bottom of the stairwell. Arkady knocked a loose bookcase down toward him. Copybooks fluttered down. Taras didn't have to shout to his brother where Arkady was. Anyone could hear.

Second floor. The music room. A piano leaning like a drunk against a loose keyboard. The tub-thumping sound of a drum accidentally kicked. All the notes a xylophone could make when stumbled into. A one-man band. Heavier feet on the stairs. Dymtrus. The next room was a flood of books, desks, children's benches. The door frame next to Arkady's head split open before he heard the shot. He javelined a bench down the hall and knew he had caught someone when he heard a curse. The last room was a nap center of dolls asleep on white beds. Arkady gathered a mattress around himself and dove through the glass of the window.

He landed on his back between seesaws, rolled to the trees and crawled under a thorn bush, feeling a prick or two, also aware of blood running down the back of his neck and into his camos, but there was no time to take inventory. In the moonlight he saw the brothers scanning trees from the broken window. He thought he might get away. He would have at least the time it would take them to go the length of the hall, down the stairs and out the front while he went the opposite direction. But they were athletes. Dymtrus stepped up on the sill and jumped. He hit the mattress and rolled off. Taras followed suit, and they were close enough for Arkady to hear their breathing. Close enough to smell a mixture of vodka and cologne.

They signaled to each other and separated. Arkady couldn't see where to, although he suspected they would go only a short distance and double back right to where he was. If he did get to the far woods, he could head west to the wild Carpathian Mountains or east to Moscow. The sky was the limit.

The woods were so loud. The electric shriek of crickets and cicadas. The invisible luffing of trees in the breeze. A man could just sink into the sound. Dead, he would.

A rock, a brick, something hit the wall of the school. Immediately, Taras, one arm hung low, hurt, ran forward and around the side of the school. One on one, Arkady took his chance. He emerged and moved to the quarter that Taras had deserted.

He had been suckered. Dymtrus was

waiting behind a big enough tree this time, but Arkady tripped in brambles, and the shot that should have taken off his shoulder was high. By the time Dymtrus had advanced to see, Arkady was on his feet again, weaving downhill between trees.

Arkady had no plan. He wasn't headed to any particular road or checkpoint, he was only running. Since the Zone was uninhabited, apart from the staff in Chernobyl and the old folks in their black villages, he had a lot of running to do. He heard Taras's shouts catching up. The brothers were behind him, one on either side. One problem was that moonlight was not real light. Branches materialized to slap his face. Roots insidiously spread. Radiation markers seemed to multiply.

He glimpsed a Woropay closer every time he dared look. How could they be so fast? The ground pitched forward, and they were herding him through deeper and deeper bracken. His feet grew heavy, clutched by mud, and he saw ahead a trail of silver water.

It was a small swamp ringed by armless, rotting trees, reeds, the plop of frogs. In the center, the hump of a beaver dam and, topping that, a diamond-shaped marker.

Arkady moved back to firmer ground.

He found no stones. A branch he picked up turned to dust. Weaponless, he met the charge of Taras, threw him over his hip, and stood to face Dymtrus. Dymtrus fought like an ice-hockey player: grab with one hand and pound with the other. Arkady took the hand, twisted and locked it behind Dymtrus's back, then ran him into a tree. He kicked Taras in the head when he returned. He hit Dymtrus below the belt. But Dymtrus clutched Arkady's knees as he dropped, and Arkady couldn't put enough force behind a punch into Taras's head. Dymtrus climbed up Arkady. Taras hit back with the gun. Dymtrus held Arkady's arms so Taras could swing the gun at a steadier target. The next conscious moment, Arkady was being turned over on the ground. Shooting him was too easy; they could have done that when they first caught up.

Dymtrus said, "I brought the pillow."

He pulled the pillow out of his tunic and sat on Arkady's chest while Taras knelt and held on to Arkady's arms. Dymtrus breathed hard through the saliva that draped from his mouth. The blood on the pillow was still damp.

Arkady's eyes sought the moon, a treetop, anything else.

Dymtrus said, "You'll go like Karel went. Then we'll put you in the water, and no one will find you for a thousand fucking years."

"Fifty thousand." Alex Gerasimov came out of the trees. "More like fifty thousand years."

In Alex's hand was a gun. He shot Dymtrus in the back, and the big man collapsed as dead as a slaughtered steer while his brother sat back on his heels in surprise. Taras brushed the hair from his eyes and had started to form a question when Alex shot him. A cigarette burn through the heart. Taras looked down at it and kept falling until he spread out on the ground.

Alex picked up the pillow. "*Je ne regrette rien.* Absolutely," he said and flung the pillow into the water almost to the diamond marker.

They carried the bodies back.

Alex said the swamp and hillside were too hot; the militia would either leave the Woropays or drag them out by the heels. Hadn't Arkady seen the Chernobyl militia in action? What kind of investigation did he expect? Fortunately, there were two witnesses.

"They were trying to kill you and I saved your life. Isn't that what happened?"

They carried the Woropays over the shoulder, fireman-style. Alex led the way with Dymtrus while Arkady, one eye swollen shut and his sense of balance badly out of kilter for being gunwhipped, staggered under Taras. Going uphill was slow work, slipping on needles with every step.

Alex said, "You're lucky I heard the shot. I thought it was a poacher in the middle of the city. You know how I am about poachers."

"I know."

"Then I heard another shot behind the school and followed the shouting. The Woropays make a lot of noise."

"Yes."

"You're not hurt?"

"I'm fine."

Alex paused to look back. "We'll take these two up to the school, and then I'll get the truck."

Arkady tripped on a root and went to one knee like a waiter with too much on his tray. He couldn't shift shoulders because he could see out of only one eye. He pushed himself up and asked, "Did you see Katamay?"

"Yes. You know what makes a full moon extraordinary? You feel like an animal, like an animal sees." Despite Dymtrus's weight, with guns stuck fore and aft in his belt, Alex slowed his pace just to accommodate Arkady. "We don't deserve a full moon. We make everything smaller. Everything big we cut down. First-growth trees, big cats, adult fish, wild rivers. That's what's wonderful about the Zone. Keep us out for fifty thousand years, and this place may grow into something."

"You saw Karel?" Arkady repeated.

"He didn't look good."

Arkady climbed a step at a time, and Alex began talking the way an adult would on a long, cold walk with a boy who was sniveling and slow, by distracting him with stories and things the boy would like to hear.

"Pasha Ivanov and Lev Timofeyev were my father's favorites, always in and out of our apartment. His best researchers, best instructors and, when he was too drunk to function, his best protection. There's always a good impulse behind the worst disasters, don't you find? And I swear, when I began working at NoviRus, it was purely for the extra money. I had no great plan of retribution."

Retribution? Was that what Alex had said? Arkady's head was still ringing, and it took all his concentration to continue moving as Alex bent a tree limb out of his way.

"My friend Yegor called from Moscow. Yes, I worked part-time for NoviRus Security as an interpreter in the accident section, which usually meant twenty-four hours of reading in a small, windowless room. Maybe Colonel Ozhogin's office was on the fifteenth floor, but we were in the bowels of the building."

"The belly of the beast."

"Exactly. Since you're underground, it always seems like night. Very space-age, with tinted glass for walls. I began wandering the halls and discovered that the technicians monitoring all those security screens were even more bored than I was. They're kids; I was the only one over thirty. Imagine sitting in the dark and staring at a bank of screens for hours on end. For what? Martians? Chechens? Bank robbers with stockings pulled over their heads? One day I went by an empty chair, and on the screen was a palace gate swinging open for a couple of Mercedeses. The cars moved to another screen, and there was Pasha Ivanov after so many years, Mr. NoviRus himself, getting out of a car with a beautiful woman on his arm. It's *his* palace. I hadn't seen him since

Chernobyl. On the screens I could follow him up the grand staircase and into the lobby. Here, I told myself, was a man who had everything.

"I wondered, what do you give a man who has everything? We were working with cesium chloride at the institute. Remember how social Ivanov was? At Christmas he threw a party for about a thousand people at his palace, collecting gifts for some charity. Very democratic: staff, friends, millionaires, children, wandering in every room because Ivanov liked to show off, the way New Russians do. I brought some grains of cesium chloride and a dosimeter in a lead box wrapped as a present, and lead-lined gloves and tongs in the back of my belt. I found his bathroom and left one grain out for him to step on and track around, and the present on the toilet seat with a card inviting him to Chernobyl to atone. I waited months, and all Ivanov did was send Hoffman, his fat American friend, to hide among the Hasidim. Can you believe it? Ivanov delegated a prayer for the dead, and Hoffman didn't even perform."

Arkady was not performing well, either. Taras was deadweight that took any opportunity — the brush of a limb, a faltering step — to slide off Arkady's shoulder.

Arkady stumbled, but he followed Alex's voice. Alex stopped every few steps to make sure of it. He laid out the story like a trail of tasty crumbs along a forest path. "Ivanov moved to a mansion in the city with a guardhouse. But all the bodyguards in the world won't help if your dog comes back from his run in the park with a grain or two in his hair, which he distributes around the house. I started a campaign against Timofeyev, too, but he was a secondary character. He was no Pasha Ivanov. Of course, after Ivanov was dead, Timofeyev was willing to come here, but before, the two of them had to behave as if nothing was happening, nothing to report to the militia or even NoviRus Security, where, incidentally, I flourished. I was every technician's big brother. I helped them study their correspondence courses for business degrees so they could become New Russians themselves. I found the code clerk a doctor he could take his sexual dysfunction to while I covered for him. Really, the plan took shape by itself. See, there's the school already, at the top of the hill."

To Arkady, the school was as distant as a cloud in the sky. He was impressed that he had come so far. Taras, dead or not, kept trying different ways to slither out of Arkady's arm. Alex steadied Arkady over a log, and Arkady wondered whether he could get close enough to grab one of the guns tucked in Alex's waistband, but Alex was on the march with Dymtrus again, setting an example, jollying Arkady along, keeping him entertained.

"Want to hear about the fumigator van? That was fun. Saturday mornings the tech for Ivanov's building was always hungover. I covered and saw the same images the receptionist saw in the lobby, and as soon as the van rolled into the service alley, I called on the security line and told him to read a list of the previous month's guests to me. This is not computerized. The receptionist has to physically turn away from the street, get the binder from a bottom drawer, find the day and decipher his own handwriting, with no view of the screens. I know all this because I have been watching him on the lobby monitor for weeks. The fumigator has codes for touchpads at the back door, the service elevator and Ivanov's floor, and I've promised him twelve minutes of distraction. In the middle of this, the tech comes back to replace me. I shake my head. He waits while I go on talking to the receptionist, because

I'm waiting for the fumigator to get out. I can see why people turn to a life of crime; the adrenaline is incredible. I give the tech two aspirin, and he leaves for water. At the same moment the fumigator comes into the alley, faster now because he's no longer pulling a suitcase full of salt, loads the van and drives off. I thank the receptionist, hang up and then watch. He puts down the binder, looks up at the camera, checks his screens, rewinds the street and alley tapes. He sees the van and he calls in the doorman, who disappears toward the back. I feel like I'm in the lobby. We wait, the receptionist and I. The doorman returns, shaking his head, and hops in the elevator. On the monitors I can see him going from floor to floor knocking on doors, while the receptionist acts super calm, with half an eye on the camera, until the doorman returns. No problem, nothing to worry about, everything's under control. Almost there, Renko."

Arkady grunted to hold up his side of the conversation. Carrying a body through a dense wood was like passing a jack through the tines of a comb. "Karel," he said.

"Karel was the fumigator, and he did a good job. Unfortunately, he got sloppy and must have picked up a grain or two of cesium. I tried a million times to explain radioactivity to Karel, and I don't think I ever got through."

"Why would he do it?"

"I was his friend. The Woropays', too. I listened to them, to their crazy ambitions. They were just boys from the Zone, they were never going to be New Russians. We were each in our different ways getting even."

"For what?"

"Everything."

Arkady was too exhausted to plumb that. "Not everything. Tell me one thing."

"Eva."

"What about her?"

"You know." With his finger Alex drew a scar across his neck.

The thorn bush behind the school reached for Taras, and Alex held back branches so Arkady could climb the last steps to the seesaw and chairs. When Arkady caught a ghostly reflection of himself in a window, he looked away before he turned completely into Yakov.

"Don't drop him," Alex said.

"Why not? You were going to get your truck."

"No. We'll carry them back to Karel."

"Back to Karel?" To the other end of the plaza? Arkady thought.

"We're practically there," Alex said. "The climb is over. Easy from here on."

That was it, then, Arkady thought. That's why he was alive instead of dead by the swamp, so Alex could make one trip instead of three. Ever the earnest assistant, Arkady had helped by bringing two of the bodies, Taras and himself. This way there were no tire treads on the ground or blood in the truck. A gun appeared in Alex's hand. Usually the distance from the school to the fun fair was a few minutes' walk. Even at his pace, Arkady wondered, how long could he draw it out?

"You first." Alex prodded Arkady to get him moving again, this time in front.

As Arkady stumbled forward he remembered a quote by someone about a walk to the gallows focusing the mind. That wasn't true. He thought of favorite music, Irina's laugh, his mother staying in bed to read *Anna Karenina* one more time, pansies on a grave. He thought of how Eva had called and called again, when all he'd had to do was answer.

"Why?" Arkady asked. "What did Pasha Ivanov and Timofeyev do to justify the deaths of five people, so far? What could

Pasha and Timofeyev have done that made you so insane?"

"Finally, an interesting question. The night of the accident at Chernobyl, what did Pasha and Timofeyev do? Well, you wouldn't think they could do anything; they were just two junior professors at an institute in Moscow. But they would sit up all night and drink with the old man. That's what they were doing when the call came from the Party Central Committee. The Party wanted him to go to Chernobyl to assess the situation, because he was the famous Academician Felix Gerasimov, who had more experience in nuclear disasters than anyone else, the world's number one expert. Since he was too drunk to talk, he gave the phone to Pasha."

"Where were you?"

"I was at Moscow University, sleeping soundly in my room." Recollection did slow Alex down.

"How do you know all this?"

"My father didn't write a suicide note when he died, but he sent me a letter. He said the Central Committee had wanted his advice on whether to evacuate people. Pasha acted as if he was just relaying answers from my father."

Ahead, Arkady saw Karel on the couch

in front of the crazy chairs ride. His sister, Oksana, bent over him; she wore the same jogging suit. Arkady recognized her by the blue shine of her shaved head. Walking one step behind, Alex had yet to notice her.

"Pasha asked if the reactor core had been exposed. The Committee said no, because that's what the control room told them. Pasha asked if the reactor was shut down. Yes, according to Chernobyl. Well, he said, it sounded like more smoke than fire. Don't sound any alarms, just distribute iodine tablets to children and advise the locals that they might want to stay inside for a day while the fire is extinguished and investigated. What about Kiev, the Committee asked? Even more important to keep the lid on, Pasha said. Confiscate dosimeters. 'Be merciless for the common good.' Pasha and Lev were ambitious guys. They just told the Committee and my father what they wanted to believe. That was how Soviet science worked, remember? So the evacuation of Pripyat was delayed a day and the warning to Kiev delayed six days so that a million children, including our Eva, could march on an undisturbed, radioactive May Day. Pasha and my father can't take all the credit — there were plenty of other weasels and liars — but they should take some."

"Your father was operating with faulty information. Was there an investigation?"

"A whitewash. After all, he was Felix Gerasimov. I woke up in the morning to go to class and there he was in my room, sober, as drawn as a ghost, with an iodine pill for me. He knew. Every May Day from then on was a drinking bout. Sixteen anniversaries. Finally he wrote the letter, sealed it, took it to the post office himself, returned home to his pistol and BANG!"

Oksana's head whipped around. Arkady wondered what he and Alex looked like as they approached in the moonlight — perhaps a single extraordinarily ugly creature with two heads, a trunk and a tail. Arkady motioned for her to get away.

"Surprised?" Alex asked.

"Not really. As a motive for murder, money is overrated. Shame is stronger."

"That's the best part. Pasha and Timofeyev couldn't go anywhere for protection, because then they would have had to reveal the whole story. They were too ashamed to save their own lives, can you imagine that?"

"It happens all the time."

Oksana slipped around the couch, and only because Arkady had seen her he heard her lightly running off. Maybe fifty more paces to Karel, who waited on the couch, the crazy chairs tilted behind him. Arkady resisted the temptation to run because he doubted he could escape an inchworm in his condition.

Alex said, "I wrote them. All I ever asked of Ivanov and Timofeyev was for them to come to the Zone and declare their share of responsibility personally, face-to-face."

"Timofeyev came. Look what happened to him."

"I didn't say there wouldn't be consequences. Fair's fair."

"As you often told Karel."

"As I often did."

At a shuffling gait, they arrived at the fun fair. Karel stretched languidly from one end of the sofa to the other. His eyes were closed, and the blood had been wiped from his chin and cheek; his beaded hair was arrayed more neatly, and each foot now bore a Chinese slipper. An older sister would do that sort of thing. Arkady thought Alex might notice, but he was too pleased with himself. A gondola creaked on the Ferris wheel overhead. Misery to be a Ferris wheel that never moved. Arkady had never seen a moon so large. A shadow of the wheel fell over the plaza.

Arkady laid Taras on the ground.

Alex simply let Dymtrus roll off his shoulder. The big militiaman hit the ground, his head striking like a coconut cracked open.

Arkady asked, "Who shot Hulak?"

"Who knows. He had an arrangement with the Woropays on where and what to steal. I assume they killed him." Alex rolled Dymtrus, who had a back wound, onto his face; he placed Taras, with an entry wound through the chest, on his back; waved the pistol to show Arkady where to stand until he achieved the geometry he wanted: a triangle of dead men — Karel, Dymtrus and Taras — with Arkady in the middle. "I think this will be a pretty convincing picture of the dangers of drinking samogon while bearing arms. Don't worry; I'll supply the guns and the samogon."

"So you didn't save me from the Woropays."

"No, I'm afraid not. You never got past here, but you put up a terrific struggle, if that makes you feel any better."

"All that's lacking is the pillow you smothered Karel with."

"*Je ne regrette rien?* You know, I'd barely covered his face. He gave a few kicks and was gone. I'd say, considering the shape he was in, what I did was a mercy."

Alex took two steps back from Arkady, into the shadow of the wheel, and raised the gun. Not too far, not too close.

Arkady's mobile phone rang.

"Let it ring," Alex said. "One thing at a time."

The phone rang and rang. When the message came on the caller hung up and immediately hit Redial. It could only be Zhenya, Arkady thought. No normal person would have such maddening persistence. The phone rang until Alex removed it from Arkady's pocket and crushed it underfoot.

That settled, the entire city silent, every window an anxious eye, Alex stepped back and raised the gun again. Oksana crept into Arkady's view at the end of the crazy chairs.

Arkady said, "Would you mind stepping out of the shadow?"

"You want to see me when I kill you?" Alex asked.

"If you don't mind."

Alex moved forward into the silvery light.

Arkady waited and gave Alex no reason to turn. There was a moment's perplexity on Alex's face as he seemed to wonder why Arkady was such an easy victim.

Then Alex twitched. He was dead standing, he was dead dropping, he was dead sprawled on the ground, and Oksana's shot had not been much louder than the snap of a twig. As she stepped out from the crazy chairs, she freed her arm from a sling she'd used to steady her rifle, similar to the single-shot bolt-action rifles that Arkady had seen at the Katamay apartment in Slavutych.

"I'm so sorry. I left my rifle with my bike. I barely got back in time," she said.

"But you did."

"This beast killed my little brother." She kicked Alex.

"He's dead." Arkady tried to steer her away.

"He was the devil. I heard every word." She got one good spit in before Arkady calmed her down and mopped up Alex's face. There wasn't a visible mark on him. His eyes were clear, his mouth set in a knowing smirk, his irises and muscle tone just starting to go slack. Arkady had to press his finger into Alex's ear to find the bullet's borehole and a dot of blood.

"Will they arrest me?" Oksana asked.

"Does anyone else know that you supply skins for your grandfather to mount?"

"No, he'd be embarrassed. You knew?"

"I assumed the skins were from Karel until I saw his condition. Then I knew they were from you."

"Can they trace the bullet?"

"A sophisticated lab could, but there are a lot of swamps around here. Tell me about Hulak." Arkady could barely stand, but he had a feeling that Oksana was a rarely seen moth, that he could talk to her now or never.

"He told my grandfather he was going to get your money and give you a taste of the cooling pond."

"You waited in a boat?"

"I fish there sometimes."

"And shot Hulak."

"He had a gun."

"You shot Hulak."

"He was dragging my grandfather into things."

"And you protect your family?"

Oksana frowned; her baldness exaggerated every expression. No, she didn't like that question. She made room for herself on the couch and rested Karel's head in her lap.

Arkady asked, "Do you know how your brother got so sick?"

"A saltshaker. He told me he was adding cesium to a saltshaker when he dropped a grain. Maybe two. He wore gloves, and nothing should have happened, but later, he ate a sandwich and . . ." Her face twisted. "Do you mind if I sit here for a while?"

"Please."

"Karel and I used to sit like this a lot."

She reached over her brother's shoulder to smooth the folds of his hockey shirt, place his hands together, primp his braids. Oksana became more and more absorbed, and gradually Arkady understood there were not going to be any more answers.

"I have to go," Arkady said.

"Can I stay?"

"The city is yours."

Arkady drove Alex's truck down the river road, down to the docks and the scuttled fleet, over the bridge and the hiss of the weir. His motorcycle was in the back of the truck. There was no other way to get there in time. For what, he didn't know, but he felt enormous urgency. Along the housing blocks, virtually empty, always virtually empty, and the twin track of a car path through a field of swaying ferns, to a garage half hidden by trees and a bank of lilacs.

He turned off the engine. The white truck seemed to fill the yard. The cabin was silent and had about it an air of darkness and grief. Wind softly heaved the trees, and the screen door slammed.

Eva was in her bathrobe, her eyes blurred, but she held her gun steadily with both hands. She stumbled across the ground in bare feet, but the sights stayed fixed on him. She said, "I told you if you came back, I'd shoot you."

"It's me." He started to open the door and get out of the truck.

"Don't get out, Alex." She kept moving forward.

"It's all right." Arkady swung the door open and stepped down so she could see him more clearly. He was ashamed, but he wasn't going away. Besides, he was exhausted. This was as far as he could go. She stepped closer until she could not miss before she distinguished him apart from the truck. He knew he didn't look good. In fact, the way he looked would have scared most people off. She began to shake. She shook like a woman in icy water until he carried her inside.

18

Zurin was put out because Arkady wouldn't sit in the VIP lounge. The prosecutor had arranged admission, but Arkady refused to spend hours waiting for the plane to Moscow with nothing to entertain him but the sight of Zurin consuming single-malt whiskey. Zurin considered a little comfort in a plush setting his due, after coming all the way to Kiev to fetch his wayward investigator. However, Arkady had walked out and settled in an Irish pub exactly where the traffic flowed into the main hall.

He hadn't seen a child in over a month. Had seen hardly any clothes but camos. Had gone nowhere without being aware of the diamond-shaped scarecrows of Chernobyl. Here people bulled ahead, eyes on the linoleum as they dragged suitcases of monstrous proportions. Businessmen as weary and creased as their suits tapped on laptops. Couples heading south to Cyprus or Morocco wore extraordinary colors to signal a holiday frame of mind. Men stood transfixed before the flight board, and though morning sun poured through the glass front of the hall, Arkady could see from the way the men stared that for them the hour was the middle of the night. It was wonderful.

After the empty apartments of Pripyat, families seemed miraculous. A baby wailed and beat on the bar of its stroller. Another in diapers decided, for the first time, to walk. Twins with round heads and blank blue eyes strolled hand in hand. An Indian or Pakistani boy was carried in a quilt like a prince by his tiny mother. A veritable circus.

"Enjoying yourself?" Zurin inquired. "You stall until I have to come get you myself, then you act as if you're still on vacation."

"Was that a vacation?"

"It wasn't work. I ordered you back seven days ago."

"I was under medical care." Arkady had the bruise to prove it.

However, Zurin had ostensible grounds for complaint. True, the prosecutor had set up every obstacle to a successful investigation of Lev Timofeyev's murder, but the fact remained that Arkady had failed to find out who had cut Timofeyev's throat.

"You could have come back with Colonel Ozhogin."

"We talked briefly. I had more questions about security at NoviRus, but he had to run."

"Ozhogin proved a disappointment. Although no worse than you. Here, this came to the office yesterday." Zurin flipped something at Arkady that hit him in the chest and dropped into his lap. "What is that?"

"It's a postcard." On the glossy side was a picture of nomads in blue robes riding camels across desert sands. On the reverse was Arkady's name, office address and the message "Two is cheaper than one." "A postcard from Morocco," Arkady added.

"I can see that. What's it about? Who is it from?"

"I have no idea. It's not signed."

"You have no idea. A coded message from Hoffman?"

Arkady studied the postcard. "It's in Russian and in a Russian hand."

"Never mind." Zurin leaned forward. "Doesn't it stick in your craw that you got absolutely nowhere in the investigation? What does that say about you as an investigator?"

"Volumes."

"I agree. Why don't you enjoy another bottle of Irish beer while I visit the duty-free shop and see if I can dig up some decent cigars? But stay here."

Arkady nodded. He was diverted enough by watching the parade. A boy walked in slow motion behind his GameBoy. A beautiful woman rolled by in a wheelchair, her lap covered with roses. A group of Japanese schoolgirls gathered for a photograph around two militia officers with a dog. The girls giggled behind their hands.

The same night Arkady had driven Alex's truck to Eva's cabin, they returned to Pripyat with her car to leave the truck behind. The following day the four bodies were discovered, and Captain Marchenko's small militia force was overwhelmed. Also compromised, since three of the dead were the captain's own men. Detectives and forensic teams were dispatched from Kiev, but their examination of the crime scene was rushed due to the background radioactivity of the site. One of the bodies was radioactive, and another was a Russian executed by a shot in the head in a totally professional style. How coincidental was it, Kiev asked, that on the night of the attack, a Russian security team under the command of Colonel Ozhogin happened to be in the Zone? It was the sort of question that demanded a frank dialogue country to country, and a thoroughgoing, no-holds-barred investigation of not only the crimes but the militia and the administration of the Zone; in short, an honest look at the entire squalid situation. Or a quick flush of the problem down the drain.

Arkady had that second beer and bought a newspaper to peruse. He thought it might be wise to catch up. Zurin seemed content in the duty-free shop, choosing among French cognacs, silk neckties and paisley scarves. The Japanese schoolgirls trooped by again. Coming the other direction was a girl of about eight years old, with big eyes and straight dark hair cut shoulder-length. She had a wand and streamer that she twirled as she skipped. He had seen her dance much the same way in Kiev's Independence Square. It was the dentist's daughter.

Arkady picked up his newspaper and followed. The waiting hall was a scene of family encampments, of slumber, of unshaved anxiety and a slow but constant milling around souvenir shops, ATMs and newsstands. The girl darted into a crowded music store, and he kept track of her by her upraised wand until she appeared in a back corner with a woman in a stylish Italian-looking traveling suit. Dr. Levinson. Victor had been concerned about the dentist's physical safety, but she could not have seemed happier, an attractive woman who could not completely contain her travel excitement. The girl collected a kiss and ducked out of sight.

The wand and streamer reappeared at a newsstand, a catchall of paperbacks and magazines, perfumes and nail polish, condoms and aspirin. A display of lipsticks was stacked three levels high. The girl squeezed through the crush and took the hand of a man choosing among brands of toothpaste. He was dressed like an American golfer in a windbreaker and cap. His hair was brown instead of bleached, and a wedding band had replaced his diamond horseshoe ring, but Arkady recognized the sloped shoulders and heavy jaw of Anton Obodovsky. This toothpaste promised whitening power and the other a brighter smile. How to decide? Anton joked with the girl, who demonstrated a radiant grin. His laugh faded when he saw Arkady coming down the aisle. Anton's eyes screwed down. He sent the girl off with a kiss and replaced the toothpaste on the shelf.

Arkady moved down the aisle as if considering the toiletries. "Going somewhere?"

"Away." Anton kept his voice down.

Arkady spoke softly, too. He played the game. “Let me see your passport and ticket.”

“You don’t have any authority here.”

“Let me see them.”

Anton pulled them from the windbreaker. He swallowed hard and tried to keep a smile pasted on while Arkady read, “Final destination, Vancouver, Canada, for Mr. and Dr. Levinson and their daughter. A Ukrainian passport and a Canadian immigration visa. How did you manage that?”

“As an investor immigrant. You put money in their bank.”

“You bought your way in.”

“It’s legal.”

“If your past is clean. You changed your name, you changed your hair, and I’m sure you changed your record. Anything else?”

“There was a Levinson. He ran out on them.”

“And you came to the rescue?”

“Yes. Two years ago. I was already her patient. But Rebecca wants nothing to do with the Mafia. We’re married, and I only get to see her and the girl maybe once a month because I couldn’t let anyone find out, most of all, my former colleagues.”

“And the hygienist?”

"Her? I had to have a cover to be around the office. Anyway, I'm sure she's having a good time in Morocco. A nice kid."

"That's what Victor said."

"I saw Victor. I dragged him around Kiev. He's looking better."

"The call you made from Butyrka Prison to Pasha Ivanov, what was that about?"

"It was a warning, or it would have been a warning if he'd ever returned the call."

"Warning Pasha about what?"

"Things."

"You'll have to do better than that."

"Come on."

"Let me help you. Karel Katamay. He's dead, by the way."

"I saw on the news." Anton backed into a lipstick display like a fighter who'd decided to absorb punishment. "Okay, I knew Karel from Pripyat, from when he was a kid. I knew what he went through. I remember the evacuation and how people treated everyone from Pripyat as if we had the plague. I was lucky I was a boxer; no one made much fun of me. It was tough for Karel. I'd hear from him a lot when he was little, then nothing for the last few years until suddenly he calls up, says he's in Moscow and needs to borrow a van. A fumigator van. He never asked a favor before."

"Did he say why?"

"He said, a stunt. A joke on a friend."

"And you got him the van?"

"What, do you think I'm crazy? I'm going to put the future of my family in jeopardy to steal a van for a kid I haven't seen for years? When I said no, that's when he told me he came to Moscow to take care of Pasha Ivanov. Trying to impress me, saying we'd get even. I told him there was no way of getting even with Ivanov, ever. What's done is done. Then I put myself away into Butyrka until the thing blew over. I called Ivanov but he never called back. I tried."

"And now you're going to run?"

"I'm not running. There comes a point when you've had enough. You just want to live somewhere normal, with laws."

"With your criminal background, how do you think you can get out?"

"Like this. Walk out the door. Get on a plane. Start over."

"What about the heads you broke and the people you ruined? Do you think you can leave them behind?"

Anton gathered his hands into fists. The lipstick display began to tremble. Arkady glanced at the waiting hall and saw Dr. Levinson and the girl standing with their assembled bags, their eyes on the tickets in his hand. He could almost see the floor open up beneath them.

"No," Anton said. "Rebecca says I take them all with me. The ones I hurt, they all go with me. I never forget."

"She's going to redeem you?"

"Maybe."

"Renko!" Zurin waved with great agitation from across the hall. "Damn it, Renko!"

For the first time Arkady saw Anton's eyes truly open, as if there were an interior never seen before. Anton opened his hands and let them hang. Arkady felt the entire hall go still.

"Renko, stay there!" Zurin ordered.

"Gate B10," Arkady read from Anton's boarding pass. He handed back the tickets and papers. "I'd go to the gate now if I were you." When Anton started to say something, Arkady gave him a push. "Don't look back."

Anton joined the mother and daughter; framed by them, he did look more human. Arkady watched them gather their carry-ons and join a general migration toward the gates. Anton put on sunglasses in spite of the gloomy lighting. The girl waved.

"Renko, will you stay in one place?"

Zurin arrived with a stamp of his foot. "Who was that man?"

"Someone I thought I knew."

"Did you?"

"As it turned out, not a bit."

They returned to the pub. Zurin lit a cigar and read the newspaper. Arkady tried but couldn't sit still enough, not when there were so many people, so many possibilities, so much life rushing by.

19

They paid a visit in December. Eva decided that one day's exposure was permissible, although Zhenya went with all the enthusiasm of a hostage. At least Arkady had the boy wear a new jacket, which was victory enough.

A light snow had fallen, giving the village a crisp jacket of white. Brambles were transformed into snowy flowers. Every tumbledown cabin was traced in white, and every abandoned chair held a cushion of snow. The entire population had turned out: Klara the Viking, Olga with her foggy spectacles, Nina on her crutch and, of course, Roman and Maria, to distribute a welcome of bread and salt and samogon. Vanko had come from Chernobyl. Even the cow lifted her head from her stall to see what the noise was about.

Maria stuffed everyone into the cabin for warm borsch and more samogon. The men ate standing up. Windows steamed and cheeks got red. Zhenya studied the oven, with its shelf for sleeping, and it occurred to Arkady that the boy had never seen a peasant cabin except in fairy tales. He turned to Arkady and mouthed, "Baba Yaga." The room was exactly as Arkady remembered: the same woodland tapestries and red-and-white embroidered cloths, the family icon high in its corner and, on the wall, photographs, the coexisting moments of a young Roman and Maria, of their daughter with her husband and little girl, of the same granddaughter on a Cuban beach.

Eva was the center of attention because Maria and her friends wanted to know what Moscow was like. Although she made light of it, Arkady knew that for Eva the move to Moscow was not always a happy situation. She'd gotten away from the Zone and found work at a clinic, but many days she felt she was occupying Irina's place or was a shell of a woman pretending to be whole. But other days were good, and some were very good.

Under the influence of the samogon, Vanko confided that since Alex Gerasimov's death, funding from Russia for ecological research had slowed to a trickle. A research team from Texas was moving in, however, and they would probably need someone local. Perhaps the

British Friends of the Ecology would like to contribute. He hoped so.

Maria laughed at everything Eva said. In her bright scarves, Maria looked like a twice-wrapped present, and her steel teeth gleamed. An almost childish glee seemed to have infected all the old villagers, an excitement that bubbled over in spite of their politeness.

Roman shyly pulled Arkady aside to say, "None of our families have visited for almost a year. Not even to the cemetery, if you can imagine."

"I'm sorry to hear that."

"I understand. They're busy people, and they're far away. I hope you don't mind if I take advantage of your visit, but I don't know when I will have three men here again. It takes at least three men. That's why I invited Vanko. Don't worry, I have old clothes for you to wear."

"That's fine with me."

"Good!" Roman refilled their glasses.

Arkady backtracked. "Three men to what?"

Maria couldn't hold it in any longer. "Kill the pig!"

Snow was falling again in soft handfuls.

Roman came out of the barn in boots

and a rubber apron. Vanko had tied one of the pig's legs across its chest to keep it off balance, but Sumo was strong and agile, and it understood in a moment that the same people who had been its benefactors for a year were going to slaughter it. Dragging Vanko in its wake, the pig squealed its outrage and terror, plunging one direction and then another while Roman hung a double pulley and rope over the barn door.

"Roman used to butcher pigs for the whole village," Maria said. "Now it's just our pig, but we share with our friends."

It was a simple proposition: Sumo would die so they would live. Yet the scene also had the feel of a country fair. Vanko was dragged across the white yard, and the old women cheered him on as if they expected nothing less than bedlam. When the pig broke for the gate, Nina, her eyes lit, steered the beast back with her crutch.

"I'm sorry," Eva whispered. "I didn't know this was going to happen."

"It's December, it's time to fill the larder. I understand Roman's situation."

"Will you help with the pig?"

Arkady made a noose from a cord. "I'll let Vanko wear him down a little more."

From nowhere, Zhenya stripped off his

jacket and tackled the pig. They rolled over the ground. The pig was fast, heavy and fighting for its life, pale eyelashes fluttering, squealing for help. Even when Sumo shook Zhenya off, he held onto the cord. A boy whom Arkady had never seen lift more than a chess piece hung on with one hand and waved with the other. "Arkady! Arkady!"

Arkady dove for the pig. He and Vanko and Zhenya were dragged over the snow until Arkady got the noose around the pig's other front leg. The pig plowed forward on its jaw, still charging with its rear legs.

"On three," Arkady said. "One . . . two . . ."

He and Zhenya used the animal's momentum to turn it on its back and slide it to Roman, who pressed down on the pig's front legs and slit its throat in one crescent-moon stroke.

The rubber apron made Roman a different, more impressive figure. He tied together the kicking rear legs, hooked them to the pulley, pulled the pig into the air upside down and kicked a zinc tub into place underneath to catch the spurting blood.

Smeared bright red, Zhenya staggered in the snow, his thin arms out, laughing. Vanko rose from his knees and lurched toward the samogon, while the pig hung kicking and squealing. Roman looked on with magisterial calm. He dug a finger into the pig's eye and plucked it out. Arkady looked at Eva as she looked at him.

"To drain faster," Roman explained to Zhenya.

As soon as the pig was still, Roman moved it into a wheelbarrow to the center of the yard, where the women came to life, heaping hay on the pig and setting it on fire. Flames swirled in the snow, orange beating against white. Once the hay had burned, Roman straddled the pig and scraped off the singed hair. Maria released the chickens, who raced around the yard pecking at blood and chasing the eye. When the pig had been burned and scraped several times, Roman washed off the blood; it was remarkable, Arkady thought, how clean an operation it was. Roman cut off a crisped ear and offered it as a treat to Arkady. When he declined, Zhenya took it.

The rest of the afternoon was spent reducing the pig. First with a hatchet to chop off the head, because it took longest to boil, then with knives to carve off the limbs. Roman sliced open the back to reveal a glistening sheet of fatback, and Maria and her friends scurried with plastic pails in anticipation of a year's hams, sausages, smoked fat.

Blue shadows had covered the village by the time the work was done, and Arkady and Zhenya had changed clothes and washed for the ride back to the airport. By the time everyone had kissed and had their farewell sit, a winter evening had settled in. So, into the car, Arkady and Eva in front, Zhenya in back, all waving to faces in the headlights. A bounce in reverse before finding the ruts that led like rails to the main road. A final burst of leave-taking and then they were free.

They could have been floating. On an overcast night in the Zone, there was no star, no lamp, no other traffic, only their headlights groping in a void. He looked at Eva. She reached to hold his hand and say, "Thank you." For what, he hardly dared say. He stole a glance in the rearview mirror. Zhenya sat straighter, as if he had shoulders.

Finding and following the road took all their concentration.

Dazzling crystals rushed to the windshield. Beads of light swirled around the car, tugged on the doors and beat against the windows.

No one slept, and no one said a word.

Acknowledgments

Many people generously offered knowledge and insight during the writing of this book.

In the United States, Jerry English, Victoria Bonnell and Grisha Freiden. In Moscow, Boris Rudenko; Detective Colonel Alexander Yakovlev and Anton; Colonel Vladimir Stoupin, commander of Butyrka Prison; Barsukova Mitrofanovna of the "Otradnoya" children's shelter; Alexei Klyashtorin, radioecologist; Andre Gertsev; Lena Godina; the journalists Masha Lipman, Andrew Jack and Yulia Latynina; Galina Vinogradova and, virtually every step of the way, Luba Vinogradova. In Chernobyl, Tania D'Avignon; Nastia and Nicolai; Alexander Teplov and Kyril Otradnov; militia station commander Colonel L. P. Korolchuk; and Rabbi Yakov Bleich, High Rabbi of the Ukraine. From Israel, Aharon Grundman.

Knox Burger and Kitty Sprague, Luisa Cruz Smith and Ellen Branco read draft after draft. Nevertheless, there will be errors and for them I claim sole credit.

About the Author

MARTIN CRUZ SMITH's novels include *Gorky Park*, *Rose*, *December 6*, *Polar Star* and *Stallion Gate*. A two-time winner of the Hammett Prize from the International Association of Crime Writers and a recipient of Britain's Golden Dagger Award, he lives in California.